HOLIER
THAN THOU

The Tome of Bill

Part 4

RICK GUALTIERI

Edited by Megan Harris at www.mharriseditor.com
Cover by Mallory Rock at www.malloryrock.com
Visit the author's blog at: http://www.poptartmanifesto.com

Published by Freewill press
Freewill Press
PO Box 175
Dunellen, NJ, 08812

Freewill Press

ISBN: 978-1-940415-06-2

For those few who had a little faith in me when I started down this crazy path.

* * *

Special thanks to: Alissa, Sheila, Solace, Jenn, Jessica, Justine, Melissa, Michael, Matt, Chris, and Jack; for helping me refine my craft and reminding me that there's no such thing as a *Dessert* Eagle...although it would be mighty tasty if there was.

Part 1

Hungry, Almost Like the Wolf

They say that man is the ultimate predator. Should he not also make the ultimate prey? It's a thrilling concept. Imagine taking that to the next level...hunting a predator that's even higher on the food chain. There's a fitting reason it's called the most dangerous game.

Running through the thick forest, I felt truly alive. The woods were pitch-black, but that wasn't enough to slow me down. My supernaturally attuned eyes cut through all but the darkest gloom as I sought out my target. She thought she could evade me, perhaps even turn the tables and win. She would soon find out how wrong she was.

As I pursued her through the forest primordial, a small voice reminded me to be cautious. She was far more dangerous than the others. I indulged myself in memories of the ones already dispatched - two humans, frail and weak. In another life they had meant something, but not out here. The one called Ed had been the first to fall. She had seen to that. Tom was next, by my own hand. I had sensed his impending betrayal and been the first to act. He had begged for mercy, but received none - such is the way of my kind.

I stopped and got my bearings. Sounds, sights, and scents filled my very being. It was tempting to throw back my head and howl primal defiance at the moon, but that would be foolish. She might be listening. Though I felt no fear at facing her, I had no intention of giving her any edge.

There...a scent, *hers*. It was intoxicating - awakening a deep need - but I pushed those thoughts away. I was here to hunt and would not be distracted quite so easily. Her smell played out across my hyper-sensitive nostrils for a moment before I bounded off into the darkness once more.

I savored the feel of the weapon in my hand. It would do nicely. She would never see it coming. It would be quick and clean...if I wanted it to be. But I didn't. She needed to know who had hunted her down. The look upon her face as she realized who had vanquished her would be too much of a prize to turn down. I smiled in anticipation and quickened my pace.

Victory was mine for the taking, as was fitting. Even amongst predators, I am at the very apex. My name is Bill Ryder and I'm a vampire, an immortal beast of the night - but that's not all. I am the legendary Freewill of vampire lore. The others speak of me and my coming in hushed tones. A great destiny has been foretold for me. Much honor and glory shall be laid at my feet one day.

Feh! Let them keep their prophecies. I do not exist for them or the future they proclaim for me. No, I live only in the here and now...and right now I was closing in on my prey.

* * *

There! A lesser being might have missed it, but not me. The fabric of her jacket peeked through the foliage. She was lying in wait, hoping for an ambush. She was a smart girl, but sadly not smart enough.

I circled her position, keeping outside of her range. None, save perhaps another of my kind, would have been able to sense my presence. Therein lay the challenge. Though not of my lofty status, she had skill and power of her own. She might well be able to sense that I was advancing upon her.

I bent low, picked up a few pebbles from the ground, and held my breath as I counted to ten. The ruse would only fool her for seconds at best, so it would have to be fast.

Now! Pebbles rained down from the sky, disturbing the area where I had been only moments earlier. Before the last of them had hit the ground, I was once again on the move. Bringing all of my speed to bear, I raised my weapon and advanced upon her hiding spot.

She never saw me coming. There was no movement from the bushes, so intent was she on waiting for me to fall into her trap.

"It's over, Sally."

I pulled the trigger.

* * *

My aim was true, but something was wrong. Though I struck her with multiple rounds, there was no movement at all. I stepped forward and cursed. It was her jacket, all right. It practically reeked of her perfume. But she herself was nowhere to be seen.

A quiet whisper floated from behind me out of the darkness.

"Dumbass."

My body stiffened as shot after shot peppered me. It was over. I, the mighty Freewill, had been vanquished after all.

The Games that Children Play

"That was just sad, Bill."

"Did you have to shoot me so many times?"

"Stop whining."

"Those paint pellets sting."

"Good," Tom cut in. "Serves you right for shooting me in the back, asshole."

"What part about it being called a *deathmatch* did you not understand?" I replied, my tone extra condescending.

"Was still a dick thing to do! We were supposed to be partners."

"There can be only one," I replied blithely.

"Yeah," said Sally, "and you're not it."

"I almost had you," I replied, climbing into the back of the Dodge Durango she had procured for the trip. We had all known better than to ask where she had gotten it. Best case scenario was that it was stolen. Worst case...well, Sally wasn't known to be shy when it came to bumping off those who stood in her way.

"Horseshoes and hand grenades," she answered as she climbed in next to me. "Besides, you tried a move that wouldn't have fooled a grunt in basic training. I mean seriously, throwing rocks? I don't think that even works in the movies."

"Hey, at least I was trying to be tactical. Wasn't that what you said I needed?"

Sally rolled her eyes in my direction. "When I said you needed some training, I didn't mean an outing to play paintball."

"I'm easing into it."

"I'm with Bill," Ed, my other roommate, said from the driver's seat. "Besides, you have to admit it was fun."

"No," she shot back. "The only thing I'll admit is that I can feel my social status dropping several notches. This is not how I prefer to spend my weekends."

"Sorry," I muttered, "next time we'll bring along a stripper pole so you feel more at home."

Tom started to chuckle, but immediately clamped a hand over his mouth. No doubt he remembered she sat directly behind him and was more than capable of tearing his spine out through the front seat if the mood so came over her.

"I get it," she said to me, ignoring him. "You need a break, something to take your mind off of things..."

"Don't start, Sally."

"But this really isn't doing anything to prepare you."

"Sally..." I warned through gritted teeth.

"It's been a full month since things went down in Canada. That's a long time to have your head in the sand when all-out war could erupt at any moment."

I turned away from her and watched the dark road slip by as we drove. The impending war wasn't what I was hiding from, and she knew it. Don't get me wrong, I was pretty damn worried. An army of nine foot apes running out of the forests at any moment, screaming their heads off, would be enough to cause anyone to lose their cool.

Hell, that wasn't even the worst of it. If the vampire nation went to war with their ancient enemies, Bigfoot (and yes that sounded just as ridiculous to me), all of our allies from the dawn of time would be drawn into it. We're talking primal gods and shit like that - beings that would be the equivalent of walking nuclear arsenals - creatures that have been itching to re-reveal themselves to mankind. Not cool.

"There's also the issue of..."

"Here she goes," Ed muttered.

"Your...*friend*," she finished, dropping her voice to a bare whisper - almost spitting out that last part.

I was sorely tempted to just open the door and dive out. It wouldn't kill me or even hurt...hopefully. Though not much to look at - five-ten, a little overweight, glasses - I was still a vampire and had access to all of their powers, like superhuman strength, speed, durability - not to mention the inability to die. Scraping my face off the pavement wouldn't exactly be a walk in paradise, but it wouldn't keep me down. With any luck I'd be up, running, and a mile away before they even stopped the car. I'd be lying if I said I didn't seriously consider it.

Still, Sally was right. I had been avoiding the issue at hand and with good reason: Sheila. The world was on the brink of global annihilation, but all I could think about was my girlfriend (well okay, *prospective* girlfriend). Had I known a year ago that I would be turned into one of the undead - and subsequently set in motion the chain of events that had occurred - I would have jumped in front of a bus.

Well, alright, maybe I wouldn't have. But I would have at least made it a point to stay home that fateful night. Sally was a piece of ass, as were many of the other members of the coven I became a member (and eventual leader) of, but she had turned out to be every bit as dangerous as she was beautiful. Had I been thinking with my brain instead of my dick, my life would have continued down its boring, but predictably safe, path. It also wouldn't have resulted in the girl of my dreams being transformed into my foretold nemesis...

"You're not listening to a word I'm saying are you?" Sally sighed, interrupting my train of thought.

"And that's different from every other time, how?" I quipped, earning another eye-roll.

Snickers from the front seat diverted her attention again. I knew she had a sense of humor, sick though it might be, but she never turned down an opportunity to remind my human friends how easily she could kill them. She took pleasure in tormenting Tom especially.

My thoughts veered again toward Sheila. She was the former administrative assistant at my job, now the owner of her own office efficiency company. She was also, coincidentally, the love of my life and the being I was destined to either kill or be killed by as predicted by vampire prophets. Relationships sure are a bitch.

It's the same with most guys. One day we meet a girl and it just clicks for us. Whether it's fate, pheromones, or our imaginations fucking with us, we find ourselves planning the rest of our lives around a person we just laid eyes on. A few eventually wind up together and happily live out that fantasy. Others, not so much. For some, I'm sure life just gets in the way. The desire is there, but the timing is never right (in other words, shit happens). As for the rest, even if they do end up together, reality eventually comes crashing in. They get old, fat, and grow to hate each other. Then there's that very small *lucky* minority in which the girl turns out to be an equally legendary creature, one who is fated to send the other's soul screaming to the dark Hell it deserves.

Guess which lottery I won.

Back to the Grind

"Drop us off at the loft," Sally said to Ed. It was not a request.

We had avoided getting back to the discussion at hand during the remainder of our drive back from Pennsylvania. Between my banter with Sally and Tom's general idiocy, she was distracted enough to keep from needling me about duties and whatnot. Unfortunately, my luck was about to run out.

"Us?"

"You heard me," she said still facing forward. "You've had enough play time. You are officially back on the clock."

"But..."

She turned and glared at me. "But *what*? Let me guess, you have important plans for the rest of tonight?"

"Well, sorta. I was going to..."

"If you say the name of that stupid game...what is it, War World?"

"World of Warcraft," Ed corrected her.

"Thank you," she replied, still facing me. "If you even think of saying that, I'm going to kick your ass right here."

Damn. Either she knew me too well or she had my place bugged. Truth be told, I wasn't sure which scenario was more likely.

"Ooh, can I watch?"

Sally turned to Tom, fangs bared. "I'll throw in a beat-down for you too if you want, meat-sack."

His mouth clamped shut and she turned her focus back to me.

"Well..." I stammered, trying to think of something else to say. Goddamnit, I hated when she was right. Unfortunately, she was right about a lot of things.

Sue me for being almost human, but I'm pretty sure the events of the past several weeks would've been too much for any sane person to endure.

I had been summoned to the world's freakiest peace summit, up in northern Canada of all places, and had gotten my ass handed to me, both physically and otherwise, by a scumbag vampire named Francois and a foul-smelling Sasquatch chieftain called Turd. Regardless, in the end - through some minor miracle - it had all worked out and war looked to be averted. I was right on the verge of being the hero when suddenly it all hopped onto an express train to Hell.

Thanks to the misguided affections of Gan, a three-hundred year old vampire princess in a pint-sized body, Turd's ugly-ass daughter wound up on the business end of a silver pig-sticker. I wouldn't have minded much - being that a clause in our treaty specified I was expected to marry the hairy she-beast - except for that little bit at the end where they sort of took offense to her murder and declared war on the vampire nation. Yeah, that fucked me big time.

Adding to the stress was having one of our ruling body's bigwigs, none other than Alexander the Great himself, outmaneuver me. The First Coven, our so-called leaders, is more widely known by the nickname *the Draculas*, and being outmaneuvered not only by one of the greatest military leaders of all time, but a senior member of that merry little bunch, wasn't exactly something to hang your head about. It's kind of like being bummed because you lost a game of Trivial Pursuit to Albert Einstein.

That Alex was happily looking forward to my part in the coming conflict wasn't helping matters either. It was yet another stupid vampire prophecy they kept beating me over the head with - *The Freewill shall lead our armies against our enemies* or some such bullshit. As far as I was concerned, he could go fuck himself...not that I was about to say that to his face.

One would think that'd be enough to send me straight to the closest bar - intent on drowning my sorrows - but fate had one more kick to the balls in mind for me...Sheila

"It's settled, then," Sally said with a tone of finality - dragging me out of my reverie. "Bill and I are heading to the loft."

"Need us to stick around?" Ed asked, drawing an exasperated sigh from me. Though his tone was innocent enough, there was little doubt of his ulterior motive. He and Sally had been dating behind my back for the past few months. Though they both claimed it was just casual, Ed had been on the receiving end of a vampire hickey from her while up in Canada. As psycho as it was - and believe me, a human trying to do anything with Sally may as well be on suicide watch - he was obviously positioning himself for an undead booty call.

"Nice try, stud," she said. "But we have vampire business to discuss. You can stick around, but I can't guarantee you won't wind up an appetizer. Double that for the flesh-ball next to you."

"Dropping off it is, then," Ed took the hint, immediately ending that line of questioning. He was smart enough to know when not to push his luck.

"No problem," Tom let the insult slide. "Besides, Christy said she's gonna pop by later."

Once we stopped, I'd considered shoving Sally out of the car and telling Ed to floor it. With the mention of his girlfriend's name, though, Tom was able to completely reverse that plan of action. The undead aren't the only ones with prophecies.

Vampires are far from being the only secret the world holds. Magic, monsters, and other fantastical shit - stuff that most of us assume exists only in the realm of movies, books, or role-playing games - is real. Not all of it, mind you, but enough to make most people crap their pants and run screaming for the hills. There is an underworld of horrific creatures existing all around us, hidden just out of plain sight. The rabbit hole goes pretty goddamn deep, too.

Christy is a witch, a real one. She can teleport, fire energy blasts, and control Tom with just a few sucks of his dick. Oh wait, any woman could do that last one.

Typically, vampires and mages are kind of like cats and dogs. Under some circumstances, they'll tangle with one another, but most of the time they're content to just go about their own business with a little posturing, but not much else. There are always exceptions, though.

I'm one of them, and that's not just an ego thing to make the bulge in my pants look bigger. I'm what's known as a Freewill, a rare type of vampire. In the distant past they led armies, crushed their enemies, and were generally even bigger dicks than normal vamps. Then, out of nowhere, they disappeared. No one knows why. For whatever reason, I'm the first in over half a millennium.

Thanks to that little detail, I've been number one on her coven's hit list for a while now (the assholes stole the coven idea from vampires, by the way). The wizarding world has a pretty big Sword of Damocles hanging above their head in the form of their own prophecy surrounding vampire Freewills, lucky me.

Supposedly, my "birth" heralded the beginning of their end. They didn't exactly take kindly to it either. Their first act, as way of introduction, was an attempt to fireball my ass into oblivion. All because my existence meant that the Icons would return.

Love Nest

"Stop here," Sally commanded.

"We're still six blocks away," Ed argued, his eyebrows visibly raised in the rearview mirror.

"Exactly," she said. "I have an image to maintain. No offense, but being dropped off after a night of paintball isn't exactly the height of coolness."

Ed shrugged and pulled over to the side, double parking in the process.

"I'll see you guys later," I said, stepping from the SUV. "Say hi to Christy for me."

"Oh, I'll do more than say hi," Tom said with a creepy grin.

"Like I really needed to know that," Sally groaned as she joined me on the sidewalk.

I smiled uneasily at Tom. He was one of my best and oldest friends, and I felt like a piece of shit lying to him, but it was for the best. When push came to shove, he was particularly bad at keeping things from Christy.

* * *

I had gotten lucky upon returning home the night I'd been *enlightened* as to the Icon's identity. Tom had been out, which was good because the first thing I did upon walking in the door was spill my guts. Ed patiently sat through my pathetic soliloquy and, upon hearing me out, had suggested it might be best to keep my fucking mouth shut around Tom.

I felt bad in doing so. He was my bud and we didn't keep things from each other...even stuff the other really didn't want to know. Hell, I knew far too many disturbing details of his and Christy's sex life as it was.

I wasn't feeling too happy about keeping it from her either. Despite us getting off to a rocky start, we had managed to come to a somewhat peaceful coexistence as of late.

Christy becoming aware of my role in the Icon's creation would probably undo all that progress, especially since I had managed to convince her I would have nothing to do with it. Sue me for not being psychic. Unfortunately, as far as I was aware, her coven, and more importantly their leader, Harry Decker, still wanted me dead. Though I was sure the truth would come out eventually, I saw no reason to give them any further fuel to add to that murderous fire.

* * *

"What should we do with this?" Ed gestured at the stolen SUV he was still driving.

Sally shrugged nonchalantly. "Keep it, sell it, burn it, I don't give a shit what you do. But you might want to consider doing so before the cops find its owner...or what's left of him."

She flashed him a wicked grin and started walking. Ed turned a shade paler in the glow of the city lights. I offered him my best apologetic glance and turned to follow Sally.

* * *

"Where are you going?"

She veered down an unfamiliar side street before we were even halfway to the loft, one of the coven's prime hangouts.

"Pit stop," she replied before walking up to the entrance of a building and unlocking a few bolts.

"New digs?" I followed her up the stairs.

"Something like that."

"Taking me up for an illicit encounter?"

She flipped me the finger over her shoulder and continued up. We arrived at the fifth floor, where a metal security door awaited. Sally punched a code into a keypad, produced a different key and unlatched another series of locks.

Intrigued, I followed her in.

"This is new," I remarked while she flipped on the lights. With the exception of a few rooms, it was an open floor plan not entirely dissimilar to the loft. However, this place had a more Spartan, utilitarian feel. Heavy load-bearing columns broke up the main room. Thick bars adorned all the windows and there were odd symbols painted at intervals along the walls. "Let me guess, this is a sex dungeon and I'm your prisoner."

"Not even in your sickest fantasies."

"You have no idea how sick some of my..."

"That wasn't an invitation to enlighten me, Bill," she walked into one of the rooms and closed the door behind her, the click of the lock echoing through the room.

I strolled over and casually gave the doorknob a jiggle. It didn't budge.

"So what is this place?"

"You know," said her voice from the other side, "you really should be concentrating on defending yourself rather than asking stupid questions."

"Why?"

"The Alma are big, but they can be surprisingly quiet when they want to be."

* * *

Oh shit! I turned and put my back against the door, scanning the room for any sign of movement.

Alma was the Mongolian name for Sasquatch. They were the physical forms of forest spirits...big hairy physical forms that smelled like shit. Worse than that, they hated vampires and were more than capable of fucking one up six ways to Sunday. The undead might be physically powerful, but a half-ton of angry ape can go a long way toward tipping the odds.

"What the fuck did you do, Sally?" I tried to make it sound tough and failed miserably in the process. Had the Draculas captured one and sent it down here for me to train with? That didn't sound so far-fetched. Older vampires can control younger ones psychically through a means known as compulsion. As far as I know, I'm the only one who's immune to it. If a vampire of sufficient age wanted Sally to do something, she wouldn't have much choice.

Normally when I think of compulsion, I imagine the vampire hierarchy using it to get chicks like her to open wide and say AH...but maybe that's just me. I had to keep reminding myself that most other vamps used their powers for slightly more diabolical reasons.

It was possible this was punishment for me mouthing off constantly to those who outranked me. Either way if one of those foul-odored monstrosities got its hands on me before I could...

Wait! A variety of scents filtered into my sensitive nostrils: Sally's perfume, some mustiness from the air vents, and the vague scent of whatever cleaner had been used on the floor here...*Pine-sol,* maybe. Nothing that smelled like a walking fur coat dipped in diarrhea.

Still, that didn't necessarily mean anything. They could have shampooed the goddamned thing just to throw me off. I crouched into a defensive position and continued watching the room.

There came a soft click from behind me - the lock on the door. Oh crap, was the Bigfoot in...

"What the fuck are you doing?" Sally asked before I could turn around.

I spun to face her, still attempting my best Kung-Fu stance, and my mouth dropped open. She wore a tight red, off-the-shoulder cocktail dress.

"Eyes up here, perv."

It took me a second to compose myself. The fact that Sally is a prime piece of ass never failed to get my attention.

"But what about the Alma?"

"Don't tell me you actually believed that," she broke out in laughter.

"There's no..."

"Of course not! What the hell would I be doing keeping one of those fucking things locked up in the middle of the city?"

"Then what is this place? Why are you dressed like that? Why did you tell me there was a Bigfoot here?"

"On that last one...why not?" she replied chuckling. "As for the others, welcome to our new safe house." I raised an eyebrow as she continued. "Considering how Starlight blabbed about all our other secrets the last time she was up in Boston, I figured I'd keep this on the down low for now. We're the only ones who know about it, and I'd prefer we keep it that way until we really need it."

"Our own little love nest?"

"In your dreams, jackass," she replied pushing past me.

It made sense, and I wished I'd thought of it. The coven owned numerous properties in the SoHo area of the city - some above ground, some below. All coven holdings were supposed to be on file up in Boston, the headquarters for vampire activity in the Northeastern

US. However, it was generally tolerated that covens were allowed to keep a few off the books for safety purposes.

Unfortunately for us, Starlight - another vamp from my coven - had been brow beaten by one of the Boston bigwigs into giving up all of our secrets some months back. The only place my group had been left in case of emergency was a safe house in Brooklyn we shared with the so-called Howard Beach Coven, a bunch of vampires who heavily disliked me.

Aside from that, there was also the apartment I shared with Tom and Ed. Needless to say, they weren't too pleased knowing that in case of emergency, our living room was the designated safe zone for a pack of bloodthirsty monsters. I should have guessed Sally would eventually take steps to rectify that.

"This must have cost a pretty penny." I said, taking in the view - including the room.

"Nothing the coven can't cover," she walked over to a full length mirror that hung on one wall. "You would know that if you ever bothered to look at our books."

"I keep asking to see them. You're the one who won't let me."

"Oh yeah, silly me. Forgot all about that. Never mind then. Just know that we're not exactly hurting for cash."

"Even with you at the helm?"

"*Especially* with me at the helm," she continued to check herself out in the mirror. "If you think I'm bad, you should have seen how Jeff ran the place. That asshole spent money like it grew on trees. Hell, he probably kept half the coke dealers in the city employed."

That wasn't surprising. The late unlamented leader of my coven, Jeff, had been the Grand Moff of douchebags, surrounding himself with guys like him and girls that were eye-meltingly gorgeous. Pity for him he wasn't a very good judge of character. Sally had been one of his minions at the time of my turning. It hadn't worked out well for him.

Sadly, my reign over the coven consisted of much less grandeur on my own part. I got to play leader at any and all functions that might end with me getting my ass beaten - all the while keeping my day job as a programmer - while Sally got a black Amex and a corner suite in the office building where she managed the coven's day to day affairs. She wasn't shy about flaunting it, either. I had little doubt the hot number she was wearing probably cost more than I got in a paycheck. "Why are you dressed like that?"

"Because otherwise I'd be naked and your reality just doesn't get that good." Bitch!

"Not what I meant, Sally."

"Fine. For starters, I have a reputation to uphold. By the way, if you even think of mentioning what we were doing tonight, I'll stake you with the erection you're probably sporting right now."

How did she know I was...? Still, her threat *did* imply touching my dick. I briefly considered the possibilities before continuing.

"Fair enough," I said. "We were out killing people. Is that better?"

"Much." A small smile played out across her lips as she checked her hair. "Getting back to your original question, I want to look nice for the party."

"Thank you. Was that so hard to just...wait, *what* party?"

"The one at the loft tonight, obviously."

"There's a party at the loft?"

"That's what I said."

"Why?"

She turned to face me. "If you have to ask for a reason to hold a party, then you obviously haven't been invited to that many."

"I thought you wanted to talk about...well, you know."

"The Icon, A.K.A. that girl you like - what's her name - Shannon..."

"Sheila!"

"Whatever. Don't worry, we will. But first we need to unwind."

"We?"

"Yes *we*, as in all of us. You're obviously stressed. One doesn't need eyes or ears to notice that. You're practically wearing it like cologne. Not a particularly flattering one at that."

"You try being all happy and cheery when…"

"Then there's me. I have to listen to you complain, which isn't doing wonders for my mental health. I mean do you see this?" She held up a strand of her blonde hair.

"Um, you're going grey?"

She flashed her fangs in anger. "No, shit for brains. Worse…split ends! Even with Alfonso's care, I'm practically falling apart here."

Alfonso was Sally's favorite stylist. Before our little jaunt up to Canada, she had taken the liberty of turning his smarmy ass into her undead minion.

"Yes, you're obviously suffering," I quipped, watching her pull out a lipstick tube.

"Don't be an ass," she puckered her lips and applied the glossy red color. "Then there's the coven, or have you forgotten about them?"

"They're kind of hard to forget about."

"You could've fooled me. You haven't exactly been leading by example since we got back."

"I've had a lot on my mind."

"Yeah, well, while you sit behind your computer jerking off to German porn, I have to deal with them all. Between half of them getting wiped out the last time that little bitch Gan was in town and you pulling a disappearing act, things have been getting out of hand. I caught Dread Stalker trying to organize a hunting party the other day. You know how *that* would have turned out, right?"

I nodded. Dread Stalker had been one of Jeff's favorites. He was a vicious killer wrapped in the form of a long-haired male model. The body count had been steady under Jeff's rule, keeping the bloodsucker in check. But when I took over and tried to curtail the blatant murdering that went on...well, you try telling a pride of lions that gazelles are off the menu.

"I was half tempted to let him go, but knew you'd probably whine about it."

"Whine about it? Sorry that I take offense at people being killed like cattle."

"Omelets and eggs," she waved a hand around. "So, anyway, I figured we all needed a break. Besides, they wanted to celebrate the good news."

"What good news?"

"Well..."

"Spill it, Sally."

She hesitated. "I sort of let what happened up north slip out."

Burning Down the House

"You *what?*"

Back when we arrived home from the frozen wasteland that is Canada - fresh from hearing the declaration of the impending global Armageddon - we'd decided it would be best to not share the *wonderful* news with the rest of the coven. Some of the more violent members of our merry little group weren't particularly happy with me as of late. Curbing their murder sprees didn't make me number one on their friend lists.

That Sally had apparently announced to the group that their illustrious leader had managed to incompetently fuck them all over by starting a war wasn't exactly music to my ears. I found myself starting to wonder if this little soiree of hers wasn't going to be a going away (permanently) party for me.

"I was starting to get questions, mostly about where you were, what was going on, et cetera. I figured a little good news would keep them distracted."

"You have an interesting definition of good news," I swung my arms in frustration. "Hey guys, guess what?

We're all gonna be overrun by giant fucking monkeys. Let's party!"

"You really are a negative Nancy, you know that?"

"Enlighten me as to the bright side, oh wise one," I spat back.

"It's not the information itself that's important - it's all about perception. Hell, turn on Fox news at six PM and tell me that's not true."

I couldn't argue with that one.

"I gave the coven an *edited* version of the events up north," she explained, "starting with your *brilliant* battle against the Sasquatch leader in which your Freewill powers proved the deciding factor."

"Turd?"

"I left out his name. Figured that would blunt some of the impact." She stopped to adjust one of her high heels, continuing her tale once she was finished. "Following their pathetic defeat, they begged for peace, not wishing to risk your wrath."

"Spreading on the bullshit a little thick, aren't you?"

"Yep, and they ate it like it was filet mignon. Now stop interrupting me. Finally, the vampire nation agreed to a new treaty, but you would have none of that. You stood up and inspired us all with a speech, reminding us of the glory of old - how we were once conquerors, a people to be feared. With you at the helm and the might of the Draculas behind you, we could reclaim our former station in life. Thus said, you stood, drew your dagger and slew their leader, proclaiming that from this day forth we would no longer be content with hiding in the shadows."

"Uh huh. For starters, that was Nergui, and it was Turd's daughter he killed."

"So what? It's not like either of them are gonna contradict you."

She had a point there. Nergui, Gan's chief assassin, had murdered the Bigfoot leader's daughter to satisfy his mistress's insane desire to keep me for herself. His mission accomplished, he had done nothing to stop the other Sasquatches from tearing him limb from limb for his crimes.

The only ones who knew the truth were...well, the shitload of beings who'd attended the peace conference. Still, I had to remind myself that I ran one little coven in the grand scheme of things. Considering most of the vamps under my leadership were vacuous douchebags, it wasn't surprising the rest of the supernatural world didn't exactly keep them in the loop.

"And they believed all of that?" I asked.

"Yep, and even if some of them didn't, they're not going to call you out on it."

"And now, in addition to all the other crap they believe about me, they think I'm going to lead them to some glorious vampire ruled future?"

"Yep. Congratulations, Bill. As far as Village Coven is concerned, you are officially the undead messiah."

Why didn't that exactly inspire me with confidence?

* * *

As we began our walk to the loft, I felt the weight of the world on my shoulders. It made me wish I had spent more time working out. On top of all of that, though, there was one more tiny detail to add to my growing list of personal baggage.

"Couldn't have told me in advance about the party, could you?" I glanced down at my jacket and camo sweatpants that contrasted with Sally's heels, tight dress and well-coifed hair.

"Would you have come?"

"No."

"Now you know why I didn't tell you," she smirked.

"You could have at least picked me up a change of clothes, then."

She rolled her eyes. "Sorry, Bill, but I don't answer to the call of 'attention K-mart shoppers'." Bitch! "Besides, it fits your story better. You look like you just came in from a training exercise in the field." She gave me the once-over and sighed, "Well, sorta."

"You didn't tell them anything about the Icon, did you?"

"Fuck no. My tongue is golden, but I wasn't about to touch *that* one."

"We can't keep it a secret forever, you know."

"I know, but I sure as shit want to try. It'll be bad enough once they know she exists, but it would be best if nobody found out it was all because of your misguided case of puppy love."

I glowered at her. She had no idea how deep my feelings for Sheila ran.

"Boston doesn't know what happened, either."

"Really?"

"Yep. I didn't even tell James."

"He's back?"

"Returned to the states a week ago. Gave me a call to see how things were going."

James is a six-hundred year old vampire and former contemporary of Marco Polo. He's also a freshly minted member of the Draculas. Leaving out something this important wasn't usually an option with them, at least for those of us who cared to keep breathing. I was happy that they didn't know about the Icon yet, but it would be less awesome once they discovered everything later, especially my connection to her.

"You didn't tell them anything?"

"I didn't talk to them, just James. No fucking way was I letting Colin know shit about anything." Colin was James's assistant, and a weasely little suck-up of a vampire. The second he learned something, you could be sure anyone who outranked him knew about it, too.

"And you didn't mention..."

"Relax, Bill. All I gave him was a mundane status report and a quick note that you were taking some time off."

I stopped and turned to face her. "Really?"

"Yes really. If I told them even the slightest thing, the entire city would be crawling with vampire hitmen by

31

now. I said just enough to make us look like good undead citizens. Hopefully this will give us a little more time to figure things out on our own."

I had been so busy feeling sorry for myself and trying to keep Christy from finding out, that I hadn't bothered to consider the vampire nation might take a *nuke it from orbit* approach. In all likelihood, Sally had saved Sheila's life.

"Th-thanks," I stammered.

"Oh don't get all drippy on me," she said dismissively. "I'm doing it more for me anyway. I don't want to have to listen to you whine about it for the next century or two."

"That's very...human of you, Sally."

"Don't push your luck," she sniffed and started walking again. "Let's go, we're late enough as it is."

"Think James would have kept it to himself?"

"Doubt it. That's why I only gave him a status report. Even if he had wanted to keep a lid on things, he'd probably still need to inform the other Draculas, especially Alex."

My fangs extended and my lips pulled back in a grimace. "Once he finds out the truth, I bet he'll be creaming his pants knowing that one of his precious prophecies has come true."

"No doubt, but the rest of the Draculas probably won't be nearly as pleased. It could cause a panic. Once word gets out, vamps halfway around the world will see the Icon hiding under their bed. With the war looming, they don't need that crap right now."

Sheila hiding under my bed? Now there was a thought. Unfortunately, any relationship with her was going to be facing some difficulties in the days ahead. Talk about an understatement. She was capable of frying me extra crispy with just a touch. That made even a handshake, much less anything more intimate, a tad difficult. Hell, that might not even be the half of it. If she was like me, perhaps she also had a few hidden tricks in her arsenal of powers.

I got sidetracked before I could ride that train of thought very far, though. As the building that housed the loft came into view, I realized something wasn't quite right. The first floor was dark.

"They closed the bar?"

"I heard they're renovating the place. Probably gonna take a couple of months too. Pity, guess it'll be nothing but take out for a while."

The loft occupied the third floor. With the exception of the bar, the entire structure was coven territory. The noise from the small club at street level drowned out any of the atrocities that occurred in other sections of the building. Though the hunters in the coven were usually careful to keep most of their activities spread throughout the city, the bar also proved handy in times of need, or so I was told. I strictly stick to the bottled stuff, although Tom and Ed were often (rightfully so) quick to question where our bottled blood came from. I try to convince myself we get it from hospitals and other willing donors, but I'm not a complete idiot. Let's just say that there are some instances where a policy of *don't ask, don't tell* is necessary to maintain one's sanity.

Remembering the night I was turned and the others in attendance that weren't as lucky as me, I wasn't overly dismayed to see the bar closed. It might mean whatever party Sally had planned would be relatively trauma free (for me and any *hors d'oeuvres* unlucky enough to be present). All things considered, I found myself hoping that they'd take their sweet-ass time renovating the place.

"Come on, Bill, stop day dreaming," Sally said, prodding me on. "I don't know about you, but I could use a few stiff drinks to drown out the dorkitude of the day."

I stopped dilly-dallying and followed her. Maybe she was right. I probably did need to relax a little. Besides which, it's not like it would all be torture. There would definitely be some eye-candy on display, and I certainly wasn't above playing Willy Wonka for an evening. Adding hard liquor to the mix wasn't bad for that equation either. Hell, a few months back I had walked in on Firebird and Vanessa, two of the looser members of the coven, topless and making out. They had been shit-faced drunk and didn't care who had watched. Talk about a fang bang. I definitely wouldn't say no if given a chance to see that show again. The last time had fueled my personal fantasies for quite a few weeks.

For the first time that evening, I allowed myself a genuine smile. Maybe Sally was right. The world could wait for one more night, especially if the night held the promise of seeing some tits.

Sadly, fate took a perverse pleasure in waiting for me to drop my guard just before blowing up in my face. That night was no different...quite literally in fact. Sally and I had just reached the front door when our world exploded in green flame.

Like Falling Asleep
in a Giant Blender

Flying is such a pleasant sensation. Nothing, save the very air around you, caresses your being - almost like being in the womb again. It was a pity flight was not amongst the supernatural powers I achieved upon awakening as a vampire.

Mind you, it was a lot more pleasant when I wasn't on fire. Go figure.

Fortunately for my muddled brain, the concussive wave that hit me had done its job quite nicely. I drifted away from the loft, or what remained of it, almost as if in slow motion. Each foot I flew felt like days passed. With no video games, internet porn, or similar distractions, it gave me some downtime to reflect on the recent past.

* * *

I don't know too much about vampire lore. What I do know, though, is: faith is power. It's not so much about God, or whoever else you pray to, as it is about the raw belief. A strong enough belief can actually tap into the magic of the world around us - magic that's not particularly friendly to vampires.

Most people are too shallow to be able to do anything with it. A few, though, are either devout or insane enough to utilize it. Tom was a good example of that latter group. Months back, he had become so enamored with a Transformer toy, that he managed to imbue it with a little of that magic. Pretty messed up, I know, but true none the less. What should have been a kid's toy was transformed, pun intended, into the equivalent of a crucifix from those old Peter Cushing movies - albeit slightly more embarrassing to be attacked with.

It's bad enough for vampires that some folks can empower small objects this way, but for truly exceptional people, it can work on a much larger scale. Many of the heroes of old were able to tap into this energy. They were known by many names: the Shining Ones, the Silver Eyes, and, more commonly, *Icons* - short for icons of faith. The source of their power was a deep seated belief in their own abilities. I'm sure this resulted in most of them being egomaniacal assholes, nevertheless their faith in themselves was so strong their entire bodies became conduits for this form of magic, rendering them...well I'm not entirely sure. All I know for certain is that they could fuck up vampires with only a touch and that their powers made them particularly resistant to other kinds of magic, too.

What were the odds that the one girl on the planet that I desperately wanted a relationship with would be amongst their number?

Apparently better than I would have guessed.

* * *

I relived that day again. I had just dragged the vampire world into a death match with our ancient enemies in the Woods of Mourning. Things looked fairly shitty, but her presence had immediately made everything else seem petty in comparison.

But it was different this time - *she* was different. Sheila had quit her job at Hopskotchgames - where I still worked as a programmer - to pursue her own destiny. We had been growing closer in the months since I had first asked her out for coffee - not as romantic as I would have liked, but a bond had formed nevertheless. I hadn't known it at the time, but my encouragement had apparently struck a nerve deep inside of her. That newfound confidence grew until it awoke the potential within her.

"*I believe in you. I believe you can do better,*" I had said. Little did I know how much better she could do. How much better she could become.

She was different that day. The way she dressed, walked, talked, held herself...it was all her, but somehow to the nth degree. She was once quiet and unassuming, but in her place that day stood someone who was utterly unafraid of the world. My God, she was marvelous to behold.

Our time together that evening culminated in the moment I had been dreaming of ever since meeting her. We kissed.

Or at least we would have. Instead, my proximity caused her newfound powers to flare up, sending me flying - not unlike what I was doing now - enveloped in pure white-hot flame.

I'm pretty sure that alone would have put the kibosh on our make-out session, but then I had to up the ante on our little game of super-power poker.

Her unexpected surge of power activated the beast within me, and I'm not just talking about being a horny, single guy either. Whatever makes me a Freewill also comes with some nasty perks. Under extreme stress, pain, or anger I change. Into what, I'm not sure, but I become much stronger and a hell of a lot meaner. I'm kinda like the Hulk if he had a craving for blood clots.

Maybe Sheila's power would have protected her, maybe not. All I knew was that I couldn't risk hurting her. Before it could completely take over, I took off. In a lot of ways, I haven't stopped running.

* * *

Since encountering Sheila and her newfound power, I'd been doing my damnedest to avoid anything supernatural - vampires, Icons, wizards, you name it. Believe me, I felt like shit about it. Not so much for the vampires or wizards, - most of them can go fuck themselves sideways with a rusty cheese grater - but for her. I can only imagine what she was going through, discovering she's not quite human anymore. Unlike me, however, there wasn't anyone to teach her the ropes or offer her a helping hand. Sally may be a bitch, but she was my lifeline in those early days. Not so for Sheila, though. If anything, she would have a price on her head should anyone else learn of her *birth*.

It figured. I'm one of the few who would willingly reach out to help her make the transition and, as luck would have it, I'm fated to be her arch enemy - according to vampire lore anyway. She's either destined to destroy me or I'm going to wind up killing her. Stupid fucking vampire prophets! What a bunch of assholes.

Of course, that's only half the issue. The other reason I haven't reached out to her is simple...I'm a goddamned pussy when it comes to women.

Especially her.

Now You See It...

The cold hard reality of my body slamming down onto the asphalt brought me back. I bounced once, twice, vaguely aware of the green sparks flying off of me as I slid into the middle of the street. For anyone watching from the sidelines, I'm sure it looked pretty goddamned awesome.

I finally skidded to a halt, hoping my vampiric healing kicked in before my nerve endings started working again. The buildings towered over me for what felt like weeks. Finally, the screech of tires and the familiar cursing that is second nature to city dwellers rung out around me. They could call me a cocksucking dick nozzle all they wanted, but at least they didn't run me over.

I blinked a few times and the faces staring down at me came into focus.

"Is he hurt?"

"Dude's completely shit-faced."

"Goddamn homeless assholes!"

"Get out of the street and get a job you fucking faggot."

Gotta love the sympathy of New Yorkers. You'd think they might be a little more concerned for my well-being considering I was just blown to fucking smithereens. At the very least I hoped a few might dial 911 because of the building engulfed in green flame just a few yards away. As weird as New York can be, that sure as shit isn't an everyday occurrence.

I shook my head and sat up, glad to find my limbs were all still attached. "Are you assholes all blind? Don't you see the burning..."

The words died in my mouth as I looked up. The building that housed the loft stood completely untouched. The lights in the bar were still out, but otherwise it looked completely normal. What the hell?

"Yep, fucker's totally high."

"I want some of the shit he's smoking."

Maybe the people around me were right. Wouldn't be the first time I had woken up and completely blanked as to how I had gotten that way.

I staggered to my feet and the small crowd, seeing that the show was over, started to disperse, eager to get on with whatever they had been doing before I had so rudely come crashing down...

Except I *had* come crashing down. My clothes were in tatters. Hell, they were still smoldering. Yet my eyes, ears, and all the rest of my enhanced senses were telling me that everything was just fine. Maybe somehow Sally had...Sally!

I walked back to the sidewalk and looked up and down the street, but it was the same as on any other night in the city. Sure, there were plenty of weirdos about, but not a vampire in sight.

I turned back toward the loft. Maybe someone in there would have a clue about this fucked up hallucination I seemed to be having.

Oh who was I kidding? Outside of Sally, most of the coven was lucky if they remembered what day of the week it was.

Like it or not, without her around, I was on my own. Oh well, I wasn't getting any answers just standing there looking like a doofus. I took another step toward the loft and in the space of a proverbial heartbeat found myself standing in the middle of Hell.

* * *

I stumbled over a pile of debris and felt a blast of intense heat buffet my face. My skin blistered from the intensity of it, and no wonder why. The gutted remains of our building stood before me, still burning with that unearthly green fire. I gawked for a moment before the magnitude of it all struck me. Instinctively, I reached into my pocket for my cell phone, but it wasn't there. Fuck! I must've dropped it when...well whatever the hell had happened. Damn. I doubted my carrier would be all too forgiving about that, albeit that was probably the least of my worries.

I turned back toward the street. "Hey! Someone call for help!"

My cry went unanswered, as people continued to walk by, not even glancing in my direction or at the unearthly towering inferno behind me. New Yorkers are supposed to be jaded, but seriously? Goddamn, these people were cold hearted bastards.

I was stuck somewhere between utter terror and outright confusion when a groan came from behind me, triggering my sensitive vampire ears.

It was coming from where the entrance had once been. It wasn't hard to figure out the source, as a moment later I heard the scrape of rubble as something pushed up from beneath the fallen masonry. *Sally!*

I rushed over and began digging. A moment later, a hand appeared from the debris. I grabbed hold of it and pulled, hoping it wasn't a human. If so, I'd be lucky to not rip their arm right off. Even relatively young vampires possess strength that would make most NFL linebackers jealous. Despite the fact that most elder vamps are complete assholes, I wished one of them was there now, so I might borrow their power. That's one of my Freewill abilities. If I put the bite down on another vampire, not only do I remain upchuck free, unlike most vamps, but I also temporarily add their power to my own. It can be quite a charge, especially if the bitten vampire is considerably older than me.

"Pull harder, asshole."

Gotta love Sally. Do her a solid and she's eternally grateful...sorta.

With one last heave, the rubble gave way and she came free. She stood up, coughing, singed, and covered in dust. Her dress was in tatters, giving me a moment's pause while I noted the color of her undergarments (pink, in case you're interested). She otherwise appeared to be okay for someone who just had a chunk of building collapse on top of her.

I took one last look at Sally, committing the image to memory for later *introspection,* and then dragged her back toward the street.

"Are you okay?"

"No," she snapped. "This dress cost me seven hundred bucks." Nice to see she had her priorities straight.

I ignored her comment. "Wait here and call 911. I'm going back to see if anyone else made it."

Before I could even grasp where my newfound sense of bravado came from, I stopped dead in my tracks. The building that stood before me was whole and untouched again.

What the fuck?

Hocus Pocus

"Please tell me you're seeing this and I haven't gone completely batshit insane."

"I can't vouch for that, but if you are, I'm apparently coming along for the ride."

"It's fine...again."

"Again?"

"I'll explain later. I want to try something. Tell me what you see."

"I see you standing there wearing a dorky..."

"Not yet! Give me til the count of five."

Readying myself, I walked back toward the loft. One step...no change. Two steps...nada. Three steps...whoa - back on the set of a disaster flick. Smoke choked my lungs and made my eyes water. The green flames had died down, but the place was still hotter than Hell.

"What do you see, Sally?"

She stood where I had left her, looking both confused and annoyed.

"Sally?"

A passerby noticed her ruined clothes and mouthed something too low for me to overhear. Her eyes flashed black and she turned toward him. Oh crap.

"Sally, stop!" I shouted, but she ignored me.

I stepped back toward her. "Down girl!" My voice echoed out louder as the heat disappeared and my lungs cleared. Goddamn it was weird.

That she heard. She turned to face me again, forgetting whatever she had planned for the dude who snarked her.

"Glad to see you're paying attention to me again."

"What the fuck are you talking about?"

"I asked you to tell me what you saw."

"No you didn't," she replied. "You just walked up to the building and stood there while some asshole with a death wish..."

"Wait," I said as her words sunk in. "Just watch and tell me if you see anything strange."

I stepped backwards until the blistering heat surrounded me. I grabbed my crotch and pumped it twice at her - all while giving her the finger. She just stood there nonplussed as she watched. That was definitely not normal, but it confirmed...well, I'm not sure what it confirmed other than something really weird was going on.

Sally's brow furrowed and her mouth moved, but there were no sounds save the destruction behind me. I stepped forward again - passing once more through the unseen line in the sand - and at once the sounds of the city were plainly audible again, including her voice.

"...and now they're trashed again."

"Huh?"

"Your clothes...they were fine a moment ago and now they're trashed again."

"That's all you saw?"

"Isn't that enough?"

"No. We need to know which one is real."

"Which what?"

"Reality," I probably sounded like an extra from *Doctor Who*. "This?" I grabbed Sally by the hand and dragged her to the point where the smoke again stung my eyes. "Or this?"

"I see what you mean." She raised her head and sniffed the air.

"Maybe we're in another dimension," I pondered aloud. "Or maybe this is some twisted future we've been thrust into."

"I don't think so."

"Why? Obviously something..."

"It's an illusion," she stated flatly.

A sinking feeling hit my gut. I remembered the gnome illusionist, Festus the Astounding, I had once played at my weekly Dungeons and Dragons game.

"Magic?"

She nodded. "I can smell it...a little trick I picked up from your girlfriend."

"*Sheila?*"

She rolled her eyes. "No, the *other* one."

It took me a moment, but then I realized she was talking about Gan. I groaned. When the little psycho was last in the city, her senses had proven acute enough to sniff out the machinations of Harry Decker and Christy. Sure, she had at least two-hundred and fifty years of experience on either of us, but that didn't mean Sally wasn't a fast learner.

"So is this really happening?"

"Yep. It's real." She put hands on her hips and surveyed the damage, her tone surprisingly calm. "The loft is gone. It's just that the rest of the world can't see, smell, or hear it."

"But..."

"Isn't it obvious? They weren't looking to burn down the whole city."

"Let me guess...just me."

"If I were a betting woman..."

"Which you are."

"Exactly. And instead of getting you, they got the rest of the coven. Guess I should thank you for making us late."

Oh shit! The whole thing had been such a mind-fuck that I had forgotten the coven was inside when the building blew.

"We have to..."

"No we don't," she said coldly, turning to face me.

"But..."

"But *nothing*. If there are any survivors, they'll have to fend for themselves. Going in there would be both suicidal and stupid. I'm neither."

Damn, she was a reptilian bitch. "Well then I'm..."

"No you're not," she stepped in front of me. "You're getting the fuck out of here with me before they decide to nuke this place again just to be safe."

"We don't even..." but I stopped protesting. I may not always be quick on the uptake, but my gaming days had taught me a thing or two about magic (sorta). Whatever was creating this barrier, keeping the destruction penned in, probably wasn't very far away. We could be surrounded by witches. If Decker was controlling them - and as leader of the only group of mages I was aware of, that was a fair bet - they'd probably be more than happy to finish the job once they realized I wasn't a smoking pile of dirt.

Goddamn it! I felt my frustration boil over and I kicked at a mound of rubble, sending debris flying. Sally waited silently, letting me get it out of my system.

At last I calmed down, realizing that I wasn't the only one affected by this. "Do you think anyone made it?"

"I guess we'll find out. Now move it. I don't want to get blasted just by virtue of my association with you."

"Yeah, because you're *so* beloved otherwise," I shot back without any real venom. "So what's the plan?"

"We get underground *fast*."

"The emergency entrance?"

She nodded and took off running toward the alleyway, where a conveniently placed dumpster marked the manhole that would lead us downward.

Rallying the Troops

I thought Sally would lead us back to her new safe house (being that it was supposedly safe and all), but I was wrong. Instead, her plan was to stay below ground until daybreak and then head to the office, the hub of our coven business activities, which also conveniently possessed a sewer-based entrance.

"But the office isn't a secret to anyone," I protested, facing her in the pungent tunnels. I'll admit part of my annoyance stemmed from not being overly joyed at spending the rest of the night wading through knee-deep shit water.

"That's the point. If any of the coven survived, that's where they'll go. We can get a headcount there. The building will also be packed with humans by then."

"You're assuming they won't blow up a group of people to get to us."

"A big assumption, I know. That sure wouldn't stop me."

Big surprise there. Still, if our attackers were the mages, that might be a different story. During our past encounters, they had gone out of their way to avoid hurting normal humans including...

"Oh shit!"

"Well it is a sewer." She crouched, entering a section of the tunnel where the ceiling was lower.

"Not that."

"Then what are you blathering about?"

"Tom and Ed."

"What about them?" She lifted a hand and casually flicked at something nasty that had fallen on her bare shoulder. I doubted she held Tom in much higher regard.

"Christy's coven...they know where we live."

"Not much we can do at the moment," she shrugged. "Cell service down here sucks, go figure. You'd better just hope that witch isn't tired of fucking your idiot friend."

She had a point. I could try to get home, but that might just be painting a big target on my apartment (my renter's insurance was high enough as it was). My roommates had been a part of my adventures since I had first been turned. If things started to get weird...well, okay, *weirder*...they'd hopefully spot it and get the fuck out of Dodge.

Sally was probably right. The office might very well be our best bet. Decker's witches might be able to take down an entire building, shielding the effects from those around it, but selectively disintegrating the couple of floors we rented might be a tad harder to disguise. If they wanted a showdown there, they'd need to do it personally. The odds would be more evenly balanced, especially since Sally kept a loaded gun in her corner suite - a Desert Eagle, a fifty-caliber welcome mat for uninvited guests.

"All right, the office it is."

"Once we get there, I'll tell Starlight to get on the horn with Boston - see what James makes of all this."

"Sounds like a...wait a second. How do you know she survived?"

Sally shrugged, pretending she found a section of the tunnel wall particularly interesting.

"Don't tell me you made her work late."

"What? It's not like the coven paperwork is going to file itself. Besides I probably saved her life. She should thank me."

Starlight was a former model turned vampire. She was both strikingly beautiful and a true sweetheart - a mother hen amongst the wolf pack. Unfortunately for her, she wasn't the sharpest tool in our shed, something Sally gleefully took advantage of. Since assuming her place as my silent partner, she had continually conscripted Starlight to act as her personal secretary. It would have been fine except, in typical Sally fashion, it was a flagrant abuse of her station. She often acted as if she was the goddamned empress of New York. Leona Helmsley had nothing on her.

Still I couldn't be too mad at her. Starlight was one of the few members of the coven, outside of present company, that I didn't want to see meet a bad end.

I considered for a moment whether Sally's flaunting of her position might actually be on purpose in case of contingencies like this - after all she had proven herself to be surprisingly insightful with regards to the perils of our lifestyle. However, I quickly kicked that thought to the curb. If Sally had some foresight that an attack was coming, why hadn't she shared that information? No, more than likely she had been enjoying her role as queen bitch and got lucky.

"What should we do once we get there? Assuming, of course, there isn't a firing squad full of pissed-off sorcerers waiting for us."

She turned around, catching my eyes wandering. I couldn't help it. Her thong had been peeking through one of the many tears in her no-longer pristine evening wear. "Well, getting changed into something less drafty is pretty high on my list."

"Aside from that." I backed up a step, not wanting to get slugged.

Sally shrugged then continued walking in the oppressive darkness of the sewer tunnel. "Your guess is as good as mine. It's my first time being directly part of a coven massacre."

"Directly?"

"Well, I do get around, you know."

"Okay." It was better not to ask, but I did anyway. "So what happened in those indirect cases?"

"Let's just say that things are so much easier when there aren't any survivors."

"That's really not helpful."

"Sorry. Attacks by outside forces are rare in recent times...although I'm thinking they're going to get more common. Most vampire *prunings* are internal matters, usually First Coven-related. When they send a message, it tends to be a permanent one."

"What about when the Khan's coven got wiped out a few months back? Weren't there some stragglers?" It pained me to even think of it. The Khan was Ogedai Khan, one of the Draculas and also Gan's adopted father. He and his forces had been destroyed by the Alma. At the time, his top assassins had been out of country - trying to execute yours truly. As a result, through some twisted logic, the whole thing had been blamed on me.

Sally nodded. "The survivors got absorbed into the surrounding covens, but it was a little different since they were all underneath his rule. I'm hoping that's not the case here because the nearest coven is our friends over in the HBC."

Ugh, not a happy thought. HBC stood for Howard Beach Coven, based out of Queens. Whereas Village Coven was - or had been - primarily a vampire frat house, the HBC was a little more hardcore. That wasn't really the issue. Heck, neither group was really my crowd. What mattered was that they sort of had a grudge against me. Though they were under new leadership these days (thanks to me...well okay, thanks to Sally), they weren't exactly itching to kiss and make up yet.

"Fuck that shit," I said.

"We're in agreement there. I guess we could always go on a massive recruitment drive."

I gave her a sideways glance.

"You're going to have to get over that shit, Bill."

"That's what I'm doing," I replied, stepping over a nasty pile of something.

She ignored my attempt at levity, continuing as if I hadn't spoken. "We can't have a coven with only three vampires and you know it, especially with a bunch of magical morons hunting us down."

"So not only do you want to kill people and bring them back as vampires, you want to immediately line them up as cannon fodder, too?"

"Well, if anything happens, at least we wouldn't have time to get overly attached to them."

"That's fucking evil."

"No, that's realistic."

"What about calling Boston and asking their advice?"

"I don't think we have much choice there," she said. "The only question is what we're going to tell them."

That *was* a good question. I just wished I had a good answer.

* * *

We waited until the start of rush hour to ascend from the sewers, figuring there'd be enough humans present to keep us from being blasted into oblivion. Unfortunately, it also meant we ran into a few people on the way up. We got a few odd glances from our somewhat singed look and slight sewer-scented odor. So much for keeping a low profile.

"Is Starlight even going to be in?" I asked as we reached our floor. "This is typically bedtime."

"Well there *was* a lot of paperwork," she replied with a smirk.

"Slave driver."

"Flatterer."

I needn't have worried, though. We had no more than stepped through the door when Starlight came running out to meet us. She wore a conservative business suit and had her long black hair tied back in a bun. Holy shit, Sally even had her dressing the part.

"Bill, Sally, thank goodness! Did you hear what happened?"

"Don't know, probably don't care," Sally pushed past her and headed for the back.

I locked the door behind us. "We have some bad news."

"I know," Starlight replied. "The loft is gone."

Sally stopped in her tracks and turned. "How'd you know?"

"It was on the radio."

Sally and I exchanged confused glances.

"What did they say?"

"It was weird. When the sun came up, the place was just burned out. None of the neighbors saw or heard anything."

"I guess they dropped their illusion once the fire was out," I said to Sally.

"Apparently so."

"Who dropped what?" Starlight asked. "I thought you were throwing a party last night."

"We definitely had a blast," I said.

"I'm not following you."

"What a surprise," Sally sniffed. "Our wizard friends decided to crash the party last night...explosively so."

"Why?" Starlight wasn't exactly the master strategist of the group, but even she knew better. She turned to me. "They were after you again, weren't they?"

I wasn't sure what Sally had told her about recent events, but it probably wasn't too extensive. Starlight was trustworthy, but that wouldn't stop an older vampire from getting anything he wanted out of her.

"Yep. They still think I'm gonna bring about the birth of the Icon."

"Don't they realize how stupid that is?"

"Heh, yeah, stupid..." I trailed off, hoping to change the subject. "What else did the news say?"

"They said the building must have been empty. They didn't find any bodies."

That wasn't good. When a vampire dies, it typically turns into a pile of ash. In a burnt out building, you'd never notice what could be a veritable vamp graveyard. Deep fried or not, if there were bodies then chances were the vamps attached to them would still be kicking and screaming.

"Don't jump to conclusions, Bill," Sally said. "If anyone survived, I doubt they would have stuck around to talk to the press."

She had a point. The second the sun came up, they would have been toast.

"I have a job for you, Star," she continued.

"I'm on it, boss."

"Get on the horn. Try every one of our lairs and also any cell phones we have on file. I want to know if anyone else made it out."

"You got it."

"Bill, you wait here. I have something to take care of."

"What?" I demanded. "Whatever it is, there's no way I'm letting you do it alone."

"I'm going to take a shower, and believe me, I'd better be alone...unless, that is, you'd like one more casualty to add to the day."

* * *

As much as I have to admit such a death would be totally worth it, I somehow refrained from peeking. I managed to cobble together a pair of pants and a shirt that fit, if didn't altogether match, from the hodgepodge of extras in the office - courtesy of past victims. Considering how often I tended to end up on fire, you'd think I'd have left a change of clothes at the office by now. Unfortunately, that and grabbing a few pints of blood from the fridge were the extent of what I could do during daylight hours. It was pointless to try calling Boston before late afternoon.

That just left checking in on my roommates. Sally asked that I be coy about that first one, as we didn't know the situation back in Brooklyn. She didn't try to stop me, though. I knew she was at least somewhat fond of Ed - much in the same way a child might be fond of a pet gerbil - and she didn't entirely hate Tom.

I called home and was pleasantly surprised when Ed answered and not some gruff voice telling me, "We have your human cattle, Freewill." (Hey, it could happen.) Sensing nothing more than general annoyance in Ed's voice (he was behind in a project at our mutual place of employment), I made up a plausible excuse involving coven-related business - asking him to pass on the message to Dave, my dungeon master, in case he called wondering why I wasn't there. It was actually as much truth as lie. Sunday was game day after all.

Dave's a doctor with lofty ambitions and a shitty bedside manner. He knows I'm a vampire, but unlike Tom or Ed, I keep his knowledge of my undead nature on the down low. Dave's been experimenting on me, his price for offering me some help a while back. Unfortunately, such things are considered a major no-no in the vampire community. If it were ever found out, we'd be in shit deep enough to fill the Mariana Trench twice over.

Once I made sure my friends were fine, the waiting game began. Sally locked herself in her office, but not before putting Starlight back to work on some bullshit assignment. Rather than sit and wonder whether survivors or assassins would come bursting through the doors, I commandeered a computer and followed Ed's lead - getting a little coding done in advance of the work week. I had a feeling I'd be busy over the next few days.

Sadly, vampire life doesn't come with a steady paycheck, at least not when Sally is controlling the purse strings, the cheap bitch. Unlike my movie counterparts like Dracula, Edward, or whatever the fuck character Brad Pitt played in that one movie, I have to hold down a day job to keep a roof over my head. My only solace: in another century or two, the interest on my meager bank savings should start to add up. Yep, it was only a matter of time before that two percent put me on easy street. And no, I don't believe that bullshit for a second, either.

* * *

Four o'clock rolled around, and we had confirmed three additional survivors by that time. That put the infernal forces under my command at a grand total of four, five if you count Sally.

Alfonso, the aforementioned undead hair stylist, hadn't been at the party. He called to let us know that one of his clients had been in need of an emergency manicure, requiring his immediate attention. Sally's squeal of delight at his survival didn't help my mood.

We might be thoroughly fucked, but at least she'd be well-coifed while it happened.

The other two were Dread Stalker and Firebird, two holdovers from the days when Jeff ruled the coven. Dread Stalker was a fucking psycho, no two ways about it. He had been one of Jeff's favorites - innocent looking on the outside, but one of the coven's top hunters. In fact, that was the very reason he had survived the previous night. He had arrived late to the party after scouting for some additional *refreshments*.

Firebird hadn't been nearly as lucky. She crawled into the office mid-afternoon, having pulled her way through the sewers. She'd been present when the fireworks started. It hadn't been pretty.

She was a smoking hot redhead. When I first met her, she'd existed for seemingly no other reason than to be Jeff's personal sex toy. Just for the record, though, she looks much hotter when she has skin. Before blacking out, she managed to tell us that she'd been standing near the windows at the back of the building when the loft went up like a Roman candle. She'd been flung through the glass and onto the street below.

After hearing Firebird's tale, Sally shrugged and walked silently back into her office. Her meaning was clear. Anyone who hadn't been as *lucky* was most likely dust in the wind by now.

Starlight and I carried Firebird to a back room, and set her up with an IV transfusion of bottled blood. The blood, combined with accelerated healing, would get her back on her feet within a day or so. Hopefully it would leave her looking less gross, too.

After we got Firebird situated, Sally popped her head out of her office.

"It's probably safe to call Boston now."

I nodded, gave the others specific orders to stay put, and then locked myself in with her. It was sure to be quite the interesting call.

The Conference Call of Cthulhu

James didn't answer his cell phone. Being the newest member of our ruling coven probably kept him busy. We tried the main line for Boston instead and hoped for the best - kind of like getting on a call with tier one tech support in India and naïvely expecting that a solution was forthcoming.

"How may I direct your call?" the bored voice on the other end asked.

"We need to speak with James," Sally replied.

"James? I don't know of any James, unless you mean..."

Sally sighed and said, "I would like to speak with James the Wanderer, esteemed member of the First Coven." She gave me a look of disgust. Sally wasn't exactly big on ceremony.

"All glory to the First!" the operator replied.

Sally hit mute on the speakerphone. "Ass-kisser."

I failed to suppress a smirk as she unmuted the phone and the office drone on the other end finished their verbal genuflecting. "The First, praise be to them, are not in the habit of taking calls. I will warn you that..."

"Oh quit the shit," Sally snapped. "It's an emergency. It's about the Freewill."

"You know the Freewill?"

"Yeah," I chimed in, "she's sitting right next to me."

"Sorry...sir," came the reply. "Praise be to the one who shall lead our armies in battle..."

"We're kind of in a rush here," Sally interrupted.

"Oh...sorry. Hold please."

Bland elevator music began to play as she muted the speaker again.

"Are they always like that?"

"Yep. Aside from James, I'm pretty sure Boston exclusively employs a legion of boot-lickers."

"And zombies," I added, remembering the not-so ravenous hordes of the undead the vampire nation liked to use as clerical help.

"They smell bad, but at least they keep their fucking mouths shut...those that have mouths, anyway. That's more than I can say for most of those assholes."

Almost as if summoned, a familiar oily voice came onto the line. "Can I help you?"

"Colin?" Sally asked, unable to disguise her dislike for James's assistant. They apparently had history, but she had never let me in on what that was. If I had to guess, though, I'd say Colin was an ex fuck-buddy gone sour. Of course when it came to Sally, I sort of assumed the same of everyone she knew.

There was nothing but silence on the other end. "Colin, are you still there?"

"Oh I'm here...just waiting for you to address me properly."

"What the hell are you talking about?"

"Since you're a little slow on the uptake, as usual, I'll give you a hint. That's Regional Coven Master, Colin, prefect for the northeastern United States to you."

"No fucking way."

"Oh yes," he replied eagerly. "James's promotion left an open spot and I, already knowing and...dare I say...*excelling* at the job, was the natural choice."

Sally's nails dug into the arms of her chair listening to him gloat. It was probably only a matter of time before she said something that would get us hung up on.

"Congratulations, Coven Master Colin." I figured it was easier to give him a little mollification. No skin off my teeth as at the end of the day he'd still be an asshole.

Sally's eyes grew wide and she mouthed, "What the fuck?!"

I gestured for her to relax. My experience in corporate America taught me how to play the game.

"Is that you, Freewill?"

"It is."

"Always a pleasure," he replied flatly.

"Likewise. We were hoping to speak to James." Bantering with Colin was pointless. He disliked Sally and his opinion of me was even lower.

"The First are not at your beck and call, nor do they speak with children. You two really should know the rules, but then again, I guess that's to be expected."

"We have a special exception from James and you know it," Sally spat.

I hit mute. "We do?"

"Uh, yeah. Unlike *you*, I haven't spent the past month jerking off to anime. Shit is going down and you're gonna be a part of it whether you like it or not. I talked to James and he agreed that the least they can do is answer the fucking phone for us."

She had a good point. I'd been avoiding reality while she dealt with it head-on.

"That exception is only to be used in times of emergency."

"You're right, Colin," Sally replied as she unmuted the phone. "So how does our entire fucking coven being wiped out by a bunch of magic-wielding assholes sound to you? Is that emergency enough?"

"Well..."

She turned beet red - quite an accomplishment for someone lacking a heartbeat. "They were trying to kill the Freewill!" she snapped.

There was a pause as Colin no doubt tried to figure out how to stonewall us some more. "Very well. I guess that does count as a potential emergency."

"Potential..."

"Don't get your panties in a bunch, Sally, my dear. Assuming you wear them, something I highly doubt..."

I snatched the phone out of the way as her fist came down on the heavy desk, leaving a visible crack in its surface.

"What was that?"

"Nothing," I replied. "Must be a glitch in the line."

"I suppose, considering the circumstances, this news should be shared," he made no attempt to hide his scorn. "Hold while I check to see if James is available to join us."

"Wait," I said. "Join us?"

"Of course, Freewill. I am in charge of the wellbeing of your coven now, after all. As this concerns me, it's only appropriate that I take the lead in investigating this *heinous* crime." His emphasis indicated that any sorrow he might've felt at my plight was only because my attackers hadn't succeeded.

If this was the new power structure, eternal life would be a very long time indeed.

* * *

Colin took a good long while. Sally passed the time with a string of angry insults as to what a fucktard he was. It was highly amusing to listen to her vent about someone who wasn't me for a change.

Finally, just when I was starting to suspect we'd been purposely forgotten, we were taken off hold.

"Hello, Sally, are you still there?" James asked from the speakerphone. Hearing him, I immediately felt a little better. In a world populated by backbiting, supernatural assholes, James was one of the few exceptions. He wasn't exactly a saint - I had once seen him tear through a gang of street thugs like they were made of tissue paper - but he had always been cool to me.

"James it's..."

Colin's greasy voice cut her off. "Eh hem! Please rise to show respect for the Wanderer, bold explorer of the shadows and esteemed member of the First Coven."

Rise? What a fucking douchebag.

"All glory to the First!" No doubt his lips were nice and puckered up for James's ass. "His eminence is recognized."

"Thank you, Colin, I'm sure," James replied dryly. It was painfully obvious that his tolerance for his former aide was limited. There was more than one reason I liked him.

"Are we done yet?" Sally asked. "Because we have..."

"The children shall not speak until the First addresses them to do so!" Colin snapped.

Motherfucker! The guy probably had the rules tattooed to his eyelids, although surely part of it was because he disliked us.

"Colin, please," James's tone showed his restraint was barely hanging on. "I think we can suspend protocol for the Freewill."

"Very well, my lord." Though Colin's words were entirely subservient, there was an undertone of *fuck-you* to his tone.

"Thank you," James replied flatly before addressing us. "I apologize for not answering earlier..."

"The First need never apologize to..."

"Colin, please!" James's voice had an edge this time. That finally shut up the little ass-kisser. The silence hung in the air for several seconds.

"Sally, my dear, please forgive me. My new duties, combined with our combat preparations, have, alas, taken up a great deal of my time."

"I can understand," she replied with a smile on her face. No doubt her expression was at the fact that Colin was probably seething at that moment.

"I'm not being flippant when I say I truly doubt that."

"Anything we can help with?" I asked, immediately realizing how stupid it probably sounded.

James chuckled. "Thank you, Dr. Death." At the time I was turned, Jeff had a dumbass rule in place that called for all members to adopt new code names, for lack of a better word, hence why coven members had names like Starlight and Dread Stalker. Dr. Death had been mine.

What can I say? I was under a bit of a pressure at the time. Although the rule, like Jeff, was long gone, a few people had grown fond of my dopey moniker and continued to use it.

"I think I can handle things," James continued. "Although it *is* an interesting coincidence that you called. I was just compiling a database of special vampires, yourself being at the top of that list."

Now it was Sally's turn to chuckle. She hit mute just long enough to ask me, "Should I buy you a helmet?"

"Fuck you."

"Excuse me?" James asked.

Goddamn it! She had unmuted us. "Err, sorry. Must be static in the line. What do you mean special vampires?"

"Exactly that. Vampires with powers outside of the norm."

"I thought I was the only Freewill." I had been under the impression that I was the only one for at least half a millennia. A brief glimmer of hope flickered within me. If there were others, then perhaps the prophecies wouldn't apply to me.

"You are, so far as we know," James replied, pouring ice water on my small tinder of wishful thinking. "But just because you are the sole being of legend doesn't mean that other vampire *anomalies* don't exist. I'm compiling a list of their abilities in preparation for the coming conflict. It could prove useful."

"Really? Like what?"

"Well...ah, I have an example you might recognize. Surely you remember Gansetseg." It sounded as if he had a smirk on his face.

"Gan is special, all right," I growled.

"Quite so," he ignored my snark. "Gansetseg was turned when she was still a pre-teen. Her body became forever locked in the state she was in at the time.

"So?"

"So, she is in a perpetual state of puberty."

"So her superpower is being hormonally imbalanced?" Sally asked.

"Partially. One of the side effects is that her body chemistry is hyper-accelerated compared to other vampires her age."

My eyes opened wide. "Speed."

"I see you noticed," James replied.

I had seen her in action during her *vacation* to New York when she followed me from her home in China thanks to a case of misguided puppy love. She was capable of moving at speeds that rendered her but a blur to even vampire eyes. At the time, she was one of the older vampires I had been exposed to, at a ripe old three hundred years, so it just appeared to be her greater powers. With a little more experience under my belt, though, I now realized she moved more like a vamp twice her age - with the added benefit of having the size and flexibility of a child.

"That's just great," Sally remarked. "Will probably do wonders for her humility."

"That, combined with her status in Asia, makes her quite indispensable to our cause." James paused for a moment. "But I'm sure you didn't call for this meeting just to ask me how things were going. Am I correct?"

"Colin didn't fill you in?" Somehow I wasn't surprised.

"I'm not your messenger boy, child," he said. Damn, I had almost forgotten the prick was still on the call, but it served as a reminder to watch my words. James could probably be counted on to be discreet, but Colin could only be trusted to fuck us over as quickly as was vampirically possible.

"Colin..." James's threat hung in the air.

"You're right, James," Sally said, swerving us back on track. "We had a bit of a night."

"Care to elaborate?"

"There was an incident at the loft..."

"An incident?" I interrupted. "The entire building was wiped the fuck out."

"Thanks, Bill," she sighed. "I was getting to that."

* * *

We explained the situation to James. Well, okay, *Sally* explained while I interrupted whenever she downplayed the situation too much. Most vamps are emotionally unaffected by mass carnage, but *c'mon*! Sure, my coven were mostly douchebags, most of whom I wouldn't miss - hell I was pretty much over it - but what happened should have warranted at least a modicum of outrage.

Sally stuck mostly to the facts, not elaborating unless pressed. She was probably hoping we'd be taken at face value. Sadly, being a wage slave, I knew what it was like to be grilled by upper management. If I was sure of one thing, it was that the hard questions were still to come.

I knew it would probably be unwise to flat out lie. I was considered special in the vampire community, but that didn't mean they wouldn't come up with some appropriate punishment to make an example of me. It would be even worse for Sally. The elders wouldn't think twice about dusting her and then pissing on the ashes.

At last, she finished with her account and then came the anticipated Q&A.

"Are you sure it was the mages who did this?" James asked.

"We didn't see them," Sally admitted, "but the green fire was definitely not natural."

"No doubt. I just find it odd."

"I don't," I said. "They haven't really gotten over wanting me dead."

"I had thought, based on your associations up in the Woods of Mourning, you had perhaps come to a measure of peace with them."

"That was Christy," I replied. "She's just one member of that group. The rest...well, not so much. If we hadn't been under a state of truce up there, I don't doubt they would've tried to blast the shit out of me."

"Thank you for the colorful observation, Dr. Death. Still, the Magi's feud is known to be primarily with you, not vampire kind in general."

"I'm well aware," I said, an edge to my voice.

"Please know I'm not trying to downplay this," James said in a conciliatory tone. "Even so, personal vendettas are considered exactly that - personal. If a force attacks us en masse, we respond in kind. However, a lone vampire..."

"I get it. We're expected to deal with our own crap."

"In a word, precisely."

"But they didn't go after just me."

"I know and, assuming it was them, that's troubling. A skilled Magi is more like a surgeon than a child with a hammer. Such an act of...*terrorism*...is unlike them."

"Know anyone else who can level a building full of vampires in the middle of Manhattan while keeping it hidden from everyone more than twenty feet away?"

"Some entities come to mind, but none who have any motive."

That was a scary thought, although it wasn't particularly surprising. I had seen enough in Canada not to be overly shocked should Godzilla, Mothra, and the Old Ones rise out of the East River and start smashing shit. It was nearly terrifying to know that as powerful as vampires are, there were beings out there to whom we're little more than bugs.

"The thing is," James continued, "the Magi have already indicated they prefer to remain neutral in the coming conflict. They have no love of us, but likewise, they have never counted the Alma as allies...nor do I see that changing. The Alma aren't particularly fond of anything in human guise, vampire or otherwise."

"Yet, despite all that, we have a brand new parking lot only a few blocks away."

"I don't dispute that. I'm just trying to find sense in the motives here."

"They have that stupid prophecy of theirs," Sally commented.

"We're aware of that. The logic of their reasoning is dubious at best, unless perhaps they are, for some reason, convinced that the rise of the Icon is imminent."

Sally and I locked eyes. Oh crap. She shook her head. Her meaning was clear...shut the fuck up. I didn't need to be told twice. Jesus Christ, what a fucking minefield.

"I'm afraid there are too many questions on the table," James said. "The loss of one coven is of little consequence to the First's plans, no offense intended. However, considering your role in the coming conflict..."

"Oh fuck," I muttered under my breath, forgetting James's hearing was supernaturally acute.

"In this, sadly, I have no say. Lord Alexander was quite adamant on this point. Your involvement raises this incident's priority."

"Go me," I sighed as Sally kicked me from under the table.

"Based on what we know, or more precisely what we don't, I see only one course of action..."

That didn't sound promising. Tom was definitely not going to be pleased if I'd put a giant crosshairs on his girlfriend."

"...we need to set up a conference call with the Magi."

"What?!"

Whatever the hell had happened to nuking it from orbit?

A friendly chat with the assholes who'd nearly vaporized me...go figure. I couldn't wait to see how that was gonna turn out. If I was a betting man, though, I'd venture to guess it wouldn't be in my favor.

Without Bad Luck, I'd have No Luck at All

"A conference call?"

"Of course," James replied. "What did you expect me to say?"

"Something with a bit more killing, for starters," Sally said.

James chuckled. "Sally, my dear, this isn't the thirteenth century. We don't take up arms for the slightest offenses, especially at this moment. We'll soon have our hands full enough of enemies. I'd prefer we not add to their number."

I bristled at the slightly offensive remark. I don't consider myself hot shit or anything, but I'm not jaded enough to shrug off attempts on my life as no big deal.

Sally raised her hands and shrugged. There wasn't much we could do to protest. By bringing Boston into this mess, we had to accept their judgment on the matter. Regardless, neither of us was quite expecting a conference bridge with the folks who, in all likelihood, just succeeded in sending about a dozen vampires screaming into the great beyond.

Talking to those psychos was not a good thing at any time, but right now, it had potential to be epically disastrous. Harry Decker and his fun bunch claimed to have known about my birth through their scrying or whatever the fuck they did. Assuming they weren't full of shit, I wasn't about to rule out their ability to do the same for the Icon. Considering they somehow thought that Sheila would be the death of them - which was hard to wrap my brain around since she wasn't a killer - there was little doubt they'd be keeping their eyes open for her arrival.

This was shaping up to be the worst conference call of my life, even worse than that time I accidentally clogged the school toilet back in first grade with my Boba Fett figure (I was pretending it was the Sarlaac pit).

Talk about a shitty situation.

* * *

Once more, Sally and I played the waiting game, as there were diplomatic channels to be opened on Boston's end. If there was an upside, it was that Colin was again forced to act as James's toady. No matter how far up in the vampire hierarchy he got, he was still just someone else's bitch. That alone was worth a fraction of a smile.

The evening stretched into the wee hours of the night. Despite my orders, Dread Stalker left at some point...probably to go and commit some heinous act or another. Hopefully he ran into some witches in a dark alley. It was a horrible thought, but fuck it - I'm not applying for sainthood anytime soon. If the asshole wanted to get himself killed, that was his problem. Starlight was kept busy with some more of Sally's bullshit paperwork. Firebird continued resting, albeit probably not comfortably. She still looked like a charbroiled chicken, but the blood transfusions appeared to be having some effect. She looked a little less *crispy* in places.

Sally and Alfonzo disappeared into her office for a while. I couldn't even amuse myself with the fantasy that he was railing her behind closed doors. I probably had far more of a chance with him than she did. No, she was probably doing something douchey like getting her hair colored. It would figure. We almost got our asses turned into Baked Alaska, and her biggest concern was whether her roots were showing.

At last, her door opened. Alfonzo exited and indicated that Sally wanted me back in her office. I was supposed to be the one in charge. *I* should be summoning *her* into my office (if I had one).

Oh, who was I kidding? I would have gladly handed her the keys to the castle. Hell, I would have dropped to one knee and proclaimed her Queen Shit if I could've turned back the clock a year and gone down a different path. Even two months back would be enough. I could have told Sheila, "Sorry, babe, but I just don't think you've got it in you to do any better." Sure, it would have completely fucked up my chances with her, but it would have been far more preferable compared to what lay ahead for both of us. My only advantage was knowing how much shit I was in. She would be blindsided.

I stopped midway into Sally's office. No, I couldn't let that happen. The call's outcome couldn't be predicted, but I had a very good idea what my next course of action was going to be.

* * *

"Greetings, Freewill," a voice on the line intoned.

"Hey, Harry," I replied flippantly. "Fuck up the launch of Farm Blitz yet?" Harry Decker was yet another on my ever-growing list of arch-enemies. He also, not coincidentally, happened to be the senior vice-president of marketing at my workplace, Hopskotchgames.

"Hardly. In fact, I expect a nice bonus from that one. Perhaps I'll buy myself a new Bentley."

"Only douchebags drive Bentleys," I spat. It wasn't much of a comeback, but rubbing my face in the fact that he pretty much wrote his own paychecks just poured salt in the wound.

"I'm sure your work relationship is truly fascinating," James interrupted, "but we have far more serious business to discuss."

"Of course, vampire," Decker replied.

"Esteemed Magi," Colin said. "We welcome you to this conclave under protection of truce..."

Truce? What the fuck?

"Will you be attending alone, or shall we extend the invitation to others of your circle?"

"I speak for my coven," Decker replied arrogantly. What a douche.

"Very well, honored guest." Colin's tone took on a sour note. "Freewill, are you ready?"

"How come Gandalf the Gay gets an esteemed and honored greeting?"

"Because he's not you."

I heard Decker chuckle. Make that double douches.

"Colin, please," James said, his tone neutral but the warning fairly evident.

"My apologies, Wanderer."

James ignored his sniveling and got down to business. As he began to speak, I locked eyes with Sally. Her look mirrored my own. She had no idea how this was going to play out either.

"Mr. Decker, the Magi and the vampire nation have been on civil terms these past few centuries."

"Indeed," he replied. "My people have no quarrel with yours...typically."

"Yes, we are aware of your issue with the Freewill. However, we consider that to be a personal matter."

I had meant to be a fly on the wall, but my mouth had other plans. "It's fucking personal, alright."

Sally rolled her eyes - yeah, saw that one coming a mile away.

"I am here on good faith, Wanderer," Decker said. "Kindly restrain your dog."

"Dog? Fuck you, you..."

"That will be enough, Dr. Death." I knew what James was capable of. Likewise I knew the influence he now wielded as one of the thirteen most powerful vampires on the planet. All of that considered, I shut my mouth quickly, obeying...like a dog. Motherfucker!

"My apologies," James said.

Sally immediately reached over and hit the mute button. "Curse out the asshole this way if it makes you feel better."

"Not as much fun if he can't hear it, but good idea anyway."

"I'm full of them."

"You're full of something all right."

"...as you can see, the situation is somewhat beyond normal. Considering the circumstances, I'm forced to investigate potential causes." Oh crap, what had James been saying? From the sound of things, he was just summing things up for Decker. Hopefully there hadn't been any questions in there for me. "Do you have anything to add, Dr. Death?"

Yep, I deserved that one.

"Err...no, I think that about covers it." I hoped I didn't just hand Decker a "get out of blowing me up free" card.

Silence resonated on the line for several seconds. "Despite our past vendetta against the Freewill," Decker said at last, "my coven did not attempt to assassinate him this evening, though it would have been well within our power."

I flipped the finger at the phone. It only made me feel slightly better.

"That is a relief to hear," James replied.

"Hold on," I cried, unmuting the phone. "That's it? He says he didn't blow up the loft and you just take him at his word?"

"Dr. Death..."

"Perhaps it would behoove you to listen, you idiotic abomination," Decker explained. "I didn't say we had nothing to do with leveling that murderous hive of filth. I simply replied to the question at hand...we were not trying to kill you."

There was silence from all parties on the line. I wasn't sure what Decker was trying to say other than to announce he had just gotten off the train at Crazy Town.

Sally's mouth opened, but I quickly waved her off. Whatever had been on the tip of her tongue was doubtlessly less than diplomatic. If anything, she probably liked being flash-fried even less than I did.

Finally James spoke again, his tone stern. "I'm not sure I follow, Mr. Decker. Please explain yourself."

"I need explain nothing. I am a dead man walking. We all are. My fate, as that of all the magical covens, is at hand. The future cannot be rewritten, but I can make sure that those who have had a hand in it shall suffer."

"And why is that?" James asked.

"Is it not as plain as the fangs hanging from your mouth?" Decker spat. "The signs are all there. Death looms over us all. The Icon has risen."

Oh fuck.

Party Crashers

"The Icon!" Colin exclaimed.

Oh shit. I was afraid of this.

"Calm down, Colin," James replied. There was an edge in his voice that hadn't previously been there. The vampire nation was preparing for war against the Feet. Yeah, that sounds stupid to me too, but what are you gonna do? Primal powers that had long lain dormant would most likely join in the fray. We were potentially looking at a global supernatural showdown that would make the battle of Helms Deep look like a slap fight in comparison. The Icon was the last person that any vampire...other than me, maybe...wanted to meet. Outside of sunlight, silver, and stakes to the heart, vamps are pretty damn tough to kill. It shows in their general everyday arrogance. To introduce a wildcard now, one that could potentially turn a legion of vampires to dust with but a touch of her hand, was a recipe for widespread panic - right when the vampire nation needed it least.

"We're aware of the prophecy, Mr. Decker. However, our own seers have..."

"Then they are as useless as that beast and the diseased harlot with whom we are speaking."

"I am so gonna rip your lungs out through your asshole, you fucking little weasel!" Yep, that's Sally. Try to kill her, and she'll hold her tongue. Call her names and she loses it.

"Everyone, please!" James shouted, attempting to regain control. "Mr. Decker, I apologize for the outbursts. Please indulge us with what you were saying."

"The Icon lives, vampire," Decker hissed. "My people have seen it. The portents do not lie. We have double and triple checked them."

"Did you find out who's naughty and who's nice?" Sally sniffed.

"Laugh if you wish, trollop. You know as well as I do that the Icon brings nothing but death. My kind is doomed by its coming, but do not think yours is immune. How many of the undead shall burn at its touch?"

I gotta say, I was starting to take a little offense to his constant referring to the Icon as an *it*. Thankfully, before the words could spill out of my mouth, I remembered what a monumentally bad idea it would be to correct him.

Even worse was the fact that Decker knew Sheila from our workplace. Hell, the asshole had once gone out on a *date* with her. If he had known back then her potential...well, who knows how that night would have played out? As it was, it ended fairly explosively thanks in part to Gan's presence. Little did I know back then that so many pieces of the fucked up puzzle of my life were in such close proximity.

Sally snapped her fingers in front of my face.

"Hey, anyone home?"

"Huh?"

"Pay attention, dipshit," she snapped. "Now's not the time to zone out."

"Oh, sorry."

She unmuted the phone while I tried to figure out what I had missed.

"Assuming that is even true," James was saying, "how can you know it's a threat? The creature could be living in a cave in Bangladesh for all you are aware."

"Not true. It is close, that much we can tell."

"You said it yourself, the Icon's power somehow counteracts against your own. You have no way of knowing..."

"DO NOT TELL ME WHAT I KNOW, BEAST!" Decker screamed into the phone as an uncomfortable whine of feedback blared on our end. "The Icon is near, perhaps in this very city. I can *feel* its presence, much like a reaper breathing down the back of my neck."

"Are you sure that's not just the men in white coats?"

Decker ignored me and continued on his insane tirade. "I was too late to save my people. My protégé was too soft - weak - to do what needed to be done..."

He must have been talking about Christy, and what he said was good to hear. She was much more pleasant to be around when she wasn't actively plotting to kill me, and it was likewise a good thing for Tom. Though he typically didn't bring it up, it bothered him that his girlfriend and me didn't always get along...murderously so. Of course, now Christy had a Sheila shaped pendulum of death hanging over her head. That had potential to be a bit awkward in the near future.

"...but that didn't mean I couldn't make you suffer."

Huh? Oh yeah, Decker was still yammering. I had been on the receiving end of his insane monologues in the past. It was easiest to just nod as he ranted. That last part, though, sounded like it might be sorta important.

"What do you mean by that?" I asked, although I had a feeling I knew where this was going.

"Fool!" he spat venomously - the spittle practically flying through the speaker. "You think we were trying to kill you last night? We purposely struck when we did."

Hmm, that sounded kind of like a confession to me.

"Are you saying you knowingly attacked one of our covens?" James asked.

"Not one of your covens, Wanderer...*his* coven, the Freewill's. All of this started with him: the portents, the prophecy, the coming war."

"I must say..." James tried to say, but Harry was still busy frothing at the mouth.

"Hear me, Freewill. Your existence has brought forth nothing but suffering..."

"Tell me about it," Sally muttered. "We have to suffer through listening to this asshole."

"Shhh," I whispered. "I want to hear this."

"...and so shall you suffer in return. My days may be numbered, beast, but I shall make sure that I spend every waking moment bringing misery to your existence. Your coven was only the beginning, so as to truly make you appreciate your sense of loss..."

Uh huh. Sure, I hadn't wanted to see my coven wind up as fertilizer, but the truth was I didn't like most of them. My sense of loss ran about as deep as a paper cut.

"...until at last, right before I myself die, you shall beg me to kill you. Only then shall I perhaps allow your miserable life to..."

"Perhaps we can work together to solve this problem."

"What?!" I knew Colin was a douche-weasel, but did I really just hear him offer help to the crazy wizard who nearly blasted Sally and me to kingdom come?

"Excuse me?" James broke the momentary silence.

"I was offering our esteemed guest assistance in solving this mutual dilemma."

"You'll forgive my confusion, Colin, but did not this wizard just admit to an act of war against the vampire nation? That hardly seems..."

"I mean no disrespect to the First, my lord," Colin sniveled. It had been a little while since he had slobbered his lips against someone's rear-end. He was due. "But I do not believe the wizard's actions were an act of war."

"The fuck?!" I yelled. "This asshole just admitted he..."

"Kindly allow him to finish, Dr. Death," James said, his tone making me think twice about continuing. "I'm curious as to where this is going. Please continue, Colin."

"Thank you, great Wanderer."

It was my turn to roll my eyes. Oh, fuck me up the ass with a chainsaw.

"I believe the Magi only acted out of desperation. They do not wish to war with us. Is that not true, Mr. Decker?"

"We have nothing to lose by acting," he replied.

"Then I believe I see a solution that might avoid hostilities between our people as well as eliminate a shared enemy..."

No!

"We will work together to find, hunt down, and exterminate the Icon."

Oh shit. Talk about a bad day getting even worse.

Planning the Offensive

"That didn't go quite as expected," Sally said ten minutes after the call ended. To my great chagrin, James had been swayed from whatever ultra-violent course of action he had hopefully been contemplating to actually agreeing with Colin. I guess I couldn't blame him, either. James was loathe to spare troops for a skirmish with the mages. As dangerous as the Icon was, combining forces seemed the safer option. Damn the gods of logic!

Despite his layering of brown-nosing, Colin's suggestion had made sense. Even Decker, batshit crazy as he was, had stopped his ranting to listen. In the end, he had agreed to a temporary truce. If the Icon could be located and eliminated, then he would cease hostilities against the vampire nation.

"You ain't whistling Dixie, sister."

"It's even worse than you think, Bill," she said quite seriously. That wasn't good. Sally usually dropped the attitude only in extreme circumstances.

"They just handed the girl I love a death sentence. Pray tell how it could get worse."

"Do you think for one second Decker is going to stop trying to kill you?"

"You think he would risk it?"

"The guy's a fucking nutcase. You tell me."

"Point taken."

"Then there's Colin. He's probably squirting in his pants with joy right now. He got to score brownie points with James and gets to coordinate our efforts in this witch hunt."

"Icon hunt."

"Whatever the fuck. Don't think for a second that Colin isn't aware that Decker will try to take you out at the first chance he gets. Don't doubt he won't do everything in his power to fuck you over until that happens, either."

I sighed and got up, feeling the need to pace. "Any more *good* news before I allow myself to fall into a spiraling depression?"

"Just this: they're going to find her."

"I know."

"I don't know if they can stop her, Bill, but they're going to find her and figure out who she is."

"Decker?"

"Count on it, and once they do..."

"They're going to put two and two together."

"Exactly."

"Then I guess we have one course of action ahead of us."

"And that is?" she asked, although she knew better than that. She was one of the quickest thinkers I had ever met.

"We need to find Sheila first."

* * *

"And what makes you think I'm going to help you? After all, the others have a point. The Icon is dangerous to all of us."

There was a brief, uncomfortable pause as Sally's words sunk in. She was right. The Icon represented a massive threat to vampires as a whole. If the stories were to be believed, the Icons of days past had cut through our ranks like a hot knife through butter.

In one of our past talks, Sally had mentioned that the biblical tale of Samson versus an army of Philistines was actually based on fact. Samson, the egomaniacally horny muscleman of myth, had actually been an Icon. His foes had been vampires. Needless to say, it didn't end well for our side. Sure, he had eventually been taken down - supposedly by that power that eventually fells all great men...*pussy* - but the actual details of his downfall had been lost to legend. Even if the Bible stories were true, I wasn't particularly in love with the idea of crushing my wannabe girlfriend under several tons of falling debris.

Still, Sally had a point. I was basically asking her to help me find and protect a person who was, in essence, a walking time bomb. Forget touch, my lips hadn't even come into contact with Sheila's (much to my chagrin) when her powers had flared. Who's to say that we might find her, and the simple act of doing so might end with our asses being fried like chickens?

Therein lay another problem. If Sally refused to help me, she held enough game pieces to sink my battleship once and for all. It would only benefit her to spill her guts. Alexander, oldest of the First Coven and the guy that shitty Oliver Stone movie was based on, had taken a shine to her despite her relatively young age. She could easily play this up and win herself a nice comfy spot at the table.

"Just fucking with you."

"What?"

"You heard me," she said, a grin spreading across her face. "I just wanted to see the look on your face. I gotta get my kicks somewhere." Bitch!

"So you're actually going to help me?" I asked, not quite daring to believe what I heard.

"Uh yeah, dumbass. What the fuck do you think I've been doing this past month? I'm already up to my shapely ass in lies. It's not like I can even claim you compelled me. You suck at it and James wouldn't buy it for a second."

"Thanks, Sally."

"I speak only the truth. So that leaves me only a couple of choices. I could fuck you over, don't think I don't know that. In doing so, though, I'd have to throw myself on the mercy of the Draculas and beg their forgiveness."

"Which they're not exactly known for giving."

"Precisely. Assuming they don't ram a stake through me and ruin my favorite bra, I'd have to team up with Colin and Decker. I would sooner be sentenced to an eternity of giving you and your roommate - the stupid one, mind you - hourly blowjobs than tell either of those twats the time of day."

I lost focus for a moment as that image formed in my mind. Sorry, I couldn't help it. Even in the midst of a dire emergency, there are some things that take priority.

"Are you finished giving yourself a hard-on?" Sally's eyes met mine. Goddamn, some days I'd swear she was almost psychic.

"Uh, I was just mentally planning our next steps."

"Sure you were. As I was saying, I'd sooner take my chances helping you. Either way, I'm probably fucked, but at least I can stomach your company better..."

I opened my mouth to comment.

"Don't get any ideas, limp dick. I've already cast my ballot and you're simply the lesser of multiple evils."

I smiled at her.

"What?" she demanded.

"You're a good friend, Sally."

"Fuck you, Bill."

* * *

"So what's the plan?"

"That's the other reason I'm helping you. You're fucking pathetic on your own. Without me, they'd figure out the whole thing in about five minutes and be up yours and your girlfriend's asses within the day."

"How about *without* the commentary? I only ask because, Decker aside, you know all the players involved better than I do."

"True," she soaked up the compliment like a sponge.

"James?" I asked.

"I don't think we have anything to worry about. First off, as I'm sure you well know, he's a little different than the other elders." I nodded. "If push comes to shove, he'd at least hear us out without getting all stabby about it."

"Yeah, but I don't see him helping us either."

"Agreed. There's too big of a spotlight on him right now. Also, I'm not sure we could convince him that the Icon is harmless and should be spared. James is reasonable, but that's a big uphill battle right there. The best case scenario would be that he keeps the crosshairs off of us."

"But Sheila still gets ganked," I said morosely.

"Sorry, but yeah. So we'll keep him as our contingency plan if all else goes to shit. If he asks too many questions, we can always play stupid."

"Let me guess, I shouldn't have a problem with that."

"Ooh, you know me too well," she replied, a saucy little grin on her face.

"So you're going to help me save her, in addition to our own asses?"

"Don't get me wrong, Bill. My ass is *always* my number one priority. But..."

"But?"

She looked almost constipated, as if the words wouldn't quite come. "I figure I owe you one...or maybe two. Besides which, if I thought for a second I'd have to spend eternity listening to you whine about lost love like some fucked up *Twilight* reject, I'd find myself a nice beach to lie on and wait for the sun to rise."

Despite my somewhat dead nature, I felt my insides warm at her words. All things considered, she had earned me not rubbing it in...just this once.

"Okay, so what about Colin?"

"He's an asshole."

"I know *that*. What can we expect?"

"His new position is pretty high ranking. Since we're under his jurisdiction, James will probably let him lead this operation. He won't want to, but his hands are already pretty full and it's proper protocol. Besides, the Icon is just one being. James still has to worry about a whole army of angry Sasquatches."

"The needs of the many, outweigh the needs of the few...or the one," I said, raising my fingers in a Vulcan salute.

Sally raised a quizzical eyebrow. "I'm gonna assume I don't want to know. Anyway, Colin will be in charge, but he's also a little fucking weasel. Unlike James, he's not about to throw his natty little ass into the fray. Expect him to be an armchair general. I doubt he'll even come down here in person...probably make up some bullshit about all the administrative duties requiring his oversight."

"That's a plus."

"Maybe..."

"Why just maybe?"

"It depends who he sends in his place."

She was right. That was a big *if*, one that could potentially save us or screw us.

Crank Call

Following our attempt at assessing Boston's role in all of this, we had tried to take inventory of all the other players. Decker and his coven of witches were definitely dangerous. The plus was we knew enough not to trust them. He and anyone under his command would fuck us over the first chance they got. That left our heavily limited resources.

"There's you and me, and the fact that they think we'll be helping them in this," Sally stated matter-of-factly.

"Not entirely true."

"How so? Need I remind you that we're covenless here."

"We have four..."

"No we don't. Dread Stalker and Firebird are nothing but liabilities. They're not going to do anything that goes against the Draculas. I wouldn't trust them as far as I can throw a car. Alfonzo's out too."

"Untrustworthy?"

"Fuck no. I trust him implicitly. No fucking way are you putting him in harm's way, though. When this is all said and done, I'm gonna need at least a week's spa treatment."

"Way to suffer for the cause, Sally."

She ignored me and continued, "We can trust Starlight, but she's a dim bulb. Someone asks the right questions and she'll squeal like a pig even if she doesn't mean to. We might be able to use her to run interference, though."

"Noted. You're forgetting Tom and Ed, though."

"I try to forget Tom every chance I get."

"Regardless, you know they're in."

"Yeah, yeah, I know. Not sure what use they'll be, though. There's also some risk there too. You bring numbnuts into this and there's no way his little fuck buddy isn't going to find out, too."

"Christy?"

"Yep."

"Maybe..." I trailed off.

"What are you thinking?"

"From the sound of things, Decker isn't too happy with her right now. They might be on the outs because of her recent change of heart." She had been as gung ho on my death as Decker when we first met. It was obvious she wasn't quite as crazy as he, but she was his loyal little coven minion nevertheless. Lately, though, thanks in part to her continuing relationship with Tom, she had started to see I wasn't quite the big bad wolf Decker had portrayed me as. There was little doubt that had caused friction between them.

"Be careful there," Sally warned. "At the end of the day there're two things against you. One: you've been lying to her this past month..."

"More like omitting the truth, I'd say."

"Don't argue semantics. Two, and most important here, you *did* fulfill your end of the prophecy. Not only did your birth herald the Icon's return, but you practically rolled out the red carpet for her."

"You think we should make up some bullshit instead?"

"No. As much as it pains me to say, Christy's too smart for that. It blows my mind what she sees in your chimp of a roommate. You need to either keep her entirely in the dark or bring her fully into the circle, but..."

She didn't need to finish. If Christy's loyalty to Decker won out in the end, it would be even worse than if we had just spilled our guts on the phone. They'd know everything, and we'd be exposed as having tried to cover it up. Might as well buy a hacksaw and cut off my own head in that case.

Once we had finished our somewhat incomplete assessment of the situation, Sally and I discussed possible courses of action.

Over the previous day, I had begun considering Mission Impossible-esque type scenarios. Sheila and I would somehow defeat the forces stacked against us...perhaps even saving the world in the process. What? I didn't say they were realistic scenarios. Hell, I could barely fill in my yearly goals at work - a master military strategist I was not. To say that put me at a slight disadvantage against Alexander the Great was like comparing a warm summer breeze with a tornado. At the end of it all, I had to admit that most of my plans involved getting nearly impossibly lucky.

Fortunately for my own ineptitude, Sally believed in making her own luck.

* * *

"...and if everything works out just as I said, the Sasquatches will be hunted down by the government, Sheila will be alive, and Alexander will be so busy dealing with the ..."

I stopped relaying my plan of action as Sally sat down and put her face in her hands.

"What?"

"Give me a moment. I have a stupidity headache."

"I suppose you have a better idea."

"Not only better, but one that actually has a chance in hell of working."

"Enlighten me please, Rommel."

Sally fixed her eyes on me, giving me her best condescending stare. "It's very simple. We're going to find her and explain the situation."

"Just like that, eh?"

She flashed her fangs. "We're vampires. We'll convince her."

"Then?"

"Then we'll give her the cliff notes version to bring her up to speed. We'll help pack her bags, steal a car, buy her a plane ticket, or whatever the fuck. Bottom line is she gets the hell out of the city and keeps running."

"That's it?"

"It's a start. With any luck, she'll be out of New York before the day is through. We can stonewall Colin's people for as long as it takes. We might even get lucky and find ourselves a nice opportunity to take Decker out of the equation."

"And Sheila?"

"She becomes a nomad. Doesn't stay in any one place for too long. If she keeps moving, maybe she'll stay alive."

"How the hell is she supposed to live?"

"She has that company she owns. She can probably grab some cash from that."

"And if it's not enough?"

"Then we'll bankroll her," she said flatly. "It wouldn't be the first time I've cooked the books a little."

My eyes opened wide. It wasn't so much the plan. It was simple enough that it might even work. But the fact that Sally was willing to stick her neck out, even using coven funds to do so - when I could barely get cab fare out of her most days - was utterly amazing to me. It was good...except for one little detail.

"She'll be all alone out there. Alone against a world of monsters. I need to go with her."

That earned me a super slow eye-roll. "Nice sentiment, Romeo. Just a few problems with your plan."

"I know we're not that close, but I need to..."

"You can't even touch her, Bill, at least not without it looking like someone just shot off a flare gun in the room. Your Freewill abilities might save you from getting cooked, but just think about how subtle that won't be. Hell, you trip on the sidewalk and bump into her...bam, suddenly you'll make the local papers at the very least."

"I'll be careful."

"Doesn't matter." She looked me in the eye and dropped the attitude. "I'm serious here, Bill, it won't work. If there are other vamps in the area, they'll be able to sniff you out. We know what you look like. Your face would be plastered on the wall of every coven from here to Indochina. Then there're the mages. You would lead them right to her. Remember how they found you?"

"But Decker said..."

"Decker is full of shit! They know the Icon is alive, that's all. Something about her abilities frigs up their magic. They can't home in on her like a guided missile."

"But they can with me."

"You'll lead them right to her. You're powerful, Bill...or you will be if you ever learn to control your shit."

"Thanks for the vote of confidence."

"But even the two of you combined can't take on the world. There's also an additional complication to your plan."

"What?"

"I'm sorry to have to burst your little puppy-love bubble, but you don't even know if she's gonna want you around. Didn't you say she seemed kind of freaked after she blasted you across the street?"

"That would've freaked out anyone," I replied, but there was no real conviction in my voice. What I hadn't told Sally was the last thing Sheila had said before I took off running.

"*What are you?*"

* * *

I decided to sort out my feelings later. As long as Sheila was alive, I could take some comfort in that. Even if she walked out of my life hating me, it was a shitload better than watching her get blasted into nothing more than a smoking crater.

"In any case, we need to find her first," Sally rightly pointed out.

When all else fails, there's always the obvious. "I guess we could try calling her."

I wasn't ashamed to admit (well okay, I wasn't *too* ashamed) that I knew a little bit about Sheila. You know, basic things that you pick up when you work alongside someone for a while: where she lived, her phone number, her favorite perfume, what she liked to eat, her favorite color...you know, that kind of stuff. Nothing creepy about any of that, right?

Sally shrugged and handed me the phone. "Dial away."

"You do realize that I'm about to call a girl at three AM to tell her that vampires and wizards are hunting her down, right?"

"The thought had crossed my mind," she replied. "If she answers, put her on speaker. I want to hear this."

"Screw you."

"Not even if we somehow live through this mess."

In my previous life of being, well, alive, I had never dared to call her up. Hell, since being turned into one of the undead I hadn't tried either. All of our interactions had been through work, at least until she'd quit. Somehow I always envisioned our first phone call being a little different than this. I sighed and began to dial.

"Hold on, Sherlock," Sally said, swatting my hand away from the receiver. "Almost forgot. Not that one."

"What do you mean? You just gave me the..."

"Here," she replied, reaching into a drawer and pulling out a box. She tossed it across the desk to me. It was a prepaid cell phone, still sealed. "Use this one instead."

"Paranoid?"

"Shouldn't I be? Don't think for a moment that Colin trusts us."

"I didn't, but why the change of heart? I thought you weren't worried about phone taps."

"When did I ever say that?"

"Back when the Khan's assassins were hunting us."

"Whole different story then. We're not dealing with a bunch of heavily-armed yak herders this time around. The Draculas may be old-school, but the Boston office is firmly in the twenty-first century. Best to assume they have access to state of the art tech. Even if not, they manage all our agreements with the local law enforcement. If they need to, they can pull strings."

Dammit! I had forgotten about that part. Vampires weren't able to exist entirely in the shadows. Vamps are strong and fast, but they're no smarter than they were in life. There were plenty of dumbasses within the undead ranks. Thus it was necessary to grease the wheels, so to speak. Treaties and agreements existed that allowed us to go about our bloody business and stay out of the limelight. In return, we agreed to concessions that basically kept us from turning human civilization into a bloodbath.

Unfortunately, I had a feeling such contracts were not going to be up for renewal. Alexander had grand designs. Not only did he plan on winning our war against the Bigfeet, but his vision also extended to remaking the world in our own image...or more likely, *his* own image. Over two thousand years ago, he had set out to conquer the Earth. Now, he was prepared to finish the job.

I pried open the box - damn plastic packaging. Even with vampire strength they're a bitch. "So we're going all *Bourne Identity*, then?"

"For some things, yes. Best not to be stupid."

I couldn't disagree on that. Too much of what had transpired had occurred because I'd gone into things acting like a clueless idiot. I'd have to try to temper that a bit in the coming days.

"It's going to look a little funny calling her up from an unlisted number."

"It's going to look a little funny regardless, calling her up at this hour and telling her to pack her bags before the boogeyman gets there."

"Touché." I began dialing.

* * *

"Well?"

"No answer."

"Are you sure you have the right number?"

"Hell yeah. I have it memorized."

"You've used it before?"

"Well, no."

"I'd tell you how pathetic that is, but I'm sure you already know. Hang up and dial it again."

"Why?"

"If it keeps ringing, she might wake up and answer it."

"I can just leave a voicemail."

"And say what?"

"...I'll just try dialing her again."

* * *

"Directory assistance says it's the right number. She's just not answering."

"Maybe she's not home."

"Where would she be at this hour?"

Sally sighed. "Oh I don't know. It's only the weekend and she's a single semi-attractive female."

I bared my fangs at her for the dig, but she didn't even flinch. It was sad. I could intimidate strangers by sheer virtue of being the Freewill, but the people closest to me...nada.

"Are you sure she wasn't seeing someone else?"

"Positive...mostly."

"There's just one problem with that."

"What?"

"One, you don't have a clue about this girl other than the goo-goo eyes you make whenever you talk about her, and two, your data is at least thirty days old. Sorry, that was more than one problem, wasn't it?"

"It's only been a month."

"You do realize that some people meet, get engaged, and are married in that time frame, right?"

"They do?" Horrific images of Sheila settling down with some corporate schlub, who wasn't me, and raising two point five kids in the suburbs suddenly raced through my mind.

"Duh! You really have no clue how this dating thing works, do you? Most of us don't clock our social lives against the geologic time table."

"But...we're meant to be together."

"Only if by *be together* you mean kill each other. Let's not forget..."

"Fuck the prophecies!"

"Probably a good attitude to take. Get your coat."

"Where..."

"To her place, obviously. Do you think the witches are going to be fucking around here?"

"Well..."

"Fine, bad example. What about Boston? They have a lot of shit on their plate. They're gonna want this bagged and tagged quickly."

I turned a shade paler at her words. That was exactly what I was hoping to avoid. "Let's go."

"Do you know where she lives? Wait, stupid question, never mind."

Gate Crashers

Fortunately, Sheila didn't live too far away. Considering the time, we decided it made sense to go by foot. The trains ran less frequently at that hour, and there would also be a lot of fucking weirdos on them. The streets were fairly empty in the more residential blocks. That allowed us to put our vampiric speed to good use. Sticking to the shadows, we maintained a pace that would have put even a world class sprinter to shame. Within minutes we were at the stoop of Sheila's building.

I paused and looked around. This was where it had happened. Though any evidence was long gone, I knew exactly where I had been standing when the best moment of my life had morphed into the worst in a white hot sheet of magical flame.

"What is it?"

"This is where I was blown across the street."

"Guys are way too preoccupied with getting blown." I glared at her. "Oh lighten up, Bill. You're depressing me."

"Let's focus on why we're here."

"Gladly. The sooner we can say bon voyage, the better. Decker and Colin can jerk each other off while they sweep the city, and we can get on with life."

"You think Decker will give up?"

"No. But I think there will be ample opportunity to kill his ass."

"Not quite my favorite type of happy ending, but I wouldn't argue against it."

"Thought not," she replied with a smirk, starting up the stairs.

"So, what do we do?"

"We get in, obviously."

"Uh yeah...heh, not quite how I envisioned my first visit to her apartment."

"I'd offer to give you some alone time, but I left the asbestos condoms in my other dress."

I let out a heavy sigh. At this rate, I'd be standing there bantering with Sally on the front stoop until the sun came up. Wouldn't that be an inglorious end to things? At the very least, though, it would give the prophets of the supernatural world a gigantic kick to the balls. That alone almost made it worth it...almost.

I pushed past Sally and pressed the bell for Sheila's apartment.

"Sure that's hers?"

"Yep. Apartment Two-B."

"There's no name on it."

"Trust me on this."

"It's kind of cute that you know so much about her, in a creepy restraining order sort of way."

"I'm sure you'd know all about those."

"Only how to ignore them. How long are you going to press that thing anyway? You could have woken up a narcoleptic by now."

"She might be a deep sleeper."

"Or, as I said, she might not be here."

"Not helping."

"Enjoying a nice evening out..."

"Sally," I warned.

"...playing a game of hide the sausage with a guy who won't spontaneously combust next to her..."

"Maybe one of her neighbors will let us in," I tried desperately to focus, despite an urgent need to clock her.

"Oh get out of the way." She grabbed the door handle and turned, twisting until the lock snapped. "Keys are for pussies."

"You're lucky there isn't a doorman," I whispered, following her in.

"No, Bill. A doorman is lucky *he's* not here."

* * *

Thankfully, the halls were empty. Nobody on the first floor appeared to have heard us breaking and entering. Sally might be just old enough to be officially off the grid, but I was still a hardworking, tax paying citizen as far as New York City was concerned. Getting arrested for burglary wasn't high on my list.

We walked up to the second floor, still unseen. Finally I stopped in front of Sheila's door.

"This is it. Should we knock?"

"We already tried that route. I'm more for the direct approach."

"What if we scare her?"

"Scare her? She can kill vampires with a touch. I think it's the other way around."

"Good point."

"Be careful in there, though. It's gonna be close quarters and she's liable to not be entirely pleased with unannounced guests."

"Sheila won't hurt us."

"Purposefully, maybe," Sally pointed out. "Just remember, even a handshake from her is gonna be like touching a live power line."

I nodded, and she stepped forward, grasped the knob and began to apply pressure. Before she could break the lock, though, wisps of smoke poured from between her fingers. A scant second later, she started to scream.

Thinking quickly, I covered her mouth with my hand to stifle the cry rushing out. I got lucky in that one moment, but less lucky in the next as she bit down on my hand. I gritted my own teeth as her fangs sunk into the meat of my palm. Motherfucker!

She yanked her hand back from the doorknob and I did the same with mine from her mouth. That last one was for both our benefit. Had Sally swallowed my blood, she would have been reduced to a quivering ball of puke. The plus to me was...well, she wasn't biting my fucking hand anymore. My God, what a mess things had become and we hadn't even gotten into the apartment yet.

"What the fuck was that?" Sally hissed as she cradled her still smoking hand.

"My latest excuse to get a shot of penicillin."

"I meant the door, dickwad."

"How the hell am I supposed to know? I'm not an expert in apartment security. I'm lucky my place even has a fucking door."

"It feels like someone was holding a blowtorch to it."

Remembering the fire safety video they made us watch in sixth grade, I placed my hand against the wood of the door. It was cold, so no fire in her apartment - a good thing overall. I sniffed the air, and it lacked the distinct smell of smoke. So what was happening?

"Do you have any paper?" I asked as a thought hit me.

"Paper?"

"Yes, paper, Sally. Don't ask why, just give me a piece."

Her eyebrows narrowed. "A piece?"

"Of paper. Come on, we don't have time for this shit. Someone is eventually going to notice us loitering out here."

"Hold on a sec." She opened her purse and rummaged through it. Finally she said, "Ah, here we go." She pulled out a crumpled slip and handed it to me.

"What is this, a prescription for skank-off?"

"It's a parking ticket, genius."

"You got a ticket?" I started to smirk. Focus was nearly impossible with Sally around.

"It's not mine. I don't own a car."

"Then who..."

"Remember that Durango I borrowed?"

"Never mind, I don't want to know." I held out the edge of the paper and pressed it against the doorknob.

"That's not how you pick a lock."

"I'm testing a theory."

After a few seconds I pulled it away and held it up. "It's not smoldering." I touched the tip. "It's not even warm."

"What are you getting at?"

"Remember that business card, the one from Sheila?" I sure as hell wouldn't ever forget it. After she had nearly immolated me, it had fallen out of my shirt pocket. Through some bizarre bit of coincidence, although I suspect it somehow wasn't that at all - fucking fate - the company Sheila had started was named *Iconic Efficiencies*. Weird isn't even close to being the word for that.

"Yeah, so?"

"It was intact. My clothes were practically incinerated, yet the card was completely unharmed."

"I remember. Didn't you say something about a portion of her power rubbing off on it?"

"I was just taking a stab in the dark at the time, but what if I was right? What if that's exactly what happened?"

I reached out toward the doorknob. I needed to be fast, being that pain wasn't something I was overly fond of. I placed the tip of my index finger against the metal and almost immediately felt the temperature begin to rise. I pulled back, but a thin wisp of smoke drifted up from it anyway.

"She can do that?" Sally asked, eyes wide.

"Beats the fuck out of me. I was hoping you'd know."

"I don't think anyone knows. Icons were lethal to vampires. I doubt any of us ever got close enough to study them for an extended period of time. If they did, they didn't live long enough to save it to our archives."

"Great."

"So how come the door itself didn't burn you?"

"I don't know. Maybe it's a conductive thing...or maybe it has to do with touch. She'd be in physical contact with the doorknob more than the rest of it."

"Okay, let's go with that. Then why..."

"Who are you people?" a voice called from down the hall. "Do you have any idea what time it is?"

Vampires have excellent senses. Unfortunately, they don't work all that well when we aren't paying the fuck attention.

* * *

"Who are you?"

Sally and I locked gazes and her eyes blackened. Oh shit. I shook my head and turned to face our accuser.

An old lady stood in the doorway of another apartment. What she lacked in height she made up for in girth. Her white hair was in curlers and she wore a pink nightgown that more closely resembled a muumuu. Considering the color, she looked like some bizarre anthropomorphic pig. I tried to push that thought from my head. If I started to laugh, her next reaction would probably be to call the cops about the drunken assholes in the hallway.

I needed to make up something before Sally decided to show this lady her own spine. "I'm sorry. I was in the neighborhood and decided to check on my...sister, Sheila."

"Sister? You're her brother?" she asked, her tone dubious.

"Yeah. My...wife and I were in the area..." Sally let out a heavy sigh behind me. I gritted my teeth. All she had to do was keep her fucking mouth shut, albeit that was a tall order for her - you could cut out her tongue and she'd still somehow find a way to be snarky.

"A bit late to be visiting," Sheila's neighbor pointed out. Outside of her size, she reminded me a lot of Mrs.

Caven. She had been my nosy downstairs neighbor...at least until she had been turned into a vampire and subsequently gotten her head blown off. I guess every building has a busybody, but this woman had no idea how close she was to losing the *busy* part of the equation and just winding up a body.

"Well, maybe we weren't *quite* in the area. I was worried. I haven't heard from my sister in a while. I mean, we usually talk every week. I was up, couldn't sleep and figured...y'know."

I was babbling, but hoped to come across as a worried relative rather than an undead monster standing in a hallway making up bad lies at three in the morning.

"I didn't know she had a brother..." I opened my mouth, but the woman kept talking. "Not that I would have any reason to know. That one mostly keeps to herself. Not the best of neighbors. Here I am, all alone. You'd think she'd come over and offer to help out..."

Oh Jesus Christ. I couldn't blame Sheila. Had this annoying witch lived in my building, I'd have learned to rappel out the window rather than meet her in the halls.

"Well?"

"Huh?" I had momentarily tuned her out.

"I asked how you got in. She better not have given you a key. That's against building rules."

Fortunately, Sally jumped in and saved my hide. "We were let in. Someone was coming out and held the door for us."

The lady's eyes narrowed. "Tall fellow, greasy goatee, ratty clothes?"

"That's the one," Sally lied. Whereas I sputtered like a twit, she was cool as a cucumber. Telling a few white lies wasn't exactly an alien concept to her.

The old lady made a sound of disgust. "Damn hippy. I think that one is selling drugs. Coming and going at odd hours and always leaving the door open. I'm reporting him to the super."

"Probably a good idea," Sally said. "You never know who's going to be let in."

"Tell me about it. People are animals these days. Freaking monsters."

"You have no idea."

* * *

Sheila's neighbor from Hell was still in the middle of lecturing us on the need to be quiet and courteous to others when Sally finally had enough.

I felt the compulsion rattle my bones a split second before I heard it.

"*GO BACK TO SLEEP!!*"

Sally slumped against me from the effort, her nice, soft parts not going unnoticed, but it had the desired effect. The eyes peering out from the neighbor's jowly face glazed over. She immediately turned around, walked back into her apartment, and shut the door.

"That was close," I sighed with relief.

"For her," Sally gasped.

I decided to let it slide. Truth be told, I was proud of her. She wasn't above gutting any humans who got in her way. I was impressed that she both showed restraint and was willing to put in the effort. Typically, compulsion is a sort of psychic command between vampires. Older vampires use it to keep younger vamps in line. It doesn't work on me, hence the name Freewill, but it's fairly common to see it done in our ranks. Compulsion also works on humans, albeit not to the same degree. It requires a lot more concentration, and typically the best results come from a powerful vampire to a weak-willed person. Sally wasn't very old, so the effort cost her. Thankfully, though, the neighbor was apparently susceptible.

"Kind of loud, though," I said, as my ears (*and cortex*) continued to ring. "Aren't you afraid the other..."

"No. Why do you think I worded it like I did? Even if I did wake up the whole floor, they're going to just turn over and go back to dreamland."

"You hope."

"If not..." Her eyes blackened again. The meaning was clear. Anyone else who decided to check on us was going to be in for a very bad start to their day.

Fortunately, we appeared to have gotten lucky. No other curious faces peeked out of their doorways. After a few minutes, it became evident that I wouldn't have to stop her from turning this place into the set from a *Friday the Thirteenth* movie.

"So what now? We just wait here in the hallway until she wakes up?"

"Or comes home."

"Will you stop that!"

"Just being a realist."

"More like a jealous bitch."

"Jealous? Of her? She's not even that good..."

"Can we focus here?" I snapped. Goddamn it. What is it about women that makes them so fucking catty about other women? It's like they can't wait to stab each other in the back. If the world were populated entirely by females, I can only imagine the planet embroiled in some Highlander-type game of "There can be only one."

"Fine. The plan hasn't changed. We still need to get in, even if just to confirm she's not there."

"Why do you..."

"Come on, Bill, she slept through the phone ringing, the doorbell buzzing, us arguing out here like two fucking morons, and then a compulsion...and no, I have no idea if that would even work on the Icon. She's either not home or she's in a freaking coma."

Damn Sally and her logic. Still, she was right. We couldn't just hang out here until the sun came up.

"How do we do it? Kicking in the door seems overkill."

"Hold out your arm."

"Why?"

"Do you want to get in there or not?"

"Fine." I held out my arm. Sally grabbed the sleeve of my jacket and tore it off.

"What the fuck?"

"Oh please, you don't look any worse than you already did. Besides, it's not like I was going to rip mine. Do you know what this thing cost?"

"At least a week's worth of private lap dances?"

She gave me a sour look and turned back to the door. Wrapping the sleeve around her hand, she grasped the doorknob and gave it the same treatment as she did downstairs. One loud *crack* later and it swung open. Being a vampire means never needing a lock pick, but it's gotta be hell on the repair bills.

"Be careful," I said. "If my theory is correct, this whole apartment could be a vampire minefield."

"I know. Hands to myself." She took a step and stopped. "Does she own a gun?"

"How the hell should I know?"

"Oh yeah, that's right. You've never been here." She placed one foot over the threshold. "How's it feel knowing I got in before you?"

"Bite me."

"No thanks. I'm just warning you, though, this bitch takes a shot at me and all bets are off."

"What are you gonna do, try to bite her? Oh yeah, that'll show her. She might even need to rent a steam cleaner to get you out of the carpet."

Sally turned to glare at me, but I shooed her forward so we could avoid getting caught breaking and entering should her compulsion fail to hold.

Once in, I shut the door behind us, taking care not to touch the handle with my bare skin.

"She's not here," Sally decreed.

I almost asked how she knew, but then caught myself. One of these days I would get used to having superhuman abilities. I took a deep breath through my nose. Sheila's scent immediately filled my nostrils. Damn, I had almost forgotten how nice she smelled.

I held my breath. What if her powers extended to her lingering scent? I waited a moment. When I didn't immediately immolate from the inside out, I let out a laugh.

"What's funny?"

"Nothing, just being stupid."

"I'm surprised you don't laugh twenty-four / seven then."

I ignored her and tried to focus, but it was difficult. Fantasies of Sheila and me running along a beach together ran through my mind as I breathed in her essence. We were in a park having a picnic. We were enjoying a day out in the...I shook my head to clear it. Jesus Christ, that was pathetic even for me. One whiff of her perfume and suddenly I had tampon commercials running through my head. Okay, concentrate, Bill. Save the *Summer's Eve* fantasies for another time.

Sheila's scent was all over the place...duh, it was her apartment. My own place probably smelled like an unholy fusion of Tom, Ed, and myself to an outsider. The more I took it in, though, the more I realized it wasn't recent. The odors were lingering, not fresh. Sally was right, she wasn't there. I'm not exactly skilled in this, but I'd say it had probably been several days since she had been...maybe longer.

I looked at Sally, who just shrugged nonchalantly.

"You're not surprised, are you?" I asked.

"Nope. I figured we had a good chance of finding this place empty."

"Why?"

"Think about it. What's the first thing you did after learning you were a vampire?"

"I went home and tried to resume my normal routine."

"Okay, you're a bad example. Think of someone whose entire life isn't centered on being a dork." Sally walked around the apartment, looking at what was on the shelves. She stared at a few pictures on an end table, presumably photos of Sheila and her...life, I guess. When she started talking again, her tone took on an odd faraway quality.

"She's had an entire month on her own. That first night, she was probably far more freaked out than you. You only had the surprise of finding out she was the Icon. She, on the other hand, had her entire world turned upside down. One second her life was normal and the next...poof, magic and monsters are real. The thing is, who are you gonna talk to about that sort of stuff? You got lucky, Bill. Your friends are the type that probably jizzed themselves the second you told them what was up."

She continued talking. For some reason, her tone perhaps, I didn't want to interrupt.

"Not so with everyone. Most people know that if they tried telling anyone that sort of thing, even their best friend, they'd just look crazy. So what does she do? I'm thinking a normal person either finds a bar or pops open a bottle of hard liquor. Maybe it all even seems like just a nightmare come the morning. She gets back into her routine, probably not even realizing that she's grabbing onto it like a drowning man with a life preserver."

"How do you..."

"She tried to move on with her life. It's amazing how a new day can make the monsters seem so far away. Who knows how long she kept it up, maybe even an entire week - but little by little, it ate into her. I wonder how many times over those first few days her hand hovered over the phone as she debated whether to call you - maybe even hoping that you would reach out first to either tell her it was all real or confirm it was a dream."

Okay, now I was starting to feel like a real shit.

"Eventually, though, it was too much. Maybe she couldn't deny it anymore or maybe her powers flared again. Hard to say on that last one, though it's possible. It might have been spontaneous or maybe she just bumped into the wrong person. From there...well, who can say? All we know is that she's not here now."

"How do you know so much?"

"Just guessing."

"Were you?" I prodded.

"Yes," she replied, a little too harshly. Almost immediately she was back to being her normal self. "And don't ask me about it again or I'll cave your skull in."

I held my hands up in a placating manner. She turned away, then began poking her head into the other rooms of the apartment.

"What are you looking for now?"

"Nothing, just being nosy. She's not much for interior decorating, is she? I think my grandmother had more style." She stopped in front of a shelf and pulled out something. "Ooh, I don't have this CD."

"Put that back," I demanded.

"Oh please, Bill. It's not exactly grand theft."

"It's not yours."

"She doesn't even listen to it."

"And how do you know that?"

"Simple. I'm not on fire right now."

Bitch!

* * *

Sheila's apartment was a bust. There were no messages on her machine and nothing to indicate where she had gone, assuming she had gone anywhere. Sally had checked her closets and, in between criticizing her wardrobe choices, said everything appeared pretty full. If she had taken anything with her, she had packed light. I haven't cased too many apartments in my time, but if I had to guess, I'd say it seemed as if one day she left as normal and simply never returned.

I wasn't sure what that meant. Colin's team, whoever they might be, hadn't had time to arrive yet. As for Decker, I doubted it was him. He wasn't that subtle. If he and his people had found out Sheila was the Icon, they would have taken out a full page ad in the *New York Times* proclaiming it.

Was it possible she just decided to leave on a whim? Maybe, but my gut was telling me no. There was one other possibility to consider, though. If she truly felt alone - thought that she was either losing her mind or becoming some sort of monster - could she have...

"What's wrong, Bill?"

"Huh?"

"You just spaced out and then turned a shade paler, if that's even possible."

"I was just thinking about what you said."

"Well, unfortunately, it's too late for that. You should have worried about getting a tan back when you were alive."

"Not that. Earlier."

"What?" she asked.

"That stuff you were saying about her being alone and trying to get back to normalcy."

"I told you not to bring it up. That wasn't about me!"

"Who's talking about you? I meant Sheila."

"Oh," she said, looking slightly embarrassed. "Okay then. What about her?"

"Well...I really don't want to consider this. But do you maybe think, she could've..."

"Could've what?"

"You know."

"I know what?"

"Been really depressed and feeling all alone...maybe she..."

"Offed herself?" she asked nonchalantly.

"Don't be so cavalier about it."

"Sorry, can't help it. We do run one of the biggest suicide hotlines in the city, you know. Tends to desensitize me."

Yeah right. To supply the coven with fresh kills and likewise keep the stupider elements from bringing too much attention to us, Sally had instituted the hotline. Using it, the coven was able to identify those whose disappearances wouldn't be noticed. Ugh, just thinking about it skeeved me out.

"Yes," I tried to shake off the dirty feeling I got whenever the hotline came up. "Do you think maybe she...hurt herself?"

"Nope," she replied as if discussing the weather.

"How can you..."

She turned toward me. Despite the fact that I was several inches taller, I got the distinct impression she was looking down upon me. "Wise up and think beyond the end of your dick for once. Decker probably wouldn't have been all gung-ho to fuck with the vampire nation if he was able to divine that she iced herself."

"That doesn't mean..."

"And, she's not gonna do it anyway for one good reason."

After a moment, I finally asked, "And that would be?"

"She's the fucking Icon, genius. You don't become one unless you truly and deeply believe in yourself. They call it faith, but let's not bullshit ourselves here. Those with self-esteem problems need not apply. Wherever your girlie is right now, she might be confused, she might even be afraid, but I guarantee she is not contemplating eating a bullet. End of story. So stop moping about like you're at her funeral because if you don't, and we're too late, you just might be."

A Typical Day at the Office

We had only a few hours until daybreak, and the weather report called for sun for the rest of the week. There wasn't much that could be accomplished on our end. Fortunately, the same could be said of any vampire team, so at least they would be in the same boat. The mages would be free to operate, but they were probably just shooting in the dark. They'd have a better chance at finding a needle in a haystack, especially in a packed city during business hours.

There was also the fact that the weekend was over and I had a project due at work. At the very least, it could take my mind off of things and give me a little time to think of my next step.

I parted ways with Sally and hopped on the subway back to Brooklyn, hoping to make it home before the sun came up and ruined my day even further.

Despite the forecast, the day was overcast - stupid weathermen, but good news for me. The trains ran on schedule and I made it back to my apartment with time to spare. Thank goodness too. Exhaustion hit like a freight train once I walked in the door. The excitement of the weekend hadn't left a lot of time for shuteye. I had work to do, but it could wait for a couple of hours.

I walked in, noted the distinct lack of dead bodies lying about (you'd be surprised what you check for when you're one of the undead), and slunk to my bedroom door.

You're probably expecting me to tell you that I opened it and Sheila was there waiting for me. Well congratulations, you're probably a fan of bad romantic comedies. Maybe you should go rent one.

Alas, the only thing waiting was my bed. But all things considered, it was enough for the moment.

* * *

By the time I awoke, Tom was long gone for the day - off to his job as an office drone in the city's financial district. That was fine. The stuff I needed to talk about was probably best kept from his ears for now.

As expected, I found Ed in our kitchen nook sipping a cup of coffee. He grabbed a mug and filled it for me when he saw me drag my ass in. Some days I don't know what I'd do without my wonderful friends.

"You can put the blood in yourself," he said, handing it over. Well, maybe they're not *that* wonderful.

As I stirred it in with some sugar, he not-so casually asked, "So how's Sally?"

"Loaded up to her neck with STDs."

"You look like shit."

"You have no idea."

I filled him in on the details of what occurred after he dropped us off. Despite my tale of destruction, bloodshed, and woe, he remained his typical stoic self. He raised an eyebrow a few times as he sipped his coffee, but that was the extent of his reaction. Guess Sally wasn't the only one getting desensitized to this stuff. It was a pity she was a soulless killing machine. Otherwise, they might make for a nice couple.

When at last I had finished, Ed put down his now empty mug. "And the reason you couldn't have told me this when you called *is*? I wasn't too busy yesterday, so I might have been interested to know that wizards could have firebombed this place at any moment."

"Sorry, man. We kind of figured it was one of those cases of ignorance being bliss. Besides, I didn't know if Christy was here or not."

"She wasn't. I think she came down with something. Tom said she must have had a stomach bug."

"Maybe she finally opened her eyes and got a good look at him."

"Could be."

"But you see my problem?"

"Yeah I guess," he said. "Although I'm pretty sure she's on the outs right now with Decker."

"I wouldn't know."

"No shit. You've been playing a one man game of hide and seek ever since..."

"I know!"

"Of course, but I'm still gonna give you crap about it."

"Have I mentioned how nice it is to be home?"

"Isn't it? Oh, almost forgot, Dave called yesterday. Said he couldn't reach your cell phone."

"I kind of lost it in the explosion. Let me guess, he was pissed I missed the game."

"Pretty much."

"He was probably annoyed that he didn't get to cut any more pieces off of me either."

"He didn't say. I told him you were probably busy with vampire business, although I got the feeling he wasn't entirely sympathetic."

"Dave lives in his own little self-centered universe. I'm pretty sure he just sees the rest of us as little more than lab rats."

"Doubtless."

"He is a good dungeon master, though."

"A skilled DM is probably worth a few missing digits."

"True enough...maybe."

Ed paused to refill his cup. "So is it safe to say that your self-imposed exile is over?"

"I don't think I have much of a choice."

"So what's *our* next step? And before you say anything, yes, we're a part of it. You need to cut that *I need to spare my human allies the danger that comes with my job* bullshit. You aren't Superman, and I sure as shit ain't Lois Lane."

I smiled. I couldn't imagine how things would have turned out for me without some awesome buds backing me up. Forget that shit you see in the movies - real friends don't completely freak the fuck out when a little something like vampirism comes along...at least not if those friends are the type who have grown up on that kind of shit.

Unfortunately, that brought Sally's words from back at Sheila's apartment to mind. It seemed like she was doing a wee bit more than speculating when she said those things. Still, it was probably a little late to feel any pity for her. She had obviously made some mighty potent lemonade from the lemons of her life. No, the person I needed to worry about was still Sheila. Despite what Sally had said about belief in oneself, I couldn't help but imagine her out there alone and scared. Of course the question was still *where*?

"Obviously we need to find Sheila."

"Did you try her office?"

"Well...no. It was kinda late. Besides, if she wasn't at home, then what would she be doing..."

"Occam's Razor, Bill. Get the obvious shit out of the way first. If that doesn't work, then you can play Sherlock Holmes."

"Heh, if that happens I'd have better luck going door to door to every building in the city and just asking if she's there."

"The beauty of being immortal is that you have the time."

"Alas, no I don't. Time is one ally I don't have on my side...or at least she doesn't."

"Well then I suggest we get our asses in gear. It's supposed to be a clear day and you're gonna need a lot of sunscreen."

* * *

"Are you certain you don't want to call Sally?"

"I don't need her permission to do anything."

"Are you sure on that?"

"Fuck you, dude." Ed chuckled. "Besides," I continued, "she was going to check in with Boston, monitor the situation a bit. Let her do her job. Besides which, if we do find her..."

"You're afraid Sally is gonna say something that gets you both blown to bits?"

"Something like that."

"She's probably gonna say far worse when she finds out we did this without her."

"Oh no!" I gasped in mock horror. "I'm pissing off Sally. What else is new?"

About two hours had passed since we'd made our decision. I needed time to prep myself for an excursion outside...and there was a conference call we both needed to be on for work.

Yeah yeah, I know, but an extra hour wouldn't kill us during the daytime, and Jim, our boss, can get a little whiney when we blow him off. It so sucks to be an immortal beast of the night, foretold to bring doom and destruction to the world, and yet still be a wage slave. I really needed to win the lottery one of these days.

Thank goodness it was cold outside. I could get away with a hat, scarf, and even ski mask without looking like a weirdo...not that I was too worried about looking weird in the city. Regardless of my coverings, I smelled like a rancid palm tree. Clothing or not, I was still slathered with sunscreen. Better safe than immolated.

"Are you ready?" Ed asked. I was never much for sun and fun even during my living days, but I still kind of envied him the ability to just throw on a coat.

"Let's roll."

We stepped to the door, ready to track down Sheila, come hell or high water, when it was opened from the outside.

* * *

Before I could do anything, the weapon pierced my chest. I looked down, seeing the stake sticking out of me. My body began to combust, regret filling me as...

* * *

Just fucking with you.

"Hey, Tom, you're home early," I said to my oldest friend.

"Hey man," Ed likewise greeted him.

Tom glanced at us both, a blank look upon his face. Without saying a word, he strode past us and into the kitchen.

"You okay, dude?" Instead of replying, he grabbed a glass out of the sink and began rooting through one of the cabinets. He pulled out a mostly full fifth of peppermint schnapps and filled half the glass with it.

Ed and I watched as he downed the contents in three large swallows.

"Bad day at the office?"

He let out a sigh. "You could say that." He filled the glass again. This wasn't good. I had paid for that liquor.

Ed turned to me and gave a shrug. We had important business to do, but Tom was a friend in need. Our mission was probably going to turn out to be a wild good chase anyway. It could wait a little while. Sheila was my fantasy, but Tom was reality. From the look of things, he needed a friendly ear or two.

"So what happened?" I grabbed a glass and handed it to him. "You might as well hit me. Friends don't let friends get shit-faced alone. Ed?"

"I'll grab a beer. You sure about this, Bill?"

I wasn't, but nodded to him anyway and proceeded to strip off my coat...and scarf, and gloves, and ski-mask.

I took a seat next to Tom as he made headway into his second mega-shot. "Did you get your dumb ass fired?"

"Are you kidding? They love me at that place. I'm the only fucker with any personality." A slight slur already hung at the edge of his voice. None of us were lightweights when it came to libations, but he was currently sucking down eighty proof liquor like *Kool Aid*. At this rate, he'd be proclaiming his love for us within fifteen minutes and puking on our shoes in the next thirty.

"Uh huh. Do tell," Ed quipped as he cracked a cold one.

Tom paused for a moment. "It's Christy."

"She finally wise up and dump your ass?" I asked, perhaps sounding a little more hopeful than I had meant to. Recently we had come to a somewhat peaceful, almost friendly, understanding with one another. Even so, I had to admit that their relationship coming to an end wouldn't exactly cause me to shed too many tears. That would make the whole scenario with my wannabe girlfriend being fated to kill his actual girlfriend slightly less awkward.

Tom's glare practically had *fuck you* written all over it. "No."

"You dumped her?" Ed speculated.

"It's a lot worse than that," he replied miserably.

"Spill, dude. What is it? Did she turn out to be a guy in disguise?"

"I'm pretty sure he'd like that," Ed said and we both chuckled.

"I don't think that's the case," Tom eyed the last few inches in the bottle. "She's been sick the last few days."

"Oh yeah, Ed told me. She got the flu?"

"Worse. She's been puking her guts out."

Ed's eyes widened. "No fucking way!"

I was about to ask what he meant when something clicked in my brain. "Holy shit, Tom. Really?"

He nodded. "She took one of those tests this morning. Christy's pregnant."

A Trip into Town

"BWAHAHAHAHAHA!"

"It's not funny."

"Oh believe me, it is," Ed cried.

"Oh God!" I said through tears, still laughing. "I just hope it inherits her looks *and* brains."

"Come on, guys, this is some serious shit here," Tom grumbled. The look on his face was cross, but his tone suggested he expected no less. No doubt he would have given the same reaction had one of us broken the news.

"I'm sure it is," I said as I got my laughter under control. "You do realize there are these things called condoms, right?" He continued to glare at me, so I added, "And you understand that you're supposed to put them on your dick, not use them as rubber finger puppets."

Ed snorted and began to choke on his beer. I clapped him on the back until he got it under control.

"Ow! Watch it," he protested.

"Sorry, sometimes I forget my own strength."

"Seriously, Tom, you were using protection, right?" Ed asked.

"Well..."

"What the fuck do you mean *well*?"

"I thought...you know...maybe she had some kind of magical birth control."

There was a moment of silence while Ed and I absorbed this declaration of brilliance.

"My god, you are a fucking idiot," I said.

"What? She uses that shit for everything else. You think she ever cleans her apartment? No, it's all fucking magic. So I kinda figured..."

"She was dispelling your magic missiles?"

"Well...yeah."

"Guess you rolled a critical hit, my friend," Ed commented.

"What the fuck am I going to do?"

"Okay, let's think this through like rational human beings. Well, Bill and I will anyway. Have you discussed her...um...not being pregnant anymore?"

"Good point," I added.

"Not gonna fucking happen," Tom replied.

"So she told you..."

"It's not even worth bringing up," he said. "You remember her and her friends up in Canada? Outside of the magic shit they were doing, they were all communing with nature like a bunch of fucking flower children. I think they're big on that live and let live thing."

I thought back to the firebombed loft. "Could've fooled me."

"Well, technically you're not alive."

"And technically you're a fag," I shot back.

"Apparently not," Ed pointed out. "Holy shit, Tom is gonna be a daddy. What the fuck is this world coming to?"

I was about to join in the laughter again when his words struck me. I *knew* what the world was coming to. A global supernatural war was brewing, one which we'd all be very lucky to survive. Bringing a child into such a world was...wait! The kid might not even make it that far. If Decker was right, the birth of the Icon signaled the end of wizard and witch-kind. Christy was amongst their number.

Saving Sheila meant I was potentially condemning Christy. I had known that and - considering our past rocky relationship - been willing to take that chance. But now things were complicated. If Christy was indeed pregnant, wouldn't I be dooming her unborn child as well? What was that baby guilty of...outside of being a product of Tom's stupidity?

Holy shit. How the fuck was I going to fix this? Jesus Christ, when it rains it pours.

* * *

By the time we got Tom settled down, we had lost our window of opportunity. In the time it would take to get to Manhattan, it would be well past normal business hours. I just had to hope that Decker's efforts had so far proven fruitless and Colin's team was still assembling itself. Fortunately, neither of them was what I would call a competent leader. Had James been heading up this effort personally, I would have been worried. Colin? Well, I probably had a little slack there.

Finally, Tom passed out, and we dragged his ass to bed. From the look Ed gave me as we shut the door, he had figured out the implications as well.

"Still in this with me?" I asked. "If you're not, I'm..."

"Oh, quit whining like a bitch," he said dismissively. "Of course I'm still in."

"What about Tom?"

"He'll be fine. Probably puke his guts out before morning, though. I'm not cleaning that shit up."

"Don't look at me," I replied before getting back to my point. "I meant afterwards"

"I know. At some point you're gonna have to tell him."

"How do you think he'll take it?"

A pensive look came over his face. Finally, he said, "For the life of me, I have no fucking idea. This whole scenario is so far out there...beats the hell out of me."

"Tell me about it."

"You will have to tell him, though."

"I know. I owe him that much."

"Yeah...but not tonight. Probably not tomorrow either."

I nodded.

"So what do we do right now?" he asked.

"Only thing that comes to mind. Call Sally."

"Sounds good to me."

"Keep it in your pants, dude."

"Bite me."

"I thought that was her job."

* * *

"You're kidding me," Sally said over the speaker.

"I assure you we are not."

"I can't believe that fucktard was allowed to breed. He's a walking poster child for selective sterilization."

"There is an argument for that," Ed replied.

"Oh well. Hopefully the brat inherits her brains."

"Yeah, about that..."

"I know what it means, Bill. You don't have to spell it out."

I sighed. Sally had the luxury, if you could call it that, of not being overly burdened by morals, ethics, or guilt. Some days I envied that.

"So anything going on coven-side?" I asked, changing the subject.

"Just battening down the hatches, so to speak."

"Any word on things?"

"I've been on the horn ever since I woke up."

"And?"

"*And* there's a good deal of freaking out going on out there. Covens all over the tri-state area are busy packing up their shit and getting to their safe houses."

"Colin?"

"I don't doubt it. He's all about secrets when it suits him, but I bet he couldn't resist telling everyone with a pair of ears how he was in charge of hunting the mighty Icon. Either way, it's not a secret anymore."

"Maybe that's a good thing."

"I guess we'll see. At the very least James will probably chew him a new asshole for it."

"Speaking of..."

"Don't bother asking. I haven't heard from him."

"Boston?"

"Nada there. They're stonewalling me. Whatever they have planned, we aren't meant to be privy to it."

"So much for respecting the Freewill," I groused.

"Colin doesn't respect anybody who doesn't outrank him. Until such time as the Draculas call you up as a general, he'll shit on you without a second thought."

"Thanks for the imagery."

"Any time."

"So where's that leave us?" Ed asked.

"Up shit's creek, but at this point I'm getting used to it."

"I know the feeling," I said.

"It's not much, but I think we should try your plan, Ed. It's better than sitting around with our thumbs up our asses."

"It's too late..."

"I meant tomorrow. The forecast changed and they're calling for clouds now, so we should be okay. I'll meet you guys at the Icon's office in the early PM."

"Think we'll find her there?"

"Who the fuck knows at this point. As I said, it's better than nothing."

"Agreed."

"Alright then, be there or..."

"Be square?" I finished her sentence.

"Actually, I was gonna say be completely fucked."

Somehow, I had a feeling we were already well on our way to that destination.

* * *

Despite being somewhat hungover, Tom got up for work. His company was performing an audit on a client and he needed to be there.

"Hopefully we'll find some irregularities," he said on his way out. "That'll make me feel better."

"I'm sure they're glad they have you on their side," Ed had replied.

Rather than tip off Tom that anything was up, we decided to head out a little later than him. It gave us both the added benefit of being able to get some work done. Our jobs weren't exactly top priority these days, but going into the global apocalypse unemployed would probably make things suck even worse. Sue us for holding onto a piece of normalcy.

This time, the weatherman had been correct. It was overcast with a chance of light rain the entire day. I could deal with being soggy. It beat slathering on sunscreen and dressing up like some sort of half-assed terrorist.

Around noon I called Sally to give her a wake-up call, then Ed and I hit the road.

According to her business card, Sheila's office was downtown in an area where a lot of small businesses were headquartered. It wasn't exactly cheap, but renting a floor there put you pretty much in the middle of the action. For those lucky to survive, it was well worth the investment. The last time I had spoken to Sheila, I had gotten the impression that she had more than survived. Her business had been thriving. As for now...well, finding out you're a being of legendary status would probably be distracting for even the most stalwart workaholic.

"Any idea what you're going to say if she's there?" Ed asked on the train ride over.

"I'm sure something will come to mind."

"Famous last words."

"Don't I know it."

* * *

"This is the place," Sally declared.

"Wow," I said, reading the building directory. "They have space on two floors. Must be doing pretty good."

"Yeah, well, she's gonna be doing a whole lot less good if Decker's fun bunch finds her first."

"Fingers crossed, guys," I said, entering the elevator. I hit the button to take us to the sixth floor where the reception area was supposed to be. When in doubt, walk in the front door.

"Fingers, toes, and a few other appendages that I'd prefer not to mention," Ed replied.

"Aw, what's the matter? Feeling shy?" Sally asked with a wicked little smile.

"Ramp down the libido, Sluterella," I said. "We're on the clock. Oh wait, that's normal for you during work hours."

"Not too late for me to call Colin and spill my guts."

"Shutting up now."

"I thought so."

The doors opened and my mind went completely blank at the thought of seeing her. After a few moments, the doors began to shut again as we stood unmoving. Sally put out her hand and stopped them.

"We staying here all day?"

"Sorry." I stepped past Ed. "Not a fucking word." He smirked, but had the good graces to heed my warning.

Glass double doors with a large *Iconic Efficiencies* logo faced us as we stepped from the elevator. The lights were on, and someone sat behind the reception desk.

"Looks like they're open," I said, half surprised to see it myself. Was it possible that, after everything that had gone down, Sheila somehow managed to go on with life, business as usual? It didn't seem likely, but the view before us was a vision of pure, corporate normalcy.

"Time to see if we can get on the calendar," Ed replied.

I nodded and stepped forward, my two companions in tow. We went through the door and approached the front desk. A young man, dressed in business casual, sat behind it.

"He's kinda cute," Sally whispered. "Do you think she and him..."

"Not now," I spat back. Goddamn, she just never fucking quit, did she?

The man looked up. "Can I help you?"

"Uh, yeah. We'd like to see Sheila." Okay, maybe not the most profound opening line ever. "Uh, Sheila O'Connell, she's the..."

"I'm aware who the president is," he chuckled. "Do you have an appointment?"

An appointment? That meant she was in. Holy shit!

"I..." My voice froze in my throat. Oh crap. All of my old insecurities rushed up. Stupid subconscious! I had fought and defeated multiple master vampires. I'd faced down a monstrous ape in the frozen wastelands of Canada. Hell, I had even survived a couple of days with Gan. Yet, despite all that, my knees knocked together like I was picking up my date for the junior prom.

"Sir?"

Was he talking to me? What was I even doing here? I kind of recall it being sorta important. I...

"Oh Jesus Christ," Ed said from behind me. "We're friends of hers...from Hopskotchgames. We were just stopping by to say hi."

The man eyed us for a moment, his eyes shifting back and forth amongst the three of us.

Finally, I found my voice. "I know she's probably busy, but we just wanted to see her for a few minutes."

"Hopskotchgames, you said?"

"Yes."

He appeared to consider this for a second. "I believe her calendar is free right now."

"Really?" I sputtered, no doubt sounding way too overenthusiastic.

"I'm sure she won't mind the interruption." He stood up. "Follow me please."

* * *

The receptionist led us deeper into the building. We walked past a few empty offices and a small sea of cubes, likewise devoid of activity. Guess it was the lunch hour.

"Be on your guard, Bill," Sally whispered from behind me, speaking at a volume that she knew only I'd hear.

I glanced back toward her and raised my eyebrows.

"When's the last time your manager saw some schlubs right off the street?" she asked in that barely audible tone. "He didn't even call to check to see if she was free."

Oh shit. She was right. The receptionist in any organization served the dual function of gatekeeper...keeping the rabble out. Hell, Ed and I definitely weren't wearing our business best and Sally...well as usual, she could have just stepped in from working a corner on forty-second street.

Duh! I was such a fucking dumbass. There was one way to tell for sure whether this dude was on the up and up. Sheila's apartment had practically been swimming with her scent. I took a deep breath and reached out with my senses. Only the faintest odor of her perfume penetrated my nostrils. There were other scents overpowering it and they were definitely not hers.

A split second after I registered the number of people in the general vicinity, Sally whispered, "Two more of them."

"This way please," our not-so-gracious host said as he held a door open for us.

Oh well, in for a penny. I stepped through into what had once probably been a good sized conference area...possibly a town meeting hall for a company of this size. It was now devoid of all furnishings. The only thing that stood in the room was another man. His dress was similar to the first, typical business casual.

As we approached, he looked at the three of us before his eyes settled upon mine.

"Welcome, vampire. We've been expecting you."

The God Squad

Click The door had been shut behind us. Nice to know some clichés still applied in life. Still, just for shits and giggles, I glanced around, glad I did. The original man guarded the door, and the third I had smelled joined him. This new joker was dressed considerably less formal than his compatriots. In fact he could have just stepped in from an afternoon of LARPing. He wore armor, chainmail if my D&D knowledge served me right. A red cloak covered his shoulders, and a sheathed sword completed the look. Somehow I was willing to bet it wasn't a prop.

Fortunately, this served to snap me out of my funk. Talking to a girl was utterly terrifying. Facing off against three probable adversaries, on the other hand, none of whom appeared to be a vampire or a Sasquatch...well, not so much.

"I'm gonna go out on a limb here and assume you're not gonna serve lunch," I quipped.

"Speak for yourself," Sally replied. *sigh* No self-control in that one.

"We knew you would come for the Blessed One, praise be to our Lord for smiling upon her," the man in front of us said, stepping forward.

"Oh Jesus," Ed sighed. "This fucker sounds like my Aunt Dottie."

"Do not take his name in vain!" the man spat, immediately losing his cool. "Thralls are no better than the devils they serve."

"Heh, you're our thrall," Sally snickered. She wasn't taking this too seriously. I could understand why. Even with Sir Lancelot back there, the threat registered pretty low compared to what we had faced off against in the past.

"Okay," I put my hands up in a placating manner. I didn't know who these clowns were, but it was a safe bet that the Blessed One he referred to was Sheila. If so, they knew something, and I wanted to know what that something was before Sally decided it was time to start pruning limbs. "We're not here to fight. In fact I think we might actually be on the same side."

"I think not, spawn of the pit," the man scoffed, reaching inside of his jacket and pulling out what looked like a rosary. He brought it up to his lips and gave it a small kiss. Great. What next, was he going to start handing out pamphlets? "I serve a higher power, one whose light you shall never know."

"Says you," Sally snapped back. "I made communion in the second grade."

I turned and raised an eyebrow. Sally as a good little Catholic girl? Now there was an image.

"Don't start," she warned.

I smirked before turning back to the holy roller in front of me. "Fair enough," I said, trying to sound friendly. "I assume you guys know who I am."

"Obviously you are one of the undead. We could smell your stench the moment you walked in the door."

"Guess it's time to switch deodorants, Bill."

"Make light of the situation all you want, strumpet of Satan," the receptionist said. "We, the Templar, have been sent to escort you back to the gates of Hell from whence you came."

"Templar?" Ed and I asked in unison.

"Strumpet of Satan?" Sally growled. Her priorities were, as usual, not quite in line with the rest of ours.

"Relax," I said to her.

"Easy for you to say, he didn't call you..."

"Oh please, you practically have that written on your business cards."

Ed chuckled and Sally threw him a glare.

"Find something funny, fleshwad?"

"Me?" he quickly replied. "Nope, just...coughing."

"Thought so."

I turned around, intent on trying to get us back on track - Sally's wounded ego aside. "The Templar? Did I hear him right?"

"Indeed you did. Know that you stand in the presence of God's true warriors."

"Shouldn't you guys be out questing for...I don't know...the Holy Grail?" Ed asked.

"Fool! The Grail was found long ago," the dude in the armor proudly proclaimed. "Even now it rests within the..."

"That will be quite enough, Brother Robert," the man in front interrupted. Heh, guess sword boy wasn't exactly recruited for his stunning intellect.

"This is all fascinating," I said. "I can respect you guys. I saw *Indiana Jones and the Last Crusade*, I can dig it. Right now, though, we need to find my friend."

"Friend?" he scoffed at me.

"Yes, I have friends," I replied, perhaps a little more defensively than intended. "Her name is Sheila and she's..."

"You are no friend of the Blessed One. Those of her caliber do not consort with those of yours."

"Can't blame a guy for trying to date out of his league," Sally said.

I gritted my teeth, trying to keep from puncturing my bottom lip with my own fangs. Must...learn...to...ignore...Sally. I mentally counted to ten before starting again. "Listen, I know this is hard to believe, but we're trying to help her."

"Help her? How, by presenting yourself so that she might cleanse this world of you with her touch?" The man openly caressed his rosary. He ran the beads through his hand as if he were mentally saying his prayers. Christ, my grandmother used to do that. It would drive me batshit at Thanksgiving.

"Not quite. I understand what she's going through and I want to keep her safe from those who are hunting her."

"You understand what she's going through? I highly doubt that, vampire."

"I do," I kept my hands up and my tone placating. I needed to make these fuckers understand that we were here to help. "I know what it's like because I'm the vampire Freewill. I didn't ask for this..."

"The Freewill!" he shouted. "We will all die before letting you have her, spawn." Okay, maybe that was the wrong thing to say. I heard the sound of steel being scraped against leather. No doubt, Sir Doofus had drawn his sword. I guess talking time was over.

"If you fuckers want to die, I'm more than happy to oblige," Sally said from behind me.

"It is not us who shall perish today, whore of Babylon." Oh crap. That was definitely not going to put her into a forgiving mood.

"Wait!" I implored, trying to rein the situation back in, but it was too late.

Sally screamed, and I turned to find her cradling her cheek, smoke pouring from between her fingers. What the hell...but then I saw it. The man who had led us into this trap held a cross out before him. Smoke rose from it as well.

"Burn before the might of the Lord our God!" the man cried triumphantly, advancing upon her. Ed rather heroically tried to position himself between them. Unfortunately, the dude with the sword stepped to move into flank.

I mentally bumped these guys up a notch in my threat book. I had almost forgotten that faith could work for normal people. The cross by itself wouldn't do dick against a vampire. It was just a piece of wood or metal under normal circumstances, but this guy believed in it - apparently enough to empower it with his faith. Suddenly all those old vampire movies made a lot more sense.

This wasn't good. Their implements would be like branding irons to Sally and me. Ed was human, so a faith empowered trinket wouldn't hurt him, but that didn't mean anything - especially against three guys, one of whom brandished a longsword.

Sadly, I couldn't help him. I had my own cross to bear - pardon the pun - in the form of the guy up front. He made good use of the distraction his friend provided. Before I could react, he looped the rosary around my neck and pressed the crucifix against my forehead. Oh crap...

* * *

"Bow before the might of our Creator," the Templar in charge hissed into my ear. He was trying to strangle me with the rosary, but my more pressing concern was the cross. Any second now it would...

Except it didn't. The only thing I felt was the cold metal pressed against my skin. It wasn't exactly comfortable, but then again, my head wasn't bursting into flames either.

I grinned despite the situation. Guess this guy wasn't as true of a believer as he claimed. Maybe that was why he had been reciting the rosary as he spoke to me. It wasn't too hard to imagine that, despite his words, deep down there was just enough doubt to keep him from getting his faith on.

I grabbed the thin chain around my neck and snapped it. I turned to my opponent and a look of panic flooded his face.

"No!" he cried. "I don't believe..."

"That is why you fail," I did my best Yoda impersonation before decking the guy square on the jaw. The Templar flew back and went down like a sack of bricks, blood pouring from his smashed nose. Ladies and gentleman, your winner by knockout.

I spun, ready to give my friends a hand, but I was a second too late.

SHRIPPP! There's a noise I was gonna hear in my nightmares. Note to self, do not piss off Sally...at least not the way this guy had. While I had been dealing with Mr. Lack of Faith, the receptionist had apparently tried to finish her off. It hadn't gone well for him.

His right arm, its hand still clutching the crucifix, flew across the room sans the rest of him. Before I could open my mouth, she was on him. One slash of her now fully extended claws and the guy was nearly decapitated. Eww. It's so much less...nasty when that happens in the movies.

She wasn't done, though. She leapt upon the man and continued ripping him to shreds. Guess she took some offense to that *strumpet of Satan* comment.

"Okay, Sally. I think you got him."

"Err Bill," came Ed's voice from the other side of the room. "Thanks for leaving the guy with the sword for me." I glanced over and found the knight holding my roommate from behind, his blade at his throat. Oh yeah, I kept forgetting that Ed's not much of a fighter. He usually brings his shotgun into situations like these. Unfortunately, the NYPD tends to take a dim view toward people walking around fully armed.

"Easy there, Robert," I said to the man wielding the sword. "This doesn't have to end badly." Out of the corner of my eye, Sally rose from her kill. She was covered head to toe with the guy's blood, a burn mark in the shape of a cross still evident on her cheek. Hmm, so much for that. "It doesn't have to end any worse," I quickly amended.

"Speak not my name, beast," the man spat. "You may end my life, but I shall take your thrall with me."

"I'm not his fucking thrall."

"Silence, thrall!"

This wasn't going well. Jeez, how the hell were we going to talk this guy down without Ed being given a really close shave? Negotiations weren't exactly my strong suit. Calling this guy a fucking twat over and over again wouldn't do much in the way of...

BANG!

Something exploded next to my head. Damn, that hurt. Sensitive vampire ears aren't always a good thing. My headache was small beans compared to what happened to Robert, though. A neat little bullet hole appeared in his forehead. With no further fanfare, his sword dropped to the floor and the rest of him followed.

I turned to see that Sally had her purse in one hand and a small pistol in the other.

"Um, nice shot," I meekly commented.

"I think I just shit my pants," Ed said, a small splash of Robert's blood on his shoulder.

"New piece?" I asked conversationally, despite the fact that I was pretty close to following Ed's lead.

"Yep," she replied brightly. "I figure this one is a little more subtle to carry around."

I glanced at Robert's body. "Yeah, real subtle. When did you decide to show up packing?"

"Are you serious, Bill? Shit's getting real. I'm not stepping my dainty ass outside without a little protection."

I gave her one more sideways glance and then stepped toward Ed. "Are you all right?"

"I'll live." He still sounded shaken but had regained his composure. He gave me a quick thumbs-up.

"So I guess it's back to the drawing board," Sally said, putting her gun away.

"No thanks to you," I replied. "Fortunately I was able to show a little more restraint." I pointed to the still unconscious, but obviously breathing, form of the Templar I had decked.

"Not bad, Bill," she said, high praise from her. "How'd you keep from getting burned?"

"Turns out his faith wasn't as great as he thought."

"Lucky you."

"Damn straight."

"I hate to interrupt the vampire love fest," Ed pointed out, "but that gunshot was pretty goddamned loud and there are other businesses in this building. We should get the fuck out of here."

I glanced over at Sally, who looked like she had practically bathed in the receptionist's blood. "Yeah, this might look a little suspicious."

"We should be right above the subway lines," she said, licking some gore off her fingers. You can always count on Sally to be classy. "If we're lucky, this place has a drainage vent in the basement we can squeeze through."

"In the mood to tour the sewers?" I asked Ed, a smirk on my face.

"Do I have much choice?"

"Yep, you can stay and get arrested," Sally said blithely. She walked over to the still unconscious form on the floor and gave him a good solid kick to the midsection. Never let it be said that Sally doesn't forgive and forget. "Let's bring this piece of shit."

"Snack for the trip?"

"You want to find your girlfriend, right? Well, dickhead here probably knows where she is."

"Think he'll talk?"

"I *know* he will."

Preying for Forgiveness

We got lucky. We managed to make it underground unseen and, more importantly, unarrested. Using the tunnels, we made our way back to the office.

"Such wonderful places you take me to, Bill," Ed said as we sloshed our way toward our destination.

"You really haven't seen the city until you trek around underneath it."

"Uuhhhh." A groan came from over my shoulder followed by a sharp crack as Sally put her fist into his face.

"Thanks," I told her.

"My pleasure."

* * *

I unceremoniously dumped the Templar onto the floor once we entered the office. It was my second forced march through filthy sewer tunnels this week and, needless to say, it didn't leave me in the best of moods.

I stopped and looked around. The office was unusually silent.

"Where's Starlight and the others?"

"I sent all of them to the new safe house earlier," Sally said, which explained why we were here and not there. Whatever this guy had to say wasn't for their ears anyway.

"Is that an iota of caring I hear in your tone?"

"Hardly. Good help is hard to find..."

"As well as a good stylist?"

"Hell yeah, and I couldn't exactly send her and Alfonzo there without the others."

"Alfonzo?" Ed asked.

"You don't want to know," I assured him before turning back to Sally. "Why don't you go get cleaned up while we figure out what to do?"

"I will after we do what needs to be done."

"You have a plan?" Ed asked.

"Obviously."

"Torture?"

"Tempting," she said. She meant it too. "But it would probably take too long. No guarantee he'll talk either. He'd probably just die screaming for Jesus and I don't have enough aspirin to deal with that kind of headache."

"What then?" I asked.

"Compulsion," she replied simply enough.

That definitely had potential, but it wasn't a certainty. Humans were difficult for vampires to control. Faith or not, if this guy was as devoted to his order as he claimed, he could potentially resist being Vulcan mind-melded.

"Think you've got enough juice to make him talk?"

"Nope." She reached down, grabbed the unconscious Templar by his shirt and dragged him to his feet.

"Then what..."

She turned her head and looked both of us straight in the eye. This time there was no hint of sarcasm or attitude. When she spoke, it was simple and direct. "Do you want to find this girl, Bill?"

"You know I do."

"And you're willing to do whatever it takes to save her?"

"Sure..."

"Don't just give me a bullshit answer here," she snapped. "I'm serious. You've been lucky up until now. You've been able to get through a lot of crap without dirtying your hands...well too much anyway, at least by vampire standards. It's different now, though. There's some serious business coming down the pipe. This is just the beginning. Whatever lines you've drawn in the sand are going to get blurry at best. I need to know that you're going to be able to handle it."

Her words didn't surprise me. Some part of me had been expecting it, probably for quite some time now - at the very least, ever since I had gotten back from the Woods of Mourning. It didn't mean I had to like it, though. Neither choice was particularly appealing. I could keep on the path I was, playing the loveable doofus (semi-loveable at the very least), but would that really end well for anyone? The other option meant possibly giving up the one thing that truly separated me from most other vamps: my humanity, or at least a good chunk of it. Could I go down that path and not turn into a monster? I honestly didn't know.

Sally and Ed stayed silent while I thought it over. Ultimately, it was my choice to make. Oh who was I kidding? Like there really was a choice.

It was time to man up.

"Do what needs to be done," I said.

Sally gave me a single nod. Her eyes blackened, and I realized what she meant to do. I couldn't help but feel a slight sense of irony. I'd been bitching for the past year about how I was suckered in and turned into a vampire against my will, and now I was giving the order to do the same thing. Sure, the circumstances were different, but the end result wouldn't be. If I had to guess, I'd bet that Night Razor was laughing his ass off in Hell right about then.

Sally lowered her mouth, fangs fully extended, to the Templar's throat. There was a crunch as she bit in, followed by a spray of blood.

"Ewww," I muttered. Well alright, maybe I wasn't manning up *that much*. Remembering that not everyone in the room was an undead monster, I turned to Ed. "How are you holding up?"

"Me? I'm fine. I see you pouring blood on shit every fucking day. If I'm not desensitized by now..."

"Yeah, but this is..."

"Necessary. I agree with Sally, shit's gonna get real soon enough. We're either in this game to win it or we might as well just cash in our chips now."

"We?" I asked for what felt like the millionth time since becoming a vampire.

"Don't ruin the moment by turning back into a dumbass, Bill. You'd still last all of five minutes without your friends."

"Speaking of which, any idea yet how to break this to Tom?"

"Not a fucking clue, dude."

A thud brought our attention back to Sally. She had dropped the Templar on the floor like ten pounds of shit in a five pound bag. She turned to us, a smile on her blood stained lips. "Tangy," she said. "I think our altar boy here has a taste for the sacramental wine."

"Is it done?"

"Yep, unless you'd care for a sip."

"Pass," I replied.

"Well then, this dipshit should be waking up in a couple of hours. Make yourselves comfortable, boys. As for me, I'm gonna hit the showers." She started walking to the back. Just before disappearing, she added, "I might be a while. Being covered in so much blood makes me feel all tingly inside." With that, she left the room.

Ed stood there slack-jawed for a moment, then asked, "Is it wrong of me to be turned on by that?"

"Highly," I said. "But if that's wrong, I don't want to be right."

If Sally had thrown that out to purposely distract us from the man who lay bleeding out just a few feet from where we stood, she had done a hell of a job.

* * *

Unfortunately, the distraction didn't last. I sat and stared at the crumpled form on the floor, remembering how it had all started for me. It had come dangerously close to ending for me that night as well. Had it not been for the fact that my antics had amused James, Night Razor would have staked me into dust and been done with it.

Despite what he stood for, his feelings toward us, and the fact that he and his buddies had spirited Sheila away to god-knows where, I found myself feeling sorry for the Templar. It was doubtful a guardian angel would come to his rescue like one had for me.

"Knock it off," Ed said from behind me as he pulled up a chair.

"What's Sally up to?"

"She's in her office trying to dig up some intel."

"Having any luck?"

"Didn't seem like it," he said. "When I walked out, it looked like she was pulling up an online poker site. Now stop trying to change the subject."

"What subject?"

"I'm not a fucking moron, Bill."

"Well..."

"Kiss my ass," he said amicably enough. "Do you know what your problem is?"

"Which one? I have lots of them."

"The problem that separates you from Tom and me."

"Hmm, let me think. Could it be that you both have heartbeats?"

"Nope. It's that we have heartbeats, but you have a heart."

"You're losing me here."

"What a surprise. Me? I'm not exactly a people person."

I feigned shock. "No! Say it isn't so."

"I know - my stellar personality often shines through like a beacon in the night. But let's face facts. If I were in your shoes, I'd have left a trail of bodies in my wake by now that might even impress Sally."

"Not likely!" she shouted from within her office.

"The walls have ears," he said in a hushed tone.

"So do the annoying ex-strippers."

"Anyway, you get my point," he continued. "Tom, he's a good guy, but I'm pretty sure the only things he's ever clued in about are his toys and whoever happens to be sucking his dick at the time."

I nodded. Tom was my oldest friend and I loved him like a brother, but Ed had pretty much summed him up in a nutshell.

"The bottom line is that he'd probably cause a bloodbath just...well, by being Tom."

"An accurate assessment, I'd say."

"But not you. You worry about these things. I mean sure, you talk big and all that shit, but deep down..."

"I'm a pussy?"

"Well yeah, but you also care. Look at all the shit you've managed to get yourself into trying to keep your coven under control. Hell, if that Nergui dude hadn't iced the Sasquatch princess, I don't know what you'd have done."

"I would have found a way out of it...probably."

"Yeah, but your first, second, or even third choice wouldn't have been to drive a knife hilt-deep into her chest."

"I guess..."

"I *know*."

"So what are you trying to say?"

"Stop beating the shit out of yourself about it. You're in a bad situation. Hell, we all are. You're gonna need to occasionally do bad things to deal with it. The thing is, I know that in every case you'll always try to think of a better way. Unfortunately, life won't always give you that chance. That's just how things roll, but it does *not* make you a monster."

"Thanks, man. I guess I'm just worried I'll start to like it if I do it enough."

"I doubt it."

"It could happen. What if I turn into another Sally?"

"Not on your best day!" she shouted out again.

"Will you stop fucking eavesdropping!" I yelled back.

"Heh," Ed whispered. "You turn into Sally and I'll just fuck you myself."

I paused to raise an eyebrow. "Okay, maybe she's a bad example. What if I start acting like Night Razor or Francois or maybe..."

"You won't. And if you do, I promise I will pull out my shotgun, load it up with silver slugs and blow your fucking head right off."

I considered that for a moment. "Or you could just try talking to me."

"I could, but what fun would that be?"

* * *

"Hold him down," Sally commanded.

"He's already tied up," I pointed out. Our former Templar was secured to the sturdiest office chair we could find. Well okay, second sturdiest. Sally wouldn't let us touch hers.

"Uh hello...he's gonna wake up a vampire. Not everyone is like you. Some don't take it too well. The last thing I want is to have him messing up this place while we chase him around."

I guess she had a point. I walked to one side and held onto his already tied arm. Ed shrugged and did the same on the other side. It was a nice gesture on his part, but I was really hoping the bonds held. Otherwise, he was gonna be sent flying. Forget just being human - Ed's not exactly a heavyweight.

Sure enough, the Templar began to stir a few minutes later. His head lolled back and his eyes cracked open. They had gone black. He opened his mouth to draw a breath and bared his descended fangs. A moment later, he ran his tongue over them and drew a thin bead of blood. That got his attention. His eyes popped wide open. It was hard to tell, what with the lack of pupils and all, but it seemed like they carried a look of horror.

"Welcome back, asshole," Sally said as she stood directly in front of him.

"Uhhh, what...what have you monsters done to me?"

"I'm sure you can figure it out." She was more at home in this role than I was. Let her handle the interrogation. She was stone cold, the ice queen bitch of the frozen north.

"God, please have mercy on your servant!" he shrieked. "Deliver me from my..."

"*ENOUGH OF THAT!!*" The Templar's eyes glazed over at her command and his prattling ceased as quickly as it began. Seeing how it worked always made me damn glad I was a vamp Freewill. It was at least comforting to know someone couldn't fuck with my head at their whim.

The same couldn't be said of our newest recruit, though. Sadly for him, his tenure in our diminished coven probably wouldn't be a particularly lengthy one.

"Bill, do you want to do the honors?"

Oh well, I guess it was time to get some practice at this. I took a breath and focused on the glassy eyed ex-Templar.

"TELL US EVERYTHING YOU KNOW!!"

All the Guests Have Arrived

"And then Father McDonally whispered in my ear, *after this you'll be a man...*"

"Okay, that's **ENOUGH!!**" Sally compelled, throwing her hands up in frustration.

"Guess, I should've been more specific," I said sheepishly.

"You think?"

"Sorry. I haven't been in charge of too many interrogations."

"One can see why," Ed commented, drawing a glare from me.

"All right," she took a deep breath. "Let's try this again. *WHAT HAVE THE TEMPLAR DONE WITH THE ICON!?*"

"The Blessed One," the turned Templar said, "is safe with my brothers. She is our guest."

"Well that's fucking great," Sally spat. "We're getting blasted and burned while your girlfriend is being treated to tea and crumpets."

I opened my mouth to comment, but the Templar wasn't finished yet.

"We have told her of your kind. We have prepared her for you."

"I believe you mean *us*," I replied. "Unless you think those are Halloween props sticking out of your mouth."

The Templar spat at me in disgust. Gross! No class with these fundamentalist types. Despite the compulsion, his sheer hatred of us was enough to let him partially shake it off.

Before he could try it again, Sally's fist smashed against his jaw with a loud crack. The Templar's head flew back, blood and spittle spraying from his mouth.

"Nice shot," Ed commented.

"Thank you."

"I thought you were going to compel him," I said, "not beat the information out of him."

"I am. That was just for the hell of it. Punching out assholes helps me concentrate."

Ed snickered until I shot him a look. Finally, Sally said, "Listen up, dickhead. *TELL ME WHERE YOU'RE KEEPING THE ICON!!*"

It was about time. We all leaned closer to listen. This was what we had been waiting for.

The Templar strained against the compulsion. Had he still been human, he probably could have resisted it. Alas, he wasn't, nor was he lucky enough to be a Freewill like me. After a brief inner struggle in which his eyes practically bulged from his skull, the compulsion won out. He gritted his teeth and tried to bite down on his lip, but his mouth opened against his will.

"She...she's in..."

"Come on, you can do it," I prodded.

"Our Lady of Innocence."

"Huh?"

"Sounds like a church," Ed said.

"Uh huh. How original," Sally commented. "Where is it?"

"I will never..."

"*WHERE IS IT!?*"

"In Mamaroneck, off of Post Street," he spat, the hatred in his eyes evident.

"You're keeping her in Westchester?" I asked.

"It could be worse," she said.

"Ever try driving up there on a weekend?" Ed asked.

"Let's focus here, guys," I said. "We still need some more information."

"We're gonna need my car too," Ed replied.

"No offense, lover," Sally quipped, "but your little hatchback isn't exactly my idea of a rescue vehicle."

"We can swipe one," I said offhandedly. "We've done it before."

Sally inclined her head in my direction and stared at me.

"What? You're the one who said to man up."

"Yeah, I just didn't expect..."

"Let's finish up here and then you can berate me. It's gonna be a long night as it is."

She nodded, an almost impressed look upon her face...*almost*. She turned to continue the interrogation when suddenly, she paused. "Shit!"

I was just about to ask her what was up when a scent - no, make that multiple scents - registered in my overly sensitive vampire nostrils. A group approached. Judging by the smell, at least some of them were vampires.

"What?" Ed asked.

"We have company," I whispered, hoping they weren't close enough to overhear us.

A moment later, there came a knock on the office's door. Time was up.

* * *

"What are you doing?"

Sally pushed over the chair holding our prisoner and proceeded to rip one of the legs off. "Covering our tracks."

"You can't just..." but I stopped myself. The guy we captured would have gladly killed us had our positions been reversed. Hell, he had already tried. Still, it somehow seemed dickish to kill him twice.

No, I told myself. It had to be done. The entire jig would be up if we were caught with him in our possession. The vamps, Colin's crew no doubt, could just as easily compel him as we had. I bit my tongue as Sally raised the makeshift stake.

The Templar only had time to draw in breath for a scream before she rammed it through his chest. There was a flash of light and he instantly self-combusted. Within moments, there was nothing left but a pile of dust.

"Where are you going?" I asked as she started walking away.

"To open the door, of course."

"What the hell are we supposed to say about this?" I motioned at the pile of ash at Ed's and my feet.

"You're the Freewill," she snapped, then turned back to the door.

What the fuck was that supposed to mean? Unfortunately I didn't have time to ask as she unlocked the door for our uninvited guests.

Oh crap!

* * *

"We welcome the faithful of the First," Sally said, almost managing to mask the sarcasm in her voice. "With your help...what are *they* doing here?"

"Have you not heard, vampire?" a familiar voice answered from just outside the doorway. "We are partners in this endeavor." Motherfucker! Harry Decker was here? I knew they had agreed to work with Colin's people, but I hadn't expected them to actually take it to heart. I had figured it was more of a mutual "we won't kill you if you won't kill us" thing. So much for wishful thinking.

Sally gritted her teeth as she said, "Welcome, oh *honored* guests." She stepped aside, but not before shooting me a glance that was more annoyance than panic. Leave it to her to only be partially put out by a bad situation.

In walked quite the interesting collection of beings, although it was fairly easy to tell who was who. A group of vampires, each dressed like a bad imitation of an Italian mobster - black suits and trench coats the attire of choice - entered. Judging by the bulges in their outfits, they were concealing weaponry of some sort. Interspersed amongst them were white-robed witches, several of whom I recognized from my little misadventure up in Canada. Last, and definitely least, entered Decker - standing out from his coven, dressed in what I guessed was an Armani suit - douche! Fortunately, Christy was nowhere to be seen amongst the magical menagerie. That would have ratcheted up the awkward factor by about a thousand.

The entire group except Decker pretty much ignored Sally. He gave her a quick smirk as he entered. Forget barbarians at the gates, we had opened up and invited them right in. This was going to require some fast talking. Sadly, I was drawing a blank.

One of the rejects from *The Matrix* approached me...apparently the Morpheus of the group. Hell, he even looked the part. He was a big guy - a few inches taller than me - dark skinned and with a bald head. He wore a neatly clipped beard on his heavy-set jaw, which showed not even the faintest trace of humor. His dark sunglasses couldn't mask the look of disapproval as he gave me the once over, but at least it was better than the complete lack of acknowledgement he gave to Ed.

"Greetings, Freewill," he said in a deep voice with minimal inflection, but enough for me to notice the slight British accent. Judging by how he'd addressed me, I'd say he had probably been briefed by Colin. Up in Boston, they kept files on most vampires. It was like the FBI, but without any concern for silly things like privacy.

"My name is Remington," Mr. Personality continued, "Remington Windsor, and before you ask, yes I am related, albeit from years past. I will be heading up this assignment. As of this moment, I am in charge of all vampire related activity in this city." He turned away.

"Related to who?" I whispered to Ed.

"I think the royal family."

"Really?" I mused. This guy had about as much resemblance to Prince Charles as I did to Sally.

"Uh yeah. Pretty sure that's their last name."

Huh, learn something new every day. Wait a second...what was that about him being in charge? What the fuck was that weasel Colin up to?

"You mean this operation?" I asked, getting his attention again.

"I said what I meant, Freewill."

"Okay," I tried to keep my cool. No doubt he was attempting to rile me up. Well fuck that. I wasn't about to give him or Decker the satisfaction. "First off, my name is Bill."

"We know what..."

"Secondly," I interrupted, "This is my coven. I'd appreciate it if you showed the proper respect." Hmm, actually he probably *was* showing the proper respect. Most vampires tended to give those younger than them about as much consideration as a hobo begging for change. I had no idea of this guy's age, but it was a safe bet he wasn't exactly freshly risen.

"Your coven?" scoffed Decker. "I see but two vampires here."

"No thanks to you, fuckface." Sally spat.

Remington turned to face me. "You will control your underling, or I will remove her from this operation." He took a step forward and his foot landed in the remnants of the Templar. He briefly looked down at it, then at me, a slight crease in his brow.

I was tempted to take a swing at him. Fuck the Templar. This dick had walked in here, proclaimed his leadership, and threatened Sally - all in the space of about ten seconds.

It was then that inspiration struck. I had ascended to the top of this coven through a combination of luck and the smokescreen that I was far more ferocious than reality. It was time to use that.

"A survivor of the wizard's attack," I casually kicked at the dust. "He wanted to flee the city. I didn't approve and was kinda hungry too."

For the first time since entering, something resembling an emotion passed across Remington's face. "You would turn on your own?"

"I'm the Freewill. You've heard the stories," I replied, putting some steel behind my voice. "They're all true."

"The beast feeds upon his kind," gasped one of the witches.

"I still have a little room left," I warned, hoping that the truce held. Getting hit with half a dozen fireballs wouldn't exactly do wonders for my already shitty week.

Thankfully, Ed tried to keep things from devolving into a straight out brawl. "Okay, people, let's not forget we're all on the same side here."

Remington (gah! What a stupid fucking name!) cocked an eyebrow in his direction. His left hand shot out and grabbed Ed by the neck, none too gently judging by my friend's reaction. My first instinct was to try to pry him off, but I stopped myself short. This vampire was most likely several times stronger than me. Doing so would have just resulted in embarrassing myself and losing what little chance I had of reining in this situation.

Instead, I casually said, "Let go of my friend, Remington."

"You are *friends* with this blood swine? What can he possibly mean to you?"

"Mr. Vesser here," Decker commented, an insufferable smirk still on his face, "is a modestly talented graphic designer. Beyond that..."

"Better than being a useless marketing droid," I snapped back, momentarily losing my cool. Goddamn, that guy got under my skin, not the least of which was because he was probably pulling in about double my salary. Fucker!

A strangled gasp caught my attention. Oh yeah, Ed. I glanced over and saw he was turning an interesting shade of purple. Not good.

"This human was my advisor in the Woods of Mourning," I said, an edge working its way into my voice. "He was partially responsible for the great victory (*yeah right*) I was able to present to Lord Alexander."

That got Remington's attention. Never discount the power of name dropping.

"Unlike you," I said, trying to keep my cool as Ed continued to turn funny colors, "*he* was a part of shaping our destiny. Although, perhaps you're right and Lord Alexander won't mind you killing this mere mortal without his express approval."

Never let it be said I can't play the game. Most vampires are arrogant pieces of shit, at least until they're confronted by a bigger and badder piece of shit. At that point they usually can't kiss ass fast enough.

My ruse worked. Remington let go of his grip and Ed was able to suck in a huge gulp of air just in the nick of time. I somehow managed to keep from letting out a sigh of relief. I looked over his shoulder and Sally gave me just the barest of nods. Guess I was doing all right after all.

Now that the immediate crisis was over, I figured it was best to try a little diplomacy. "We will respect your authority here, on behalf of the Boston office."

"We will?" Sally shot out. It sounded like genuine outrage, but it was hard to tell with her. It was entirely possible that she was giving me another opening to assert myself. Either way, I took it.

"Yes we will," I said in what I hoped sounded like an authoritative tone. "In return, I expect Remington, Mr. Decker, and their respective contingents will respect the hospitality of our coven."

There was a beat as everyone considered what I said. Finally, Decker replied, "The Magi are nothing if not respectful to our gracious hosts." The smirk never left his face. He knew he had us over a barrel. What a dick.

If his tone registered with Remington, he gave it no notice. "Very well. You will heed our authority, give us your full cooperation, and in return we shall respect your coven's traditions. Speaking of which, is this truly all that remains?"

"There are a few other survivors," Sally said.

"Recall them immediately," Remington ordered, still facing me. Had it not been for the presence of several other potential hostiles in the room, I have little doubt she would have tried staking his ass right then and there.

"Easier said than done," she replied. "They're under strict orders for radio silence." Radio silence? No doubt Sally was making it up as she went along. It was a good idea, though. Bringing the others into this would just complicate matters, especially with the pile of Templar dust lying about.

"And why is that?" Remington asked coolly.

"Ask your buddy there," Sally said, the snark coming through. "Despite our little arrangement, they're a bit paranoid about working with the wizard...rightfully so, if you ask me."

"I did not," he said, finally turning to face her. The tone of his voice sounded dangerous. Apparently he was not particularly fond of being talked back to by his inferiors. Two of the vamps closest to Sally pushed back the edges of their coats. Holy shit! Were those silver stakes they were packing? Fuck me. Where the hell did they get those things? Was every vampire but me practically rolling in cash?

"They're helping out," I said, trying to steer Remington's attention back toward me. Outside of James, who understood our relationship, Sally's status as my partner wasn't really common knowledge. In most cases, a coven has one master. Everyone else was just a piece of crap as far as other vamps of status were concerned.

"Helping out?"

"I had them fan out across the city," I said, taking my turn at making shit up. "They're keeping their eyes and ears open for word of the Icon."

Harry Decker immediately stepped past Remington and got right in my face, so close that I could see remnants of his lunch stuck between his teeth. Gross. The word *Icon* had apparently unhinged him a bit. "What do you know? What have you heard about the Icon, Freewill? Tell me!"

"First off, mouthwash is your friend. Last I heard, they're following up on a few leads. As soon as they know something, we'll hear about it."

It was complete and utter bullshit, but the beginnings of a plan had begun to form in my mind. With any luck, we'd be able to regain whatever edge we had lost when these jokers rolled into town. Sadly, it didn't fill me with much hope. Resting everything on a little luck was a sucker's bet, but it was better than nothing.

The Great Icon Hunt

Remington established the entire floor as his team's base of operations. Much to Sally's chagrin, he commandeered her office as his personal HQ. While his people took over the other offices and their computers, the witches set up shop where the hotline was normally manned. I allowed myself a chuckle as they pushed desks out of the way to make room for a circle of sorts. I guess they were doing some sort of magic, but it basically looked like a bunch of women sitting in a circle and chanting nonsense. In a way, it reminded me of my mother's book club.

Sally was forced to give Remington the keys to all of our coven locations, including safe houses. I couldn't help but notice, though, that she conveniently left out the new one - the building where the remnants of our coven were actually holed up. In its place, she gave up the warehouse in Brooklyn we jointly shared with the Queens-bound Howard Beach Coven.

She was doing her part, and now it was my turn. Fortunately, I had begun to formulate a plan. The vampire nation is surprisingly modern in many ways, but they have the same downside that parents of kids today have. Many of the older ones have had to adjust to the new technology of modern times. I was willing to bet that none of the hunters from Boston moonlighted as system administers in their spare time. I could potentially use this little oversight to my advantage. I just had to be patient.

The frantic activity kept up throughout the night, with us being relegated to watching from the sidelines while, at the same time, being watched. The mages didn't trust me and Colin couldn't stand me, a fact he had undoubtedly imprinted upon his team. Though we were all supposed to be on the same side, the three of us were treated as little better than detainees. Considering that we really were working against them, I had to begrudgingly give them a little credit for that foresight.

As dawn neared and Remington's team made preparations to hunker down for the day, I approached him.

"What is it Freewill? We're very busy correlating data here."

"I'm sure you are." It was obvious they didn't have clue one where to begin. They were shooting blind, perhaps hoping that the Icon would just show up at our doorstep and announce herself. "I'll get right to the point. I need to go to work."

Remington looked up from Sally's computer, a mask of confusion upon his face. "Excuse me? Are you not right where you are supposed to be, overseeing your coven?"

"Sally handles a lot of the day to day stuff. I actually have a job, so as to keep myself in touch with the human world. It's helpful with regards to strategizing for the coming conflict." Yeah, I was laying it on a little thick, but telling him the truth - that I worked because I needed the paycheck - would have looked just ever so slightly pathetic.

"I think your *strategizing* can wait a day. Hunting down the Icon is our top priority."

"I disagree, but regardless, I'm just standing around out there watching your people work. I could be back after nightfall."

"Absolutely not," he said. "It's too risky to allow you to go out there by yourself. If the Icon were to track you down, it could be catastrophic to our cause."

His lack of faith in my abilities aside, his meaning was clear. Translation: you aren't fucking going anywhere.

"Very well. Can I at least go home and get my laptop?"

"Negative. You would never make it back before sunrise and I can't spare the men to watch over you during the day."

Grrrr! Fine, it still wasn't over. I had one more ace up my sleeve. I paused for a moment and crossed my fingers. "What about Ed?"

"Ed?"

"Sorry, my human advisor."

"He is of no consequence."

"I know, I tell him that all the time. Would there be any objection to him going to get my stuff?"

Remington's eyes narrowed. No doubt he smelled a rat. He couldn't quite come right out and say it to my face, though, and we both knew it. Colin had obviously ordered him to make my life as difficult as possible. Still, I had friends in high places - one of whom just so happened to be Colin's immediate superior. Thus they couldn't just outright accuse me of anything without proof. Check and mate.

"How long will it take?"

"Rush hour hasn't started yet. Two hours, maybe a little more."

"I'll be timing him...for his own safety, of course."

"Of course. Thank you for helping me to maintain my cover." Asshole.

* * *

I spoke to Ed as softly as I could, telling him to bring back our work computers and nothing else. I didn't need him playing the hero and grabbing his shotgun. It was doubtful he'd make it back without being arrested, but even if he did, he'd just be walking into his own funeral. Twelve gauge slugs, even silver ones, weren't going to be very intimidating against a whole platoon of vampires and mages.

Speaking of the magical morons, I couldn't help but notice they let Decker leave unhindered. Guess it was okay for him to go to work, but as for me, I could end up on the fucking bread line for all these assholes cared.

Motherfuckers! One of these days I really need to convince Sally to just put me on the goddamn payroll already. Fucking cheap ass vampires.

Okay, so I lied about that first part. I also asked Ed to grab me a coffee along the way. I had a feeling there wasn't going to be much sleep for me during the day ahead. It would be just my luck to pass out right as a break came that would let us to lose these pricks and save Sheila from...well, whatever fate she was embroiled in.

As Ed left, Sally gave me a questioning glance. I needed to bring her up to speed. Whispering to Ed about the laptops was one thing, but spilling my guts to her could prove to be a bad idea if anyone was listening. Fortunately, I had that one covered too. She was the one who had told me to act like the Freewill, after all.

Once the sun came up, our vampire guests decided to grab some sleep. The witches kept at their chanting, but some of them started to nod off. It had apparently been a long series of days and nights for them, what with searching for the Icon and blowing up my coven. That was good. Once their numbers were whittled down, I stood and stretched. I took a deep breath and turned to Sally. This needed to look convincing.

"I need a shower to relax," I said to her, making sure to keep my tone as haughty as possible. "Let's go." I phrased it as a command, something that a coven master would say...hopefully. I hadn't ordered too many women into the shower with me. The few times

I'd tried, it came out sounding more like wishful pleading.

Sally, unsurprisingly, raised an eyebrow at that. All right, time for the coup de grâce.

"*NOW!!*" I compelled at her.

For a moment, she didn't move. That wasn't too surprising. Sally's older than me, so compelling her would be next to impossible. There was also the fact that I sucked at it.

Still, the others didn't know that. For all they were aware, I was the all-powerful Freewill for whom the normal rules of being a vampire did not apply. A second passed, and I feared that she was going to tell me to go fuck myself. Without warning, though, she stood up, a blank look on her face. I turned toward the back and began walking, listening as her footsteps followed.

As I passed a few of the still conscious vamps, a shadow of a smirk appeared on their faces. This was the kind of thing that most vampires loved to see, the strong forcing their will upon the weak. Bunch of dicks.

We reached the showers, and I locked the door behind us. Taking my cue, Sally immediately began turning on all the faucets.

Once the room was nice and noisy, she walked over and whispered, "I assume you're going to give me a reason to not kick your ass."

I nodded. "Thanks for playing along."

"Just don't make it a habit." She threw back her head and screeched, "OH GOD, YES!"

"Um..."

"Do you want this to be convincing or not?" she asked, her voice low again.

"Oh, yeah."

"Then spill. Even I'm not that good of an actress."

* * *

I filled her in on my plan, telling her to be ready to go come sundown - in betwixt her continued cries of stuff like "MORE!" and "HARDER, MASTER, HARDER!" Fake or not, she made it damn difficult to concentrate. I found myself wishing I hadn't lost my cell phone the night before. This shit would have made a nice ringtone.

We both ran our heads under the water before shutting things down. I may be new at the deception game, but even I knew enough to be leery of someone who takes a shower and walks out as dry as they went in. Before we left, Sally made a show of rumpling her clothes a bit, to give them that hastily dressed look. It was probably wrong of me to think it, but regardless of how this whole mess turned out, I had little doubt this interlude would be filling my fantasies for weeks to come. Sue me for being shallow.

By the time we got out, Ed had returned, computers in hand. He gave us a quizzical look as we emerged. Sally, being the bitch that she is, turned to me as we approached him and breathily gasped, "Thank you, master," before changing direction. I was used to daylight hours, but they weren't her specialty. She had mentioned in the shower grabbing a few hours of sleep. At least one of us would be fresh for the night to come. It might save us from doing something stupid.

"Do I want to ask?"

"What?" I said innocently enough. "Just taking advantage of my lofty station in life." I took some amusement from torturing him, especially considering he had an eye for Sally. What good are friends if they can't fuck with one another in even the direst of situations?

Taking my laptop, I set myself up at one of the desks - making sure that no unfriendly eyes were in a position to look over my shoulder.

I then proceeded to get to work...seriously. What I had planned would need to wait until it started to get dark. It wouldn't be realistic otherwise. Additionally, I actually did have a project due. On top of everything else, I really didn't need my boss, Jim, crawling up my ass right at that moment. He's just the type to freak out over deadlines while everyone else is busy trying to stave off the apocalypse. Some people just have no sense of perspective.

At around three PM, I figured it was time to get the ball rolling. I logged into an encrypted proxy I occasionally used to...err...*borrow* movies online. Despite my confidence that Remington wasn't exactly a master hacker, there was no point in taking chances. At the very least, it made sense to cover my tracks a bit. It would be just my luck to have someone run an IP trace and notice that the source of what I was sending was right there on the same network.

* * *

Right on cue, about fifteen minutes after the sun went down, Remington stalked out of Sally's office. He walked over to where she stirred and rudely nudged her with his boot.

"Wake up. You're with me."

"Huh?" she asked sleepily.

"Let's go. I need you to confirm the authenticity of something."

He didn't bother waiting for her reply. Reaching down, he grasped her by the arm and dragged her to her feet, steering her toward her office and shutting the door behind them.

I immediately fired off an email to Ed. It comprised just three words: *Wait for it.*

Double Agents of Chaos

"We have a lead!" Remington barked. "I want to be on the road in five."

"The Icon?" a witch asked.

"Quite possibly."

"We need to inform the master."

Remington gave her a curt nod. "Tell him to meet us there."

"Where are we going?" I asked, as if I didn't have a clue.

"*We* are not going anywhere, Freewill," he stated. "My team and the Magi have a possible Icon sighting in Hoboken."

"You do? How?"

"Amazingly enough, via members of your coven. I intercepted some instant messaging chatter between them."

Heh, intercepted...yeah right. I made sure that shit popped up front and center on Sally's PC.

"If they're from my people, I need to..."

"No," he said, his tone implying he wasn't to be argued with. "You, the woman, and your human will remain here."

"But..."

"It is for your own safety," he said. He didn't even try to mask that fact that his concern was complete bullshit.

"We're a part of this," I protested, laying it on thick.

"It's Starlight, Bill," Sally said, drawing a glare from Remington. "She could be in trouble." Heh, she almost sounded concerned.

"The safety of your coven-mates will be our top priority," Remington told her in such an offhanded manner you could almost hear the scorn between the lines.

"This is unacceptable," I replied, going for the Academy Award. "Boston will hear about these improprieties." I wasn't even sure of what I had just said, but it sure as shit sounded snippy.

"Feel free," he said, knowing that my protests would go in one of Colin's ears and out the other.

Despite our best *efforts*, Remington wouldn't budge. It was going perfectly. These dipshits and Decker's minions would be heading west, while we'd be going northeast. That would give us plenty of time to...

"Harris!" Remington shouted.

One of his trench-coated minions stepped forward. "Yes, sir."

"I want you to stay here." What?! "The Freewill needs to be protected."

"Of course, sir."

"At *all* times," he added.

Motherfucker! The asshole was leaving a babysitter to keep an eye on us. I doubted they really suspected anything. Well, okay, Decker most likely did. Colin, on the other hand, probably just wanted to keep me from fucking things up for him. Either way, though, it was something I hadn't planned for. We needed to find a way to lose this guy.

* * *

"Settle down, we're going to be here for a while," Harris smugly said.

I racked my brain, trying to think of a way to distract him long enough for us to disappear. I considered asking Sally to turn on the charm, but I had a feeling her commitment to our cause wasn't quite *that* solid.

Heck, even overpowering him was problematic. Harris was most likely older than Sally and thus stronger than both of us. I could always try to bite him, absorbing his strength as my own. The problem was, even if we managed to knock him out, there wasn't anything to keep him from ratting us out once the others got back.

I was still considering my options when Sally walked out of her office wearing a jacket.

"Let's go," she casually said to Ed and me.

"How?" I asked as Harris rose to his feet.

"Like this."

In one swift motion, Sally reached into her jacket and produced a massive handgun - one that dwarfed the weapon she had used at Sheila's office - her Desert Eagle. A thunderous *BOOM!* sounded and Harris's head disappeared in a spray of blood and brains. A moment later, his body disintegrated into dust.

While I waited for my hearing to return, Ed mouthed, "Holy shit!" That was the understatement of the day.

"What the fuck did you do, Sally?!" I yelled.

"I cleared the road. Look, no more obstacles. You're welcome, by the way."

"You didn't have to kill him."

"Seemed like the path of least resistance to me."

"Um, not that we're ungrateful or anything," Ed said, "but didn't you just commit the equivalent of vampire high treason?"

"Probably," she replied, putting the still smoking gun back into her jacket. I don't know how I missed it when she first walked out. It left quite a visible hump under the material.

"And isn't that bad?" he asked. "Bill, didn't you say these Draculas don't fuck around with shit like this?"

Sally actually cracked a smile. "I'm touched by your concern, and just for the record, you're right. Under normal circumstances, I might as well have just blown my own head off right there."

"But?" I prodded.

"But, it's not like he's going to tell anyone now. Is it really a crime if there aren't any witnesses?"

"I guess you have a point."

"Of course I do. Now let's vacuum him up and get moving. We need to find a car, and it's not like one is going to steal itself."

* * *

We got caught in rush hour traffic heading toward Westchester. It greatly slowed us down, but hopefully the others would be busy for hours to come on a snipe hunt over in Hoboken. If not, we'd still have a huge head start. It wasn't like they knew where we were going. Even if they suspected us, we would still be the veritable needle in a haystack.

The upside was the delay gave us time to fill in some gaping holes with our plan. There was always the possibility that the Templar moved Sheila someplace else and we'd come slinking back to the city empty-handed. In that case, we'd have some explaining to do. After a bit of back and forth, we decided to fall back on some tried and true Freewill-related bullshit - I went nuts, snacked on Harris, then led Sally and Ed on a merry chase through the city for the entire night. It was pretty weak, but still better than *so sorry, but we killed your man so we could attend an all-night Star Trek marathon.*

* * *

Thankfully, the car that Sally jacked had a built-in GPS. Once we got past traffic, we were able to find the church with no problem. It was a good sized place situated right next to a Catholic middle school. Just great. It wasn't bad enough that we were going to desecrate a church, but a school too. Oh well - if you're going to do something morally reprehensible, you might as well go all the way.

At first glance, it all looked to be abandoned. Construction tape blocked off the parking lots of both structures, warning of renovations. No doubt it was a smoke screen set up by the Templar.

We instructed Ed to park a few blocks away. No point in being obvious about our commando raid.

"Okay," I said once we had parked, "we know these guys are hostile to us. It's probably too much to hope that we can talk our way through them."

"I wasn't planning on trying," Sally remarked, pulling out the massive handgun again and slamming in a fresh clip.

"No," I said, putting my hand over the gun.

She swatted it away. "Never touch a girl's piece without asking first, Bill."

"No killing unless absolutely necessary."

"Oh pl..."

"We don't know what's going on in there. If you run in acting like it's the fucking O.K. Corral, you could accidentally hit her."

"Or worse," Ed said.

"Worse?"

"Yeah," he continued. "Didn't you say she seemed pretty freaked when you vamped out on her?"

"Yep, but can you really blame her?"

"No, but I likewise couldn't blame her if she freaked out seeing two vampires, one of whom was blowing people away with a hand cannon."

"Your point?" Sally asked.

"If she gets frightened, she may try to bolt..."

"If that..."

"Or she may try to fight," he said. "Let's not forget that she's the Icon. Even a handshake from her can fuck up both of your days."

Sally seemed to consider this. "Fine. No shooting...unless I have to."

"Fair enough."

"That's all we can ask for," I added.

"Just between the three of us, though," she said, opening the car door, "I hope I have to."

* * *

"Which one?" Ed asked from our vantage point, hidden behind some bushes just out of sight of the church.

Despite the construction notices, dim light shone from both buildings. Not overly subtle of the Templar, but they must not have been aware we had forced one of their men to squeal.

"Church first," I replied, my tone more confident than I felt. "That's what the Templar said. Should be easier to check. If we don't find her there, then it's time to go to school."

"How do you want to do this?" Sally asked.

"How? I figured maybe we'd just sneak around to the rectory and try our luck."

"And yet somehow you're supposed to lead our armies against the Feet," she sighed.

"Hey," Ed asked her, "you didn't happen to bring along an extra peashooter, did you?"

I cocked an eyebrow at him. "I thought you were with me on the no shooting thing."

"I am, but like Sally said, shit could happen. If it does, need I point out to you that I don't have vampire strength on my side? I'd prefer to not end up with another sword at my throat."

"Sorry, babe," Sally replied. "I only brought enough for me." She paused for a moment. "Besides, you don't need one."

"Why?"

"Because we're going with Bill's plan of trying the back door."

"We are?"

"Yep, we just need a distraction. Congratulations, Ed, you've been promoted."

"How..."

Without further warning, Sally grabbed him by the lapels of his jacket and dragged him down to her level, pushing his head to the side. Before I could stop her, there was a flash of fang as she buried her teeth in his neck.

* * *

"What the fuck?" Ed hissed, holding the side of his bleeding neck.

"Oh stop whining," Sally replied dismissively. "I didn't get anything major. It's just deep enough to look authentic."

"Authentic?" I asked.

"Yep. Ed here is the victim of a vampire attack. He's gonna go rushing into the church screaming for help, just like in the movies. I bet our Templar buddies will practically trip over themselves coming to his rescue."

"Actually that's not bad," he replied. "Although you could have warned me. That hurt like fuck."

"Stop being such a baby."

"Um...will this..."

No doubt anticipating the question, she cut him off. "No. You're not going to turn."

"You're sure you can control it? That other guy..."

"I *meant* to do that. I'm not a fucking newb. Trust me. I only turn who I choose to."

"Like Alfonzo?" I asked.

"Yes," she said. "Speaking of which, hold on a second." Sally pulled a cell phone out of her pocket and began dialing.

"Who are you...?"

"Hi, Star? It's Sally..."

"Do you really have to give her more work *now*?"

"Shhh! I'm talking here, asshole. No, not you..." She turned her attention back to the phone and stepped away from us.

"Bill, if she's wrong and I do turn..." Ed's voice wavered.

"You want me to stake you?"

"Fuck no! I want to make sure I get a good spot in the coven."

"Oh."

"And I swear, if you *ever* try to compel me I will kick your ass."

"Ooh, I hadn't even considered that. The possibilities..."

"Believe me when I say I would gladly wait an eternity to pay you back for any shit you pull."

"Wouldn't doubt it for a second."

Sally rejoined us, her call over.

"What was that about?"

"I told Starlight that shit's about to get real and I wanted her and the rest of them to get the fuck out of the city. There's a coven in Philly we're friendly with. She's heading there."

"Good idea," Ed said.

"It'll also keep them from getting caught and spilling their guts on our little charade," I pointed out.

"Bingo," she replied.

"So all is good then?"

"Maybe," she said with a shrug. "Starlight and Alfonzo are good to go. Firebird is still pretty messed up, so she won't give them any problems."

"Dread Stalker?"

"Not sure. He wasn't there. The asshole went out despite my orders to the contrary. I think we'll need to have a *talk* with him when this is over."

"Whatever, fuck him for now. As long as he doesn't do anything monumentally stupid, we have bigger fish to fry."

"Agreed." She turned to Ed. "You're up. Give us an Oscar winning performance...your life depends on it."

* * *

Sally and I made our way hopefully unseen to the rectory. Assuming the Templar weren't tricked out with high tech surveillance equipment - which seemed a fair assumption, considering their armaments from the day before - we'd be hard to track in the dark. We made it to the door and waited a few minutes to give Ed the time it took to make for a pathetic display of human chop meat.

"What if she doesn't want to come with us?"

"Huh?"

"I asked what we should do if she doesn't want to come with us."

"Uhhhh..."

"Yeah, I thought so. Great to see you planned for contingencies."

"I just want to get to her and explain everything. It's ultimately her choice. This doesn't become a kidnapping mission if she says no." I tried to convey a tone of conviction, but was freaking out inwardly. Unfortunately, speaking to women - especially those I had a hopeless crush on - was one of my weaknesses. I just hoped I could be persuasive. Either way, I'd be winging it big time.

Sally forced the door, managing to make very little noise in the process, thank God. But before she could step inside, I put a hand on her shoulder.

"Remember, no killing unless necessary."

"Define necessary."

"Maybe I should go first."

* * *

Fortunately, most churches aren't exactly mazes. We got lucky in that the rectory was empty. It allowed us to make our way, unchallenged, to the main hall. We peeked out and got a good look at the open area before us. There was a commotion at the far end, no doubt Ed relaying stories of all the damn vampires running about. I could hear multiple voices, but couldn't tell exactly how many. The lingering incense of past masses likewise made it difficult to tell how many different scents there were.

It didn't matter, though. We saw enough to know that this probably wasn't the right place. I doubted they'd let Sheila just run out at the first sign of trouble.

There were no guards present and, more importantly, no sign of her anywhere. The church was a bust.

"Time to ring the school bell?" Sally whispered.

I nodded, and turned to retrace our steps out of the building.

Once outside, I broke into a full run, closing the distance between the church and the school within seconds, Sally hot on my heels. There was no point in fucking around. Ed's distraction wasn't going to last forever.

"It's a big building. Where do we start?" she asked, as if I had a clue.

"Whatever room is closest. Maybe we'll get lucky."

"Do you really believe that?"

"Not even remotely."

Unsurprisingly, Sally chuckled. She knew me almost as well as I knew myself.

"Most classrooms have too many windows," I said, trying to apply logic to the situation. "If they're keeping her prisoner, I'd guess the auditorium or maybe gym would be the best place. Windows tend to be high up and there probably won't be too many entrances to guard."

"Good thinking, Bill," Sally said, almost sounding impressed.

"Nah. I'm just still young enough to remember high school."

* * *

If they had her anywhere here, I was willing to bet it was the school. We circled to one of the side doors and immediately saw movement through one of the windows. Unlike at the church, the entrances were guarded.

"There's only one," she said, as we neared the door under cover of darkness.

"At least at this entrance."

"Seems kind of light. Think it's a trap?"

"Probably, or they could just be understaffed. I can't see Templar being a popular career choice."

"Oh I don't know, beats being a programmer at a shitty little startup."

"Bite me," I quipped. "Oh well, guess there's only one way to find out."

"Yep. You get the door, and I'll take care of the guy inside. We just need to make it fast."

"And if there's an alarm?"

"We resign ourselves to being completely fucked." Gotta love Sally's optimism.

Fortunately, on at least the first part, things were under our control. Fast goes hand in hand with being a vampire.

I counted to three, then we raced top speed from where we had been hiding. I grabbed the door and yanked, putting all of my vampire strength into it in case it was locked. It wasn't, and the damn thing tore right off its hinges with a quick, but far too loud, squeal of metal.

Before I could do anything else, Sally was already inside. I put the door down and heard a brief commotion which culminated in a thud and then silence.

I stepped in and found her standing over the downed form of a man. Judging by his red cloak, I'd say we had bagged our first Templar of the evening.

"Is he?"

"Out cold," she said. "Courtesy of my mean left hook."

"Thanks."

"Don't mention it. Just remember later on, if the killing starts, I at least tried."

"That's all I can ask."

No alarms rang out or footsteps sounded in the hall beyond. Our first objective was complete: we were in.

I stepped into the hall and took a deep breath. Multiple scents assaulted my senses. It was confusing. I couldn't tell how many or how recent.

I looked at Sally and cocked a quizzical eyebrow.

"Must be because it's a school. Tons of kids coming and going, a lot of whom are probably not into regular bathing."

That wasn't good. It potentially negated one of the few advantages we had. I took another whiff just to be sure and got the same result...wait! There was a familiar scent mixed in with the rest. I knew it well, probably too well. Under different circumstances, my familiarity with it would probably warrant a restraining order.

"She's here, or at least she was."

"Are you...oh who am I kidding? Of course you're sure. How long have you been stalking this girl anyway?"

"Don't start."

"Jeez, just rent a fucking prostitute already."

"Sally..." I warned.

"Okay okay. Lead the way, lover boy."

I did, although there wasn't much of a trail to follow. Aside from brief whiffs here and there, it was hard to isolate her from the rest. We were back to just searching door to door.

We passed several dark classrooms. A cursory glance didn't reveal anything in the first few, so we kept going. I was still willing to hedge my bets on the gym or some other large room - maybe the cafeteria. It seemed logical to me, although that didn't mean much considering most of my concept of logic stemmed from *Star Trek* reruns.

We continued down the hall, unhindered. It was a little too quiet. I began to get the distinct impression that this was a giant roach motel and we were the bugs.

Of course, with any such trap, you need some bait. Rounding a corner, I began to suspect we had found it.

* * *

A light came from the double doors ahead of us. We approached and peeked through the window. It was the gym, and it wasn't empty. The bleachers were closed and the basketball hoops all cranked up. Multiple man-sized, wooden figures stood in a circular pattern at the center of the room. On the far side lay several hay bales with targets attached, arrows sticking out of them. The whole thing had the feel of one of those Kung-Fu training arenas you see in the movies.

The person who stood in the center of it all, his back to us, complimented the atmosphere. He wore a bulky red cloak, similar to the other Templar we had seen, and brandished a sword. From what little I could see of his arms, the rest of his outfit consisted of heavy chain mail. The hood of the cloak covered his face, but that didn't seem particularly important at the moment. What did was the skill and speed with which he swung the sword. The person moved amongst the training dummies, swinging and striking out with deadly precision. Despite the apparent weight of the armor, his movements were fast, agile, and deadly.

"Holy *Connor MacLeod*, Batman," I gasped.

"Robert must have been at the bottom of his class," Sally commented.

The figure continued in his movements, a graceful symmetry to it all. At last, he struck the sword into the wooden floor with surprising strength and then knelt before it, facing away from us.

"What do you think?" I asked.

"I don't see any other leads. Let's go see what they know." She had drawn her gun. Considering the skills of the warrior before us, I couldn't begrudge her doing so. If things went sour, I'd prefer he eat a bullet before we lost any of our favorite limbs.

We opened the door as quietly as we could and entered. The figure remained where it was, still kneeling in front of the sword, almost as if in prayer. Despite our stealth, I had the distinct impression he knew we were there. It was kind of creepy.

We crept to within twenty feet of where he still knelt. I stopped and motioned for Sally to do the same. Armed or not, I didn't want to get within sword range of this person. I opened my mouth to announce our presence, but the warrior spoke first.

"They said you would come."

Whatever words I had been about to say died in my throat. I knew that voice.

The figure lifted its head, the hood falling away. Light blonde hair spilled out onto *her* shoulders.

We had found the Icon.

Part 2

Iconic Encounter

Sally and I shared a quick glance. "You didn't tell me she was a fucking ninja."

I opened my mouth to reply, but before I could find my voice, all of the gymnasium's doors opened, including the one we had entered from. Multiple Templars, all holding crucifixes out before them, entered the room and quickly converged upon us. Yep, it was a trap...how surprising.

"Congratulations," one of them said. "A great honor is bestowed upon you. You will die within the presence of the Blessed One. May God have mercy upon your tainted souls."

Sally spun, bringing her gun to bear, but as fast as she was, we were too outnumbered. Several Templars rushed her before she could properly aim. Under different circumstances, there was no doubt she could fight off a crowd. Sadly, each warrior that converged upon her brandished a cross. A quick succession of flashes proved that while not all were faith empowered, more than enough were. She screamed and went down, the gun skidding out of her grasp.

"Sally!" I managed to take a single step before I was likewise dogpiled. Unlike last time, my skin burned as crosses came into contact. Motherfucker, it hurt. Imagine being attacked by a bunch of assholes with blowtorches and you might have a clue.

As I went down, Sheila spun around, a look of confusion on her face. "Bill?"

Sadly, the only noise I heard after her voice was the sound of my own skin sizzling.

* * *

I couldn't let it end this way. Despite the pain, I began to fight back. Unfortunately, I had no leverage. I opened my mouth to scream, but they shoved a crucifix in it. My tongue began to fry - not the most pleasant of experiences. The Templars pressed more crosses against me, increasing the pain tenfold.

Suddenly, I saw red. My instincts told me it had nothing to do with their weapons. The monster inside of me was trying to claw its way free. Without even realizing I was doing so, my fangs elongated and I bit down, snapping the crucifix into splinters.

A part of me welcomed the change, knowing that in my transformed state I could easily shrug off these Templar assholes. The sane part of my mind, however, freaked the fuck out. Sure, I could save myself and might even save Sally, but I'd surely kill every single other person in the room, quite possibly including Sheila. No! I had come too far to let that happen.

I began to fight two battles: one against the Templar and their faith-empowered weapons, another inside of my head trying to force the creature back into its metaphorical cage. Neither was going to be an easy victory. It's hard to win any fight, even a battle of wills, when you're being distracted by little things like your own flesh burning.

The pain began to recede and I realized that I was losing that latter fight. My muscles tensed and I flung half the group off of me with but a shrug. Oh no!

I opened my mouth to scream for Sheila to run before I completely lost myself in the change, but she spoke first.

"Stop."

"But your holiness..." one of the Templars protested.

"Now!" There was such authority in her voice that even I would've probably stood at attention had the assholes not been covering me.

Within the space of seconds, though, they were off of me. Holy shit...emphasis on the holy part. Such was my surprise that for a moment I forgot about everything else: Templars, Sally, and - oh yeah - the fact that I was about to turn into a rampaging monster.

Or was I?

Once the Templars backed off, I saw her. A lump in my throat replaced my surprise, my breath completely caught. She was even more beautiful than I remembered...although that might have been the addition of the sword and cape. What can I say? The geek in me loved the shit out of her new look.

It was only then that I realized I was still me. The change had stopped. I wasn't sure if it was her voice, the distraction, or the way my heart skipped a beat - had it been capable - when I saw her. Whatever the case, I didn't care.

OUCH!

Okay, maybe I *did* care a little. The rage receded, but my nerve endings started firing again, reminding me that I was covered in second and third degree burns.

Speaking of burns...oh shit, Sally!

As difficult as it was, I managed to peel my eyes away from Sheila and toward where I had last seen my partner in crime. The Templars had likewise backed away from her, although they still surrounded us on three sides, crosses bared. One false move, or the wrong word from Sheila, and we'd be thoroughly fucked.

Sally had been hit far worse than me. One side of her face was scarred nearly beyond recognition. Cross shaped burns marked wherever there was exposed skin. The look on her face was one of pure unadulterated rage. Had she been in my shoes, as Freewill, this place would've become a bloodbath.

I quickly realized that might still happen. She scrambled to her feet and her claws elongated. She meant to have her pound of flesh.

Oh crap.

* * *

Screw it, if Sheila could do it, so could I. "Sally, that's enough."

"Fuck that..."

"Stand down!" I roared. Damn, that almost sounded convincing. I couldn't help but glance at Sheila out of the corner of my eye, hoping I had scored a few points.

Sally glared daggers at me, no doubt pissed off, but amazingly she did as told. Phew! That was a close one. Unfortunately we weren't out of the woods yet.

"Why are you here, Bill?" Sheila asked, her tone stern but curious.

"We're here for you." Her hand tightened its grip upon the sword she now stood behind.

"Let me rephrase that," I quickly amended. "We're here to *save* you."

"Save the Blessed One?" a Templar scoffed. "She is already saved. All your kind can bring are damnation."

"Oh for Christ's sake..." I said, before nearly all of the Templars drowned me out.

"BLASPHEMER!"

Oh yeah, poor choice of words considering the circumstances. "Sorry." I held up my still burnt hands in a placating manner, then turned back toward Sheila. "It's true, though. You don't have to be afraid of me."

"I'm not," she replied, her voice unwavering.

"Really?" I asked, perhaps sounding far more surprised than I had meant to.

"Not at all." Way to crush a dude's ego.

Okay, I needed to focus. "Listen, I'm sorry for sneaking in here. I realize that doesn't exactly help substantiate what I'm saying, but the only reason I didn't just try knocking on the door is because your buddies here started it."

She raised an eyebrow.

"At your workplace. We went to Iconic Efficiencies looking for you."

Another of the Templar spoke up. "And what became of our brothers?"

"Self-defense is a bitch," Sally replied. Jesus Christ! Did she want to get us killed?

I desperately tried to think of something to say to keep from getting a dozen crosses shoved up our asses. Thankfully, just then a distraction came in the form of my awesome roommate.

"Blessed One!" a voice called from one of the entrances.

"These beasts lie," a Templar cried out as he entered. Two more followed him, one on each side of Ed. They led him, but he wasn't restrained. "This is one of their victims. He came to us in the church, seeking refuge from these abominations."

"Ed?" Sheila asked, recognizing him. Score one for having friends who worked at the same job.

"Hey, Sheils," he replied nonchalantly as he stepped away from his escorts and approached her unhindered. "How's it going?"

She noticed his neck wound, blood still dripping from it onto his shirt. A look of concern came over her face. She glanced over at me, suspicion in her eyes. "Did Bill do this to you?"

"No," Ed said, still conversationally. "This little love bite is courtesy of Sally." He motioned over at her.

"Nice to meet you," Sally replied.

"But..."

"It's not like that," he said, interrupting her. "We did it to distract your buddies. Last time, they took a 'stab first, ask questions later' approach."

"Blessed One..."

"I want to hear him out," Sheila said, cutting off the Templar minion. Thank goodness Ed had come along. I'd worried that it would be too risky for him, but he had become our saving grace. His word carried a lot more credence around these parts than from us vampires.

"He is obviously their thrall, oh Holy One."

Or maybe not.

Sheila raised a bemused eyebrow. She knew Ed. He was a lot of things, but a mindless sycophant wasn't one of them...especially for me. "So you're Bill's thrall now?"

"Not in this lifetime," he replied with a smirk.

Her gaze again moved to the wound on his neck. "Doesn't that hurt?"

"Well yeah, but I'll live."

Sheila's eyes suddenly got a faraway look in them. She stepped toward Ed and raised her hand. Slowly she placed it over the still oozing gash on his throat.

"What are you doing?" he asked, a bit confused.

"I'm not sure," she replied. As her hand touched the ugly looking bite, it started to glow. A soft white light emanated from it. Ed let out a gasp, but didn't flinch from her touch. Some motherfuckers have all the luck.

I took a step forward, but Sally caught my arm. Oh yeah, all the unfriendly Templars in the room. They might take my intentions the wrong way. I needed to remember that.

It didn't matter anyway. Whatever Sheila did ended as quickly as it began. She removed her hand, spotless despite touching the wound, and the light started to fade. Guess her Icon powers included an anti-dirt barrier or something...handy.

Ed's neck glowed for a moment longer where she had touched it. When it was over, the bite mark was entirely gone: no scar, no magical sutures, like it had never been there. Fucking wild.

"You can heal people?" I asked.

She turned to me, the same question in her eyes. "I guess so."

"Tis a miracle!" one of the Templar shouted. "Praise be!" They all dropped to one knee in silent prayer, leaving only the four of us still standing.

Ed touched his newly mended neck, an impressed look upon his face. "How come you can't do anything cool like this, Bill?"

I shrugged. "Guess she got bitten by a different radioactive spider."

To my surprise, Sheila actually chuckled at that. She understood nerd humor? Be still my unbeating heart. As if I needed further convincing that she was my dream girl.

Unfortunately, the moment of levity was brief. Sally and I were still stuck in a lion's den. Should any of the Templar decide that their time would be better spent cooking us than listening to our banter, we'd be in for a hell of a fight.

"You're in danger," I said, trying to get us back on track. Immediately all of the unfriendly eyes in the room looked up and trained upon us. "Not from me, assholes."

"Bill's telling the truth," Ed said, no doubt understanding a little backup would keep me from continually shoving my own foot in my mouth. "There's some really bad stuff coming down the road."

"I know," she replied.

"You do?" Ed and I asked simultaneously.

"We have prepared the Blessed One for your arrival, vampire," one of the Templar said, rising to his feet. His hand never strayed from the wooden cross hanging from his neck. He had been one of the goons who had dogpiled Sally. Unlike the dude she had turned the previous night, this one's cross was the real deal faith-wise.

"Benjamin, please," Sheila said. She was on a first name basis with these fucktards? Well, okay, I guess that made sense. Here they were, revering her like some sort of saint. It would probably figure that, at some point, they might introduce themselves. Still, Benny the Templar? Not exactly an awe inspiring title.

"Yeah Benny," I added. "Simon says chill the fuck out." Hmm, maybe that came out sounding a bit more catty than I'd intended. I guess the fact that she wasn't begging me to rescue her grated on me more than I cared to admit. Sheila's eyebrows rose in my direction. "Sorry. It's been a long day. What have the Templar told you?"

"That darkness is coming."

"You have no clue, sister," Sally commented.

"Anything more specific?" I asked, ignoring Sally.

"I'm not sure how much I should say." Sheila fixed her silver colored gaze upon me. "They told me about vampires. That's what you are, right?"

I averted my eyes from hers. It was hard not to get lost in them. "Well, yeah."

"A spawn of the pit," snarled Benny.

"So was your mom," I shot back. *sigh* This *really* wasn't going how I had imagined. "Sorry...again...but yes, I'm a vampire."

"They tell me your kind has been lying in wait for me."

"Yeah, I guess that's sorta true. Vampires have prophecies about the Icon."

"Icon?"

"That's what you're referred to in our circles. It's short for Icon of Faith."

"Interesting."

"You gotta admit," Sally interjected, "it's a bit less pretentious than Blessed One."

For perhaps the first time, Sheila turned her full attention to Sally. "Are you his..."

"Hah! Not if I live long enough to see the sun burn out." Gotta love how Sally can really prop up a man's ego when she wants to.

"Yep," I replied, "you'll still be whoring yourself out for lap dances even as the lights go out for good."

"You'll have to excuse them," Ed said. "They do this shit all the time. I think they secretly enjoy it."

"So have you?" Sheila asked me.

"Um, do I enjoy trading barbs with Sally?"

"No. Have you been lying in wait for me? Is that the whole reason you started working at Hopskotchgames? The reason you were always nice to me? Was it all a game until you were sure I was..."

"No!" I exclaimed. "It wasn't like that at all."

"Do not believe him," Benny said. "He has had an eternity to master his deceit."

"Deceit? Bill couldn't fib his way out of a paper bag."

"Thanks, Sally."

"Just trying to help."

"Bill hasn't been trying to deceive you and he definitely hasn't been stalking you," Ed said. "Well, not like that anyway. You see, Bill has been..."

"Shut up," I warned. If I was going to proclaim my love for her, it would be at a time and place of my own choosing. It certainly wouldn't be by my roommate, and it definitely wouldn't be in front of a room full of zealots itching for an excuse to kill me."

"Relax," he said, "I was just going to tell her that you've only been a vampire for about a year."

"Really?" she asked, turning toward me.

"It's the truth. Remember when I brought in that excuse about needing to work from home?"

She glanced back to Ed. "And you knew?"

"From the very start."

"And has he ever..."

"Bill? Hell no."

"And you're okay with it?"

"Yep. At the end of the day, fangs or not, he's still just Bill." I glared at him for a moment, to which he replied, "You know what I mean."

"Fine, assuming I believe you..."

"Do not believe them!" Benny warned, stepping in front of us. "They are the children of the Prince of Lies."

"I want to hear them out, Ben," she said. Her tone was gentle, but there was a firmness to it that couldn't be denied. Benny acquiesced to her, with a quick bow. Was she really their prisoner? If so, there was definitely some weird reverse Stockholm Syndrome shit going on.

"If you ever believed anything I ever told you," I said, stepping forward, "believe that I have never *ever* meant you any harm."

"So you weren't there because I was...what did you call me...the Icon?"

"I didn't even know you were the Icon until you nearly blew my head off a month ago."

There was a pause as she considered this. I held my breath for her answer, not the least of which was because she could seal our fate with just a few words. Finally, she looked me in the eye and said, "I believe you. I'm not sure why, but I do."

There were grumbles from the Templar. I was relieved as shit, but they obviously weren't.

"Good, because you need to believe me again. What I was saying earlier about you being in danger was real. I'm here to help you."

She stared at me hard for what felt like an eternity, but was probably just a second. At last, she said, "Ben, take your men out please. I'd like a word with Bill and his friends."

"No, Your Holiness. We cannot..."

"Yes, you *can*," she replied, that tone of authority back in her voice. Holy shit, I almost didn't recognize her as the same person who handled the paperwork for our group at work. Here stood a person who could have put our CEO in his place, no problem. "I'm in no danger."

"You can't believe them."

"Even if they're lying," she replied calmly, "I am quite capable of taking care of myself." She laid her hand on the hilt of her broadsword.

Goddamn she was hot. *Red Sonja* had nothing on her. All she needed was a chainmail bikini and...I shook my head. I really needed to save the fantasies for later.

Benny and she stared each other down in an unspoken battle of wills, but it didn't take a genius to see that it was over before it even began. After a few moments, he averted his gaze like a dog who'd just been whacked on the nose with a newspaper. "As you wish, Blessed One. We shall be right outside should you require our assistance." He nodded to the others, and they began to spread out toward the multiple exits. The move was obvious. They followed her orders but made sure there wouldn't be any easy escapes in our future. My opinion of Benny begrudgingly went up a fraction of a notch.

Unfortunately, my respect of his security measures was immediately undone as a blur of movement near one of the entrances caught my eye. The figure moved fast, but not fast enough to escape my vision. The black trench coat gave him away, but even had it not, the fate of the Templar nearest that doorway would have. The guard fell to the floor, his intestines splayed out before him.

Vampire claws can have that effect on a person.

Hitting the Fan

The first vampire wasn't alone...not even remotely. Before I could shout a warning, two Templars burst into green flame.

The training of the Templars wasn't anything to sneeze at, though. In the space of seconds, they began to fall back from the entrances - drawing their weapons and assuming defensive stances. It was impressive. Unfortunately, it just wasn't enough.

Before they could form ranks, several witches materialized out of thin air atop the closed bleachers. From there, they'd have the high ground and couldn't easily be reached. Decker was amongst their ranks...the fucker. Unfortunately, I only had that moment to take in the scene as Remington and his men poured through the doors.

Several of the Templars had their crosses out before them, but it wasn't going to do them any good. Remington's people were trained killers. A faith empowered cross wasn't much good if the hand that held it was ripped out at the shoulder.

Worse yet for the outclassed holy warriors, Decker's coven rained fire down upon them from afar. A

Templar would successfully fend off a vampire, only to be engulfed in supernatural flame. It was like the world's most realistic LARPer gathering...most lethal, too, by the look of things.

All of this happened in the space of a few seconds. It wasn't enough time for Ed and I to do anything more than gape at how quickly things had turned to shit.

Sally, though, had been in far more scrapes than either of us. She uttered a quick curse and threw herself into a dive - the Desert Eagle still lying on the floor her obvious goal.

She almost made it. Three of the nearby Templars, no doubt misinterpreting her actions, threw themselves on top of her and again began pummeling her with their crosses.

I considered the odds and came to the conclusion that she could probably handle herself against that number. She'd have to.

"Ed, protect Sheila!" I shouted, momentarily forgetting that he was the least likely creature in the room to protect anyone.

Even amidst the din of battle, I heard a voice question, "Sheila?" It was Decker. Oh fuck. He stared at her, mouth agape.

"Harry?" she asked, even as she hefted the sword and assumed a defensive stance in the middle of the room.

Recognition turned to rage as Decker put two and two together. "The Icon!" he screamed, pointing at her. "Kill it!"

Oh shit! Several of the witches turned toward her and began invocations. I didn't wait for them to finish.

"GET DOWN!" I shouted even as I hurled myself at her.

It was a mistake.

In my haste to protect her, I had forgotten that we were absolutely incapable of touching without things turning explosive.

* * *

Whatever force I would have plowed into Sheila with was redirected back at me tenfold. There was a white hot flash and then I slammed into, and through, the bleachers at the far end of the gym. I barely had enough time to register how much it hurt.

Well, okay, that's not quite true. It hurt like a motherfucker. Fortunately, it wasn't all for naught. The undead projectile I had become hit hard enough to knock several of the witches off balance. Their shots went wide, or at least I assumed they did. I was too busy seeing stars to tell for sure.

"Bill!" It sounded like Ed's voice, although it was hard to tell amongst the screaming and blasting going on.

I tried to clear my head and stand, but it wasn't going to be that easy. It felt like I'd been hit by a speeding car. If I didn't shake it off quickly, there was no telling what would happen. I was so close. There was no way I was going to lose her now.

All of this was my fault. I had obviously not been nearly as clever as I had thought. Decker and

Remington had somehow tailed me. Even an idiot could tell that much. That made it ten times worse. If she died now, it would be entirely on my head.

Fortunately, fate is occasionally kind to even me. A pair of Templars drove one of Remington's troops back in my direction. Mustering my strength, I waited until he was nearly within reach and sprang at him. Not caring one iota for anything except protecting my friends (and the girl I really hoped would be more than a friend), I grabbed the vamp from behind and sank my teeth into his neck.

The vampire let out a surprisingly high pitched scream - freaking pussy. Christ, even I can take a hit without sounding like a fucking five year old throwing a temper tantrum. He wasn't the only one freaked out, though.

As the vampire's blood flowed down my throat, I heard the Templars gasp in surprise as well. Guess they hadn't been expecting that either.

The vamp I was latched onto was strong, far stronger than me. He was at least a century in age. That being said, strong or not, it can be kind of difficult to shake someone off who's holding on with a death grip while digging into you like some kind of human-sized tick. It also didn't hurt my cause that any forward momentum on his part would just take him straight into the waiting crosses of the Templars.

I took great gulps of blood, feeling the power course through me. Within seconds, the damage I had sustained was healed. Gotta love that. Better than a *Band-Aid*.

Sensing I had gotten all I was going to get from this vampire, I pulled my teeth out and wrapped my arms around his neck. With a twist, bone snapped. I let go and he dropped to the floor. What I had done would have instantly killed a person, but not a vamp, though. Still, he was definitely out of the battle for now...one less foe in a room full of them.

"Thank you for that, fool," a voice said from behind me. I turned to find Harry Decker standing about ten feet away, a big grin on his face. Guess the dude had finally gone off the deep end.

"For what, powering myself up so that I could kick your ass?"

"No, for leading me to the Icon and now giving me an excuse to watch you both die."

Realization sunk in just a moment before he shouted, "The Freewill has turned on us! He's in league with the Icon!"

I guess I kind of deserved that one. Thankfully, when I absorb the power of another vampire, I get the full deal: strength, speed, heightened senses and reflexes. The last two were of particular interest right at that moment. Decker's coven must have been waiting for his signal, for no sooner did he raise his voice then several pinpricks of light shone in my peripheral vision. I dove to the side just as the spot where I had been standing was turned into a miniature Bikini Atoll. The area erupted in multicolored flame, leaving a crater where the floor had been. The vamp I had bitten was caught in the blast and immediately immolated. Even the

Templars who had been threatening him were blown back by the shockwave. Guess these guys weren't fucking around.

I weaved into the battle so as to deny them an easy target. Most of the participants were currently occupied, so it gave me a moment to take stock of the situation. The Templars were slowly losing ground. The vampires were far faster and stronger. The firepower of Decker's coven augmented their numbers. I couldn't see Sally. Hopefully she wasn't currently in a state more fit for lining a cat box. I shook my head. No, Sally was a survivor. I had to trust in that. I had other people to worry about, anyway.

Speaking of which, I managed to spy Sheila and Ed. True to what I had asked of him, Ed was...oh wait, no he wasn't. He was actually hiding *behind* Sheila. Three vamps had closed on her. She stepped back, holding her sword up in a defensive stance, but there was uncertainty in her eyes. Oh no!

The vamps saw the same thing and lunged at her, their silver stakes at the ready. Goddammit! She was too far away. Even with my stolen strength there was no way I was going to be able to...

SNICKT!

What the fuck? In one smooth move, she spun, swinging the sword in a graceful arc. The blade connected just as the vampires came into range. There was an explosion of dust as three silver stakes clattered to the floor. Holy shit! It had been a ruse on her part, a good one too. Jesus Christ, I wasn't sure if she was the Icon or the second coming of Chuck Norris.

"Templar to me!" a voice rang out. Still weaving amongst the combatants, I saw Benny break away from the witch he had been grappling with...real manly. A room full of vampires, and he chooses to tussle with a girl.

Cross raised, he made his way to Sheila's side - much to my consternation. If the dude had designs on my woman, we were gonna have words about it. I'd kick his ass if he so much as...

A clawed hand swung out at me, one of Remington's vamps - obviously heeding Decker's warning. Jeez! No honor amongst the undead. No doubt Colin had some say in this. It wasn't hard to imagine him giving orders dictating that the preservation of my life was low on the priority list.

I stepped into the blow before he could remove a chunk of my face and grabbed the vamp by the lapels of his trench coat. I flung him to the side with everything I had and he went flying, right into the outstretched cross of a nearby Templar. I may not be the most impressive physical specimen on the planet, but I had gotten more than my fair share of ass-kickings since being turned. Even someone like me is bound to learn a thing or two from continual beatings.

Benny's voice rang out again. A half dozen Templars raced in from the entrance in full battle gear, armor and gleaming swords at the ready.

The cavalry had arrived.

* * *

And, just as quickly, they were gone. Decker's witches had been ready for them. No sooner had they come charging into the room when their armor began to glow bright red. The Templar knights were roasted alive inside of their own chain mail before they could take five steps. So much for the reinforcements. I could appreciate these guys' adherence to traditional weaponry, but they'd have been much better served with a couple of shotguns. As any gamer knows, a low level mage is pretty much a glass cannon. Add a few levels of experience, though, and you do not fuck with them unless you want to die a messy death. Jeez! Did none of these guys ever pick up a twenty-sider?

Oh well, that was neither here nor there. I found it hard to feel any sympathy for them, considering their attitude toward me. I still had my primary mission, and that meant saving the one person in the room who could incinerate me with a friendly handshake.

To do so, however, I'd need to get us the fuck out of there. Sooner or later the combination of Remington's and Decker's forces would prove too much. Sure, it would save me the trouble of embarrassing myself at some future date - pathetically trying to lead our armies into battle against God knows what - but still. I was fond of my ass and not quite ready to kiss it goodbye yet.

Fortunately, I had a secret weapon at my disposal...a dumbass wizard named Harry Decker.

* * *

"You cannot escape your fate, Freewill!" Decker shouted, raising a hand to point me out.

I had fought my way to the far wall and then huddled there trying to make myself look as small as possible.

"Die like the coward you are!" he screamed.

Like I said, a total dumbass.

Multiple blasts of energy converged on my spot, just as I'd planned. Using the stolen strength still coursing through my veins, I jumped. Vampires can't fly, but we could sure as shit make kick-ass NBA center guards. I must've cleared over ten feet vertically, more than enough to take me out of harm's way.

The furious spellcraft exploded against the wall, blowing a hole in it large enough to drive a van through. I landed and could see the parking lot through the smoke the explosion had created. Thank you, Mr. Decker.

The inferno caught all, save me, by surprise. I used the distraction to race back into the fray, my eyes scanning the battle.

Sheila and Ed were still fighting off vamps (well okay, she was anyway). I pushed my way through the combatants, shoving several to the side, enough to make a path. Fighting my way to them, I grabbed Ed by the arm and spun him to face me.

"Get her out of here!" I shouted.

He nodded and tapped her on the shoulder - almost losing his head in the process. She swung her blade at him and only managed to change the trajectory at the last moment. It was close, so close he probably lost a few hairs off the top of his head.

"Sorry," she said.

Ed blinked once - most likely evacuating his bowels in the process - then somehow managed to compose himself. "Let's go."

They started to make their way to the newly created exit, Benny hot on their heels. Sheila expertly used her sword to keep clear the path I had made. God damn, I really needed to ask her where she learned that stuff.

There was only one other minor thing to worry about.

"Sally!"

"One second!" A Templar came flying through the air in my direction.

She was still squaring off against the guys (two of them anyway) who had tackled her and, from the look of things, she wasn't particularly happy. My distraction, however, had allowed her to get to her feet and turn the tide in her favor.

She had one from behind, her teeth sunk into his neck - arterial blood spraying. His remaining companion tried to close in, but Sally's claws flashed out. He went down missing even more of his throat than his recently chewed on buddy.

Not bothering to wait for her to follow, I ran over, grabbed her by the wrist and dragged her toward the hole in the wall.

"You ruin all my fun," she protested, helping me slash and claw through anyone standing in our way.

"It's what I live for."

* * *

We dodged several more potshots from Decker's coven, but at last managed to make it out. The remaining few Templars, having seen Sheila make a run for it, redoubled their efforts against Remington's forces. They weren't going to last long, but it would hopefully cover her escape - as well as mine and Sally's (although I doubt they cared about that latter part).

Emerging from the school, the wind hit my face, bringing a few droplets of rain with it. Apparently the weather had changed since we had entered. Odd, I could have sworn the forecast called for clearing skies.

"Come on, Bill," Ed cried out. "What, did you die in there?"

"You're a barrel of fucking laughs, you know that?" I replied as we caught up with him, Sheila, and - of course - Benny. Fuck me. There's always gotta be a third wheel on every couple's outing.

He whispered something to her and pointed at us. Sheila immediately raised her sword as we neared, her eyes narrowing on Sally. "She killed those men."

I guess Benny had noticed Sally's little temper tantrum back there.

"It's not like that," I said, feeling my own temper start to fray.

"I don't..."

"No, *I* don't care," I snapped back, "They attacked first. Sally was just defending herself."

"But..."

"But nothing. We don't have time for this shit. I told you, we're here to help. Now put the fucking sword down!"

Much to my surprise, she actually took a step back. A moment passed and she lowered the blade. Holy crap! Where the hell had that outburst come from? Sometimes it was like I didn't even know myself.

"Wow, Bill," Sally said from behind me. "You just got ever so slightly sexier."

"Not now, Sally," I replied. "We need to get out of here before..."

Unfortunately, it was already too late.

Remington and his vampires swarmed out of the break in the wall. Before we could react to this, several flashes of light shone on the far side of us. Decker and his witches appeared from out of thin air, cutting off our escape.

Though we and the Templars had taken out our fair share of enemies, we were still outnumbered at least four to one. There were only two words that came to mind to describe the situation: *Game Over*.

Love Triangle

"If you could only see the look on your own face, Mr. Ryder."

"I imagine it would still be only half as dumb as the one on yours," I shot back at Decker. Never let them kill you without a snappy retort, I always say.

The situation didn't look good. Vampire hitmen and a coven of pissed-off mages surrounded us. I was still amped on that other vampire's strength but wasn't sure how much longer that would last. Sally looked like she had been dipped into a deep fryer. Benny had his cross, although I wouldn't count on him to do much more than stab me in the back with it if push came to shove. Ed...well, let's be honest, aside from any witty comments he might have regarding the situation, he was tits on a bull.

That left Sheila. She was definitely the X-factor there, but even she could only swing that sword so fast. At some point her back would be exposed, and there was little doubt one of our enemies would be more than happy to take advantage of that.

"Step away from the Icon, Freewill," Remington moved to stand by Decker's side.

"Freewill?"

"Did he not tell you, my dear?" Decker asked, trying to pour a little salt in my wounds. He was well aware of my not-so-little crush on her. Apparently everyone in our office knew.

"We haven't exactly had much time to chat," I replied.

"You're in on this too, Harry?" she asked.

"Obviously," he said, a sneer on his douche face. "Alas, had I known what you were during our little dinner date some months back...the night would have ended much differently."

"I could say the same thing," I snapped. "If I had known what a fucking asshole you were, I wouldn't have been so quick to save your ass...even less so if I had known you were a wizard."

Sheila looked between us. "Was everyone at Hopskotchgames some kind of monster?"

Ooh, that stung. Was that how she saw me now? Well okay, I *was* currently covered in blood and gore. That wasn't exactly helping my credibility.

"You're lucky," Ed said. "At least you didn't have to go out on a date with Barb from HR. Talk about a many-tentacled beast."

"Enough of this chatter," Remington barked as lightning flashed in the sky. There was a storm coming, in more ways than one. "You will step away from the Icon now, or we will not be held accountable for your fate."

"You really expect me to just walk away while you fry my girlf...err friends?"

"Who said anything about you walking away? You are a traitor to your kind. You will surrender and be brought before your superiors for punishment."

There was a little too much glee in his voice for my personal edification. Knowing vampire justice, I had to assume that probably didn't involve just a slap on the wrist. Hell, I'd be lucky if they killed me. In special cases, vampires could draw out the torture of their enemies for an eternity. Knowing my luck, I'd definitely be considered one of those.

"I think I'll take my chances," I replied, putting a little swagger into my voice. Hell, they didn't need to know I was practically ready to shit a brick. If anything, it might make a few of them slightly more cautious as they moved in to fuck my day up further.

"Dibs on Decker," Sally said.

"No fucking way," I tried to keep a grin on my face. "First come, first served." I turned my eyes toward Ed. He gave a shrug and smiled back. I liked his odds far less than my own, but his look said it all. He knew the risks when he signed on to this crazy-ass adventure.

Benny could go suck a fat dick as far as I was concerned. I turned to Sheila and met her eyes for what might have been the last time. "I've got your back."

"Really?" The question came out honestly, with no sarcasm.

"You can trust me." I meant every word of it.

"Why?"

Because I am deeply madly in love with you would have been my answer. Fortunately for me...err, sadly, that is...or whatever...I didn't have the time to sputter out a reply. Our enemies converged upon us.

Oh well, at least they saved me from embarrassing myself.

* * *

Remington's goons had come into the fray ready for a fight, armed with silver stakes. That meant only one of two things: either silver was equally effective against the Icon - something I had absolutely no idea about - or they were expecting trouble from me. When a vampire really wants to mess with another vamp's outlook on life, that's what they use. It reacts badly with vampire blood...explosively so. Think of throwing a magnesium flare into a puddle of water, except it happens inside of our bodies. It also has the added effect of really screwing up our healing abilities. Depending on a vampire's age, minor injuries can heal themselves in minutes or less. Add some silver to the mix, though, and you slow things down enough that the vamp is left vulnerable in the middle of battle.

Considering who was behind their little expedition, I had little doubt they'd arrived fully expecting me to cause some problems. I had never gone out of my way to make an enemy of Colin, outside of maybe one little joke revolving around reformatting his precious work computer. Even so, he had taken an instant dislike to me. Part of it was probably the friends I kept. Sally and

Colin had history. I wasn't sure why James tolerated his continual existence, but then he was already a bit of an odd duck amongst vampires. He had his reasons...just as I had my own for doing what I did.

"Take the Freewill alive, kill the rest," Remington ordered. His tone implied that he wouldn't be overly concerned should I be captured sans a few of my limbs. What a surprise. It figured that the jerk would...

"I'll hold them. You take everyone else and run."

"Huh?" I grunted, pulling my focus away from Remington.

"I said," Sheila repeated, "take the others and get out of here. It's me they're after. I'll keep them busy."

Hold on, that's what *I* was supposed to say. Damn the crazy times we lived in and its confused gender roles.

"No chance," I replied, adding some false bravado to my voice. If I was going to die in her presence, I might as well look cool doing it. "We all leave or none of us do."

"Don't I get a say?" Sally asked.

"Maybe later," I said, ducking the first blow that came my way as our enemies converged on us. The battle was on...again.

Or maybe not.

Four of Remington's vamps rushed me, two high and two low. There was no time to dodge. They smashed into me like a herd of runaway water buffalos. I went down, cracking my head solidly against the pavement.

Hopefully my friends were putting out a better showing than me.

I saw stars, but I had been hit harder during my day. I struggled against my attackers, but they had numbers and leverage on their side.

They also had weapons. One of them raised a stake high above his head. My arms were pinned, so there was no way to defend myself against it. My life, and afterlife, flashed before my eyes as it descended. I prepared myself for the doubtlessly unpleasant sensation of turning to dust, but at the last second, they heeded their orders to take me alive.

The vamp slammed the stake down into my shoulder with enough force to plow straight through me and into the asphalt below. Goddamn, that hurt! Worse yet, I was pinned like a bug.

Oh wait, that wasn't the worst. Sparks and flame began to shoot out of the wound as I cooked from the inside out. I wasn't sure whether it would kill me or not, but after a second or two, I began to wish it would.

In between trying not to cry like a little girl, I tilted my head to see how the others fared. It didn't look good. Sally had likewise been ganged up on. Two of Remington's vamps held her arms, while a third worked her over with his fists. So much for not hitting a girl.

Another vamp knocked Benny and Ed effortlessly to the ground. Benny's cross clattered off into the darkness, making him pretty much useless for doing anything other than breaking someone's fist with his face.

That left Sheila. At first I thought she was keeping the other vamps at bay with her kickass sword moves, but it was a ruse. The vampires weren't even trying to get to her.

"Watch out!" I screamed. It probably came out much higher pitched than I intended, being that my shoulder was currently auditioning for a spot on the Macy's Fourth of July fireworks display. It didn't matter, though - I was too late.

This was the opening Decker's coven had been waiting for. Multiple beams of pure magical force struck Sheila from all angles. She was enveloped in a blinding red light, flame leaping out in all directions.

"No!" It couldn't end like this. I bit down on my lip, drawing blood but using the pain (well, *other* pain) to clear my head. The sight of her fiery death distracted the vamps who had pinned me, and I used it to my advantage. I brought my free arm up in a fist.

I caught two of the vamps straight on the jaw, knocking them into the others and off of me. Before any more could join the fray, I grabbed hold of the stake, said a silent prayer to whatever gods are in charge of pain management, and yanked with everything I had.

FUUUUUUCCCCKKKK!!

Yeah it hurt a bit. At last, though, it came out with a squirt of blood and sparks. Unfortunately, I wasn't sure I could do much to take advantage of my hard-won freedom. That move had used up the last of my stolen strength.

As if to accentuate the point, Decker casually strolled over and kicked me in the jaw, putting me flat on my back again.

"Let me guess," I said, testing my mouth to make sure nothing was broken, "this little party crashing was your doing?"

"Of course," he replied, planting another blow in my side for good measure. He wasn't above kicking a man while he was down. "The others weren't sure, but I *knew* you were somehow connected to the Icon. I gave my coven daughters strict orders to scry your movements the moment you were out of their sight. Imagine my lack of surprise when you led us right to her. You are ridiculously predictable."

I gritted my teeth while trying to come up with a witty comeback. Unfortunately I had nothing. Decker was right. I had been outmaneuvered, pretty fucking easily by the sound of things. Even so, I couldn't let him know that. I needed to...

"What?!" His eyes opened wide and he suddenly focused his attention elsewhere. I looked up and turned my head to follow his gaze.

Was it even possible? Sheila had been driven to her knees by the force of the attack, but a white glow was spreading out from her - forcing the witches' magic back. It was like watching the Enterprise's shields hold against a photon torpedo barrage. She knelt at the center of the torrent of power. Sweat poured off her forehead from the effort, but she looked otherwise unhurt. Un-fucking-real!

Another boot to the head caught my attention. I glanced up, dazed, to find Decker adding his own magic to the attack.

"It matters not," he growled. "She can't hold us off indefinitely."

"Looks like she's doing pretty good so far," I gasped, trying to find enough strength to do more than make pithy remarks.

"Sir!" One of the vampires ran up. "We found this inside." He held out a familiar looking weapon - Sally's hand cannon.

"I'll take that," Decker said, glee in his eye. He cocked back the hammer and raised the massive handgun. "Hold the humans," he commanded. What the?

"Do it," Remington added, stepping to his side.

Two of the vamps dragged Ed and Benny to their feet. They looked beat to all hell, but they were still alive...for the moment.

"Hear me, Icon!" Decker shouted. "Drop your guard or the humans will pay for your sins with their blood." So much for mages not hurting normal people. That nobility shit went right out the window when it was convenient.

Several of the witches gave each other worrisome glances. I guess a battle was one thing, a full-on execution was quite another. Even so, they didn't cease their attack against Sheila. When push came to shove, they were more concerned with saving their asses than protecting their karma.

Even through the light show surrounding her, Sheila appeared to weigh her options. She was actually considering it. Goddamnit, didn't she watch TV? That shit never worked. She seemed to forget that even if Decker let them go, they were still surrounded by a pack of angry vampires...vampires who were no doubt thirsty after all the fighting going on.

Her eyes flickered to Ed and Benny, then back to me. She gave a single nod and the glow that surrounded her dimmed.

The witches' attack began to close in on her, but that still wasn't good enough for Decker. He turned the gun on her and took aim.

"And now, Icon, you..."

A screech sounded in the night, drowning out the rest of his threat. It was as if someone had stuck a bobcat into a blender and set it to liquefy. What the fuck?

Before the last of its echoes had died away, there came a blur of movement, too fast for my weary eyes to follow. When it was over, Decker stood there a moment longer - a look of pure surprise on his face - before keeling over dead. His throat had been completely torn out.

* * *

Before I could process Decker's sudden and unlamented demise, I heard a whistling noise followed by a thunk. I turned just in time to see the vampires holding Ed and Benny turn to dust. Silver throwing knives clattered to the ground along with their ashes.

I'd seen weapons like that before. Come to think of it, I had heard a screech like that too. Hell, I was still hearing it in my nightmares.

No fucking way.

One of Decker's witches ran toward his body. They certainly were a devoted bunch. Not too bright or cautious for that matter, though. Another whistle and thunk found an arrow buried nearly to its fletching in her chest. Someone had brought a bow to a magic fight and they were winning.

The rest of Decker's crew wasn't quite as keen on following their leader down to whatever Hell he was being carted off to. They immediately ceased their assault and disappeared in bright flashes of light. So much for their alliance.

That just left Remington and his vampires.

They backed off from Sheila and Sally and reformed ranks, although it seemed their resolve was shaken. I couldn't blame them. If what I was thinking was true, they were up against a force that they stood no chance against. It's really hard to fight one-hundred percent batshit crazy, especially if that crazy wasn't alone.

Almost as if in response to what was coming, the skies opened up and it began to pour. I'd like to say the cold rain felt good on my gushing shoulder, but it really didn't.

Remington stepped to the forefront of his group and stalked over to me. Taking charge, he turned and started barking orders. Four of his men loosely surrounded Sheila - taking care to block her escape while staying outside of her reach. She was obviously still their primary target. The rest of us were just icing on the cake...at least some of us. At the very least, I'd make a nice trophy. Not sure the same could be said for the others.

The rest of his men took up defensive positions around us all. I tried to rise, but Remington's boot forced me down. I was still trying to catch my second wind and once more found the back of my head clonking down upon the pavement...but hey, at least this time it was wet pavement.

He turned to the darkness beyond the parking lot's lights and spoke, his tone conveying confidence and authority...no doubt to help inspire his shaken men. "Show yourselves! I am here on the authority of the First Coven. Surrender now and perhaps mercy shall be..." *SPLORCH!*

A splash of blood washed down upon me as his speech was cut short. Blinking it out of my eyes, I looked up to find a hand protruding from the front of his stomach. It was petite in size, like that belonging to a little girl of perhaps twelve years of age.

"I do not ask for mercy, nor am I predisposed to offer it."

The hand withdrew from Remington, who promptly fell to his knees, clutching his ruined midsection. It wasn't a mortal wound, for a vampire at least, but I had no doubt that was purposeful. Vampires are tough and they heal very fast, especially the older they are, but there's nothing wrong with our nerves. Being gutted hurts like a salt-encrusted motherfucker. Trust me I know.

Gansetseg - the crazy-ass vampire princess who had started a war simply to keep me from getting hitched - stepped out from behind him, casually shoving him to the side. She gave her hand a shake, sending droplets of gore flying, visible even in the rain.

She stepped over and looked down upon me. At that moment, lightning flashed. Silken black hair framed her fair skin, accentuated by her bright green eyes...eyes that betrayed a soul far older than the body it inhabited - a soul that was nuttier than any fruitcake I'd ever had the displeasure of sampling.

"Hello, my beloved. It has been far too long."

Irresistible Force Meets Immoveable Object

"Tell your men to withdraw," Gan said. It was not a request. She made the slightest movement with her hand and half a dozen figures jumped down from the rooftop of the school. They wore traditional Mongolian battle gear, the type assassins favored. I knew it well, having been exposed to it more times than I would have cared.

Half of them held hand crossbows, and the others brandished throwing knives. Though Remington's men had the number advantage, none were equipped for ranged combat. Even for a novice like me, it was blindingly obvious that most of them would be cut down if they tried to go on the offensive. This wasn't even counting the threat Sheila and I still represented...well, okay, that she did. The best I could currently do was sputter out some scathing one-liners. Sadly, even in that I was at a disadvantage. I found myself at a complete loss of words. Where the fuck had Gan come from, and what was she doing there?

Still, it was best not to look a gift horse in the mouth. While Remington's troops were weighing their options,

I decided to take stock of the situation. Wincing from the effort, I managed to prop myself up on an elbow and take a look around.

Ed had made his way over to Sally and was trying to help her up. In typical Sally fashion, though, she brushed off his efforts and got to her feet on her own. The downpour made it hard to tell, but I could have sworn she mouthed something as she laid eyes upon Gan. I highly doubted it was anything kind.

Benny had made his way back to Sheila's side, not that she needed any help. She continued to maintain a defensive position, but I couldn't blame her. For all she knew, she was still surrounded by enemies. Considering Gan's unpredictability, I considered that a smart move, although it was surprising that her small force hadn't attempted to take Sheila down yet. Maybe they didn't know she was the Icon, albeit I highly doubted that. They couldn't have missed the light show a scant few minutes earlier.

Two of Remington's men came to his aid, lifting him to his feet. One of them turned to the rest. "Stand down."

"Leave this place now," Gan commanded, her tone eerily calm - the authority in it unmistakable.

Still supporting their leader, Remington's men sheathed their weapons and slowly melted away into the shadows. Just before leaving, though, Remington managed to turn back to us. His eyes locked with mine, their meaning clear: he wasn't finished with us. Still, he was finished for now. I'd take what I could get.

That left just one little problem.

Gan stood in place for a few minutes longer, no doubt extending her senses to make sure the others were doing as they were told. I used the momentary calm to refocus on her. She was dressed similarly to her troops, albeit her outfit seemed of much finer quality. Big surprise there. The only oddity was the yellow *Spongebob* backpack that hung from her back. Oh yeah, I had definitely lost my fucking mind.

At last, she turned to one of her people and nodded. He stepped forward and I realized I vaguely recognized him. Monkhbat, or something like that.

"Follow them. Once you are sure they have complied, you are to track down the Magi. Kill any you find."

Monkhbat gave a deep bow then took off into the darkness. The others followed him, slipping away into the night with a disturbing amount of stealth.

I finally got back to my feet, keeping one hand over the wound in my shoulder. Unfortunately, it was a pointless effort as I was bleeding out from both sides, the stake having punched clear through me. Goddamn, it hurt, and it was probably going to continue doing so for hours to come thanks to the silver.

I gasped at the pain, and Gan turned to face me, a solemn look upon her face.

"My apologies, beloved."

Huh? She caught me by surprise with that one, so much so that I ignored the *beloved* comment for the moment.

"Why?"

"For robbing you of your impending victory." Was she watching a different fight than the one I was in? "Sadly, when I saw the wizard, my impulsiveness got the better of me. I did not think of anything, save repaying him for the embarrassment he caused me in days past."

Gan had been present when Decker had first made his move against me. Needless to say, he'd majorly pissed her off. The dude had a talent for doing so, although - I noted - he wouldn't be using it any longer.

I turned to where he lay, a look of surprise still upon his now ashen face. Water pooled in his open eyes and mouth. It was a bad way to go, but the guy had been a serious asshole. I wouldn't be losing any sleep over his death anytime soon.

Still trying to wrap my brain around both her apology and assumption that I was about to win anything other than a one-way trip to the Draculas in chains, I numbly replied, "That's all right, Gan. Um, thank you for the assist and for saving my friends."

I was treading carefully. For all I knew, Gan was seconds away from launching herself at Sheila. If that happened, all my efforts to save her might still be for naught. I couldn't allow that. I dropped my eyes to the ground and spied Sally's discarded gun. If Gan decided she was going to tangle with us, my best bet would be a little fifty-caliber dissuasion.

"Yes," Gan replied, stepping toward Sheila, who stood with her sword at the ready. "I remembered what you told me from before about your friendship with the human." She indicated Ed. "I still find it a curious custom, but I shall respect your wishes."

"I'm sure Ed appreciates that," I replied, watching her walk toward the group. As she stepped away, I slowly bent and grabbed the weapon. Hopefully the safety was off...oh, who was I kidding? It was Sally's gun. I doubted it even had a safety.

I stood up, the heavy gun in my right hand, and followed after Gan. If she tried anything I'd, well...probably miss badly. I was a suck shot, but it was better than nothing. I was still too tapped out to fight, especially a three-century old hellion.

Sheila stood her ground, no fear evident on her face despite everything that had happened. As the little Spongebob-toting demon approached, though, her silver-colored eyes widened in recognition.

"Becky?"

* * *

Oh yeah, I had almost forgotten they'd briefly met. In a lame attempt to cover the fact that she and Decker had just barely escaped a nasty death, I had told her Gan was my niece. It was one of the poorer lies of my life, and I was still surprised that at the time I hadn't immediately been called on it.

Gan stopped about ten feet from where Sheila stood, Benny standing behind her being...well, kinda useless.

261

I raised the gun and pointed it at Gan's back. If she so much as twitched the wrong way...

Then she did the thing I least expected. She put her hands together in front of her and bowed. Okay, did I miss something? Was it possible she didn't know that the person standing before her was the legendary bane of all vampire kind?

"It is an honor to meet you, Shining One. Your arrival has been foretold." So much for that theory. Gan was apparently well aware of who she was in the presence of. What the hell was she doing, then?

"Am I missing something here?" Sally asked, stepping forward.

Gan glanced back and smiled at me over the huge hand cannon. "I see you still keep company with the whore, Dr. Death. I would have thought you would have grown tired of her."

Even in the middle of the storm, I saw Sally's fangs extend. Oh crap.

"All right," I said, stepping forward, lowering the gun in the process. "Let's all calm down."

"Dr. Death?" Sheila asked.

"Heh, it's kind of a nickname...long story."

"Trust me, there's a good deal of irony involved," Sally added.

Sheila looked utterly perplexed, probably for a combination of reasons. "Who is this?"

Gan let out a giggle. It made her sound much younger than she really was. Bowing again, she replied, "I am

Gansetseg, Shadow Mistress of Asia and heir to the throne of the great Khans."

"Um...nice to meet you, Gansetseg," Sheila replied, sounding about as confused as I felt. She turned to me. "She's not your niece, is she?"

"Heh, sorry about that. It was the best I could come up with at the time. She's actually..."

"I am his betrothed," Gan interrupted.

"What?"

"No she's not!" I shouted.

"Of course I am," Gan replied as if it were written in stone. "We are destined to be together."

"Like them a little young, don't you?" Sheila asked, causing Sally to chuckle. Bitch!

"It's not like that. For starters, Gan is three hundred years old."

"Three hundred and twenty six to be exact, beloved."

"Stop calling me that." Jesus Christ! As if this whole thing wasn't difficult enough.

"You cannot escape your destiny."

"Watch me."

"You're a vampire too?" Sheila asked. She was still holding her sword, but appeared slightly more relaxed.

"Of course, Shining One."

"Then why..."

"Why what?"

"Why aren't you busy trying to tear her a new asshole?" Sally finished for her, as usual doing the exact opposite of diffusing the situation.

"Uh, yeah...something like that." Sheila said as she gave Sally a sideways glance. Oh, I was so fucked. Next time I really need to mount a rescue mission alone.

"Is it not obvious?" Gan replied.

"Not really."

"That is also Dr. Death's destiny. It is the fate of my beloved to kill you."

* * *

"Heh, she doesn't mean that," I quickly added.

"Of course I do. The prophecies are quite specific, up to a point. My father insisted I study them intimately."

"Your father?" Sheila asked.

"Do not listen to them, Blessed One," Benny hissed from behind her, caressing his recently retrieved cross. "They are deceivers, each and every one of them."

"Please, Benjamin. Not now."

"Dr. Death, this human is insolent," Gan mused. "Is he your friend as well?"

The threat was obvious, but Benny seemed oblivious to it. "I am no friend to these *minions* of Satan. I shall not..."

"Ben, you need to..." Sheila began to warn, but I cut her off.

"Yes, Gan. That's us, all good friends here. Best of buds in fact. He just has an odd...err...sense of humor."

Both Sheila and I fixed him with hard glares. We were trying to save the fuckhead's life and he didn't even realize it. Fortunately, she held some sway over him. He finally averted his gaze from hers and lowered his eyes. Heh, dude was totally whipped. Oh well, it beat him being flayed alive...barely. The guy was a tool.

Seeing that Benny had been reined in, Sheila turned back toward the pint-sized she-demon. "You were saying, Gansetseg?"

Gan continued as if she hadn't been interrupted. "My father, the great Khan, had me study the words of our prophets. Dr. Death is the reborn Freewill of our people. It is his destiny to lead our forces in battle in the coming days. The twilight of man is at hand. Many will fall as we clash against our ancient enemies..."

Holy shit. In the confusion, I had completely forgotten about that. "Yeah, a clash that *you* caused," I said, stepping in front of her and pointing my finger accusingly.

"You are welcome, my love."

"That wasn't a thank you! You sacrificed Nergui and started a fucking war."

"What war?" Sheila asked.

"The war that my beloved is destined to be victorious in," Gan replied, ignoring my outburst. Grrr!

I remembered the gun in my hand and tightened my grip on it. It was so tempting. All I had to do was shoot the little bitch's head clean off.

"Wait," Sheila said, interrupting my violent fantasies. "They called you the Freewill earlier too, right Bill?"

Uh oh. "Yeah, it's kind of a stupid name."

"The Templar told me of something they called the Night Spawn."

"Yes," Benny said, "a demon of unspeakable..."

"Benny, do us all a favor and shut the fuck up. You're not helping." I hoped he got the hint that time. Goddamn, he was dense.

"How dare you..."

"Listen, dude," Ed said, stepping up to him. "You don't seem to be grasping the picture here. You see Dora the fucking psycho explorer over there?" he asked, hooking a thumb toward Gan. "Let me tell you, she doesn't fuck around. If I were you, I'd keep my fucking mouth shut before she decides to turn you into a walking Capri Sun."

"I do not fear death. I am..."

"Benjamin, enough!" Sheila snapped, the authority once more coming through her voice. "Please don't interrupt again."

I flashed her a brief smile of gratitude. Amazingly enough, she returned it. Regardless of whatever bullshit the Templars had been filling her head with, it seemed she finally understood that I was on her side.

"The Templar spoke of this Night Spawn," she continued. "They said it was a creature beyond the normal vampires, one that couldn't be controlled..."

"Yeah, that's probably me. The other vamps can't compel...err...control me. Really pisses them off," I replied, somewhat mollified. It was nice to know that others had different names for me, ones that were a whole helluva lot cooler sounding than Freewill. Night Spawn...I could get used to that.

"Yes," Gan said, taking over the conversation again. "One and the same. Your destinies are intertwined, Shining One. In the final days of the war, as our enemies wane, you shall stand tall - the last defense of humanity against the coming darkness. You and Dr. Death shall clash in a battle of glorious proportions."

"And Bill is going to kill me?"

"No," I insisted.

"The seers cannot tell. The outcome remains a mystery," Gan replied, again ignoring me. "But I have faith in my beloved. It is his destiny to conquer you. Once that is accomplished, I shall stand by his side so we may rule this world for all eternity."

"Whoa there," I said. "Why do I have the feeling that the seers don't have anything to say about that last part?"

"They do not need to. I know it in my heart. There can be no other outcome."

"I'm not going to kill Sheila."

"Of course you are, just as she will be the death of the Magi. It is your..."

I interrupted her. I had heard enough destiny bullshit to last me the next several lifetimes. "Okay, enough of this. We're tired, most of us are hurt, and I'm sure the police will be along any moment now to..."

"They will not," Gan said calmly. "My followers have already dealt with them."

"What?!" Sheila and I exclaimed.

"Do not fear. I can assure you, they were dispatched with utmost efficiency."

"You killed them?" Sheila asked, shocked. Oh boy. This had potential to turn ugly.

"Of course," Gan replied. "Uncontrolled humans cannot know of our existence, at least not until we are ready to rule them."

"Uncontrolled?" Ed asked. Gan just admitted to wholesale slaughter and *that* was the thing that bothered him? Jeez, talk about fucked up priorities.

"Does Dr. Death not hold you under constant threat of death?"

"Gan, Ed is my friend. I already explained that."

"Hold on, a second here," Sheila said. "How many people did you kill?"

"All of the authorities within a kilometer radius."

"What do you mean *threat of death*?" Ed asked.

Sheila rounded on him for that. "What is wrong with you? We're talking about people dying here."

"Says the girl with the three foot broadsword," he quipped.

"This isn't a joke!"

"Isn't it?" Sally replied. "Listen, you're new to this, I get it. I was there once too." She raised her hands and continued in a faux panicky voice. "'Oh my, you're vampires. Killing people is sooo evil.'"

"Is your whore always so melodramatic?" Gan asked.

Now it was Sally's turn to lose it. "You want to see melodramatic, you little..."

"Enough!" I growled, amazed to find myself the lone voice of sanity. "More walking, less histrionics please."

"And you're okay with all of this, Bill?" Sheila asked me, semi-accusingly.

"No," I replied, stepping toward her. "I'm about as far from okay as you can get and still stay sane, but it is what it is. This is the hand I've been dealt. I'm doing the best I can. I hate to say it, but Sally has a point. The world you knew is done, over, finito. This..." I waved my hands about, "is what we have now and it isn't a very nice place to be. It's bloody and corpse-filled and it's only going to get worse." I lowered my voice. "You were never supposed to be a part of it. I'm sorry about that."

"You need not apologize for destiny, beloved."

ARGH! I spun toward Gan. "What are you even doing here? Aren't you supposed to be back in Mongolia terrorizing your subjects?"

"Your concern for my people makes my heart swell, but fear not. Our defenses are quite adequate. Should the Alma attack in my absence, they will find their mettle well tested."

Sheila asked Ed what the Alma were, but I decided to let him field that one. I was still dealing with Gan. "That doesn't answer my question."

"Patience, my betrothed." Motherfucker! She liked saying that a little too much for my personal comfort. "I am getting to that. I have been watching you..."

"What?" A chorus of voices, mine included, replied.

"Yes. Ever since my father's death, I have kept watch on your actions from the seat of power in Boston. There are people loyal to me amongst their number."

"You've been spying on me?"

"Of course. Would you have me do any different? Word reached me two days ago of the destruction of your coven and your involvement with the Shining One."

"I knew Colin wouldn't be able to keep his fucking mouth shut," Sally commented under her breath.

"Needless to say, I ordered my assassins to commandeer an aircraft immediately."

"That's fascinating Gan, truly it is," I replied, trying to keep the conversation away from the topic of mass murder. I doubted she and her people simply *asked* to borrow a plane. The peace we had was pretty tenuous as it was.

"Not to mention creepy as all hell," Ed muttered.

"Don't think I'm discounting that," I said, "but first things first. We should probably get the fuck out of here."

"And you're just assuming I'm going to come with you?" Sheila asked, stopping us as a group.

"Well...yeah."

"I am coming with you, Dr. Death." Gan added cheerfully.

"You are?"

"Of course."

"Sorry, we didn't bring a kiddie seat with us," Sally quipped.

"Your whore is being insolent again."

"Yeah she does that," I replied, immediately dragging Ed between Sally and me, before turning back to Sheila. "You need to come with us. It's not safe here."

"It was until you arrived."

Ouch, touché. "They would have found you eventually, trust me. Decker was obsessed and vampires don't give up easily."

"Do not listen to him," Benny chimed in, having found his voice again. "Let's go back. Perhaps some of my brothers survived."

"I highly doubt that," I replied.

"Brothers?" Gan asked.

"Yes, vampire. We are the Templar. Humble servants sworn to do God's bidding."

At this, Gan actually started giggling, drawing all of our attention to her.

"What's so funny?"

"Don't you see, beloved? This just proves my point on destiny. The Templar were believed to have been wiped out at the time of the last known Icon's death."

"Last known Icon?"

"Yes," Benny replied. "Her Holiness, Jeanne d'Arc."

"Joan of Arc?"

"The same. The Blessed One wields her blade."

"I *do*?" Sheila asked, obviously as surprised as the rest of us.

"Don't tell our other roommate that," Ed replied. "He'll have it up on Ebay within the hour."

"How dare you profane..." Benny started, but Gan cut him off.

"See, it *is* destiny, beloved."

"Wasn't Joan of Arc burnt at the stake?" Sheila asked, still eying the broadsword with awe.

"It depends which history you believe," Gan replied offhandedly.

I ignored the rest and concentrated on leading us out of there. It was really starting to come down, and it wasn't exactly a warm summer rain either - probably because it wasn't summer. In addition to being horrifically wounded, now I was cold and wet. Add Gan to the mix, and the day wasn't exactly going swimmingly.

* * *

Fortunately, Sally tends to go big when she steals something. We'd be in for a bit of a problem had we driven up in a Prius. Thankfully, the Nissan Armada we came in had plenty of room for us all, even including Benny and Gan. Don't get me wrong, I'd have been happy to leave them both behind, but neither was to be dissuaded. Gan insisted on coming with me so as to be witness to my glorious fucking destiny.

As for Benny, he practically glued himself to Sheila...something which I was not particularly pleased with. As much as I try my best to not be the monster most other vampires are, I really wouldn't have argued with the suggestion to just off him and be done with it. For starters, he was obviously not friendly. I had little doubt he'd fuck Sally and me over at the first chance he got. Then there was the fact that he was really fucking annoying, what with his constant Bible thumping. Yeah, murder might be a tad overkill for that, but sue me for being petty.

Once it was settled that all of the uninvited guests were coming along for the ride, that left just one other little problem.

"I will not leave the Blessed One's side," Benny said adamantly

"There's no fucking way you're sitting behind me, asshole," Sally snapped.

"I will sit next to Bill," Gan declared as if it were law, which in her mind it probably was.

I sighed. "Okay, enough of this," This must have been what it'd be like to chaperone the world's most fucked up class trip. "Ed, you're driving."

"But I insist..." Benny started, getting in my face.

My fangs involuntarily extended (well, it might have been *slightly* voluntary). Benny immediately produced his cross, which I slapped out of his hand, sending it once more clattering away into the stormy night.

Sheila tensed up in my periphery. Rather than gut him, though, as I'm sure they were both expecting, I simply said, "Get into the goddamn back seat."

I turned to the others. "Sally, you're with him. If he tries anything, fuck him over...you should be used to doing that in a car."

She opened her mouth to say something, but I talked over her. "Gan, you're with me in the middle row."

"Of course, belo..."

"Just get in before I change my mind. As for you," I said turning to Sheila. "Put the sword in the trunk and ride shotgun. I'll be sitting behind you, so please try not to disintegrate me."

"You won't turn your back on Ben, but you expect me to turn mine on you?" she asked. I guess it was a fair question.

"Yes. I know I haven't given you many reasons tonight, but you have to know that you can trust me. This is going to sound corny, but you need to have a little...faith."

"Why?"

Before I could answer, Gan stepped in front of me. "Is it not obvious? It is because he is in love with you."

The Long Ride Home

True to form, I immediately tried to backpedal upon Gan's spilling of my beans.

"What?" I sputtered, feeling my face turn red - something I still didn't understand, given my lack of a heartbeat. Weird-ass vampire physiology...go figure. "That's ridiculous. I don't..."

"Of course you do," Gan replied, sounding almost bored. "It would be obvious to even a stranger." She turned to Sally and Ed, who weren't doing a particularly good job of hiding their smirks. "Have you never noticed?"

Ed just shrugged and turned away. Sally, who looked like her head was about to pop off with laughter, said, "Nope. Not here. Bill's really hard to read...good poker face, that one." Bunch of fuckers!

"You really should consider replacing her. Your whore is not particularly insightful." That wiped the smile right off Sally's face and almost distracted everyone from the topic...at least until Benny had to start in again.

"Hah, as if the spawn of Satan could know such a thing as love."

275

"Gan, remember what I said about him being my friend?" I asked through gritted teeth.

"Yes, beloved."

"If he's not in that car within three seconds, I'm rescinding that status."

Needless to say, Benny was seated with at least a second and a half to spare.

Ed, possessing at least a modicum of tact, walked around the vehicle and climbed in. He started the engine, the exhaust visible in the cold, wet night.

At least Sheila had the good graces not to laugh directly at my face. That would have crushed me far worse than any of the combatants that night were capable of doing. Instead, we both stood there, neither of us seeming to enjoy the uncomfortable silence that had descended.

"Heh, maybe we should talk...later."

"Yeah, later," she agreed, a look not unlike shell shock on her face.

Thankfully, Gan was there to help further ruin the moment.

"It is all right, my beloved. I am not upset."

She wasn't...oh yeah. This was the girl who had started a supernatural war rather than see me married to a Sasquatch. I hadn't even considered what that could mean for anyone else.

Picking my words carefully, I replied, "I'm...surprised to hear that, Gan."

"Do not be. I have no need to be concerned. You are destined to destroy her. There is no escaping that fate. When it is done, then we shall be together for all of eternity."

Talk about killing the mood.

* * *

We drove mostly in silence for an hour, the battle in Westchester far behind us, but the storm continuing to intensify. To say things were a bit awkward, well that was the fucking understatement of the century.

Nearing the city, Ed broke the silence. "Where to? I assume we're not going back to the office."

"The office?" Sheila asked.

"Vampire HQ," he replied.

"Nope. At this point everyone and their mother knows where it is. I wouldn't doubt that Remington and his men have already regrouped there." I turned in my seat to face Sally, who sat there thumbing through a magazine while ignoring Benny. "We need someplace *safe*," I said, throwing in a wink in case she didn't get the hint.

She narrowed her eyes at me. The new safe house was an unknown to everyone outside of the two of us.

"It's not like we have much of a coven to keep safe right now anyway," I added.

"You think I give a shit about that?" she replied. "Do you realize how much I paid for that fucking place? I doubt they're going to give us the deposit back."

"Do you have a better idea?"

"How about your place?"

"My place?"

"Yeah. It's not like we haven't crashed there before."

"I would hope you have purchased a new bed since last time, Dr. Death," Gan said. "The old one had an offensive odor to it."

Sheila turned around in her seat, wide-eyed. For a split second, a white glow surrounded her, no doubt a result of her surprise. My skin began to spark at even that small display.

"It wasn't like that!" I said, far more defensively than I cared to. "I was just...you know...babysitting."

"Babysitting your fiancée?"

"She's *not* my fiancée."

"Of course I am, beloved. We are destined to be..."

"Ed, could you crash us into the next telephone pole you see?"

"Don't look at me, man. I'm enjoying this shit."

I'm glad someone was.

* * *

After much bickering, we finally decided on a course of action. We would hunker down in the safe house until we could think of something better. Gan's forces would be seeking shelter from the day, but she assured us they could track us down the next night. I wasn't about to argue with that logic. After all, she had once claimed to be able to sniff me out anywhere I went...something she had proven herself more than able to do.

First, though, we made two stops. Sheila had only the clothes she wore, and it wasn't exactly casual wear. Ed and I were in the same boat. Benny...well, he could go fuck himself. We decided to stop first at our apartment in Brooklyn to grab some stuff as well as check on Tom. He wasn't a part of this, but that didn't mean he wouldn't be dragged into it. Decker had known where I lived, which meant his coven more than likely did. Right before being snuffed, he had dropped all pretense of protecting humans and outright threatened to kill Ed. It was probably safe to assume his coven might likewise become desperate. I didn't want to drag Tom into this. He had enough shit on his plate, but he needed to be warned. Maybe he could go to Jersey for the week and stay with his parents.

After that, we'd make a stop at Sheila's apartment. It was likewise a risk, but fortunately we had an ace in the hole. Gan's senses were hyper-alert. If there were vamps or witches watching either of those places, she'd be able to sniff them out. I just hoped it wouldn't come to that. Hopefully they'd gotten enough of a bloody nose for one night. I was beat and my arm still hadn't healed - good thing this wasn't our vehicle, because it was going to be a bitch getting all the blood stains out. I really wasn't in the mood to get into another knock-down, drag-em-out fight at least not until I got a chance for some shuteye.

The same could probably be said for all of us. At least Sally's healing had kicked in. Her hair had started to grow back and she was now covered in only second degree burns. All in all, it was a marked improvement over how she had looked earlier in the evening.

We crossed over the Brooklyn Bridge and suddenly, the night sky lit up. The car swerved as if in response. Ed was both exhausted and caught completely by surprise at the display. Thankfully it was very late and traffic was light, so we didn't hit anyone.

He rubbed his eyes. "Was that red lightning?"

"You saw it too, huh?" Sheila asked.

"That's not normal," I commented.

"Indeed it is not," Gan replied, her voice calm as if she saw this sort of thing every day. Hell, she lived in the deserts of Mongolia. For all I knew of the place, maybe she did.

"I guess the Mayans were right after all," I joked.

"No, their math was faulty," she said matter-of-factly. "They were off by a goodly amount."

"How comforting to know."

"Do not fear, my love. This storm is just a sign that it is beginning."

"What's beginning?"

"Our glorious uprising. The forces beyond the veil are gathering their strength."

"Why?"

"It is so they can join what you have started, Dr. Death. They are preparing for war."

Well, wasn't that just dandy like fucking candy?

Home Not-so Alone

Sally offered to wait in the Nissan. Benny agreed to stay with her...as in I overheard her whisper something to him about removing his intestines if he tried leaving. That was fine with me. I had no interest in letting the dickhead cast judgment on my home. He'd probably declare it a pit of sin or something stupid like that. Not that I would *mind* it being a pit of sin, but still...

Gan followed me like a lost puppy, wishing to see my *secret headquarters* again. As for Sheila...well, I'd love to say she was all enthusiastic about visiting my place. Hell, inviting her over was at the top of things I meant to do before I died (again). The circumstances, though, were somewhat less than ideal. Whatever I had so meticulously fantasized about was not going to come to pass. In the end, though, she had to use the bathroom. Oh well, it was better than nothing. Beggars can't be choosers and all that.

Figuring I might as well make the best of a bad situation, I asked Gan to sniff out the area as we walked toward the building entrance.

"I do not sense any vampires in the vicinity."

"That's good..."

"There is the aura of magic, though."

"That's not so good."

"It is lingering. This mage has been here often."

"Oh," I replied, immediately feeling a sense of relief. "That's just Christy..."

"I know this scent. She is the witch who attempted to torture us some months back."

Oh crap.

"Torture you?" Sheila asked.

"Long story," I replied. "She's Tom's girlfriend now."

"Your other roommate is dating a witch?"

"Like I said, it's a bit of a story."

"She will meet the same fate as her master," Gan declared. "The human will join her. Consorting with our enemies is punishable by death."

"Hold on," I said, stopping and turning to face her. "Tom's my friend. Christy's off limits too. She's...well, one of us now."

"A vampire?" Sheila asked, confused.

"No, she's one of the good guys. She had a change of heart up in Canada. We're cool now."

"I am not *cool*," Gan said. "In fact I am quite incensed. Her slight against me cannot go unpunished."

"No. Besides which...she's pregnant."

"Your roommate is dating a pregnant witch?" Sheila asked, starting to get a broken record vibe. I guess all this could be a little odd to someone who wasn't quite up to speed.

"Then I will share her with you, beloved," Gan said. "The blood of expectant cattle is quite rich. We save it for only the most special of occasions..."

"I didn't need to know that..."

"Such as when you visited my father's kingdom some months back."

"You're kidding, right?"

"Of course not. Were you not aware?"

"No!"

I sensed Sheila's eyes narrowing at me again. Jesus Christ! Regardless of my intentions, if the conversation kept going in this direction, it was only a matter of time before she ran to get her sword.

Thinking quick, I asked Gan, "Do you smell that?"

"I smell nothing. There is no..."

"There it is again." I put on my best bullshit voice. "My Freewill senses are tingling and they're picking up the presence of...our enemies."

"I am not aware of..."

"Are you doubting me, Gan? I thought you said you believed in me. Maybe we're not as..."

"I do, beloved!"

Hah! Despite her age, knowledge, power, rank et cetera, Gan still had the emotional fragility of a teenager. It was perhaps the one advantage I had over her, so of course I was going to abuse the hell out of it.

"Good, then I think it might be best for you to circle the block while we're upstairs. You know, to keep an eye out for our foes."

"But the witch..."

"Don't worry. I have the Icon with me. Between the two of us, we can handle any witches that happen to be hanging out in my apartment."

"Very well. I shall keep the streets safe for your return."

"Yeah, you do that."

* * *

The second the door was shut, I turned to Sheila. "You'll have to excuse Gan, she's..."

"Crazy as a shithouse rat wearing a Spongebob backpack?" Ed offered.

"Yeah, what he said."

We made our way up the stairs, unmolested by either the forces of the netherworld or any overly nosy neighbors, where I unlocked the door to our apartment.

The lights were on.

"Tom must still be up," I commented.

"At this hour?" Sheila asked, already on her guard. Damn, becoming the Icon sure did instill a bit of a paranoid streak in her.

"He's had a lot on his mind," Ed replied. "It's not every day you knock up a girl with enough eldritch firepower to level a house."

Almost as if in response to our discussion, we heard the toilet flush.

"Or he just had to pee," I said.

"Could you fuckers be any louder?" Tom's voice called from inside of his bedroom. He stepped out wearing a pair of shorts and a t-shirt. He had bags under his eyes and a growth of stubble, making me think his bender from the previous day wasn't quite over yet.

"I swear..." He stopped mid-rant when he saw Sheila. "Sorry, I thought maybe you guys were with Sally." He looked her up and down, no doubt noticing her Templar battle garb. "Who's the LARPer?"

"Hi," she said. "I'm Sheila. Sheila O'Connell."

"*The* Sheila?"

"Ixnay the eilaShay, asshole," I snapped. Jeez! Was everyone looking to spill their guts about...wait a second. If Tom was here, who flushed the toilet?

Oh crap.

There was shuffling in the bathroom. I quickly turned to Tom, grabbing him by the shoulders.

"What's she doing here?"

"Why wouldn't she be?"

"I thought you were freaking out."

"I was...well okay, I still am...but I sat down and thought real hard about it."

"Really?" Ed asked.

"Fine, some drunk at the bar told me to stop being such a fucking pussy...but he was right. I'm not a kid anymore. Hell, I'm almost twenty-six. Isn't it about time I took some responsibility with my life?"

Ed and I shared a quick glance. "She fucked with your mind again, didn't she?"

"No."

"At least that you know of..."

The bathroom door opened and Christy came out. She was wearing a long nightshirt over a pair of shorts and looked absolutely green about the gills.

"Hey, guys," she said groggily, wiping her mouth with the back of her hand.

Sheila stepped forward before I could say anything, a look of concern on her face. "Are you alright?"

"Morning sickness," Christy said. "Runs in my family. According to my mother, she puked her guts out for ten months straight."

"One for good luck?"

"Something like that," she replied with a weak grin. "I don't think we've met."

"I'm Sheila."

"*The* Sheila?"

Oh Jesus motherfucking Christ!

"So I've been told," she replied after a glance back at me.

Christy reached out and their hands touched in a friendly shake. I held my breath. I knew what happened the last time I had tried to touch her. If it was anything like...

Or not. Christy wasn't blown through a wall or even set ablaze. Whew! That was a close one. For a second there I thought...

Then Sheila started to glow.

It figured. What a fucking night.

Witch Way to Go

A soft white glow emanated from Sheila for just a moment. Maybe it was a subconscious reaction to Christy's energy. I had no way of knowing for sure. Christy, for her part, remained unharmed, but her eyes opened wide. She pulled back as if she had touched something electric.

"No," she gasped, backing up.

"Uh, did I miss something here?" Tom asked. "Do you two know each other?"

"Didn't you see that?" Christy shrieked, near panic. "She's..." Here it comes. "The Icon!"

Ed and I looked at each other, most likely sharing the same thought. It was time to duck because a fireball was no doubt incoming...

"Please."

What the?

"Please," Christy repeated, tears filling her eyes. "Don't hurt my baby."

Well, if I didn't feel like an absolute piece of crap before, I sure did now. Getting shitstomped by Turd, the Sasquatch chief, was a piece of cake compared to dealing with stuff like this.

There was only thing that could make it worse.

"Ed, get the door," I quickly whispered.

"Princess Peach?" he replied to which I nodded. He knew exactly what was on my mind.

As Sheila and Christy continued to face one another, each with a look of abject horror on their face, Ed moved to lock and bolt the door. The last thing we needed was Gan barging in and turning this place into a scene straight out of a *Saw* movie.

"Okay, everybody calm down," I said. "Nobody's killing anybody here. Isn't that right?"

Sheila rounded on me. I took a step backward, and it had nothing to do with her being the equivalent of a human blowtorch to vampires. "How can you even say that?!"

"I..."

"Dude," Tom said, sliding up to me. "A word, please."

Oh boy.

He grabbed my arm and dragged me over to his bedroom.

"You two...play nice," he said, shutting the door on us.

"Bill, I say this as your friend...what the fuck is wrong with you?"

"This isn't quite how things were supposed to work out."

"No shit," he said, turning away from me and fidgeting with the action figures on his dresser. *Man at Arms* was slightly out of line where he stood, flanked by *Zartan* and *Panthro*. Don't ask. "So, let me see if I have this figured out. The girl who I've listened to you whine about..."

"I haven't whined about her."

"Correction, whined like a bitch about. So she's the Icon, the legendary archenemy of vampires who also happens to be destined to kill all magic users..."

"Well...

"Including my pregnant and way overly emotional girlfriend. Is that about right?"

"Destiny is one hell of a motherfucker," I mumbled in reply.

"Did you know what she was?"

"No. I just sort of stumbled on her wearing King Arthur gear in the street and invited her up for coffee."

"Not joking, Bill," he said, turning to face me. He didn't look particularly pleased, and not in the normal Tom sort of way.

"Yes I knew. Ed did too."

"How long?"

"About a month," I replied. Then, after listening and noticing the distinct lack of things blowing up in the other room, I broke into a rambling account of what we had been out doing and why we were there.

"Why didn't you tell me?"

"Because..."

"I'm your friend, or at least I thought I was."

"I know and I'm sorry. I, Ed and me...we knew you'd tell Christy."

"Yeah, and?"

"And she'd freak out. I had just gotten her to stop trying to kill me. I'm sorry, but I kind of panicked. I thought she'd tell Decker and they'd hunt her down."

"Sounds like that's what happened anyway."

"Tell me about it."

"How'd you get away?"

"He sort of wound up...dead."

"Oh shit. Christy and he were on the outs, but they were still close."

"I know."

"What happened?"

"Gan," was the only word I needed to say.

"She's not..."

"Outside somewhere, hopefully not turning the neighborhood into a crime scene."

Tom sat down on the bed and began rubbing his eyes. "What the fuck were you thinking?"

"Do you think I planned this? Come on, man, you know me better than that."

"Do I? What else are you and Ed hiding from me?"

"That's it, I swear."

He stood and walked over to where I was standing. He looked me in the eye, suddenly seeming far older than when last we spoke. "I think you guys need to get out of here."

"We were just on our..."

"And you need to keep her the fuck away from my girlfriend."

I opened my mouth to protest that all of the prophecies were bullshit, but I found myself unable to believe it. Things had gotten far too weird as of late. I simply nodded.

"I mean it. I..." he seemed to struggle with the words, his eyes getting all glassy for a moment. "I...love Christy. I won't let either of you hurt her."

Whoa! I was sorely tempted to ask if he was sure she wasn't mucking with his head again, but I had a feeling that would get me little more than a punch to the jaw.

I nodded and turned back to the door. I opened it and stepped outside, immediately stopping at what I saw. I hadn't known what to expect, but it sure wasn't this.

* * *

Sheila and Christy sat on our couch, talking and laughing like they were old friends. I looked past them to our kitchen nook, where Ed stood. He simply raised his hands and shrugged.

I walked over to him and quietly asked, "What's going on?"

"Don't ask me. I understand women only slightly better than you do. How's Tom?"

"Ditto on the don't ask."

"Kind of figured that."

We turned back to find him warily approaching the two.

"Are you alright, honey?" he asked cautiously.

"Yeah, I think I am. She took cooking classes at the same school I do."

Tom continued to look suspicious as the two resumed their conversation. I took the moment to turn to Ed and say, "Let's get our shit and get the fuck out of here, before things turn any weirder."

"You don't have to tell me twice."

* * *

I made two pit stops before packing. The first was to the bathroom to peel off my blood soaked shirt and jacket, then wrap up my shoulder in a goodly amount of bandages. It had finally stopped bleeding, but thanks to the silver it probably wouldn't heal up for at least a day. Next was the fridge, where I grabbed a couple pints of blood.

That being done, I quickly packed enough clothes for a few days, sucking down the blood whilst in the privacy of my room. I remembered my adventure up in the Woods of Mourning. At one point, I was badly injured and had seriously considered making a snack out of Ed. This wasn't nearly as bad, but I wasn't keen on taking chances. All things considered, I felt I was walking a tightrope between humanity and full-blown monster. I didn't want to do anything to tip my balance over to the wrong side.

We wouldn't be able to avoid the situation with Tom forever. No doubt there would be a confrontation in our future that would make his past rants about toys seem preferable. For the moment, though, we had a city full of assassins to deal with and a supernatural storm gathering strength outside. Jeez, talk about stress.

I finished packing and returned to the living room. Sheila and Christy were still chatting. It was oddly comforting to see neither of them letting that whole *destined to kill you* thing get to them.

Ed joined me a few moments later, a backpack in one hand, a long blanket-wrapped object in the other.

"Shotgun?" I asked, already knowing the answer.

"Fuck yeah. These days I feel almost naked without it, especially when I'm hanging around your playmates."

We both walked over to Tom. I wasn't sure about Ed, but I sure as shit was treading on eggshells. I had never seen him so serious.

I tried to play it as cautious as possible. "Be careful."

He nodded. "Thinking of maybe taking her down to my folks' place for a bit."

"That'd be a good idea. I don't think the city is going to be friendly for anyone who knows me, at least for a couple of days."

"When has it ever?" A small smile cracked on his face. It wasn't much, but it told me that the Tom I knew was still there. Hopefully we'd get through this - just another blip on the radar of life...maybe.

Sheila and Christy said their goodbyes, still amiable. When she was done, Tom walked us to the door.

As he let us out, I turned and handed him a slip of paper. "This is where we'll be. It's a safe house. If anything weird happens..."

"I'll call you," he replied.

"Actually call Ed. I lost my cellphone the other night. Long story involving exploding vampires."

"We'll have to catch up when this is all over," he said, then closed the door behind us.

I sighed and started down the stairs. That was part of the problem, wasn't it? I really had no idea when, if ever, it would be over.

Alone Time

Our apartment had been uncomfortable, but fortunately not dangerous...to us at least. I held out hope that our next stop might be the same. Hopefully it would also be somewhat less likely to involve the police than the first.

We walked out of our building, where I motioned for Ed to escort Sheila back into the SUV. I'm not stupid. I had unleashed Gan upon the streets unsupervised. Sure, I had spared Tom and Christy a rather unpleasant evisceration at her hands, but in doing so I had to wonder what horrors I had inflicted upon my neighborhood.

It didn't take me long to find her, mainly because she found me first. I had started walking, softly calling her name. I got about two buildings down when a voice hailed me from above.

"Welcome back, my love. Did you deliver swift death upon the witch and her consort?"

I practically jumped out of my skin, wondering where it had come from. Looking up, I saw that Gan clung to the side of an apartment building, at around the third floor level. Her claws were dug into it, giving her purchase. She looked like some kind of fucked up Spider-Man groupie.

"Get down here, Gan!" I had hissed up at her. Jesus Christ, the concept of being subtle was just not in her vocabulary.

"I was keeping watch for our enemies," she replied, letting go. She fell the entire distance, landing on her feet as if it were a minor inconvenience. "I have already dispatched two spies, no doubt thralls to the vampires who were harassing you earlier."

"Dispatched?"

"Yes. They shall trouble us no more."

So much for me winning any future good neighbor awards. Needless to say, we got the fuck out of there as quickly as possible. Much longer and she'd turn my little section of Brooklyn into a mass grave.

A short while later we were in Manhattan again, at Sheila's apartment building, after another uncomfortably silent drive over. Fortunately, Gan kept her mouth shut - contently staring at me with her puppy-dog eyes. Sheila's neighborhood was quiet at that time of the morning, dawn not too far off. Still, this was the city. Someone somewhere was awake, probably not too far away. I decided to not risk another bloodbath.

"Gan, roll down the windows and take a sniff, but stay in the car. I'm hoping we don't need to send up any unnecessary foot traffic just for a few changes of clothes."

She did so and declared the place to be clear of anything non-human. That was a small comfort. The storm was continuing outside with no sign of letting up. If what Gan had said earlier was true, the non-human population could potentially soar in the near future. But that was a worry for...well, maybe as soon as the next day for all I knew.

It was probably stupid of me, but I didn't want to risk alienating Sheila any more than I had already done for one evening (which was probably a lot). Guess I still had at least some of my humanity left since I was pretty much making decisions as if I were a smitten teenager.

"Do you want to handle this alone?" I asked her, feeling at least a couple sets of eyeballs stare at me questioningly.

She seemed to consider it for a moment, then replied, "Actually, would you mind coming up? I might need a little help."

"Really?" I eagerly asked, once again losing an opportunity to play it cool.

She nodded and unlocked the door.

"I must protest," Benny said from the backseat, where he still sat with Sally. "I cannot allow her Holiness to go anywhere alone with such untrustworthy company."

To my surprise, Gan agreed. "I must concur with the Templar, Dr. Death. I wish to be witness should you fulfill your destiny."

You've got to be kidding me. I raised my hands and massaged my no doubt soon to be aching temples. "Stay put, Gan. I promise I won't fulfill any prophecies while I'm gone. I'll make sure you're around when I do that, cross my heart."

"Thank you, beloved!" she replied brightly, causing Sally to snort a quick burst of laughter from the backseat.

"Stay here, Ben," Sheila said. "I'll be okay."

"You should take your sword," he replied, "just in case."

She threw a glance at me and I nodded. If it would keep current company from throwing a hissy fit, what did it matter?

* * *

She pulled off her cloak and wrapped the sword in it. Icon or not, it would be just our luck to run into a cop. Nobody would be fulfilling any destinies if we all found ourselves on the inside of a jail cell.

"Just watch where you're swinging that thing," I joked, following her up the stairs to the front door.

"I'll try," she replied, putting her key in the lock.

"Where did you learn all the Inigo Montoya moves anyway? Must have taken you years."

"Huh?" she asked, still working on the door.

"The sword. I would have never taken you for a fencing aficionado."

"I'm not. I had never even picked one up until about two weeks ago."

"Really?" Hmm, wonder if that was some kind of Icon power. Seemed likely. Despite what many of us might fantasize, one does not typically pick up a sword and immediately become Conan the Barbarian.

"Go figure. Hmm, this is odd. My key doesn't work."

I was about to remark on that when I remembered my little breaking and entering adventure the day before. Guess they had replaced the lock.

"Allow me," I said. She stepped aside and I moved in, taking care not to brush against her (as much as I might otherwise want to). I grasped the knob and used Sally's trick of just twisting until it broke. *snap*

"Handy." She pushed open the door.

"Yep, being a vampire has its moments." It was good to be joking with her again. I had missed it. Sadly for me, the laugh ended once the door shut behind us.

"I didn't want to say anything in front of the others, Bill, but..."

"Listen. I know what everyone keeps saying about us. It caught me by surprise too...*really*."

"What are you talking about?"

"Uhhh...what are *you* talking about?"

"Back there in your apartment," she said. "That poor girl."

"Christy?"

"Yes. She was scared out of her wits, all because of me."

"You have to understand, she's been getting that prophecy crap shoved down her throat for God knows how long. It wasn't anything personal."

"But it was. She honestly thought I was going to kill her."

"Like I said, she's been force fed that for a while. Besides which, she's kind of emotional now what with being pregnant."

"That makes it even worse," she said as she stepped in front of me and locked her eyes on mine. Goddamn, she was beautiful. Err...no, had to focus. "I want you to promise me something."

"Anything," I replied automatically, giving it absolutely no thought whatsoever.

She opted to ignore my pathetic eagerness, and just continued talking. "If I ever become...*that*, you need to promise that you'll kill me."

"What?!" I shouted, before remembering we were in an apartment building. I quickly lowered my voice. "*What?*"

"Exactly what I just said. I'm not a murderer and I'm sure as hell not a baby killer. I won't become that."

"I know..."

"No, you don't. How do we know what the future holds, what we'll both turn into with time? All I know is that I don't want to become whatever it is that they think I will."

"I...I...why me?"

"Because if what they say is true, then you're the only one who can."

Goddamn, I hate logic.

* * *

I had no choice but to agree. Hadn't I asked Ed the very same thing less than a day ago? It would have been hypocritical of me to do any less...not that I'm above doing so, mind you, but it was *her*. There was literally nothing she could ask that I wouldn't agree to. Had she ordered me to rip off my own legs to help prop up one of her tables, I'd have gladly done so.

I just had to hope that this prophesied future, one that we both feared, wouldn't come to pass. Hell, I wouldn't let it. I'd die first...for real this time.

Whoever had replaced the front door hadn't bothered to do the same with Sheila's apartment. Her door swung in freely when she tried it. Needless to say, I made it a point to play stupid with that one.

I waited in the living room while she gathered her things. It gave me a chance to reflect on the hilarious sense of humor that life seemed to have. Hadn't it been my dream to be invited up to her apartment? Now there I was and, even if the opportunity somehow presented itself, there wasn't a damn thing I could do about it...at least if I didn't want to wind up barbecued. Why was I the only person on the planet with this problem? You never see this shit in the fairy tales. Prince Charming didn't get blasted through a wall when he finally kissed Cinderella.

Fortunately, once she returned, that train of thought was immediately derailed. She had changed out of her Templar gear into something more casual - which was to say, utterly breathtaking to me.

"That's better," she sighed, stepping out, a large duffle bag in one hand, her sword in the other. "That outfit's practical, but not very comfortable."

"I was meaning to ask you about that."

"The armor?"

"No, the Templar. I just didn't want to do it around Benny. I don't think he likes me much."

"I'd say that's an understatement. They're a little...*zealous*."

"You don't say."

"Truth be told, they're a little grating at times, but..." she trailed off.

"They were all you had?"

"Don't get me wrong, they've been great. They explained what was happening to me, looked out for me, and helped me explore what I could do."

"Listen, I'm really sorry. I shouldn't have left you alone like that," I said, suddenly feeling the need to spill my guts. Guess it was easier to do when the peanut gallery stayed behind in the car. "I meant to...tell you..."

"That you were a vampire?"

"Sorta, but after that...incident...between us."

"Incident?" she asked, a wry smile on her face. Oh crap. I could feel all of my old insecurities racing to the surface. Another second or so and I'd become a stammering idiot.

"Yeah...I sorta freaked."

"Hah, I know what you mean," she said. "I must've picked up the phone to call you at least a dozen times."

"Really?"

"Don't sound so surprised, Bill. I still have everyone's contact info from back when I worked for Jim."

"It's not that, it's...never mind."

"But anyway," she continued, "for whatever reason, I just never finished dialing. Then there was my business. I couldn't ignore it...although that probably doesn't matter now. I haven't been at the office in weeks. They probably all think I've gone crazy there."

"You're the CEO. You're allowed to be crazy."

She chuckled, and it was music to my ears. I could listen to her laugh all day.

"Trust me," I said. "It's better this way."

"Better? There are a lot of people dead out there tonight. I'm not sure I'd call that better."

"It is. I know it might not be much consolation, but the Templar knew what they were getting into. They were as prepared as they were going to be. At the very least, their eyes were open to what's out there. What if they hadn't found you and those others had instead caught up to you at your office? It would have been a slaughter."

She nodded, then was quiet for a moment. It had been horrible of me to say, but that's what our lives had become. It really was a choice between the lesser of many evils these days. If people were going to die, and they were, it was preferable that they at least have a stake in the game.

"So, enough about me," she said, almost as if this were...a date. "What's the story between you and that girl?"

"Sally? It's an interesting..."

"I meant your fiancée." Once more the grin was back on her face.

"There is no story there. She's a deluded little girl who happens to have crush on me that borders on fanatical." I tried really hard to ignore that it was a description that could easily apply to me...except maybe for the little girl part.

"Little? Didn't she say she was three-hundred years old?"

"I meant in size. In everything else she's a massive pain in the ass."

"It's kind of cute," she teased.

"Minus maybe all the stuff about leaving a trail of bodies in her wake?"

"Yeah, and also her slightly disturbing wish to watch you kill me."

"That's Gan...a whole lot of disturbing in a tiny package."

"So what are you going to do about her?"

"Figure out a way to get her back home to Mongolia as soon as I can."

"Speaking of which, how..."

"Trust me, it's another long story; one that begins with Sally Fedexing my ass over to Asia."

"You'll have to tell me about it some time."

"Oh believe me, I could fill up a book with all the crap Sally pulls."

"Are you and her..."

"No. She has a thing for Ed...I think. Ed has a thing for her, at least. It's hard to say. As for us, she's kind of my business partner."

"She's obviously your friend too, that much I can tell."

"Sometimes I wonder."

"I don't. From what I hear, vampires aren't too big on my being alive."

"That's an understatement."

"I'm beginning to see that. Yet she's sticking by your side, and I don't get the vibe that she's doing so for the same reasons Gan is."

"Sally's...hmm...let's just say she's never boring and leave it at that."

"Okay. Shall we get out of here? They're gonna wonder what we're up to."

"I can only imagine what they're saying."

"They do seem to have some opinions on the matter," she said, a smirk on her face.

Heh, was it getting hot in there or was it just me? I so desperately wanted to blurt it out, but I just couldn't. It was like my tongue had decided to take a vacation. So instead, I opted for what I typically do...wuss out.

"We should probably go down before they come looking for us. Trust me, you don't want Gan in here."

I grabbed the bag from her, being mindful to not get too close. I might be delusional in certain things, but I had been nearly killed enough times for one day. There was always tomorrow.

"That's odd."

"What?" I turned to find her staring at one of the shelves as we prepared to leave.

"I could have sworn I had more CDs than this."

Fucking Sally!

* * *

Sheila closed the door behind us, doing her best to wedge it shut with the busted lock.

"Let's be quiet," I said. "I don't want to wake your neighbor again"

"Wait...what do you mean *again?*"

Oops.

sigh "Fine. I came looking for you the other day."

"You did?"

"Well the other night actually, but yeah, once I heard you were in danger. Anyway, the crazy old lady across the hall came out and gave me shit about it."

"Who?"

"The one who lives over there, in Two-F," I replied, pointing it out.

"Nobody lives there. It's been vacant for six months..."

Almost as if on cue, the door opened and the fat old lady stepped out. This time, though, it was a little bit different. She was still fat - let's not kid ourselves here - but instead of a muumuu, she wore the red cloak of a Templar and held a cross out before her.

"You've gotta be kidding me."

"Away from the Blessed One, beast!" she screeched. So much for not waking up the whole building. "Back, demon! Back, I say," she cried, brandishing the cross in front of her Weeble-like body.

"Oh fuck this," I muttered. Not in the mood for this shit again, I drew back my fist and decked her fat face. She went down with a - dare I say it - meaty thud.

It was only then that realization hit me. I had just punched out an old lady in front of a girl I was desperately trying to impress - perhaps not my finest moment.

"That was..."

"Yeah, I know, probably not the most chivalrous thing to do," I said.

"No, she's a Templar."

"One who obviously missed a few training sessions."

"What was she..."

"Keeping an eye out for vampires is my guess. I'd suggest we maybe continue this discussion in the car. I wouldn't doubt there are a few fingers dialing 911 behind closed doors right now."

"I'm assuming you've done things like this before."

"You get surprisingly used to it."

I glanced down where the tubby Templar was still laid out cold. I gave Sheila a quick shrug then led the way back outside. It was amazing how quickly this sort of thing became almost routine.

Destiny is a Bitch

If the cops were summoned, it wasn't until after we made our escape. I was worried that Sheila would be a bit cross with me for cleaning that fat bitch's clock. Fortunately, she saved all her ire for Benny during the car trip to our safe house.

"What was that woman doing spying on my apartment?"

"I see you met Sister Bernadette." He shot a quick glare at me. "I take it she failed in her duty. Tell me, did this creature dispatch her?"

"Nope," I replied. "Didn't even ugly her up...at least not any worse than she already was."

"She's fine...mostly," Sheila said. "Answer my question, Benjamin."

"Of course. My people are keeping watch at all your former places of congress."

"Or they were," Sally muttered under her breath.

"Why?" Sheila asked.

"Because we knew they would come looking for you. Considering our current predicament, I'd say we were right to be cautious. I only wish we had more of the faithful amongst our ranks. Perhaps then, this night would have ended differently."

"Yeah, that fun bunch back in Westchester might have won."

"Do not try to paint yourself as my ally, vampire. I know what you are. One day, God's light shall shine upon thee, and thou shalt be found lacking."

"That's it," I sighed, feeling my temper snap. "Ed, pull into the next side street you see."

He looked into the rearview mirror. "You got it, Ms. Daisy." Asshole.

"I knew you would show your true colors," Benny said, a note of triumph in his voice. The fucker obviously had a martyr complex.

"I begin to doubt that this human is your friend, beloved."

"Not now, Gan. You're right, Benny. It's about time I showed you what I'm really about."

Ed did as asked, once more double parking and letting the engine idle.

"Get the fuck out," I said.

"What?"

"You heard me. I'm tired of you, your friends, and having crosses shoved down my throat every time I turn around. So get out. Find a church and pray to God...maybe he'll see fit to make you less of an asshole."

Benny stared at me suspiciously. He obviously thought he was about to become the rope in a game of vampire tug-o-war. He was wrong, though.

I got out of the car, lowered the back seat for him, and held the door.

"Let's go. If we get a ticket, it's only going to make my mood that much worse."

He climbed out, trying to keep an eye on Sally, Gan, and myself simultaneously. He was smart with regards to those first two. Hell, I wasn't entirely sure they'd let him go without snapping his neck as a parting gift. Sally, though, looked as if she could have cared less. As for Gan, I guess she was trying to score some brownie points. Either way, it was fine by me.

Benny stepped out and faced me. "And the Blessed One?"

"She's free to do as she pleases. No one here will stop her."

"Your Holiness," he called to her. "Let us leave these serpents to their foul fate."

I stepped over to the front and opened the door for her. "I meant what I said earlier. I'm sorry if things didn't go the way I planned, but I really was trying to help."

"I know you were, Bill," she replied, then added after a moment, "I'm good where I am."

She was?!

Woo! Go me! Guess I've still got it.

"But your..."

"I've made my decision, Ben," she replied, not entirely unkindly. "I've seen a lot of ugliness tonight, but despite what you think, Bill isn't the cause of it."

"You can't be serious. They will..."

"I am. You claim to know a lot about faith, Benjamin, but your problem is that you're too narrow in your beliefs."

"I have..."

"Faith in God, I know, but faith goes beyond that. Sometimes you need to have faith in people too."

"These creatures aren't people."

"Speak for yourself," Ed huffed from the driver's seat.

"I think that's a matter of perspective," Sheila replied.

"What has this creature done to you? Has he somehow defiled you with his evil influence?"

Heh, I wish.

"Ben, thank you for everything. I wish things had turned out differently, I really do, but at least I'm glad you survived. I won't forget what you or your brothers have done for me. Please be safe."

"You cannot go with this creature. It will be the end of you."

"Somehow I don't believe that. Have a little faith, Ben. I know I do." With that, she pulled the passenger side door shut.

I gave Ben a smirk of triumph as I stepped past him. Hey, I wasn't above a little pettiness. He's just lucky I didn't raise my hand to my forehead and give him the L sign.

"This isn't over, spawn of Hell," he whispered to me.

"Get in line, Benny," I replied, climbing back into my seat. "See you at the next church revival."

* * *

We ditched the car about a mile away from the safe house. Ed and I wiped it down for prints while the others grabbed our stuff. That done, we all headed toward our destination. Thank goodness we made it back when we did. Despite the rain, the horizon started to lighten. Another hour and things might be getting a bit toasty for my own comfort.

Sally wasn't happy about using the new safe house, but she'd have to deal. At least I had been able to rid us of Benny. Even if he managed to round up more of his holy rollers, they wouldn't be able to do much to bother us.

Gan was a completely different problem, but it was pointless to bother worrying in her case. Not only would she be near impossible to lose, but even if we did, she could pretty much sniff me out wherever I might be. At least this way we knew where she was. She'd hopefully cause less chaos with our eyes on her.

We reached the building and Sally let us in, disengaging the security system in the process. "Welcome to the former safe house of Village Coven," she announced to the group, holding the door open for us in mock invitation.

"Coven?" Sheila asked. "I thought that was witches."

"Stole the idea from us," Sally said. "Come on, you can have the spare bedroom. It has a security door with a heavy lock."

"I'm not afraid."

"I know," Sally replied. "It's mostly to keep you from feeling Bill's eyes staring at you all day. He can be a little pathetic like that."

"What about the rest of us?" Ed asked before I could chime in with an appropriate response to her asshole remark.

"The main bedroom is mine. If anyone has a problem with that, they can go fuck themselves sideways. The rest of you can sack out wherever you can find a spot...that includes you too, stud," she said directly to him. "I'm too tired to play with my food today."

Well that was...disturbing.

"I don't suppose you have anything to eat here that doesn't clot?" he asked. She just stared at him for a moment, her look saying it all. "I didn't think so. Oh well, dibs on the love seat."

Being a gentleman, I offered Gan the couch. She attempted to entice me into sharing it with her - all the while Ed tried to stifle laughter from where he lay. I respectfully declined and found a comfy section of floor. If I had learned anything from my college days, it was how to crash just about anywhere if the situation called for it. Hard surface or not, I was out within minutes.

* * *

I awoke some hours later, I'm not sure how many, but it probably wasn't too long. One of the advantages of being a vampire is that I needed much less sleep than during my living days. Even so, enough fatigue could knock me out for the entire night...or day. Perhaps that had been the case now. I couldn't see any light through my closed eyelids. Maybe I had actually slept through the day. It was possible, considering the wounds I had sustained.

I opened my eyes to check the time and had to stifle a scream.

Gan's smiling face beamed down at me from about six inches away. "Good day, beloved. I have been watching over you."

Damn, Sally was right. It *was* creepy.

I sat up and immediately scooted away before she could try to get more comfortable. Once out of her reach, I took a look around. The storm had abated, but clouds still covered the sky. No wonder it was still dark.

"What time is it?"

"It is still morning. You have been asleep for about four hours."

Damn, that meant the full day was still ahead...a day of being cooped up with Gan. How lovely.

"The others?"

"Asleep. We are the only ones awake."

"Shouldn't you still be catching some shuteye too?"

"I was. I awoke once I heard you stirring."

"You heard me stirring?"

"Of course. I am entirely in tune with you, my love."

Yeah, definitely creepy. Thank goodness I didn't own any pet rabbits for her to boil.

"Well, let's not wake the others."

"I would not dream of it. This is the first moment I have had you all to myself. I do not wish it to end sooner than it must."

Well, that made one of us.

"How is your shoulder?"

I gingerly touched it. It was pain free, which was good. I reached into my sleeve and under the bandages. The bumpy texture of fresh scar tissue greeted my fingers. In a few hours even that would be gone. Had it not been a silver weapon, it would have done so hours ago, but oh well. Regardless, being a vampire definitely had its perks.

"I'll live."

"I know."

sigh

I got up, walked over to the kitchen and opened the fridge. Just as Ed had suspected, it was full of blood - but thankfully no body parts. Oh well, this was New York. It's not like you could throw a rock without hitting a falafel stand. He and Sheila would be fine.

I grabbed a few pints and tossed one to Gan. She liked it fresh, but I preferred she not gnaw on my friends. To help keep her from balking, I raised mine in a toast. "To your...health."

"To our future, Dr. Death."

"Uh yeah." I took a long sip from mine. "So what are you doing here, Gan?"

"I told you..."

"I know you did, but still, aren't you worried?"

"Worried? Why would I worry?"

"You said you had spies in the Boston office, right?"

"Correct."

"Well then you have to know that the group last night was operating on the authority of the First Coven."

"Of course. Even if I did not know, I could easily surmise that."

"Then you have to know you're going against them in your actions."

"Obviously, beloved."

Grrr, again with the beloved bullshit. It was enough to make me want to get a running start and dive straight through one of the windows.

"Okay, am I missing something here, then? These are the First. You don't go against them."

"Are you not doing so right now?"

"Well, yeah...but that's different."

"How?"

"It's...hard...well...it just is."

"That is...fascinating, Dr. Death," she replied, throwing her own little smirk at me. Great, I was being humored by a reject from *Monster High*. "My own motivations are simple enough."

There was a moment or two of silence. "Care to enlighten me?"

"The war is upon us."

"I kind of noticed, right around the time that Nergui killed Turd's daughter."

"Yes," she said, a thoughtful smile on her face. "He died an honorable death. Loyal to the end, although I never expected less. Did you know that Alexander himself suggested I send him?"

"What?!" I replied, spewing blood.

"Yes. He visited my domain and told me about the gathering."

"So he manipulated you," I said, feeling some sympathy for her. She had been as much a pawn as I had. "He knew that if you suspected how the Humbaba Accord would end, combined with your feelings for me, it would cause..."

I stopped as she broke down into giggles. "Oh, Dr. Death, you are truly funny. It is one of the reasons I love you so. Alexander tried to manipulate me, that much is true, but my father did not raise me to be a fool. I saw through his guise the moment he began to speak."

"Wait, so you knew he wanted to start a war?"

"Of course. He could not have made it more obvious."

"And you still did it?"

"Certainly. I had the same vision as did he. I knew that destiny was upon us."

"Why you little..." I snarled. For a split second, I lost all sense of anything except that this little bitch had purposely and willingly set the world on a collision course with annihilation.

Before I could stop myself, the Freewill monster inside of me reared its ugly head, and I threw a punch at her still smiling face.

* * *

Or at least I tried to. As quick as I was, Gan ducked to the side effortlessly. My fist hit nothing but the empty space where she had been.

I pulled back, stunned she had moved so fast. Fortunately it gave me pause to push the anger back down again before it could take another swing.

"Ooh," she replied, still grinning. "I do so enjoy seeing the fire inside of you."

I took a deep breath and mentally counted to ten. "Do you realize what you've done, Gan? Really, do you?"

"Obviously, my love. In fact, I see things far more clearly than even Alexander."

"I don't think you do. If they find out you're going against their wishes, they're going to..."

"Kill me? I think not. You underestimate me, Dr. Death. My father's followers are now my followers and the breadth of his fealty was wide indeed. Besides which, they will most likely never know of this so-called treachery on my part."

"How can you be sure of that? You let Remington and his men go."

"Your point?"

"My point is that they've probably already gone crawling back to Colin for reinforcements, ratting us both out in the process."

"Doubtful. The First are not tolerant of failure, regardless of cause. Should Remington return to them in any state other than victory, it would reflect poorly on him. As leader, he would be expected to have prepared for any contingency. That he did not would be ill-accepted as excuse."

"You think he's still in the city?"

"Of course. There is no question that he will try again."

That wasn't good, although I'd be lying if I said I was surprised to hear it. Vampires don't like to lose. That's probably even more so when embarrassed by a pint-sized foe like Gan. Something about receiving a beat-down from a little girl doesn't sit well with most guys.

"But what if this makes it back to the First?"

"What if it does?" she replied contemptuously. She muttered something in her native tongue. I had no idea what it was, but it sounded vaguely unflattering in tone. "Unlike most, I do not fear the First. Their time is drawing to a close."

Whoa, that was unexpected. Gan was a little (read: a lot) nuts, but I hadn't taken her to be suicidal.

"What do you mean by that?"

"Is it not obvious?"

"Pretend that I'm stupid."

"As you wish. The coming war will bring with it upheavals the likes of which this world has not known since the ancient days."

"I kind of guessed as much."

"Alexander thinks his time has come. He believes that it is his destiny to finish what he started so long ago."

"And?"

"And he is wrong, my love. He arrogantly assumes he is the only conqueror amongst our people. He is not. My bloodline is stronger. I am descended from Temujin, the great Khan himself. My grandfather, then father after him, ruled over far more of this world than Alexander ever dreamed. I have even heard rumor that the First originally targeted my grandfather, but refrained at Alexander's insistence. The reason they ultimately turned my father was because he was equally as brilliant, but less enamored of conquest. Alexander assumes that my father's descendants are likewise cowed. It shall prove to be a fatal oversight on his part."

Had my jaw not been connected to the rest of my face, it would have surely hit the floor and rolled away. Up until then, I had thought that all other vampires were utterly obedient to the First. Sure, there were individual power plays going on. Hell, it was practically an everyday occurrence. However, when the Draculas said jump, everyone within earshot lined up and did so - no questions asked. I wasn't stupid enough to think it was all blind loyalty, but I assumed fear of their wrath took over where that left off. I could understand that. A powerful enough vampire could compel just about anyone they wanted, save me maybe. If that failed, well I had gotten a taste of Alexander's power. The dude was scary strong, as in powerful enough to kick the shit out of the Sasquatch chieftain.

"And what are you going to do if Alex doesn't cooperate? He doesn't strike me as the type to lie down and die when challenged."

"That is easy, my love. I shall offer my troops the benefit of my wisdom and experience." Being insecure apparently wasn't an issue for Gan. "That will enable them to route Alexander's forces, already weakened from the conflict with the Alma."

"That doesn't handle the little problem of Alex and the First Coven," I pointed out.

"Obviously. His favor with the others of the First is strained at best right now. I have little doubt some can be swayed to stand against him. As for Alexander, that is simplicity itself. You shall kill him, beloved."

Me? Oddly enough, I wasn't surprised to hear that. Goddamn, how I hate being the chosen one.

Snack Run

"Could you maybe be a little louder, Bill? They can't quite hear you in Jersey," Ed griped, joining us in the kitchen.

I'll admit, I might have forgotten to keep my volume down after Gan filled me in on her *genius* plan revolving around me being insane enough to fight Alex. Fuck that! I had an inkling of what James was capable of. I wasn't about to tangle with him and he was a good thirteen-hundred years younger than Alex.

Gan had pointed out that obviously - she sure liked that word - I would need to tap into my hidden Freewill powers to stand a chance in Hell. She didn't seem to realize I had no control over that. Knowing my luck, it would fizzle out when I needed it most. I'd be so busy quaking in my boots that I wouldn't be able to summon the necessary anger to transform. Ignoring that, there wasn't any guarantee that Alex still wouldn't just fuck my shit up.

Ed started rummaging through the cabinets looking for something resembling coffee. I used that as a distraction to end the conversation and step away. I gave Gan a quick warning about not snacking on my friend, then excused myself to take a shower. Being a vampire is dirty work on the best of days, downright disgusting on the rest. Considering who was slumbering in the other room, I had no intention of walking around smelling like ass if I could help it.

Much to my eternal horror (and Ed's amusement...asshole), Gan offered to join me. Of all the people present in the building, Ed included, she was the absolute last one I wanted making that offer. I thus politely declined - giving her some bullshit about being shy - and then locked the door the second I was through it. Thank goodness it was another security door. Apparently Sally had them on every frame in this place. I'd have to thank her profusely for that. It wouldn't stop Gan if she really put her mind to it, but it made me feel better nevertheless...much the same way that a flimsy cage at the circus makes people feel better about the tigers just a few feet away from them.

* * *

I was pleased to find that the wound on my shoulder had finally healed. About time, too...goddamn silver stakes. Hmm, I should have kept one. It might have made a nice gift for Sheila since becoming the Icon had apparently made her all badass. Sure, it might not exactly be a necklace or a - dare I say it - ring, but it was both expensive and practical. Hard to beat a present like that. Oh well.

Anyway, it's amazing how much more alive a good shower can make one feel, even someone as dead as me. For a few minutes, it's like it can almost wash the troubles of the world away. Of course, it would have been somewhat more satisfying had Sally stocked the place with soap that didn't smell like a fruit salad, but beggars can't be choosers, I suppose. Either way, it still beat smelling like shit.

I toweled off and got dressed, taking a little extra time to groom myself. What? Even in the middle of horrific danger, there might still be time to flirt.

KNOCK *KNOCK*

"Let's go, Bill!" It was Ed.

"You should have gone before I got in," I commented, still brushing my hair.

"Hurry up. You're not getting any better looking."

I ignored him, wondering if Sally kept any floss in here.

"Open up or I'm telling Gan that you changed your mind."

sigh

I opened the door and stepped out, giving Ed my best stink-eye in the process. "You have the bladder of a girl."

"So says the vampire who smells like passion fruit," he replied, pushing past me and closing the door.

I debated flipping on the TV. There wasn't much I wanted to watch, but maybe Spongebob was on. If so, it would keep Gan busy. She had developed a slightly disturbing fascination with that cartoon. However, noticing that Sheila's bedroom door was ajar distracted me from that plan of action. My sensitive vampire ears heard voices coming from within.

Noticing Gan preoccupied with something in the kitchen, I crept to the door and knocked on it.

"Everything all right in there?"

"You can come in, I'm decent," came the reply.

"Like that would stop him," another voice commented - Sally's.

What the?

I pushed open the door and found the two of them passionately making out.

Sorry, that was just my imagination filling in the blanks. Wishful thinking and all that.

In actuality, Sheila sat on the edge of her bed while Sally stood a safe distance away, leaning against a dresser. All of Sally's wounds from the night before were healed and her hair had fully grown back in. One would never have guessed that just ten hours earlier she looked like she could have been Hayden Christensen's stunt double in *Revenge of the Sith*.

"What's going on?"

"I was filling her in on the plan," Sally replied.

Oh yeah, I had almost forgotten about that. Truth be told, I was purposely trying to, but I could only delude myself for so long. We couldn't stay there and fend off the forces of the Draculas indefinitely, hoping that they'd eventually get bored and give up. There was also the fact of Gan's presence. Sooner or later, bad things were going to happen with her around. She was a walking powder keg, one who had little to no regard for human life. She was also really fucking annoying, what with her constant beloved bullshit. A small part of me was afraid that after hearing it a million times my brain would melt and I'd actually start to believe it. Talk about scary.

"You okay, Bill?" Sheila asked.

"Sorry, thinking of something unpleasant."

"I know what you mean," Sally said. "I chipped a nail in last night's fight."

"My heart bleeds for your loss," I said dryly before turning to Sheila. "So what do you think about it?"

She gave a small smile. "I guess there is something vaguely romantic about living life on the run, moving from town to town, never settling."

"Lonely too."

"Yeah," she replied. "There is that."

"You know...I was thinking..."

"Here it comes," Sally sighed.

"Don't you have some spiked heels that need sharpening?"

"Nope, did that last week. Besides, it's so much more entertaining to watch you squirm."

"Am I missing something here?" Sheila asked.

"Only the obvious," Sally said. "Bill was gonna offer to come with you."

"Thanks, Sally, I think I..."

"However, he knows deep down it wouldn't be a good idea."

"I do?"

"Yes, you do. The mages can track you. They've done it before. Hell, they did it just last night. Likewise, so can any vampire of sufficient age, especially those that you've managed to piss off - of which there is a sizable amount."

"The older vampires don't like you much?" Sheila asked.

"Bill here has a singular talent for upsetting the status quo of the undead world."

"That almost sounded like a compliment, Sally," I said.

"It almost was," she confirmed, moving toward the door. "I'll leave you two to discuss this further. I'm not in the mood to test my gag reflex today."

"I don't suppose you could keep Gan busy."

"Don't push your luck," she replied, stepping from the room.

She hadn't bothered to close the door and I didn't move to correct that. I had no illusions of privacy by that point. Even if the door was enough to keep us from Sally's ears, provided she didn't immediately plaster herself against it - something I wouldn't bet against - Gan could probably hear a fly take a shit from a mile away.

"She's right about being tracked," I said. "Hell, we'd probably have Gan knocking on our door ten minutes after arriving at a new destination."

"I don't doubt it. Still, you would actually do that for me?"

I wanted to scream, "FUCK YEAH!" but I figured that might be slightly overkill. Instead, I just nodded while trying my best to keep a fairly neutral expression. No need to come across as some sort of crazed stalker.

"I can't say I would mind it." Really?! "It sounds like a lonely road ahead for me. It would be nice to have a friend along." Friend? She didn't say friend, did she? Fuck me!

"Yeah...it would be," I replied, trying not to sound as if I was about to curl up into a little ball and cry.

"It would be even nicer to have someone who was more..."

What? For fuck's sake, why did she have to trail off there? "More what?" I asked disinterestedly.

She smiled softly. "Nothing, I guess."

Goddamn, I hate when women do that. It leaves just enough doubt for a guy to have hope, without actually committing to anything. I swear, some days it's almost enough to make me want to put on assless chaps and try playing for the other team. Yeah yeah, I know, it's not like I was any better. Here we were, two adults...fuck that, *two beings of legend*...neither of us quite brave enough to say what was on our mind. I had little doubt that Sally was laughing her ass off if she was eavesdropping (about a one-hundred percent chance of that, I'd say). For once, I couldn't blame her. Hell, had this conversation been happening with either Tom or Ed (with a woman, not me!), I know they sure as shit wouldn't hear the end of it anytime soon.

Okay, I needed to get a grip. A sense of perspective is everything in cases like these (were there other cases like this?), and the truth was I was trying to have an intimate conversation with a girl I couldn't even shake hands with.

"So...what are you going to do?" I asked as neutrally as I could.

"I think we both know the answer to that. There's a part of me that wants to stay and fight, a part that almost *needs* to do that. It's weird. That's not me. Up until less than two months ago I would have won a Ms. Passive Aggressive pageant."

"You've changed."

"I think we both have. But I am what I am now. Still, there's nothing wrong with my brain." Or the rest of her, for that matter. "I know a hopeless battle when I see it. I can't fight every vampire and wizard on the planet by myself."

"That's not all that's out there."

"So I hear. I'm not sure I want to know more."

"You probably don't have a choice."

"Tell me about it. Either way, I can't fight off an army with just a sword."

I was tempted to argue against that. She had done pretty damn well against Remington's forces, after all.

"I don't want to die," she continued, "but I'm not afraid of it. What I am afraid of is the people I care about getting hurt because of me. My mother, the rest of my family, my friends..."

She stopped short of saying potential boyfriend, but I didn't really expect it anyway. It didn't matter. I knew what she meant, even if I couldn't say for certain I would do the same thing. If the last year had taught me anything, it's that I'm apparently not bright enough to know when to run from a hopeless fight when I see it...or keep my friends out of harm's way. It just proved what I already knew: she was a better person than me. Like I needed any more proof that she was out of my league.

God, I hate this. Fuck fairy tales and those who believe in them. That *happily ever after* shit is definitely the exception and not the rule. Don't get me wrong, there are probably people out there who meet their soul mates and then spend the rest of their lives in blissful happiness with them. Then there are the rest of us. Some are lucky in that they never meet that special one. It sucks, I'm sure, but probably not as much as meeting them, realizing it, and then fucking it up somehow. Sometimes the timing isn't right, sometimes people are too stupid to make a move when the opportunity presents itself, and sometimes it turns out that you're destined to be eternal arch-enemies. Any way you look at it, things don't work out. I can only imagine how it is to live out the remainder of one's days with a constant "What if?" always there, just at the edge of your periphery. Hell, for someone like me, that could stretch out into an eternity of torment. Oh yeah, that sounded like fun.

There I'll be, miserable for centuries. Then one day, maybe three-hundred years from now, I'll be strolling through Starfleet Academy and notice a girl who's the spitting image of Sheila. At that point I'll think that maybe fate has given me a second chance. I'll make plans to convince her that she's the reincarnation of...holy shit! Yeah and maybe change my name to Edward Cullen while I'm at it. Screw that. I'd sooner ram a silver stake through my own crotch than live out some fucked up *Twilight* redux.

Fortunately, Ed spared me any further mental torture when he popped his head in. "Are you two done making goo-goo eyes at each other because I'm starving to death? There isn't anything to eat here that probably wasn't begging for mercy not too long ago."

"What do I look like, fucking Colonel Sanders to you?"

"A white suit and goatee..."

"Your point?"

"My point is that I'm heading out to grab some food." He turned toward Sheila. "As the only other guest that eats people food and not people, do you want me to bring you back something?"

"Actually, if you don't mind the company, I think I'll join you. Just let me freshen up a bit first."

* * *

It figured, within the next hour, the sky cleared up enough so that errant rays of sunlight shone through. I doubted it would last long, considering the ominous clouds on the horizon and Gan's assertion this was only a temporary pause in the gathering storm. It was enough, though. To say I was jealous of Ed would be an understatement. Not only could he go out in the daylight with Sheila, but if he was so inclined he could even hold her hand without combusting - not that he should ever even think of trying, at least not if he wanted his ass to stay unkicked.

I had put up a minor protest at the suggestion. After all, did we go through all that crap to rescue her from the Templars (who weren't exactly holding her prisoner to begin with, but let's not mince words) just to let her walk out the door unguarded? The others, though, considered the risks to be minimal.

"The witches can't track her and it's daylight, so that means no vamps," Sally said matter-of-factly.

"Wait, but they can track me. So if that's the case, they might have already zeroed in and..."

"Nope," she replied with a tone of finality.

"Yeah, they can. We know this already."

"Not here," she said proudly, hooking her thumb at one of the marks painted on the walls. I had noticed them the other day, but paid them no heed.

"Yeah, so? Is tribal art making a comeback?"

"That is not art, beloved." Gan took a good look at them as if for the first time. "If my memory serves me correctly, those are scrying guards. I am impressed," she said, addressing Sally. "Where did you obtain the knowledge of these?"

"What, no whore comment?" Sally asked.

"I thought it was implied."

"You little fuc..."

"Yeah, where did you get these?" I interrupted before she could say anything that might encourage Gan to do something more violent than just call her names.

Sally glared at me and gritted her teeth. "James told me about them not too long ago when we were discussing our little wizard problem. He wasn't sure they'd actually work, but I figured what the hell? Considering this place hasn't been blown to bits yet, I'm comfortable thinking they're doing their job."

"Damn," I replied. "I need to get a few of those tattooed on me."

"They do not work that way, beloved," Gan explained, having come from a culture where mysticism was served as a side dish with supper. "They must be properly grounded to channel the energy back into the earth. The granite beneath this city would act as a perfect conduit for this."

"You knew that too?" I asked Sally, impressed.

"Well, I might have gotten lucky on that one," she admitted.

"Are we good here, then?" Ed asked. "As fascinating as this all is, I'd really like to get some calories down my throat."

I turned to Sheila, "Are you sure? It could still be…"

"It'll be fine, Bill. We're in the middle of the city during the day. Aside from getting a little wet if it starts raining again, what's the worst that could happen?"

Damn, I hate when people say that. It never ends well.

Hormonal Imbalance

"This isn't good," I said, mostly to myself.

"Are you still harping about it?" Sally asked. "They've only been gone for half an hour. I'm sure they're..."

"Not that! I should've told Ed to bring me back something. I don't know about you, but I like a little texture with my blood. More filling that way."

Sally and I sat in the living room of the safe house. Gan had gone to take a shower after a little incident between her, a blood pack, and the microwave. She might know a shitload more about vampire history than I did, but I took some comfort that I at least knew how to program a remote control. That had to count for something.

Speaking of the remote, Sally and I were watching the news. Apparently they had taken notice of the freak storm and were attempting to make sense of it. The meteorologists were practically creaming themselves trying to come up with theories. *Good luck with that*, I thought. Oh well, at least we seemed to be in the eye of the storm, if that was even applicable. Maybe the extradimensional creatures causing the ruckus had decided to break for lunch.

Sheila and Ed must have been having those same thoughts as right then there came a knock on the door.

"Our wayward gourmets return," I declared, standing up. "Hopefully they brought a little extra."

"Doubt it," Sally said. "I'm sure they enjoyed a nice romantic lunch for two."

"Bite me," I growled, eliciting a titter of laughter from her. Bitch!

The knocking continued. "Okay, okay!" I shouted. "Relax!" I opened the door, continuing, "Gan's in the can, so if you got a hold of some bad burritos..."

I trailed off as neither Sheila nor Ed stood in the doorway.

Wide-eyed, I stepped aside as Christy entered, clearly agitated about something.

"I need your help, Bill," she said. "It's Tom."

* * *

"How the hell is she here?" Sally asked, bolting from her chair.

"First things, first," I replied, closing the door behind Christy. "What about Tom?"

"He's not...himself."

"What?" Sally asked. "He finally grew a working frontal lobe?"

Christy ignored her barb and continued, "He's...it's hard to explain. But I know one thing for certain: it's all my fault."

Before I could question her further, a voice from behind me said, "There are a great many things that are your fault, witch. It is about time you paid for them."

* * *

Thankfully, I was standing between the two of them, otherwise things could have ended badly right there.

Christy barely had time to utter a surprised, "You!" before Gan was across the room, a blur of motion. I got lucky more than anything else. Acting purely on instinct alone, I threw myself directly into her path. She was faster and stronger, but I had size on my side. We both went down, myself thankfully on top.

I tried to restrain the murderous munchkin, but it was a losing battle. It was like trying to wrestle down an angry badger. It didn't help that Sally just stood there watching us, a bemused look on her face.

"Gan, stop!" I yelled, still trying to get some leverage over her. "Christy is here...uh...because..."

"The witch is here under truce," Sally said at last.

"She is?" I asked. "Err, I mean, yeah she is. It would be dishonorable to kill her under such conditions."

Gan ceased her struggle immediately. She might be in charge of a small empire these days, but she had gotten lessons about honor banged into her head by her father for the last three centuries. She still had a response to it like some sort of small, psychotic Pavlov's dog.

"You killed my master."

Oh crap. I had nearly forgotten there was an angry hormonal witch in the room, too. Guess Tom had spilled his guts about Decker. I'd have to remember to *thank* him for that, but first I needed to not die.

I looked up to find Christy surrounded by an angry red glow. Any second now she was going to unleash hellfire at Gan and...oh, will you look at that...I was right in the line of fire. How the hell do I keep finding myself in these situations?

"Christy," I warned, trying not to sound like I was staring down the barrel of a human-shaped photon torpedo launcher, "the truce goes both ways."

"But she killed..."

"You came here about Tom. We can't help him if we're all dead."

Thank goodness that seemed to get through to her. The glow around her dissipated and her whole demeanor seemed to deflate. The immediate danger over, I let out a breath. At some point I was going to need to put together a spreadsheet, cross-referencing allies who happened to want each other dead. It would be helpful should I ever decide to host something like a fondue party.

I got off of Gan, moving nice and slow in case she decided that her personal honor could go fuck itself.

When she didn't do anything more than stand up, I said, "Gan, please go sit over there. Christy, you there," pointing to spots on opposite sides of the living room.

They did so and I continued. "I'd offer you a drink, but I'm assuming you haven't developed a taste for O-negative." The pleasantries taken care of, I got to the point. "What's wrong with Tom?"

"It's my fault."

"I am certain it is."

"Not now, Gan," I pleaded. "What's your fault, Christy?"

"Tom...he's not in his right mind."

"And this is surprising, how?" Sally asked.

My eyes opened wide. He had definitely been acting strange earlier. I had assumed that perhaps he...well...was finally growing up. Aside from him being pissed at Ed and I for keeping Sheila's alternate identity a secret, I was actually kind of proud of him for stepping up. But now... "Go on."

"I think I've been influencing him subconsciously. I didn't mean to, but I've been so scared and upset and..."

"Hormonal?" Sally offered.

"Yes, that. Back when I first learned I was a witch, my power would occasionally flare up, but I was a teenager then. I learned control and it hasn't happened in a long time, but I think maybe...no, that's not fair. I *know* it's been happening. I've been projecting all of my fears like a beacon."

"What's that you always say, Bill?" Sally asked. "The Force lets you control weak minds."

"Sally..." I warned.

Christy just ignored her, though, and went on. "Then, after I heard from my sisters that the Icon was alive, I got even worse. I didn't mean to, Bill. Hell, I didn't know she'd be so...nice."

"It's okay, Christy," I said soothingly, despite a stress migraine building behind my eyes. "Explain."

"Preferably in small words," Sally added. Apparently her attitude had grown back along with her skin.

"I think I've been brainwashing Tom without being aware of it. Everything I've had in me, all my fears, worries, thoughts about our relationship...it's all been emptying into him."

I nodded. "I'll admit he did seem a little...off. Still, he wasn't acting all that strange. He looked like he had everything under control."

"He might have, but then things got worse, *a lot* worse."

* * *

Christy explained how three members of her coven had arrived at our apartment sometime after we left. They had been in pretty dire straits. Apparently Gan's people had been hunting them through the night and doing a damn good job at it. At one point they had gotten separated from the rest and made a run for it. They had no idea what had become of their sisters, but it didn't sound like they were hopeful. Having seen Gan's assassins in action, I wouldn't have put money on the other witches. They were tired, scared, and their leader was dead. If the assassins hadn't finished the rest off yet, it probably wouldn't be long.

That was bad enough, but they had also told Christy about what had befallen Harry Decker - apparently in much greater detail than I had passed on to Tom.

"It was too much for me to handle. I mean, he had raised me like his own child for years. The stress of everything finally caught up to me. I must have fainted. When I finally woke up, my sisters had already left and I found Tom putting his shoes on."

"What happened?"

"When I passed out I must have had a psychic overload."

"Directly into Tom's head," I surmised.

"Yes, I'm afraid so. He was ranting on about protecting me and our baby. I tried to talk some sense into him, but he kept on rambling. He said he was going to find my sisters so he could tell them about the Icon and where she was hiding."

"Did he know where to find them?"

"I think so. He mentioned something about the office."

Oh crap! Forget the mages - he was likely to find a group of unfriendly vamps waiting for him there instead.

"Wait!" Sally interrupted. "How the hell did Tom know where to find *us*?"

"After he left," Christy explained, "I found a piece of crumpled paper on the table. It had this address on it in your handwriting, Bill."

"Your handwriting?" Sally asked in that sweet tone that told me she was anything but pleased. "You told that dipshit where this safe house is?"

"I...was worried. I figured if they needed to find us and..."

"Blow the shit out of us?"

"Not quite what I intended."

"Your intentions have paved an entire super fucking highway to Hell, you know that?" she said, throwing up her hands in frustration.

I tried my best to ignore her. Despite the clusterfuck that things had turned into, I was quite impressed with Christy.

"And despite everything, you still came here to warn us?"

"Of course," she replied. "I already told you, I don't believe that you're purposely trying to kill anyone."

"That is where you are wrong, witch," Gan interjected. "My beloved shall be the death of this world."

"Thanks, Gan. Any chance you could maybe...oh I don't know...not help?"

"I only speak of your fate. What does it matter if others know of it? Destiny cannot be changed."

"Watch me," I said before turning back to Christy. "They're going to come after us, aren't they?" Yeah, I've always had a singular talent for stating the obvious.

She nodded.

"Except that they haven't yet," Sally said. She explained to Christy what had happened two nights earlier: the destruction of the loft and the subsequent massacre of our coven. In typical Sally fashion, she told the story as if it were nothing more than an annoying afterthought. Christy, however, listened with growing horror on her face.

"My gods, I had no idea. I knew Harry was getting desperate, but I didn't think he would..."

"He did," Sally stated flatly. "But that's not why I'm telling you. Am I correct in assuming it would have taken a lot of juice to do what they did?"

Christy appeared to mull it over, but then nodded again. "Most, if not all, of the coven. To cause that amount of destruction without it spilling over would require a lot of control and concentration."

"Control and concentration that three tired witches on the run probably wouldn't have."

"No. In their current condition they'd be able to fight, but without knowing who or how many were in this place, it would be too risky. My sisters are desperate, but they're not suicidal."

"I guess that explains why we're not lying in a pile of rubble," I said. "They're going to want reinforcements."

"And that means Remington's crew."

"Oh crap!" I said. "The sewer entrance. They could be..."

"I doubt it," Sally said. "We'd be swarming with them already if that were the case. Even if they suspected a below ground entrance, they wouldn't be able to easily find it. The subway system is bad enough for out-of-towners. The sewers are a fucking rat maze. They're also narrow. Unless they took us by surprise, we'd be able to hold them off down there."

"Kind of like in *300*?"

Gan looked confused at that. "What does my age have to do with killing our enemies?"

"Different concept, Gan," I explained before addressing the others again. "So you think they're going to wait until after dark and then come a knocking?"

"Probably," Sally said.

"In the meantime," Christy added, "I'm sure my sisters have been watching this place."

"Do you think they know you're here?" I asked.

She gave me a sad smile. "Possibly."

Wow, she had really risked almost everything by coming here. "Thank you, Christy." I meant every word of it.

"Just promise me one thing," she replied.

"Name it."

"This destiny your *friend* mentioned. I want to know you're going to try your damnedest to change it. I'm counting on you. Tom's counting on you. And so is my baby."

No pressure there.

No Escape from New York

Sally opined that our best course of action was to leave before the attack came. She was relatively sure that Remington's vamps wouldn't know the sewers. I knew for certain Tom didn't and Christy mentioned that it wasn't a place her people tended to frequent. As soon as our friends got back from their little lunch date, she wanted us to get the fuck out of there. Once out in the open, Gan could attempt to track down her assassins. With their help, we could hopefully end this.

"There's just one small problem," I pointed out. "Tom. If he was dumb enough to head to the office, then we need to save his ass."

"Your friend is most likely already dead."

"Thanks for the encouragement, Gan, but I'm a glass is half full kind of person."

"There's still hope," Christy said. "My sisters won't be keen on killing an innocent. I might be on the outs with them, but they still know what he means to me."

I wasn't quite willing to put my faith in a group of witches who had tried to fry my ass more than once that week. Speaking of faith, though... "Does Tom still have that amulet you carved for him?"

Christy nodded. "He wears it all the time."

That figured. She had made a crude amulet for Tom while up in Canada. It bore the likeness of *Optimus Prime*. He used to have the original action figure and had been able to channel faith through it much the same way the Templars could do with their crosses. Though the toy was long since broken, Christy's magical amulet had allowed him to focus that faith again. Yeah, Tom was a little fucked in the head.

"As long as he has that on him, he might have a chance. Even so, we need to get to him quickly."

"He is the one who has betrayed us, my love."

"Not of his own accord," I pointed out. "Tom's my friend. I owe it to him...in more ways than one."

"Okay, so we wait for Gan's assassins," Sally said. "Tell them not to kill any particularly stupid humans they come across, and then storm the office."

She had meant to be sarcastic, but the truth was my plan was pretty much as simple as that. I told her as much.

"A direct assault would be foolish, Dr. Death," Gan declared. "For anyone less than the Freewill, that is."

"That's what I'm hoping."

It was settled, then. Now all we had to do was wait for Ed and Sheila to get back and then we could head out and see what could be done to make that plan a reality.

There was only one small problem.

They didn't return.

* * *

"Where the hell are they? It doesn't take this long to grab a slice of pizza."

"Maybe it was really good pizza."

"Could be," I admitted. "Can I borrow your cell?"

Sally handed it over, amazingly enough without further comment. Jokes aside, she knew this was serious business...for me at least. Once again, I felt a sense of gratitude fill me with regards to her involvement. She literally had almost nothing to gain by this insane endeavor of mine. Hell, if anything, the vampire world would be a little safer with Sheila's removal and she knew it. The same went for Christy. She was there to save Tom, obviously, but she could have easily ratted us out at any time. That they were both willing to have a little - dare I say it - *faith* in me was heartening. I vowed to not let either of them down. There had to be a way to win that didn't result in disaster for any of us.

I just wished I had a clue as to what that was.

* * *

I dialed Ed's number. He'd be likely to answer, especially the second he saw it was coming from Sally's line. Talk about living dangerously.

It rang once, twice, and then on the third ring it was answered. Thank goodness. Maybe Sally was right about it being especially good pizza. This was New York, after all.

"Hey, Ed. It's Bill. Just checking up on..."

"Hi, Bill," Tom's voice said from the other end.

It's amazing how much difference a day can make. Had this happened at any other time, the worst that either of us would have expected was a quick, "Put Ed on the line, douche."

Now, though, I'm sure I would have felt my heart skip a beat had it been capable of such.

I drew a breath and replied, as nonchalantly as I could, "Oh, hey Tom." Christy's eyebrows shot up in a look of panic. Hell, the only one in the room who didn't seem surprised was Gan. She barely even blinked.

"So..." I tried to think of something to say and drew a complete blank. "What's up?"

"*What's up?* Really?" Sally hissed, throwing me an eye-roll for good measure.

I put my hand over the speaker and replied, "Do you mind? I'm talking here."

"Bill, are you still there?" Tom asked, his voice eerily bereft of emotion.

"Yeah, I'm here. Sorry, got distracted."

"You need to watch that. That's always been one of your problems, the inability to focus."

"Uh...yeah. So, I was calling to ask Ed a question. Can you put him on?"

"I'm afraid not. The others don't want him talking right now."

Oh crap. "The others?"

"Christy's sisters..."

"Okay, then..."

"and the vampires." Oh fuck!

"You need to get away from them, Tom. They're not safe to be around."

"Ironic coming from you."

"I'm well aware, but you know me. I'm your friend."

"Are you?" he asked, his voice growing harsh. "I thought so, Bill, but then you lied to me. You lied to me about her. She's going to kill Christy and you *lied* about her!"

"Relax..."

"Do *not* tell me to relax."

Things were not exactly looking hopeful for a civilized chat. Whatever Christy had subconsciously done, it had turned his brain into a festering pile of angry mush.

"Tom!" Christy yelled, walking over to me. "Whatever you're doing, you need to stop."

"Christy?" he asked over the phone. "You have her?!"

Uh oh.

"It's not like that..."

"It wasn't enough to deceive me. You had to kidnap her too? I swear to God, I'll..."

Sally reached over and snatched the phone from my hand. Before I could protest, she hit the button to end the call.

"What the fuck are you doing?!" I screamed at her. "He's out of his flipping mind and for all we know they have Ed and Sheila. So what do you do? You hang the fuck up on him. What? Are you low on minutes or something?"

"Listen, Sally," Christy said. "I know you don't really like Tom, but…"

Sally just held up a hand and said, "Five…four…three…two…"

RING

"Damn, so close," she remarked. "Watch and learn. I've done a few of these in my day."

I was about to reply with something pithy, but came to the conclusion that I really didn't want to know.

She let the phone ring twice more before answering in her best polite tone, "Hello?"

She had the phone up against her ear, but even so, I could hear Tom ranting and raving, almost incoherently so.

"Bill's busy. He can't come to the phone right now. No, *you* listen, meat-wad. Shut up or we start pulling her fingernails out."

Almost immediately the voice on the other end went silent. Sally smiled and threw us a wink. "Now, what you're going to do is be a good little Happy Meal and put somebody on the line who's not a complete fucktard. Actually, scratch that. Who's there with you?" She listened for a moment then continued, "Put one of the witches on."

I began to catch on. Tom was rapidly becoming a full-fledged, frothing at the mouth psycho, one who held absolutely no sway with any of the parties involved.

Remington, on the other hand, was rational, but would be completely unfazed by our having "kidnapped" Christy. Under normal circumstances, witches are pieces of shit to vampires and vice versa. Once this joint venture was concluded, I had little doubt it would go back to that status quo. Therefore, it reasoned that the only ones who might be willing to negotiate would be Christy's former coven-mates.

Someone else was now speaking to Sally. It sounded like a female voice. I love being right. It was just up to Sally to be able to put a gentle enough spin on things to...

"And why should I give a shit? Go right ahead and pull his arms off for all I care."

Or not.

"What the..." I started, but was shushed by the last person in the room I expected.

"Patience, my love," Gan replied from her seat on the couch. "Your whore has the situation under control." She kept talking, not noticing the finger that Sally quickly shot out at her...or maybe not caring. I had no idea whether that meant the same thing in Mongolian culture as it does here. "I am impressed. She is handling things from a position of strength which we do not have. It is most admirable. You may wish to consider giving her additional duties beyond your pleasure."

Sally's eyes narrowed and she opened her mouth to say something, but the other conversation drew her attention back. "Yeah, I'm still here. I was just enjoying watching the Freewill break your sister's fingers." She put her hand over the receiver and addressed Christy, "Feel free to scream. That never hurts in these types of situations."

* * *

Sally finally hung up, holding the connection just long enough for the other end to catch some cries for mercy that Christy was busy faking.

"Pack of morons," she commented.

"So? What's going on?"

"They want to do a swap."

"Christy for Sheila and Ed?" I asked.

"Not quite. Christy *and* Sheila for Ed."

"What?"

"I know," she replied. "They must think you and him are going steady or something, although I could see how someone could assume that."

"Not that! What do you mean, Ed for Christy and Sheila? I thought they had them both."

"So did I. Imagine my surprise when they said they didn't."

"You didn't sound surprised on the phone," Christy pointed out.

"Never let them see you sweat, sister."

"So if they don't have her, what the fuck happened?"

"No idea," Sally replied. "I figured that asking would tip our hand just a little."

"That makes sense," Christy said. "The vampires wouldn't be out right now, and I'm not sure my sisters could have taken the Icon by themselves, at least not without drawing a lot of unwanted attention."

"I'm assuming you mean by blowing up a lot of shit."

Christy nodded.

"So that still leaves the question of what the hell happened to her."

Gan sat up and cocked her head. "I believe we are about to find out."

I hate when vampires say stuff like that. It's never a good thing. A few moments later, the sound of rapidly approaching sirens confirmed that feeling.

Call me cynical, but I had to assume they weren't here to give us a friendly police escort.

Such Wondrous Places
You Take Me

Straining my ears, I heard the front door downstairs open followed by hurried footsteps running up. A frantic pounding began on the apartment door a few moments later. There was a quick pause as we all took a moment to exchange glances.

"Anyone expecting a package from Fedex?" I asked. "Didn't think so."

I walked to the door and began to open the locks.

"Hold on," Sally cried, racing to her bedroom. A scant second later, she returned with her Desert Eagle. I'd hate to be a door-to-door salesman assigned to her part of town.

"If whoever's there isn't a glowing blonde, duck real fast," she warned.

I was starting to feel a bit panicky about this, but then I noticed Gan still seated, an almost bored expression on her face.

"Relax, Sally," I said, opening the door.

Sheila ran in. Unfortunately, I didn't step aside fast enough and she barreled into me. Heh, in all the excitement I had almost forgotten about that whole Icon thing.

That's okay, though. The subsequent flash of light - followed by my being flung across the room - reminded me quite nicely. I slammed into the wall and bounced right off, landing in a heap on the floor. I had to give Sally credit - this place was constructed solidly.

"Oh my god!" Sheila shrieked. "I'm so sorry, Bill."

"It's alright," I replied, groggily picking myself off the floor. "I'm starting to get used to it." I woozily turned to Sally. "Concrete?"

"Cinderblock," she corrected.

"I'll keep that in mind."

"We need to save Ed!" Sheila gasped, obviously out of breath.

I shook my head to clear it. "We know."

"Are you okay?" Christy asked her, ignoring the fact that I just got slammed into a wall at thirty miles per hour. I tried not to take offense at the oversight.

"I'm fine," she replied. "I just need to catch my breath. There's one small problem, though."

There came the sound of the door being kicked in downstairs. "Let me guess," Sally said. "You brought company?"

"Sorry."

"So much for this being a safe house," Sally remarked. "Get the door. It's reinforced. Should slow them down."

Gan stood up. Her claws extended and her eyes blackened. "Why not simply dispatch them?"

"That kind of goes against us keeping a low profile."

Sally replied, "I think we're already past that. Come on, grab your stuff. We'll take the back stairs."

"I thought you couldn't go outside," Sheila said. "It's still daylight out."

"We're not going out, girlfriend. We're going *down*." I immediately started chuckling. I couldn't help it. "Into the sewer, you fucking perv."

"Sorry."

"Don't be sorry. Just be fast."

* * *

Christy helped me quickly gather mine and Ed's stuff, especially his shotgun. That would be a particularly bad trinket to leave behind for the cops to find (ignoring for a moment the refrigerator full of blood). He'd also no doubt want it once we rescued him.

That is, if he was even still alive, a voice in the back of my head pointed out. No! That was a bad thought. Of course he was still alive. Tom wasn't that far gone. He couldn't be. I refused to believe it.

Thankfully, Sally was right about the door. When she said reinforced, she meant it. It had apparently been designed to keep vampires at bay. It was going to take an entire SWAT team to knock it in...not that I intended to stick around long enough to test that theory.

Sally grabbed a few spare clips of ammo, while Sheila quickly donned her Templar armor and strapped her sword to her side (and yes, it *was* hot). Gan, well, she just stood there looking bored and maybe a little disappointed that I wasn't going to let her dismember the nice policemen. Oh how nice it would be to finally see her boarding a plane back home...although first I had to live long enough to do so.

"We all set?" I asked.

There were nods all around, followed by a large hollow boom against the front door. Guess they had brought up a battering ram. It was time to go.

* * *

We lowered ourselves down the manhole in the basement, sealing it behind us. Eventually the cops would figure out how we had escaped, but by then, we'd be long gone in the warren of tunnels underneath the city.

Gan, Sally and myself were fine in the dark (albeit I could do without the dirty and/or smelly parts), but neither Sheila nor Christy had night vision. Fortunately, Christy had magic on her side. She muttered a quick incantation and a soft glow began to emanate from her. It illuminated the tunnel enough to keep them from breaking their necks.

Sally took a look around, then turned to Sheila, smiling. "Aren't you glad you met Bill?"

She chuckled in return. "Oh I don't know. Some drapes...maybe a scented candle..."

361

"Okay, enough with the jokes," I said, leading the way. "Let's get moving."

"Not that way," Sally corrected. "No way in hell are we leading the cops directly to the office. Let's take the scenic route. Besides which, it'll eat time until it gets dark."

* * *

Sheila filled us in on her *lunch date* as we walked through the dank tunnels, the squeak of rats accompanying us in the dark.

They had stopped at a Greek restaurant for some gyros - note to self: Sheila likes gyros. The attack had been both quick and efficient. Three witches, no doubt the same that had visited Christy the night before, simply walked in the door. It had been Ed who had spotted them, remembering their faces.

It was all over before anyone even knew what had happened. The witches had simultaneously fired a spell, but it hadn't been aimed at Sheila. It landed directly in front of her, exploding out in a concussive wave. Her power had flared up to protect her from harm, but she had still been thrown back by the force of the blast. The rest of the lunch crowd, Ed included, hadn't been so lucky. They had all been knocked instantly unconscious. Sheila had recovered and grabbed a steak knife from the table, but it had been too late. Just as quickly as they had entered, the witches left...but not alone. They grabbed hold of Ed's unconscious form and blinked out in a flash of light.

"So where did the cops come in?" I asked, stepping in something semi-solid that I really hoped was just mud.

"That's why I was so long in getting back. I stuck around to make sure everyone else was all right. Unfortunately, a few of them freaked out and called 911. I think maybe they thought it was a terrorist attack."

"Because a gyro shop is the first place suicide bombers target," Sally commented.

"So you ran?" I asked.

"Not quite," she replied, continuing. "The police were there within minutes. They wanted to take me in for questioning and I...."

"What?"

"I sorta..."

"Kicked the shit out of them?" Sally surmised, a note of approval in her voice. "Nice. Welcome to my world."

"Don't let it get to you," I said. "It's almost impossible to live this kind of lifestyle without committing multiple felonies."

"Yay me. If only mom could see me now." She seemed to consider this for a moment and then asked, "Bill, what about your parents?"

"My parents? They live down in New Jersey, happily spending my inheritance."

"No, I mean do they know?"

"Three words: no fucking way. I get enough shit from them as it is about not having a...well...girlfriend. Heh...anyway, no. Aside from the time I accidentally bit their cat, I try to keep them as far away from the vampire lifestyle as I can."

"You bit their cat?"

"Closest Bill's gotten to any pus..."

"Thank you, Sally. I think we get the picture. Like I said, it was an accident. Let's leave it at that."

* * *

Once the small talk petered out, we got down to business: discussing what needed to be done once we got to the office. Aside from Gan, who could have cared less, we all agreed that saving my roommates was the number one priority. Well, okay, Sally was closer to Gan's attitude with regards to Tom. There was likewise little disagreement on the subject of Remington and his vampires. They needed to either be driven out of town for good or outright eliminated. Even Sheila, the relative newb of the group, didn't have much problem with that. Remington was a dick, after all.

It was in the *hows* where we broke down in disagreement. Gan, easily the most experienced strategist amongst us, favored a full-out frontal assault. She considered the foes ahead of us unworthy of anything more complex. Thinking back over the past year, I had to concede she maybe had a point. Compared to, say, Turd or Alexander, Remington wasn't all that terrifying. Still, a direct assault would be the best and easiest way to get my roommates, not to mention possibly the rest of us, killed. There was also the fact that a lot of Gan's plan seemed to revolve around me gloriously cutting through our enemies like some sort of vampiric lawnmower. She didn't seem to grasp that I wasn't quite the demon beast she had convinced herself I was.

Christy wanted us to pop in then back out via her magic, but even she had to admit it was dicey. We didn't know where or what condition Ed was in. If we weren't quick enough, there was also the possibility of her coven sisters blocking our escape. Personally, I was discouraging that plan because I wasn't too big on her participation to begin with.

"When we get back to the surface, you should go home. You've done enough for us," I said.

"No way," Christy protested. "I caused this. I'm going to fix it."

"We'll bring Tom back. I promise."

"I'm not doubting you, Bill, but you'll need my help."

"We'll be fine, besides..."

"Besides *what*? If you're thinking I'm going to betray..."

"It's not that," I replied. "It's just...well, your...*condition*..."

"That's why you want me to leave?"

Sally and Sheila barely managed to conceal snickers.

"What? Am I the only one thinking of this?"

"I'm only a few weeks along, Bill. It's not like I'm waddling around like an elephant yet."

"Chivalry is not dead," Sheila commented.

"Maybe undead," Sally added, causing all of them to giggle (except maybe Gan). Jeez, try to the do the right thing...

Even Gan had to admit that Christy's power could come in handy. We would still be outnumbered by witches, but she was fresh whereas the others had already been through hell courtesy of us and Gan's merry bunch. I didn't like it, but their arguments were sound.

Great! Now I was endangering an expectant mother. Between that and punching out the old lady yesterday, all I needed was to maybe push a couple of orphans down a flight of stairs and my game of gross negligence BINGO would be complete.

Maybe I should reconsider that course of action Sally and I had mapped out for Sheila. I should probably do it myself...not with her, mind you...just pick an opposite direction and start running. In the long term, it would almost certainly be safer for everyone. It was something to think about, although perhaps after events played out.

At the moment, we had more pressing concerns, such as a kidnapped roommate, a psychotic friend, and a whole building full of people who wanted to kill Sheila (and wouldn't bat an eye at wiping out the rest of us in the process). If we were able to pull this off, it would be a miracle.

Sadly, in that regards, I found my faith a little lacking.

Under New Management

Sometimes the direct approach really is best. Even if it's not the smartest way of doing things, it takes a lot of complexity out of the equation. That might not be the way dudes like Alexander roll, but it helped me keep things straight. What can I say? When it came to games of strategy, I was always more of a checkers guy anyway.

Gan mentioned that she sensed vampires ahead of us in the sewer tunnels which told us they had all of the entrances covered. It wasn't particularly good news, but not surprising either. There was no way they were going to let us get the drop on them, especially since they were in our home court. They'd probably be expecting us to try that route anyway, take out the sentries and fight our way up - only to find ourselves surrounded. Well fuck them. If I was going down in flames, I'd do it my own way.

That didn't mean we had to be complete dumbasses, though.

After a little subterranean reconnaissance, we cautiously surfaced in an alley about half a block away from the office. It wasn't a particularly smart place to come up, considering how packed SoHo was even after sundown. Fortunately, it was a small enough space, with a Goodwill bin at the far end blocking our view from the street. The only ones liable to see us might be an errant wino or two. Hell, that might even be pretty damn funny - to send them off running, screaming about CHUDs surfacing in the Village. Sadly, though, there were no drunks or stoners to be found. The alley was empty.

"Gan, care to check on your people?" I asked, hoping beyond hope that they were in the vicinity. She was a fucking nutcase, but she was on my side at the moment. I could deal with her beloved bullshit if it meant having a goon squad of assassins backing us up.

She closed her eyes and inhaled deeply through her nose. She repeated the action three times, then sighed.

"Well?"

"Regrettably, they must still be occupied. I do not sense them nearby. They are not within the city limits."

"Maybe my sisters won," Christy offered.

"I think not," Gan replied evenly. "Still, it is admirable they have managed to elude their fate for this long. They will be remembered as respected foes."

That didn't sit too well with Christy, but I put a hand on her shoulder to comfort her. It served the secondary purpose of potentially stopping her if she decided it would be a good time to vaporize Gan. At the very least, I preferred she wait until the bullshit ahead of us was finished. After that, she could have fun blasting away for all I cared.

"Okay, let's all calm down here. We need to focus," I said, trying to be the voice of reason amongst this motley crew. "We're here to save Ed and Tom."

"What if your friend does not wish to be saved?" Gan asked.

"He doesn't get a vote. That's my call. If need be, we might need to neutralize him, but that's it." Heh, I sounded like a character straight out of a Tom Clancy novel.

"Snapping his neck would neutralize him without killing him," Gan rather unhelpfully pointed out.

"No. He comes out in one piece. Don't cross me on this."

Much to my surprise, she didn't just outright laugh at my somewhat toothless command. Instead, the terrible little tyke inclined her head and gave me a big smile. "As you wish, Freewill."

Gah! I was playing right into her hands by taking charge. Jesus Christ, I really was fucked no matter what I did.

Okay, I needed to focus. The time to curl up in a little ball and whine about Gan would come later.

"Either way, we need to remember that neither of them are Remington's main focus here. They're just using Ed to draw Sheila out. The Icon is going to be their main target. Always keep that in mind and don't let her out of your sight."

Sheila raised a bemused eyebrow, and I could almost immediately feel pinpricks of sweat break out on my brow. Talk about unnecessary distractions.

"Any problem with that?" I asked, doing my best to feign a sense of authority.

"I can take care of myself, you know," she said.

"I know, but we're not taking any chances. Trust me - even the most straightforward dealings with vampires can turn into gigantic clusterfucks pretty damn easily."

"What about you, Bill?"

"He's used to clusterfucks," Sally replied.

"No, I mean I got the impression they were after him too."

"Not the same thing," I said. "They're going to want me alive as a trophy for the Draculas."

"Draculas?" Sheila cocked her head to the side. Goddamn, she was cute.

"The First Coven...our ruling body."

"For now," Gan added, drawing a quizzical glance from Sally. *sigh*

"Any questions?" No one responded to my mostly rhetorical inquiry. Thank goodness - I had absolutely zero answers to anything they might ask. Hell, I was barely cognizant of what day it was.

Sheila, Gan, and Christy led the way out of the alley, weapons concealed as best they could. Despite it being *my* plan, I held back a few steps and motioned for Sally to do the same.

"Not bad, Bill." She kept her voice low so that the others, save Gan, wouldn't be able to overhear. "You almost had me convinced you were actually in charge of things."

"Thanks, Sally. I need you to..."

"Keep an eye on your girlfriend? Yeah, I garnered that."

"No," I replied, much to even my own surprise. "I want you to watch out for Christy."

"Really? That's new. Wasn't too long ago you wouldn't have shed any tears tripping over her corpse."

"Things change."

"Who'd a thought you a softie for kids?"

I dropped my voice to a bare whisper. "I guess so...at least ones that don't want to marry me."

"I'm impressed Bill. I don't say that often...nor am I planning to start, but I am. It probably doesn't mean much, but just for the record, I hope things work out for your gal pal."

So did I.

As we turned to follow, something cold and wet hit the back of my neck. The supernatural storm had started up again, but this time snow was falling. So intent had I been on the mission ahead, I hadn't noticed that the temperature had dropped. Large white flakes fell all around us.

I took a look around. "Heh, kind of reminds me of Canada."

"Me too," Sally replied. "Unfortunately, we both know how that worked out."

* * *

I led the way to the entrance of the building where the office was housed. It was an active business space, home to a few legit companies - non-vampire related, of course. Past sundown, however, we mostly had the place to ourselves. Thank goodness for the rush-hour exodus. Usually we tried to be courteous neighbors, regardless. After all, despite vampires having certain back-alley deals with the authorities - stuff that kept the eyes of the law mostly turned elsewhere - there was no need to call undue attention to ourselves.

I doubted that would be the case tonight. The office was well insulated against sound, to muffle any errant screams that rang out, but I had a feeling that things had potential to get a whole lot noisier. I felt bad for any workaholics who decided to stay late this evening.

I was certain there were eyes watching us from above as we entered through the front door. No doubt they were wondering what we were up to. Hell, so was I.

Once inside, we noticed the place was deathly still. There was no security guard stationed in the lobby, a status quo Sally made sure was maintained. She once told me that in the years since the coven had rented out their floors, there had been only one attempt at burglary - an attempt which had ended *very* badly for the would-be thieves. She considered it her token attempt at being a good neighbor to the other tenants.

Even so, there should have been some cleaning crews milling about at that hour. A sinking feeling hit my gut. I had a hunch that Remington and his crew hadn't bothered to wait for the building to clear out at quitting time. That wasn't good. Vampires have connections, but there's simply only so much that can be covered up without questions being asked.

I pushed it out of my mind for now. If that had happened, anyone there was long past our helping. As for the rest, well, Sally could handle any real estate issues that arose.

Goddamn it! I paused for a moment and let this sink in. Had I really given almost no consideration to the potential lives lost in such a massacre? Was I that far gone already? Maybe Tom wasn't so off base with his accusations. It was something to ponder once this was all over and done with.

We considered the stairs. It was probably the far more sensible choice, but I opted for the elevator primarily because of Christy...although I kept that to myself, as she would have probably protested. Well screw her. I had enough on my conscience as it was.

Speaking of Christy, though, I actually found myself damn glad she was with us. I'd tried to warn her off earlier, but now realized her presence was probably the only thing keeping us from being blasted apart where we stood - her sisters' influence upon the situation no doubt. Considering what happened in Westchester, Remington no doubt knew he needed the witches' help. That meant playing by their rules.

Thankfully, we had some rules of our own to spice up their little game.

Free For All

The elevator dinged at our floor.

"Show time," I said to my three companions, hefting Ed's shotgun. Its weight was comforting. Perhaps it was time for me to get one...assuming I didn't manage to shoot myself first.

Sheila drew her sword and Sally brandished her massive handgun, which she immediately pointed at Christy's head.

"The safety's on, isn't it?" Christy chuckled nervously.

"Best not to ask questions you don't want the answer to."

The elevator opened and before us stood the hall leading up to the double doors of the office. It, too, was empty.

"Beginning to feel unloved here," I commented.

"You shouldn't," a quiet voice whispered from the opposite side of Christy. The only person standing there happened to be the one holding a broadsword out in front of her.

"What was that?" I asked. There's nothing wrong with my vampire ears, but I needed to make sure my imagination wasn't playing tricks on me.

"Focus, Bill," Sally hissed.

"But..."

"Eyes front, mind clear, mister!"

"Yes ma'am." Goddamn it. We needed to get this shit over with and fast. It was high time Sheila and I had a good long talk with absolutely no bullshit between us...which of course was an easy thing to plan up until the point it actually happened.

Oh well, maybe I'd get lucky and not survive.

We walked up to the doors unhindered. I reached out to grasp the handle, but stopped as a little bit of inspiration hit me. Fuck it! If it was good enough for a John Woo film, it's good enough for me.

Putting my vampiric strength to use, I raised my foot and kicked the doors. They flew inward with the sound of wood splintering. Thank goodness. How embarrassing would that have been had they not moved?

"Slick," Sally commented before falling quiet again.

A phalanx of vampires stood awaiting us on either side of the doorway. I'm not the best at reading people, especially undead killers, but I could have sworn there were at least a few nervous glances amongst their number. I could dig that.

It wasn't hard to imagine why. I, the Freewill - (supposedly) destined to lead our forces against our ancient enemies - stood on one side. Sheila, the equally legendary Icon - defender of the human race and prophesied destroyer of the Magi - guarded the other.

Between us stood our prisoner, while Sally brought up the rear - her ridiculously large handgun making up for her non-legendary status. Talk about over-compensating.

All of the office-related furniture had been removed from the room. The space before us appeared to be set up as if in anticipation of a battle.

"Son of a bitch," Sally grumbled. She had put a lot of work into the office, and no doubt this was more than enough to convince her that Remington needed an extreme amount of killing.

Speaking of the devil, he stood about ten paces in front of us. Three witches, obviously the same that had visited Christy, stood to his left. Tom brandished his own firearm on the right. I'm not a gun nut, but I could have sworn it was the same one Sally had used at Sheila's workplace. Guess Remington had been going through her stuff. No sense of privacy with some people. The pistol didn't make as big of a hole as Sally's favorite piece, but it had the advantage of being quick - as well as not knocking someone on their ass the second they tried to fire it.

Either way, though, that didn't really matter. Tom was armed against us, and from the look on his face, he wasn't averse to using it. Goddamn it. If we got out of this alive, I was buying the fucking idiot a tinfoil hat to protect against this happening again.

Tom's eyes filled with worry at the sight of Christy, then met mine. It was all I could do not to look away. I had never seen such a look of pure unbridled hatred on my friend's face. Not even that time when we were in fifth grade and I accidentally stepped on his *Lava Lord* action figure. It practically broke my heart. Even if he was out of his fucking mind right now, I nevertheless made a promise to myself to make things right with him.

Movement behind Remington revealed more vamps and someone else. I had little doubt who. We were there for a prisoner swap and without some prisoners the whole thing was a little pointless.

Remington took a step forward.

"That's far enough," I said. I gulped and took a deep breath. My next words were so *not me*, that I wasn't even sure I'd be able to do it with a straight face. "Another step and the witch's brains will be decorating the walls."

In response to my threat, Sally pulled the slide back on her gun with a click. It was meant to send a message and it did...even to me. I had to remind myself that she was a cool character. She had to be. One false move and Christy would have nothing but a fine red mist where her head used to be

"You bastard!" Tom growled, raising his own weapon. I had never seen him pick up any ranged weapon more lethal than a paintball gun, so it was doubtful he'd be anywhere close to a dead shot with it. He probably had as much chance of hitting himself as he did me. Even so, I really didn't care to test that theory.

"Please, Tom," Christy whimpered so realistically that I couldn't be entirely sure she was acting. Hopefully she wouldn't decide to hedge her bets on the side with the number advantage. She had to know that wouldn't end well for her or Tom. Once their mission was accomplished, I wouldn't put it past Remington to take advantage of Decker's weakened former coven and wipe them out. Vampires weren't at war with the mages, but one less player on the battlefield wouldn't exactly hurt our odds.

Remington held up a hand at him. "I can assure you, everything is well under control."

Tom's eyes nervously played between us, but he finally lowered the gun.

"There, that's better now. There's no reason for there to be bloodshed."

Yeah right. That was such a load of bullshit I'd probably need to clean my shoes just from standing so near him.

"Let's get this over with," I said. "The witch for the human."

"Nice try, Freewill," Remington replied. "But the deal was the human for the witch *and* the Icon."

"Maybe I'm altering the deal," I said, dropping my voice a few octaves. "Pray I don't alter it any further."

I heard a sigh behind me...Sally. Jeez, she just couldn't throw me a bone, could she?

Behind Remington, the barest of smiles appeared on Tom's face before once more being buried in whatever alien thoughts were clouding his mind. He was still in there somewhere. I just hoped the others had seen it too. I really preferred he not get utterly annihilated during whatever was about to transpire. I had no idea how things would play out aside from one little detail: it would most likely be violent.

"The witch is meaningless to me," Remington said, eliciting worried glances from the ones beside him, "although not to my allies. Still, the Icon is our main quarry. The deal is both for one. If the Icon steps forward quietly and unarmed, I might even be willing to let details of your treachery slip from my report."

"You're too kind."

"No, I'm really not. For the life of me I couldn't understand why you would choose to side with this creature," he said, dismissing Sheila as little more than some animal. To say it pissed me off would be an understatement. "But then I was enlightened."

"Huh? What do you mean?" I asked, somewhat confused. The only one from his group who had known Sheila and what she meant to me was Decker, and he was currently pushing up daisies in upstate New York.

"All in good time. First things first, Freewill. Speaking of treachery, I'm curious. Where is that other one, the little vampire who came to your rescue up north?"

"She didn't come to my rescue." I muttered. "Well, not much anyway."

"The details matter not. What does is that she is a traitor to the vampire race, even more so than you. I shall see her punished for more reasons than one." His hand moved to his midsection, where Gan had none-so-gently eviscerated him. It was obviously healed by now - Remington wasn't exactly a child by our standards - but most vamps didn't exactly approach such matters with an attitude leaning toward forgiveness.

"She's dead," I said flatly, a small part of me enjoying the wishful thinking that accompanied the statement. "After you left, the surviving Templars rallied against her. They killed one another."

Remington raised an eyebrow Spock-style. "Well now, that is truly fascinating. I'm utterly surprised to hear it, especially considering the news to the contrary I recently received."

"News to the..."

Remington turned and spoke over his shoulder. "Would you care to come in, Dread Stalker? Bring your new minion with you."

Dread Stalker?! Fuck! It figured. Leave it to a holdover from Jeff's days to dick me up the ass.

* * *

Dread Stalker would have been bad enough. A few words from that asshole and all our lies from the very start would come tumbling down like a house of cards. Don't get me wrong - a small part of me couldn't blame him. We had kept him in the dark, and he would have obviously thought we should be out hunting the Icon like good little vampire drones. Then again, if he had just followed fucking orders like he was supposed to, this wouldn't be an issue. The asshole was supposed to be out of town.

"You've betrayed us, Freewill," Douche Stalker said, entering the room. "I believed in you. You killed Night Razor and now this." I didn't really hear him, though. He could have been professing his love for me and asking for my hand in marriage for all I knew. My focus was entirely on who was by his side.

Benny entered alongside him, a brand new set of fangs protruding from his mouth and the glazed look in his eyes indicative of a vamp under compulsion. Motherfucker! The assholes had even stolen our trick.

Sheila gasped, "Ben? What did you do to him?"

Remington chuckled in response. "Do? We've given him a great gift, my dear. I can assure you, he's quite happy with his new station in life. Why, his first act upon awakening was to enthusiastically tell us everything he knew about you, Ms. Sheila O'Connell, daughter of Marsha from Syracuse."

Oh shit!

"You son of a..."

"Tsk tsk, I wasn't finished. You needn't worry. Your family is of no consequence to us...for the moment. As for Benjamin here, fret not. He has been well treated. We even rewarded him for his newfound loyalty."

"Rewarded?"

"Yes, with the flesh of the living."

Remington nodded and a few of the vamps behind him stepped aside, revealing Ed. Now it was my turn to let out a gasp. My friend was on his knees, his eyes rolled back in his head. That wasn't what caused my breath to catch, however. On the side of his neck, still dripping blood, was a fresh wound...a vampire bite - one that I had little doubt was made far less carefully than the nip Sally had given him just days earlier.

As cool as I tried to play it, I couldn't keep a look of shock from immediately appearing on my face.

"So sorry, Freewill," Remington cooed, "but you know how famished the freshly risen can be. Why, there was simply no stopping him."

I had no idea what to do or say, so was surprised as anyone by the words that popped out of my mouth. "Nobody kills this asshole except for me."

Remington, for his part, appeared slightly less than terrified. "If you had only taken that attitude when and where you were supposed to, this wouldn't have been necessary. You have no one save yourself to blame. Now, I repeat what I asked earlier. Where is that little urchin? Don't bother lying. Benjamin here was quite happy to spill his guts when he was finished spilling your friend's. We know she still lives. So where is she? Hiding in the stairwell? Perhaps hoping the back entrance isn't guarded? Maybe she's crawling through the ducts even as we speak, thinking perhaps we were that easy to sneak up on." He flashed me his long canines in a sneer. "My men are trained killers, you amateurish fool. What possible course of action did you think we wouldn't consider?"

"The windows."

"What..."

CRASH Wow, couldn't have planned that better if I'd tried. Gan burst through one of the plate glass windows behind Remington's men almost exactly on cue, no doubt a result of her superb vampire hearing. It had been her suggestion to do the human fly impersonation. It wasn't the most subtle thing from the street, even with the storm outside, but it was the perfect cover against being spied from inside of the building.

In the time it took those thoughts to be processed, three of Remington's men collapsed into piles of dust, a result of her claws tearing through necks and abdomens like they were tissue paper. Note to self: don't tick off Gan.

She wasn't finished, though. Before anyone else, ourselves included, could react, Gan screamed out something in Chinese. Under other circumstances, it would have been complete gibberish to me, but she sent it out as a mass compulsion. The act of doing so is partially psychic, so my brain filled in any gaps my ears didn't understand.

"*SURRENDER! ON YOUR KNEES, LIKE THE PIGS YOU ARE!!*"

I only had a moment to consider that her order didn't make much sense. Did pigs even have knees? I'm immune to the mind control portion of compulsions, but they still ring in my head like a fucking gong. I was momentarily staggered by the force of the compulsion, but I was easily the least affected...at least of the vamp crowd.

Nearly the entire population of the room dropped their weapons and kneeled as commanded. Unfortunately, that included Sally. Her gun clanked as she dropped it and obeyed. On the bright side, at least it didn't go off. It would've been just my luck to have the back of my knees blown off.

Sadly, that was one consequence I had forgotten about when we had planned Gan's entrance. Compulsions can be a focused thing, or sent out as a mass effect - kind of like a principal addressing a school over the PA system. Sadly, at least as far as I'm aware, they can't be both. You send it out to the entire room and the entire room will be knocked on their asses. No selective channeling there.

I shook my head to clear it and surveyed the scene before me. Hands suddenly grasped my shoulders. I spun, almost decking the source out of surprise, but thankfully held myself in check. It was Christy using me as support, the compulsion having gotten through even her defenses.

Of my group, only I was left unaffected. Wait, scratch that. I looked past Christy and saw that Sheila stood there looking no more confused than if someone had farted in the room and not admitted to it. Was it possible her powers shielded her from vampiric compulsion too? It made sense. Icons would probably be considered much less of a threat if someone could just command them to jump off a cliff. I locked eyes with her and she gave me a quick thumbs-up.

Most of Remington's men were down. Dread Stalker and Benny were likewise kneeling. Tom had been knocked off his feet and he sat with a dazed look on his face. Christy's sisters were less affected, much like Christy herself. They looked shaken, but otherwise would have their wits back amongst them shortly. The only one of their number who seemed to be holding his own, unfortunately, was Remington himself. Oh shit, he must have been older than I thought.

His lips pulled back in a snarl.

"*IGNORE THE LITTLE TRAMP!!*"

Whoa! It hit me with a force equal to Gan's. It had a ripple effect amongst the vampires in the room. Their eyes immediately cleared and they began to rise. I put my arm around Christy as the shock jolted her.

"*BACK ON YOUR KNEES!! OBEY ME!!*" Gan replied, raising her voice.

"*KILL HER!!*" came the counter order.

Jesus Christ, it was a fucking compulsion battle. I hadn't seen one of those before. Just for the record, I really hope to never see one again. My head pounded from the sheer power of their exchange. Fuck me! I was going to need an industrial sized bottle of Tylenol after this thing was over.

They continued with it, each one trying to overpower the other. The vampires in the room looked like jack-in-the-boxes, alternately rising to defend Remington and dropping to their knees before Gan.

Christy held her head and sobbed from the force of the continued assault. Her coven-sisters had likewise been knocked for a loop. They were all practically falling over each other, trying and failing to mount a defense. That was nothing compared to Tom, though. He was out cold, a thin trickle of blood dribbling from his ears. That was probably for the best. I peered past him toward Ed. Sadly, my other friend was still out of it. I feared the worst. If I remembered my own turning correctly, his heart was probably slowing down even as that thought hit my head.

We needed to end this status quo. Fortunately for us, we had the Icon on our side.

"Enough of this!" She stepped forward and flung her sword across the room at Remington, channeling all her rage at the target most deserving of it. For most of us, this would be an utter embarrassment. Swords are unwieldy. Hell, for most people, even a throwing knife would go clattering harmlessly off into a corner somewhere, causing no more harm than to the thrower's ego.

Not so for Sheila. The blade flew through the air - end over end on a course straight toward its intended target. Holy shit, she was badass.

Sadly, Remington saw it too.

"PROTECT ME!!"

He smiled as he sent out the compulsion. Unlike the others, I could sense this one was focused.

The effect was immediate.

Benny launched himself obediently in front of Remington just as the broadsword finished crossing the distance.

"No!" Sheila cried, but it was in vain. The sword impaled him neatly through the chest. The shock of dying, for good this time, must have cleared the compulsion from his head. Even as he disintegrated he raised his hand and made the sign of the cross over his own forehead - finishing just as his body exploded into a shower of dust. The poor bastard. He had been an asshole, but he deserved better.

The sword, with nothing left holding it, landed with a clank at Remington's feet.

"You monster!" Sheila screamed and launched herself in his direction.

Things were getting out of hand, no doubt something Remington was counting on. Thankfully I remembered the plan and still had enough of my wits about me. Being mindful of her powers, I grabbed Sheila's cloak before she could take more than a few steps, and yanked her backwards - sending her off balance. Even so, my hand got a quick sizzle for my troubles.

Before things could spiral further out of control, I turned to Christy.

"Are you still with us?"

Her eyes refocused and she gave a quick nod.

"Do it!"

* * *

On the way over, through scenic underground New York, I had considered the spell the witches had used to kidnap Ed. It had sounded like the metaphysical equivalent of a stun grenade. I had asked Christy if it were something that could be cast by just one mage, or if it required multiple hands - much like vaporizing the loft had. She had immediately gotten my drift.

Now, in the middle of the melee, she stepped in front of me, still wobbly but determined. Raising her arms, she uttered a quick chant. A moment later, a concussive wave of pure energy exploded out from her in three directions. Sally, Sheila, and I were the only ones spared the effect.

Of our enemies, only Remington saw it coming in time to react. He tried to leap back, hoping to avoid the blast, but was a moment too slow. It caught him mid-air, sending him ass over teakettle to crash into the far wall - leaving a nice sized dent in it. Good. I found myself hoping it hurt.

All the rest, Gan included, were bowled over as if an invisible freight train had plowed into them. There was no helping her, but she knew to expect it. The others, though, hadn't considered that maybe, just maybe, Christy wasn't on their side.

The effort cost her, though, and she stumbled. Fortunately, my vampire reflexes were up to snuff and I caught her before she could hit the ground.

She blinked a few times and caught her breath. As I helped her to her feet, she said, "That was everything I had. It won't last long, though."

"It'll have to be enough," I replied, quickly turning to the rest. "Sally, you take care of Tom..." Sheila stepped forward, but I grabbed her arm. My hand immediately sparked, white flame engulfing it. Fuck me! I pulled back, trying to keep from crying in the process. Fortunately it got her attention. "You get Ed. I think he needs your help most of all."

"But..."

"Revenge is later," I said. "Rescue comes first."

That snapped her out of it. She gritted her teeth, but nodded.

"Christy, wait by the door," I continued. "Lord help me, but I've gotta grab Gan."

* * *

Sheila kept to her part of the plan, but that still didn't stop her from throwing a vicious kick at one of Remington's men as she walked past. She really was a girl after my own heart.

Sally retrieved her gun - gotta have priorities, I guess - then raced over to Tom. She muttered a quick, "Dumbass," under her breath, but otherwise did as asked. She lifted him up and tossed him over her shoulder like a sack of potatoes. It was good enough. Alive was the priority, gentle was not.

Gan was already starting to shake off the effect of Christy's blast. That meant Remington wouldn't be far behind. No time to waste. I picked up her diminutive form, ignoring her groggy whisper of, "Greetings, beloved," lest I think better of things and just leave her crazy ass behind.

Christy was waiting for us. She was still shaky, but appeared to have regained her composure following the frappe treatment her brain had received during the compulsion tug-o-war. Everyone had retrieved their intended targets. Sheila struggled a little with Ed, lacking our vampire-born strength, but fortunately he wasn't a particularly large guy. Double fortunate was that he hadn't completed the transformation yet. Otherwise, he would be a lot lighter (but much hotter) in her grasp.

"Time to vacate the premises."

Had we more time and resources, I might have suggested a mad staking party before leaving, but I doubted we'd get too far before a defense was mounted.

Speaking of staking, Sheila was missing something important. "You forgot your sword."

"Oh shit!" she replied, but then glanced toward Ed and shrugged. We were out of time and she knew it.

The elevator wasn't there waiting for us, but I wouldn't have wanted to try it anyway. With us holding all the cards, it would be a no brainer for our enemies to snap the cables. The ensuing plummet wouldn't (hopefully) kill me, Sally, or Gan, but it would almost certainly finish off the non-vamps. We made a run for the stairwell instead.

Immediately upon opening it, voices floated up from below.

"Do not let them escape!"

Fuck! We'd have the high ground against whoever was below, but all they needed to do was stall us long enough for the others to wake up and box us in. With Gan out of it and Christy's batteries still recharging, I didn't like those odds. Goddamn it. Remington had outmaneuvered us after all.

"The roof," Gan slurred from my shoulder. "We can leap to the next building over...carry the humans with us."

Well maybe *she* could. I wasn't quite so sure my legs were up to the task. There was also Sheila to take into account. None of us were picking her up, at least not without suffering the last sunburn we'd ever experience. Still, it was worth a try. At the very least we might be able to box Remington's people in at the top of the stairwell. That would give us a fighting chance to figure out a way to escape.

The good thing was that the office wasn't exactly situated in the tallest building in Manhattan. Unfortunately, it was tall enough and my coven's floors weren't anywhere near the top. But hey, what's a nice brisk hike when one of your group is pregnant and the rest are lugging dead weight?

Fortunately, Gan snapped out of her daze only two floors later. The downside was that Remington was probably on the move again as well. She wanted to bring up the rear, and I was tempted to take her up on the offer. However, I knew her temper, having seen it in action. Once she got pissed, she stayed that way. She'd most likely head down to try and take on the entire group single-handedly. Don't get me wrong, I gave her even odds at pulling it off, but it struck me as a potentially lethal idea to separate our group...especially if she failed.

Being that she was by far the fastest, I sent her ahead up the stairs instead. If there was anyone above us, she could take them out. If not, it would give her a few extra minutes to scout out the roof situation.

That being done, I took Ed from Sheila, lightening her load so that she didn't run the risk of falling behind. I'm no hero. I won't stake my life on the whole *all of us get out or none of us do* stratagem, but that didn't mean I wasn't going to try. Gan aside, perhaps, I didn't consider any of our number to be expendable. My conscience from this whole affair was muddied enough. I didn't want any further tragedy weighing it down.

By the time we reached the rooftop, Christy looked like she was ready to puke...not an ideal outcome considering she was the vanguard of our upwardly mobile group. Fortunately, she managed to refrain from raining magical stomach nuggets down on us. I could only imagine what Sally would have said at that. Stab her, burn her, or beat her and the reactions were tolerable. Mess up her look, though, and...well, I'd sooner take my chances surrendering to Remington.

Gan waited for us at the top. As the last of us exited the stairwell, she moved to guard the door. I was about to ask if she could perhaps do something to jam it shut, but she was way ahead of me. She snapped off the handle on the inside of the door, slammed it closed and grabbed hold of the frame on either side of it. I was tempted to ask what she was doing, but then I heard the squeal of metal. Hot damn! In a move straight out of a comic book, she bent the frame in, deforming it enough so that it would be near impossible to open without breaking through. It wouldn't stop our pursuers for long, but it would give us a few minutes.

I took a look around. The snow storm had intensified since we had last been outside. It looked like blizzard conditions were settling in, coupled - of course - with the occasional flash of unnaturally colored lightning. There was at least one plus, though. Whatever happened up there would be difficult for outsiders to see. It wasn't much, but at least we wouldn't end up on the eleven o'clock news.

My oh-so-important check on the weather done, I turned to bark out orders to my group.

"Sally, you cover the door with Gan. Feel free to give anyone who knocks some fifty-caliber foreplay."

"My favorite kind," she purred.

"Sheila," I said, gently laying Ed's still form down on the cold wet rooftop. "Can you..."

"Already on it," she replied, kneeling by his side. She removed her cloak and placed it over him to try and keep him warm. Hopefully her healing touch wouldn't be too late.

"Christy, can you...I don't know...*fix* Tom somehow?"

"Yes, but not here. It's going to take time."

"Fuck. Nothing you can do in the short term?"

"I don't know. Maybe a big enough shock would clear his head temporarily, but I can't be sure."

"We should kill the human," Gan said emotionlessly. "He will only serve to betray us."

"Don't start," I growled, before turning back to Christy, partially to make sure she wasn't about to blast the little psycho. "Leave him be. If we can't take care of it here, then don't try waking him up."

Orders given, I took a few seconds to scan the nearby rooftops. Nothing was even close to level with ours. It was either a fifty foot climb up to the next or an even bigger drop on the other side. Motherfucker!

I walked back over to Christy. "Think you can maybe *apparate* us out of here?"

"I keep telling you it's not called that."

"Sorry, Hermoine. Fine, teleport, transport, whatever the fuck."

She thought for a moment, then shook her head. "I might be able to send myself. *Maybe* I can take one other person with me, but it's a risk either way. I'm still kinda shaky."

Remembering an early scene from *Star Trek the Motion Picture*, I shuddered. "Okay, catch your breath. We'll save that option for last. If need-be, we can..."

"Bill!" Sheila cried. I turned to find her with two fingers pressed to Ed's still oozing neck. My heart sank as I knew what she was about to say.

"His heart...it stopped beating."

Destiny's Red-Headed Stepchild

O h god, no! "Sally!"

She was there in an instant, leaving Gan to guard the doorway alone. Kneeling, she examined Ed.

"He's started changing," she said. It was always hard to tell with Sally, but I could have sworn there was a look of worry in her eye. Maybe she had taken more than a casual liking to him after all.

I turned to Sheila. "Can you help him?"

For perhaps the first time since we had reconnected, there was a look of actual doubt in her eye. "I...I'm not sure."

"Leave him, beloved," Gan called over, keeping her eyes on the door in front of her. It wouldn't be long now. My sensitive vampire ears could hear pounding on the stairs. They were coming. "He shall wake up in darkness and be one of us."

I thought about that. She was right. It wasn't necessarily the end for Ed. Still, I considered my current life. I at least had the advantage of being immune to vampire compulsion. Ed would be easily controlled. Sure, I might do it a few times just to dick with him, but it would only be for laughs. Other vamps didn't have quite that sense of humor. I didn't want that life for him. There was also his waking state to think of. Some took the transition to vampire better than others. There was a chance Ed could rise up completely feral. If so, that could end badly for a lot of us.

I opened my mouth to voice my opinion, but Sally spoke first.

"Can you try?"

I opened my eyes wide, and she met my glance. "He'd make a shitty vampire anyway. It's much more fun to lord it over him as a human." She tried to make her voice sound casual, but I could tell it was an act. I smiled at her and, to my surprise, she returned the expression. Gotta love sharing a moment. I just wished it would happen at times that didn't involve imminent death.

"Please do what you can," I said to Sheila.

"I don't know, Bill..."

"I do." I locked eyes with her. "I once said I believed in you. I meant it. I *still* do."

Now it was her turn to smile. God, she was radiant. Forget burning at her touch - the look on her face was enough to make me melt. Once more, I found myself cursing fate that times like these only seem to happen when I'm just about to get a new asshole torn.

A soft glow began to emanate from her. It wasn't very bright, but I could feel her power even from where I knelt. Hefting Ed's shotgun, I nodded to Sally and stood up. The most we could do there was get barbecued if her powers flared. We would be best served standing guard with Gan. We could give Sheila a few extra minutes to work her magic, while at the same time welcoming Remington's goons with a twenty-one gun salute.

* * *

We didn't have to wait long. Footsteps sounded on the other side of the door. A moment later, there was a loud thud, followed by a fist shaped dent appearing on our end.

"You know how to handle that piece?" Sally asked.

"Nope, but how hard could it be?"

Even amidst the impending danger, she was able to spare me an eye-roll. Nice to know some things never changed.

A sharp sizzling noise caught my ears from behind. I quickly panned my head and saw...well, I'm not sure. Sheila had her hands pressed to Ed's neck, but was having a hard time at it as his body had begun to convulse. Christy left Tom's side to come over and try to hold him down. I was tempted to help her, but more of our foes hammered the door. It began to bow inward.

Gan's claws extended, ready to meet the oncoming rush.

"Stand back," I warned, raising the shotgun.

"You need not explain the obvious, beloved," she replied. "I merely prepare for when they get past you." Gotta love her confidence in me.

"Sally?"

"Wait for it. Let them get nice and tightly packed...now!"

* * *

The poor door - vampires pounding on it from one side, us blasting away with heavy ordinance on the other. It never stood a chance. Pity it wasn't the one we were trying to beat in this fight, otherwise this would have been a cakewalk.

Just for the record, I really need to take some shooting lessons - or stay the hell away from guns altogether.

After I got used to the recoil from Ed's shotgun, my first blast doing little more than blowing a chunk off the corner of the door, I quickly emptied it - firing shot after shot, feeling like a badass as I pumped the chamber. Of course, that resulted in a big hole in the door, maybe one or two vamps taken out of the mix, and a dry click as I realized I didn't grab any spare ammo when we left the safe house.

"Just like a man to blow his load quickly," Sally commented, continuing to squeeze off tightly controlled shots.

"Blow this," I snapped, swinging the gun around and driving the butt of it into the face of the next vamp who tried to get through. Unfortunately that didn't end quite as awesomely as I had hoped. A hand shot through the broken door, grabbed the stock and shattered it. Damn. Ed was gonna be pissed when he...if he...oh crap!

In between the thunderous report of Sally's mini-cannon, I turned and shouted over to Sheila, "How is he?"

She looked up, tears in her eyes. "I don't know."

* * *

Gan stepped up to the door and started kicking ass, giving Sally a chance to slam home a fresh clip.

"Go check on him. We've got this," she said.

"Are you..."

"Go!"

That got me moving.

Sheila and Christy were dragging Ed over to the side, making sure he was out of harm's way at least for the first assault.

"What happened?" I asked, fearing the worst.

"We're not sure," Christy said.

"I put my hands on his neck, but it wasn't like last time. His skin started smoking and there were sparks."

"Is he...?"

"No," Sheila replied, still sounding uncertain. "I was afraid that might happen, or that maybe he was too far gone, but then he took a breath and his heart started beating again."

I let out a breath of my own, feeling my eyes getting misty. "So he's going to be all right?"

"Like I said, I don't know. He's still out cold and then there's *this*." She indicated Ed's throat. Gone was the wound, but what was left in its place wasn't exactly inspiring confidence. An ugly burn in the shape of Sheila's hand covered the side of his neck.

"What the hell?"

"No idea."

"Me neither," Christy said. "I don't think we're going to know for sure until he wakes up."

"*DROP YOUR WEAPON!!*"

Oh shit! Remington was doing it again. The compulsion didn't wash over me as loudly as some of the earlier ones had. It had been focused...Sally!

I spun just as Gan commanded, "*DO NOT LISTEN TO HIM!!*" but it was too late. Remington's command had done its job. The distraction allowed his men to pour through the small opening. Three of them tackled Gan. She immediately threw two off, but she couldn't fight them and continue guarding the door.

"Christy, please watch over Ed."

"I can..."

"I know," I replied. "Blast anyone who gets too close."

Sheila stepped toward me. "I'm with you. Don't even think of telling me to stay back."

"Wouldn't dream of it," I said with a smile. If I was going out, I could think of nobody else I'd rather have at my side. "Let's show them what legends are made of."

* * *

Perhaps that last line was a tad arrogant. Apparently, the first thing a legend is made of is their big mouth. I caught one square on the kisser from one of Remington's goons. It hurt, but didn't put me down. If I had learned nothing else from my short tenure as a vampire, it was how to take a punch. Luckily, the vamp who hit me wasn't all that strong. I had taken worse.

He followed up with his left, brandishing one of those silver stakes, but I saw it coming, caught his arm and used his own momentum to swing him around, right into Sheila.

He fell into her waiting arms which she used to grasp the sides of his head. The white glow enveloped her body and within a moment - *poof*.

"Holy fuck," I cried. "Remind me not to piss you off."

"I'm a woman. You should know that already," she replied with a laugh before launching herself into the fray.

I grabbed the stake from the recently dusted vamp and followed her, taking a quick survey of our odds.

They didn't look great. Five of us versus a dozen or so vamps and three witches. ***BANG!*** Make that two witches. Sally had recovered her weapon and used it to ventilate a four inch hole in the chest of one of Christy's former coven sisters.

Speaking of which, I looked back over my shoulder to check on our magic-using ally. She was as good as her word. She had surrounded herself and Ed with a purplish force field or some such. One vampire threw himself into it and was flung back as if from a catapult.

That would do nicely. Hopefully we could handle the rest.

I came up behind a vamp who was trying to flank Sally and shanked him through the spine with the stake. Not the most sporting thing to do, but screw them. As Sally once told me, vampires have a very liberal view on what constitutes a fair fight.

As he disintegrated in a shower of dust and sparks, an unholy screech filled the night. Gan was back on her feet, and she was not happy. Two of Remington's vampires fell aside, their throats torn out as testament to that. Hmrph, show off.

It was utter mayhem on a roof where the most exciting thing in the recent past was probably some occasional nude moonbathing by my coven. Damn my libido! Why did I have to think of that right at that moment? The momentary distraction allowed another of the vampires to close on me and rake his claws painfully across my chest, drawing a spray of blood. I decked him right back, using the stake like a makeshift club.

A flash of light caught my eye as the remaining two witches engaged Sheila. They were pummeling her with rays of red energy. Both screamed out a chorus of curses as her faith aura sprang to life, easily blocking their own power. Talk about middle finger of death. Sheila didn't have the same offensive capabilities as they did, but she was a tank when it came to absorbing punishment.

Speaking of punishment, that was exactly what Sally dished out. Flipping her gun around, she used it to smash the face of another vampire who was within reach. Hope the Draculas had a good dental plan.

OOMPH! Double that, because I was gonna need it next. In the chaos of the fight, I had missed Remington. Unfortunately, he hadn't missed me. A blow connected with the side of my head, sending me flying. I landed hard, skidding across the slick rooftop.

"I think I shall amend my plans, Freewill," he spat. "Damn your place in the coming war. You have proven far too annoying to live."

* * *

Out of the corner of my eye, one of the frustrated witches turned away from Sheila and attempted to blast Gan instead. Sadly, for their side, Gan was far too fast. She grabbed one of Remington's vamps and dragged him in front of her, using him as an inhuman shield. She was doing a damn good job of evening the sides.

That was all the attention I could spare her, though. Tenuous footing or not, Remington closed the gap between us with frightening speed. I had barely gotten to my feet when he appeared right in front of me.

Fortunately, I was no slouch either. I threw a punch which connected squarely with his jaw. Take that, fucker!

And take it he did. He barely flinched - not even a step back to make me feel a little better. That didn't bode well. I realized I had been getting arrogant about these things. I had been dealing with so many ancient horrors as of late that I forgot how big a threat a vampire of Remington's age could be. Jeff, the former leader of my coven, had been a measly one-hundred and twenty years old and had thoroughly mopped the floor with my ass when we finally tussled. Judging by his little compulsion game with Gan, Remington was about three times that.

I needed to tip the odds. Thankfully, as the vampire Freewill, that's one of the things I do best...aside maybe from getting sucked into stupid-ass prophecies against my will.

I swung the stake at Remington, fully expecting him to block me...which he did. When he grabbed hold of my arm, I pulled him in, preparing to take a bite. He was expecting that too, though. He other arm shot out and caught me by the throat, squeezing until I felt my air cut off.

"Did you think I wouldn't have read your file, Freewill? I am not a rank amateur like some of us here. What good is your much vaunted power now? What use is your ability to resist compulsion? Where is your beloved destiny?"

Beloved? He must've been talking about some other Freewill. It was of little matter, though. Arrogance, coupled with idiotic monologues, was a staple of vampires over a century old. Oh they so loved to hear themselves talk. Me? Well okay, I liked hearing my own voice too, but since this guy was currently wringing my neck, that meant I needed to be a man of action (ooh, I liked how that sounded).

Time for the old standby...a knee to the crotch.

BLAM!

Remington's shoulder exploded in a spray of blood and muscle. His scream was almost enough to mask the whine of the heavy caliber bullet which exited his body and passed by so close that I felt my hair move.

"You're welcome!" Sally yelled out.

"I had it under control," I gasped once Remington let me go. "I could've..."

Well, maybe I didn't. Even in his wounded state, he backhanded me with his undamaged arm, once more sending me to the ground.

I landed and even amidst the storm, the crackling of energy, and gunshots; I heard his footsteps approaching. He meant to finish the job.

Pity for him that I had no intention of letting that happen. I dug into my pocket for the secret weapon I had brought. It was time to play my trump card.

Top Of The World, Ma

"Take this, Dr. Death," Gan had said, pulling me aside just as we were leaving the safe house.

"What is it?" I asked, trying my best to conceal a sigh. I figured she was trying to give me an engagement ring or maybe her favorite dolly.

Instead, she had handed me a small glass vial filled with a thick red liquid.

"Is this..."

"My blood, beloved. You may find it useful in the coming conflict. I would be honored if you would add my strength to your own."

To say that I was infinitely more than creeped out would be an understatement. Sure, other vamps had freely given me their blood in the recent past, more than once while in Canada, but this was different. Those times had been practical. With Gan, it felt disturbingly intimate. An involuntary shudder passed through me at the very thought.

Still, fucked up or not, I had to admit that it could come in handy. Gan's age alone made her powerful, but her perpetual state of puberty made her special amongst vampires. I wondered if that would be transferred to me as well and immediately wanted to slap the shit out of myself for the thought. Then again, what if I refused and we wound up in a situation where I could've saved my friends...I could've saved Sheila...if I only had that extra little jolt?

In the end, logic had won out over good taste and I had pocketed it, vowing to only use it in an emergency.

Being that Tom was insane, Ed was dying, we were outnumbered, and - oh yeah - Remington had decided to give special attention to killing my ass, I decided that this might - just might - constitute something close to an emergency.

I popped the cap on the vial and sucked it down just as Remington grabbed the neck of my jacket and dragged me to my feet. It wasn't a lot, just a few drops, but I could feel it hit my stomach like a grenade. It wouldn't last long, but hopefully I wouldn't need it to - especially since I didn't know whether I would inherit a bit of Gan's crazy as part of the deal.

Remington spun me around and my fist immediately shot out, faster than I would have thought possible, catching him square on the chest. He flew through the air, hitting the slushy rooftop and skidding right toward Gan, who stood waiting. I couldn't see very well with the snow coming down, but I could tell there was a big grin on her face. Goddamn, I was never going to live this one down.

Oh well, neither was Remington if she had anything to say about it. I guess I could live with that.

I turned my attention to the others. Christy stood over Ed...make that *kneeled* over him. Her shield was still up, but it and she were both faltering. One of the other witches, a look of sheer hatred on her face, had turned her power on it and was attempting to break through.

"Deceiver!" she cried. "You would dare side with these filthy beasts?"

"Just for the record, my name is Bill, not filthy beast," I said a split second later, standing right behind her. I'm sure she would've had something snippy to say, but I didn't give her a chance to reply. In an impressive display of unsportsmanlike conduct, I clonked her on the back of the head - knocking her out. Hopefully she'd stay down for the rest of the battle. Heh, I could get used to this super speed thing. I felt like the Flash.

"Thanks!" Christy gasped.

"Anytime," I replied before taking off again. Sheila was busy fighting off the remaining witch, as well as four vampires. Without her sword, she wasn't able to keep them at bay as well as before, but she was definitely holding her own. Unfortunately, they had her cornered in such a way that she couldn't finish one off without another moving in to harass her. I aimed to fix that.

"Over the edge with them all!" Remington cried from behind me.

That didn't sound particularly appealing. It was a hundred and fifty feet to the ground. I stopped and looked back. Gan had been approaching the asshole, looking to finish him off, but I saw now that three of his followers were stalking her.

I turned around and saw they were doing the same to Sheila, inching her closer and closer to the edge. Even if a fall like that didn't kill them both outright (a big if, especially for Sheila), it would certainly cripple them enough to make them easy pickings.

Stark realization hit. For all my speed, I couldn't help them both. So that's what cruel irony feels like.

I thought the choice would be a disturbingly easy one, but amazingly I found myself hesitating. For all the trouble she caused, I still couldn't bring myself to want to see Gan dead. Don't get me wrong, all of her *beloved* bullshit wasn't starting to seep into my brain (yet). Still, she had helped me (and yes, she had also fucked me over quite nicely too). Regardless of how deluded she was, all of her actions toward me seemed to be dictated by love. Sure, it was a twisted, crazy version of love - one that was horribly tainted by an insane lust for power that would, no doubt, get me killed - but it was love all the same. There was also the fact of her being a little girl. Age aside, I always had a soft spot for the kids in horror movies. Maybe I was better off quitting the vampire business and getting a job in daycare.

Or maybe I was better off paying the fuck attention. An arm encircled my neck in a chokehold. In my enhanced state, it didn't feel particularly powerful, but it was enough to keep me in place for a second, which is apparently all the owner needed.

"This is for Night Razor," Dread Stalker's voice hissed in my ear. "At last he shall be avenged!"

I had a sneaking suspicion of what was coming next. I wrenched myself to the side as best I could. It was both just enough and not nearly so. The stake missed my heart (judging by how I didn't turn to dust), but punctured several of my other favorite organs. I assumed that included my lungs, considering how I suddenly couldn't even draw breath to scream.

A gurgle of blood escaped my throat as I tried to shake the asshole off. He held on for dear life, though. Despite the blow not being fatal, he knew it was both debilitating and painful...although perhaps not enough for his liking. I felt him grab the stake and twist it a few times, just to be a dick.

A fire erupted in my chest...silver. Fuck me! I needed to get it out. It would only be a matter of time before it incinerated me from the inside.

Unfortunately, both for me and my allies, it proved to be a potentially fatal distraction.

I heard cries of "Bill!" and "Beloved!" I whipped my head around, taking stock of their respective situations, and saw that things had gone from bad to worse. In my desire to save them both, I had instead doomed them.

Gan was able to take only a single step toward me before two of Remington's goons plowed into her in a dive tackle. The impact carried all three of them over the edge. I couldn't even scream her name. She let out a shriek and then disappeared from view.

Unfortunately, I also had no time to mourn her.

To my horror, I saw that Sheila fared no better. She had managed to dust one of her tormentors, but then saw the trouble I was in. Her aura momentarily faltered. The lone remaining witch immediately took advantage of it. A beam of red hot hatred lanced out and struck Sheila full on.

At the last second, her powers flared around her again, but the impact knocked her off balance. The three remaining vampires grabbed a hold of her and dragged her toward the edge. They ignited almost instantaneously, burning like pyres in the night. As the last of them vanished into ash, though, he threw his full weight against her. It was just enough to overbalance her. She went down, her momentum taking her over the edge.

"NO!" I cried out, somehow managing to find my voice again.

* * *

"The bitch is dead, and now it's your turn," Dread Stalker literally spat in my ear. Fucker needed to learn to say it, not spray it. Sadly for him, I didn't plan on letting him get the chance. He was going to pay for what he had taken from me.

I was about to try a judo flip to get him off my back (how hard could it be?), but my attention faltered. Something very important had caught my eye.

Sheila had gone over, but she hadn't fallen...yet. I could see the fingers of one hand, still barely grasping the ledge. Saving myself could wait. I had more important matters to attend to.

My insides still burning, I made good use of Gan's borrowed strength and dove the distance to where Sheila had gone over, carrying Dread Stalker with me. I landed on my stomach with the asshole still on top (fortunately I didn't have any wind left to knock out of me), and slid to the edge. Reaching out, I caught hold of her hand just as she was about to lose her grip.

"Gotcha!" I gasped right before being immediately engulfed in a world of white-hot pain.

The ruptured organs and internal damage from the stake were bad enough, but they were nothing compared to the agony that raced up my arm.

I ignited, the fires of faith determined to devour me, but still I refused to let go. Dread Stalker proved to be smarter than I thought. Realizing what was happening, he tried to disengage from me.

Oh no you don't! The second he removed his arm from my windpipe, I bit down with everything I had, holding him in place. The fire that was consuming me, spread to him too, and he began to scream - enough for both of us.

A savage thought raced through my mind, amidst the pain. *Music to my ears, asshole.* A funny thing happened then. Though still burning, I noticed it didn't hurt nearly as badly as it should. A moment later, I realized why.

The world flashed red and my fangs elongated even further, burying themselves to the bone in Dread Stalkers arm. It was my body's defense mechanism - against the Icon's power, against death itself. I was changing.

No!

I fought it. If it happened now, all my attempts to save her would be for naught. The second it was finished, I would surely attempt to kill her. Knowing what I was capable of in that state, I didn't like her odds - disarmed as she was.

There was no way I was going to allow that. I'd die first.

Inching to the edge, I looked over. She was there, her body alight with energy. My God, she was marvelous...like an avenging angel. Almost as if in response, the rage flared up, fighting me, but I held onto her visage. There's only one thing that can conquer such animalist hatred: pure love...or so the fairy tales say. I desperately hoped they were true for once.

I began to lift her, forcing the rage down - doing all I could to keep the change at bay. I doubled my resolve. I would save her, even if it killed me in the process. She was worth it.

She was also badass.

Seeing my predicament, as soon as I had raised her high enough, she lifted her other hand in a fist and swung it over my head. In the space of an instant, all of her power focused on the killing blow. Her aim was true and she connected squarely with Dread Stalker's chin.

His body became ash almost instantly. *Good riddance, dickhead.* Unfortunately for me, I sensed I wasn't far behind.

That's when a curious thing happened. Sheila closed her eyes. A smile lit her face and she let out a small sigh of contentment.

All at once, the glow around her faded to nothing and with it went the pain. The white hot agony that had consumed me at her very touch was gone. I had managed to control my power and now she was doing the same. Gone was the burning power of faith and for the first time since this began - hell, for the first time *ever* - I felt her. My hand continued to grasp hers and all I felt was her skin against mine. For something so mundane, it was absolutely incredible.

I pulled her up over the edge. I must've looked like shit, but I smiled nevertheless...right before collapsing. Oh yeah, I was still staked. Goddamn my faulty memory.

I fell flat on my face, my insides continuing to turn to charcoal. Oh well, this wasn't such a bad way to go. I kind of felt like Leonardo DiCaprio at the end of *Titanic*, right after he saved Kate Winslet. Hmm, come to think of it, I had always hated that ending. Oh well. It could be worse. I could've been living out the fucking awful finale to *Avatar*.

I heard screams and shouts, but they suddenly sounded very far away.

"Tom!"

Tom? No, silly. My name is Bill. Jeez, talk about...

"Hold on," a sweet voice said from seemingly miles away. "I've almost...got it!"

JESUS MOTHERFUCKING CHRIST ON A POGO STICK!

Reality came screaming in to fill the void the stake had left. It, along with a good chunk of me, was wrenched free. My senses rushed back, including a massive shitload of pain.

"Are you alright?" Sheila gently rolled me onto my back, letting the nice, soft asphalt dig into the gaping hole in my backside. Icon she may be, but Florence Nightingale she was not.

"Peachy," I strained to say.

"I'm serious."

"So am I...sorta."

"That was pretty crazy. You could have, well...you know..."

"You're worth it."

Wait a second...did I actually just say that? Holy crap, I did! Thank God for getting stabbed, beaten, and almost immolated, because it finally gave my insecurities a chance to take a fucking siesta.

We had only a scant second, but in that time, nothing else mattered. We enjoyed our moment. Unfortunately, that's all it was. I remembered that the battle wasn't over yet. I tried to stand and fell right back down on my ass.

That's when I heard the scream.

* * *

"You fucking little prick, I'll kill...urk!"

It was Sally. That got me moving again. I clawed my way back to my feet in time to see her go skidding across the rooftop, her body still glowing from the attack. I had forgotten we still had one witch left to deal with.

"Check on your friend. I've got this," Sheila said.

Her aura flared to life again and she ran off to the right.

I didn't want to leave her, but I couldn't turn my back on Sally. My indecision had already cost Gan her life. I didn't want to add anyone else to that list.

I lurched over to find her semi-conscious. The witch had hit her full on, but was apparently low on juice from the continued battle. What should have been a killing blow had merely dazed her, thank goodness.

I pulled her to a sitting position, and that's when I noticed the mark on her forehead. It was a circular burn, but it was the image charred into it that caught my eye. Two large windows on its chest and a crude faceplate covering the mouth - Tom's amulet!

Still horribly wounded, I stood nevertheless and glanced around. Tom wasn't where we had lain him down. I looked toward Christy. Still standing over Ed, she was fighting off the last of Remington's vamps, the strain evident on her face. It was taking everything she had. Her eyes met mine and I saw the panic in them. That'd been her voice I had heard earlier.

I stepped forward to help her out, but she shook her head. She closed her eyes, gritted her teeth, and the power flared out from her - almost blindingly so. When I could see again, the purple glow was gone, and so were the two vampires. Piles of dust lay where they had stood.

Christy looked at me, mouthed, "Go!" then her eyes rolled up into the back of her head and she collapsed next to Ed, completely spent.

That she hadn't abandoned my roommate, even when she saw her boyfriend wake up, said a lot about her. It was time to return the favor.

Sally was going to be okay, so I limped over to the other side of the roof. Rounding an air vent, I found Sheila straddled atop the witch, pummeling the shit out of her. Say what you will for magic, but sometimes all that's needed is a good right cross.

One last punch and the witch went limp. Well damn, that was easy.

Oh wait, no it wasn't.

I took a step forward and that's when I heard the click of a slide being pulled. Tom stepped around an air conditioning unit, not ten feet from Sheila's position, Sally's Desert Eagle in his hands. He had it pointed at her head. Even a total shit shot like me wouldn't be able to miss at that range.

"Tom!" I wheezed, catching his attention. "You don't want to do this."

"You're wrong, Freewill," he replied. "She has to die." Was he really that far gone?

I needed to reach him somehow. Sadly, even with the last of Gan's speed, there was no way I'd be able to cross that distance before he could squeeze the trigger. There had to be something...that's it!

I remembered what Christy had said. Perhaps a big enough shock could temporarily bring him to his senses.

"Think about Christy," I urged. "Think about the baby."

"I am," he said, focusing again on Sheila who had started to rise. "Don't even think about moving. You're the cause of all this misery."

"She's not, Tom...I am."

"I know. I meant *you're* in the collective sense."

"Oh. Well...um...this isn't you. You're not a murderer."

"Maybe you don't know me very well after all. This *is* the real me. I'd do anything to protect my child."

"The real you..." I trailed off, a thought hitting me. Maybe I was going about it all wrong. I knew Tom. Hell, I had known him for twenty years. I remembered things about him that even he had forgotten. I knew the *real* him.

His finger tightened on the trigger. I only had one chance at this. Hopefully I knew him as well as I hoped.

"I'm glad Optimus Prime got broken."

"What?" His eyes shifted back toward me.

"You heard me. Shit like that's for immature assholes anyway. What are you, a fucking five year old?"

He blinked at me, outrage on his face. Holy shit, was it actually working? I needed to crank it up a notch.

"Yeah. In fact, you know what? I can't stand any of your toys."

"You need to stop..."

"Once this is all over, you know what I'm gonna do? I'm kicking in the door to your room and taking a blowtorch to every single fucking thing you own."

"Don't even..."

"Try selling He-Man on eBay when he looks like a hunk of melted shit."

"Goddamn it, Bill," he said, a familiar whining quality entering his voice. "How many times do I have to tell you to not touch my collectibles? Do you know how much money those fucking things are..." He stopped mid-sentence and began to blink rapidly, his stance becoming unsteady.

After a moment, he shook his head. Finally his eyes cleared and he looked over at me, recognition on his face. "Dude, where the hell am I?"

Holy crap, it had worked. I couldn't believe it. It was kind of pathetic, seeing what really snapped him out of his funk. Okay, *very* pathetic...but who cared?

He looked down at the gun in his hands. "No fucking way!"

I stepped over to him as quickly as I could. "It's okay, Tom. It's..."

"When did I get a vintage *Megatron*? Do you know how much this thing is worth?"

Oh for Christ's sake! I suddenly didn't feel so bad for what needed to be done. After all, Christy did say it was temporary.

"Tom, believe me when I say I'm sorry for this."

"Sorry for wh...OOF!"

He didn't get a chance to finish, as my fist connected with his jaw - dropping him like a ton of bricks. He hit the rooftop, out cold - the gun clattering out of his grasp.

Letting out as deep a breath as my charred lungs would allow, I turned toward Sheila. She stood up from where the unconscious witch lay and we approached each other.

"Is he going to be all right?" she asked, her eyes dancing between me and Tom's still form.

"His head is harder than you'd believe. He'll be fine. More importantly, are you okay?"

"I'm right as rain." She looked back at the fallen witch, then lifted her fist triumphantly. "Who'd a thought I had it in me?"

"Me, for starters."

"I can see that. Thank you for believing in me."

I shrugged, not knowing what to say. After all, my belief in her had caused all of this.

"Thank you for everything," she said.

"I'm not sure you should be thanking me. I..."

"Showed me that I was special? Who could find fault in that?"

"I ruined your life."

"No, you just opened a new chapter in it. That's what life is all about - endings followed by new beginnings."

"It's the endings I'm worried about."

"I'm not, especially now that I know I have you watching out for me."

Holy moly! Did she just say that? Despite the cold, my palms got all sweaty. This really wasn't the best time for us to have a moment. We were in the middle of a supernatural storm, having just barely beaten a group of trained killers. And yet, somehow it felt right...almost like a touch of destiny.

She held out her hand to me, the glow disappearing from it. I tentatively reached out and took it.

* * *

Nothing happened. Holy crap...*nothing happened*! We stood there, actually holding hands like two normal human beings.

I could barely believe it. It was the most wonderful fee...

BLAM!

The bullet just barely grazed my ear, drawing blood. For a second, time stood still as realization dawned. If I live to be a thousand, there will never be a moment as terrible as that one.

Sadly, the world resumed its normal pace far too quickly.

Sheila's head snapped violently back. The force of the impact threw her off her feet, her hand slipping from my grasp.

She landed, unmoving, amongst the slush that was building up on the rooftop.

"Oh God, no!"

"Oh yes, Freewill," an English-accented voice said from behind me.

I turned to find Remington standing there - one arm in ruins, a massive bullet wound rendering it all but useless. In his other hand, though, he held the same weapon which had earlier been used against him: Sally's Desert Eagle.

"I am not so easily beaten," he said. "You would have been wise to consider that. Alas, you were not. To think our people would put any stock in such a pathetic being as yourself."

I had nothing to reply with. My whole form...my whole world...was numb.

He glanced past me to where Sheila's body lay. "You sicken me, you know that? Who would have guessed you would choose her over your own kind?"

"Always," I spat back, my voice sounding deeper than normal, something that I found not altogether surprising. I considered things - a cold rationality washing over me. In the space of a few days, his team had tried to take everything from me. In the space of a second, he had succeeded.

"Do not fret, Freewill. I meant what I said earlier. You will be joining her in Hell."

His voice hardly registered with me as he raised the massive weapon and pointed it my way. The numbness began to leave me and in its place a red rage descended over my vision. The creature inside of me demanded freedom. For perhaps the first, and last, time, I was inclined to oblige. What did it matter anyway? What point was my life, my humanity, with her gone? What possible future could I have without her?

Future, hah! All that talk of destiny had been for naught after all. Remington had proven it with just the pull of a trigger. I was almost tempted to thank him. In his own sick way, he had freed me. First, though, I had something else in mind.

I had nothing left...save the meaningless prophecies, the death I had been supposedly fated to bring this world. So be it.

I felt the remnants of my clothes tear as my body enlarged. Remington and the gun in his hand suddenly seemed very small, almost insignificant, to me.

"Impressive," he said dispassionately, then pulled the trigger. A dry click was the only response.

The grin disappeared from his face as I leapt. The red rage consumed me, burying everything human...perhaps forever. The part of me that was still Bill Ryder faded into the darkness, glad to be gone from a world that held only pain. Remington's screams were my only company as I let it take me wholly.

And Now for a Slightly Different Epilogue

"And what happened then?"

"We bugged out of there pretty goddamned fast. Even with the storm, it must've looked like a hell of a fight from the street. I could hear sirens in the distance. It seemed like a good time to beat feet."

"I'm not blaming you. It was a prudent course of action," James said, his voice resonating from the Bluetooth earpiece I wore. I had no idea where he was calling from. Could have been Europe, for all I knew, but I was just glad it was him. As fun as gloating would have been, I wasn't in the mood to deal with Colin's bullshit.

"Thanks, I just hated having to run like that."

"Places can grow on you."

"Screw that! All of my stuff was there."

"Ah, Sally, you always have your priorities straight," he said with a chuckle. "Speaking of which, let me see if I have my facts in order. The others are expecting a report, although considering the turn of events, I highly doubt they'll give it much more consideration other than to note *case closed.*"

I didn't need to ask further. I knew what he was talking about. The news anchors were practically orgasming onscreen amidst all the chaos. It had been the first thing I had flipped on after reaching the safe house, just to see if anything had been reported about the battle atop the office.

I needn't have worried. There was so much out of the ordinary going on, that a few fireworks in SoHo were barely a blip on anyone's radar.

"...the freak storm, which appeared to have come out of nowhere, continues to pound the tri-state area. Meteorologists are still stumped as to its cause or when we can expect it to end. Some local amateur photographers managed to snap some stunning photos of the strangely colored lightning associated..."

"One witness described the scene as a modern day Roanoke. Overnight, the small trading village of Buffalo Valley, located at the Northern tip of Manitoba, seems to have disappeared. Authorities are stumped, claiming it's not just the town's residents which are missing, but the buildings as well. They claim it's as if the forest simply swallowed the small..."

"...Museum officials are refusing to comment on reports that the statue of Osiris - dating back to the twelfth century BC, and currently on loan to the Smithsonian - began to cry what witnesses described as tears of blood..."

"Police still have no leads on what has been dubbed the Mamaroneck Massacre..."

"...the Icon then wiped out Remington's forces to the last man before Dr. Death was able to intervene, is that correct?"

"Huh?" I pulled my attention away from my nails. They were going to need another coat of gloss. My active lifestyle as of late was playing hell on them. "Yep, that's what happened," I replied offhandedly.

"How about our allies in this joint venture? Did any of them survive?"

"Nope. Decker went down early in the fray. None of his coven made it either." I had personally seen to that little detail before leaving, making sure to be the last one to vacate the premises. I almost laughed at the irony. Decker and his band of magical harpies had convinced themselves that the Icon would be the death of them. Amusingly enough, they'd still be alive if they hadn't gotten involved in the first place. Talk about a self-fulfilling prophecy. Oh well, I wasn't going to be shedding any tears for those assholes anytime soon. Although...

I grabbed a pen and jotted down a note. I might as well send Starlight up north to see if she could track down his body. I wouldn't mind using Decker's skull as an ashtray. It was the least he could do for fucking up the loft.

"It's a pity about Remington," James continued. "His skills were held in high regard by the First."

"Yep, a pity," I replied. A pity the asshole didn't suffer longer. In the end, though, he did scream just like a little girl as Bill was tearing him a new asshole. That was relatively satisfying.

"I dare say, Colin has brought down far more scrutiny on his stewardship of this endeavor than he had hoped."

I perked up. Finally, this conversation was getting interesting. "How so?"

"Remington's team had been needed elsewhere, to help shore up defenses at our keep in Northern Siberia. Colin managed to convince them otherwise, that this would be a glorious victory. Needless to say, his decisions in all other matters are currently being questioned."

"I'm sorry to hear that," I lied, not bothering to conceal it in my tone. James knew my history with that prick.

"Actually I'm not. Colin's leadership skills might be...underdeveloped, but he was an excellent assistant. The truth is I miss him in that regards. There's a chance I may be able to swing a reassignment for him as my personal attaché. That would make my considerable workload somewhat more bearable."

I tried and failed to suppress a giggle. It would be so awesome to see him kiss everyone's ass for a promotion only to wind up as James's secretary once more. Perhaps there is such a thing as cosmic justice. The laugh also provided me with a needed release from the current stress I felt. It helped mask the worry worming its way through my gut.

Goddamn it Bill, where are you?

* * *

James finally finished his debriefing. I had little doubt he suspected I was leaving details out. He was both smart and perceptive that way. Whereas several centuries of life taught most vampires the joy of hearing their own voices, it had taught James a far more valuable lesson: how to listen. Fortunately, that was coupled with honest to goodness common sense. He knew when to let unimportant minutia slide, especially if it meant keeping things from turning into a full scale avalanche of stupidity.

"Do I have the facts straight?" he had asked, his wry tone indicating he knew I fudged the details a bit. That was fine. We both knew there weren't any witnesses, at least none that would contradict my story.

"Exactly as I remember them."

"Excellent. You'll let me know when he returns, won't you?"

"I will," I replied before hanging up. It was the only part of the conversation I hadn't exaggerated or outright lied about.

I had set up a small nook in the living room to act as a makeshift office, until such time as I felt it safe to return to our actual office. Once I put the phone down, Starlight entered, a pot of fresh coffee in hand. I was almost tempted to smile at her, but refrained. It was bad for my reputation. I knew how James felt about Colin. It was the same with Starlight, except for the fact that she wasn't a back-biting little dick.

Following the battle, I had called her and given the all clear. She had packed up immediately and wasted no time in returning. The others, Firebird and Alfonzo, would be back the next night. I couldn't have cared less about Firebird. She and I had never gotten along, tramp that she was. Alfonzo couldn't return fast enough, though. Gods knew I deserved a scalp massage and a good conditioning after all this shit.

I reached up and felt my temple. The burn from the meatwad's amulet had finally started to fade. He was lucky he was Bill's friend. Because of that, I was probably only going to kick his ass for attacking me. The fact that he wouldn't remember doing it or why, at least after Christy got done mind-scrubbing him, would only make it that much more amusing.

"How are the newbs handling things?" I asked Starlight, taking a business-like tone.

"I set them up at the warehouse with some supplies. They're adjusting."

"Any possible runners?"

"I compelled them to stay put, just in case."

"Good."

Remington's thugs had gone on a mad killing spree at the office, slaughtering any of the other tenants they happened to catch. Talk about fucking up our lease! It turned out, though, that they had been sloppy - not finishing the job with a half dozen or so. That was fine by me. Village Coven just so happened to have a few openings in its ranks. Hopefully one or two might even be worth the trouble of letting them live. Either way, though, that was a problem for tomorrow. For now, I needed to concentrate on...

There came a knock from the front door.

Starlight glanced at me quizzically, but I shrugged. It couldn't be the cops. James had wired a goodly amount of funds to the right parties, convincing them that the raid from the other day had been a mistake. The same would eventually be done with the office. Sadly, it was going to take a bit more time considering the mess that had been made there.

"Think it's him?" she asked, a hopeful tone in her voice. She was such an optimist. It was almost sickeningly cute.

I took a sniff and frowned. No, it definitely wasn't Bill. In fact, it wasn't anyone I wanted to see. Still, I guess it was either open up or have her break down the door.

I stood to smooth my dress - a cute little black number, appropriate for my current mood. Appearances were important, even for company I couldn't stand. "Open it," I said with a barely concealed sigh, sitting back down again.

Starlight opened the door for Gan, the little Mongolian princess bitch. She was accompanied by one of her lackeys...the same one who had been led on a merry chase by the witches.

She walked in like she owned the place. Big surprise. God, what I wouldn't have given for a trapdoor leading to a shark tank, but oh well. Maybe next safe house.

I turned to Starlight, not wanting her to eavesdrop. "Alice," I used her real name, as I often did whenever I wanted her to be sure I wasn't fucking around, "would you be good enough to go out and get us some coffee?"

Not grasping my meaning, she glanced at the steaming carafe she had just set down, a confused look on her face.

I so hate when people don't get the hint. I grabbed the pot and threw it across the room, where it shattered against the wall. Subtlety has never been one of my virtues.

"Oops."

That got her moving. She stepped past Gan and left, closing the door behind her.

Once it clicked shut, I raised an eyebrow at my guest - only partially because of the Spongebob lunchbox she was carrying. Goddamn, what a weirdo. "I was wondering what had happened to you."

"How so?" she replied.

"That was a pretty long drop from the top floor."

She shrugged as it were nothing.

"So what happened?" I asked once it became obvious she wasn't going to elaborate.

"It is simple. I survived. They did not."

Okay then. Ask a stupid question. It didn't really matter, though. I hadn't doubted she would get little more than a sprained ankle out of the ordeal. One simply doesn't get lucky like that.

"If you're looking for Bill, you're gonna be disappointed. He's missing."

"I am well aware. I am here to see you before I depart."

I couldn't hide my surprise. She hit me with three big question marks at once right there. Not wishing to seem over eager, I figured I'd save that part about her leaving for last.

"You're aware? How?"

"His scent is gone," she replied simply enough.

Her and that creepy nose of hers. She had once told Bill she could track him anywhere. It was probably how she was able to find us up in Westchester. Either that or she had chipped him like a dog...a distinct possibility. Still, if she couldn't sense him now...

"How do you know he's not..."

"Dead? Do not be so naive," she said dismissively. It was all I could do to keep from launching myself across the desk and throttling her. "Had he died, his scent would have lingered with his ashes. This is different. It is hard to explain. It is as if it simply...changed. One moment it was there, the next it vanished."

"Changed is a good word for it," I said. It wouldn't hurt to let her know that part. "He completely lost it after the Icon got iced. He transformed and tore

435

Remington to shreds. When it was all over, he just took off running. He was gone before I even fully realized what was happening. I haven't seen him since."

Now it was her turn to look surprised. Her eyes opened wide, excitement shining in them. "You *saw* him?"

I nodded. It had been the first good look I had gotten of him after a change.

"Was it as marvelous as I have heard?"

I considered this. I had to admit it was definitely not what I had been expecting. I'd have to remember that when he got back. It bore...consideration. To Gan, though, I simply nodded again. No point in going into further details. It would only encourage her.

"What of the others?"

"Remington's forces were obliterated to the man. Ditto with the mages."

"No, I mean the others who sided with us - more specifically, the witch and her human. Our alliance is over. I meant what I said about punishing them for their treachery."

I don't know why, but the lie came out of my mouth without even a moment's hesitation. "You're too late. After Bill changed, he went nuts. They didn't make it. I'm lucky I did."

Gan raised an eyebrow. She might look like a little girl, but she was perceptive. For all I knew, she could smell the deception on me. Fortunately, I was no amateur when it came to untruths. The best way to fake out a watchful eye was to marinate the bullshit in a little bit of truth. When it comes to cooking up lies, I am an Iron fucking Chef.

"I assume you have no quarrel with Bill's other friend. I managed to pull him out with me, dead weight that he was."

"Why would you do that?"

Now *that* was the first good question she had asked. Why had I done a lot of things as of late? There I was, saving Christy and Tom's asses. I had put my own on the line for Bill and his wannabe girlfriend. Hell, I was even developing a soft spot for his human roommate. What the fuck was wrong with me?

It was a rhetorical question. I knew the answer: Bill was what was wrong with me. He had started off as a means to an end, a way for me to finally claw my way out from being Jeff's plaything. At some point, though, things had changed. Despite my best efforts, he had become the first real friend I had made in decades. The fucker's humanity was starting to rub off on me. Now, with all this Icon crap, I even found myself thinking back to my own early days of being turned...something I really was not particularly nostalgic for. What was the world coming to?

Rather than give Gan that insight, though - not that she would care - I simply said, "I was curious as to what would happen to him."

"He is awake?"

"Not yet."

"You should kill him."

"Why?" I asked, genuinely intrigued. It wasn't like her to take an even passing interest in a human, other than as lunch perhaps.

"He is...an anomaly. Turned by one of us, yet saved by the Icon. He is undoubtedly changed by the experience...but into what, I do not know. The seers speak not of such a thing ever occurring. Such an aberration is not foretold."

I hadn't considered that. I figured he'd either wake up normal, or turn anyway regardless of the Icon's ministrations. Now I was more intrigued than ever. Talk about living in interesting times.

"I'll take that under advisement."

"Do so. Alas, I cannot see to it myself at this time."

"Oh yeah, you had mentioned something about departing," I said offhandedly, the sarcasm zooming way over her diminutive head.

"Yes. I must leave for home. The Alma have made their first strike against my forces. It was repelled easily enough, but I do not doubt they were simply testing us. I wish to be there to ensure they are laid low like the dogs they are. The rest of my people are securing transport even as I speak."

"How'd they fare?"

A look of irritation passed through Gan's face for just a moment. I'd be lying if I said I didn't take some amusement from it. "One of the Magi, perhaps two, escaped. There is no sign of them. My assassins are well aware of my *displeasure* at such."

Well that was just fucking great. "Shit really is starting to pile up."

"Crude, but apt. Indeed it is. Do not fret, though. I shall return when it is time for my beloved to fulfill his destiny." She took my silence as cue to go on. In reality, it was because I was confused. "I had thought that the eve of his glorious fate was upon us. I have since come to the conclusion that he needs further maturing. His destiny is still yet to come."

She stopped as her eyes focused on something leaning against the wall behind my desk. I knew exactly what she was looking at.

Without invitation, she walked around me. Gingerly she reached out toward it, but then pulled her hand back without touching it.

"The Icon's sword?"

I nodded. "I figured it would raise too many questions if the cops found it. Besides, it's an antique. Seemed a shame to leave it behind."

"I am surprised you could touch it."

"I can't, at least not without my hands blistering to all hell. Fortunately, Remington didn't need his trench coat where he was going. It made for an excellent oven mitt."

"Interesting," she said, strolling to the front of my desk, a thoughtful look upon her face. "She will no doubt want it back when the time comes to face my beloved in their final conflict."

I guess she had missed that part earlier about the Icon buying the farm. "I hate to burst your bubble, but you might want to consider that the whole prophecy was nothing but bullshit."

"Why?"

"Wasn't it foretold that Bill would kill the Icon, or the Icon kill him. Well it didn't happen."

"I know. That is obviously still to come."

"Newsflash, sweetheart - since you missed the show - but the Icon is dead."

"No, she is not."

"Yeah, she is. I was there. She took a fifty-caliber slug to the face. You don't get up from that."

To both my surprise and undying irritation, Gan actually started to giggle. It quickly turned into a full-on chortle. I looked to her companion for some clue, but he just stood there silent and stoic. Lot of fucking help he was.

"Oh, I thank you," she said after a few moments. "I have not laughed like that in some time."

"Am I missing something here?"

"Indeed, child. Tell me, was your weapon consecrated in the sacrament of the Black Tngri?"

Black what? My only reply was a blank stare, not understanding a word of her gibberish.

"My apologies. It is known in the West as the Ritual of Baal."

Yeah, like that helped at all. "Never heard of it," I replied, reaching up to twirl an errant strand of hair that had fallen out of place.

"That is not surprising. Very few of our kind have. Even during the days when Freewills and Icons waged war openly on the battlegrounds, it was a secret known only to a handful. Still, I would have thought the other vampires would have come prepared with sanctified weaponry. Odd they did not."

"I'm not following."

"To put it simply, if it were so easy to kill the Shining Ones, they would not be considered the great threats they are. We would have merely launched volleys of arrows at them from afar and been done with it."

My mouth dropped open. She couldn't be right. Wouldn't James have known about this? I could understand Colin being in the dark, but I found it unlikely one of the Draculas wouldn't know. What the hell was going on?

"To that end, I shall leave Monkhbat here when I depart."

"Huh?" I muttered, entirely distracted by her revelation. The phrase *holy shit* didn't begin to do it justice.

"I *said* I shall be leaving Monkhbat behind."

What? "Not even gonna try hiding that you're spying on us, are you?"

"No," she replied smugly. "He shall remain here as my eyes, but I do not leave him as a burden to you. He shall be entirely at your disposal. Use him as you will to help rebuild your coven."

"And he'll be reporting in to you at every step of the way?"

"Of course."

I considered this. It irked me, but perhaps the devil you know is better than the one you don't. Before then, we hadn't even been aware she was keeping an eye on us. Now at least...

"Entirely at my disposal?"

"Yes. He shall serve you loyally. Albeit take care..."

"Let me guess, don't cross the line or he'll turn on us?"

"No," she replied, looking slightly offended. "I simply wished to convey that you should keep your commands simple. His English is not so good."

"Oh."

She turned to leave. "Farewell, Sally. We shall meet again."

Sally? What happened to whore? "Wait a second. You said you stopped by to see me, not Bill."

"Ah yes," she replied, addressing me over her shoulder. "I had almost forgotten. I wished to convey to you my respect. You have proven yourself far more capable in this endeavor than I had foreseen."

"Thanks...I guess."

"Dr. Death has chosen well for his second. He could do far worse. I am comfortable leaving, knowing he has you to guide him."

I was nearly stunned. That was the closest the little witch had ever come to being remotely civil with me.

"I'll do my best," I replied, finding myself at a loss for a wittier comeback.

"I know you shall," she replied before once more turning to leave. "There is just one more thing."

"Yes?"

"Have a care, whore. Bill is still mine. Should I perceive that your intentions for him are anything more than the physical services you provide, I shall kill you without a moment's hesitation."

With that, she walked out.

Motherfucking little bitch!

* * *

I finally put down the phone. Several hours had passed since I had ordered Starlight to get me the numbers of every morgue in the city. Gan's warning had completely freaked me the fuck out.

After Bill had run off, the rest of us had gotten off the roof ASAP before the authorities could arrive. I hadn't even given consideration to Sheila's survival. Hell, I had seen Remington plug her at close range with a silver bullet. Something like that would have put down a vampire of even James's power. It was nearly inconceivable that someone could take that and live.

Now, having made call after call, I was forced to reconsider. No one even remotely resembling her appearance had been delivered to any of the bone houses I had contacted.

* * *

Two hours later, my questions were at least partially answered. After sending Monkhbat out on a bullshit errand to get him out of my hair, I had turned on the police scanner. Turns out an ambulance had gone missing shortly after our battle ended. It had just been found parked in an alley in northern Manhattan, the driver unconscious. There had been nobody else on the scene. Nothing had been stolen except for the driver's coat. The address the ambulance had been en route from when it disappeared: the office.

My feelings were decisively mixed. On the one hand, I was sort of glad. She gave Bill hope and I didn't want to see that die. The flip side of that, though, was she was also a distraction for him, a dangerous thing in these times. Her survival had been Bill's - *our* - goal. Everything we'd gone through over the past few days hadn't been for naught after all, but it also meant all of those fucking prophecies were still in play. Fate wasn't finished with us. That was perhaps the most frightening thought of all.

Then there was that ritual Gan had mentioned. Had James purposely kept Colin in the dark, letting him send those vamps on what was surely a suicide mission? In that I had more questions than answers.

444

Either way you looked at it, things were just beginning. I stepped to the window and surveyed the darkness beyond. The weather had let up a little, but I wasn't fooled. If anything, this was the calm before the real storm.

"Bill, where are you?" I said to myself more than anyone.

"Any sign of him yet?" a voice asked from behind me, Starlight.

"No, but he'll be back."

"How can you be sure?"

"He always comes back," I said with more certainty than I felt, the burden of leadership finally beginning to weigh on my shoulders. "The dopey little fuck is full of surprises."

She was silent for a moment, but then asked, "So what do we do now?"

I smiled. That part at least was easy. Freewill or not, this coven wasn't rudderless. Not to toot my own horn, but I could keep the fires burning until he got back. "We do what we need to. We rebuild and recruit."

"I thought we weren't supposed to..."

"There're bad things coming, Star, and I want this coven up to full strength again. I don't know what's out there, but I don't want us caught with our pants down again." A small grin tugged at my lips as I said that. It was something that Bill would have had an assholish reply to. Amazingly enough, I actually missed the sound of his voice.

"And then what?"

"And then we hold tight for the Freewill to return."

"To lead us into battle?" she asked, repeating the oft-said prophecy.

"Maybe," I replied, keeping my true feelings on the subject to myself.

"But what if he doesn't?"

"He will," I said, silently adding *I hope* to that. A thought then hit me. With it came a smile and even a little chuckle at the irony of it all.

"What's so funny?"

"Bill will be back and maybe things will even turn out okay in the end." I turned and put a hand on Starlight's shoulder. "We just need to have a little...faith."

THE END

Bill Ryder *might* return in:
Goddamned Freaky Monsters
(The Tome of Bill, part 5)

Can't wait for more Bill? Follow his ongoing misadventures on Facebook at
www.facebook.com/BilltheVampire

Author's Note

This has been yet another installment in the ongoing saga of a foul-mouthed, undead geek named Bill Ryder. I find myself nearly flabbergasted in writing this note, in that I can't believe how quickly things change. When I wrote the closing words for *The Mourning Woods*, Bill's third adventure, I was speaking to an audience of perhaps a couple dozen at most. Now, well, I suspect that number may have grown ever so slightly. To say it blows my mind would be an understatement. I am absolutely humbled by the awesome people who have decided to take a chance on a monkey-clicking hack from New Jersey.

So... is it getting hot in here, or is it just me?

My stage fright issues aside, each new book in this series brings with it fresh challenges. This one is no exception. As Bill and his friends become further immersed in the dangerous world of the undead, I find myself facing a dilemma of sorts: How to marry the character's growth (and maturity) while keeping these books fun. Even ignoring that roadblock, it can be an uphill battle. Everyone's tastes in humor are different. I laugh at things my wife finds about as funny as a train wreck and vice versa. The larger the audience the greater chance one is going to bomb for at least a few. No pressure there.

Needless to say, Bill's world has been becoming quite a bit darker as of late and the challenge for me has been to find that balance between keeping his perceptions quirky and realizing that there are some situations that he would have to be either insane or cataclysmically stupid to laugh off. In other words: to find a way to make people smile yet not be discouraged into thinking Bill is a hopeless dipshit.

But oh well, that's part of the fun for me. It keeps me on my toes and hopefully you on the edge of your seat wondering what he'll do or say next. Whether I have succeeded in my quest, I leave in your capable hands, dear reader.

Either way, writing these stories brings me great enjoyment. I sincerely hope you feel the same reading them.

Rick G.

About the Author

Rick Gualtieri lives alone in central New Jersey with only his wife, three kids, and countless pets to both keep him company and constantly plot against him. When he's not busy monkey-clicking out words, he can typically be found jealously guarding his collection of vintage Transformers from all who would seek to defile them.

Defilers beware!

Rick Gualtieri is the author of:

Bill The Vampire (The Tome of Bill - 1)
Scary Dead Things (The Tome of Bill - 2)
The Mourning Woods (The Tome of Bill - 3)
Holier Than Thou (The Tome of Bill - 4)
Sunset Strip: A Tale From The Tome Of Bill
Goddamned Freaky Monsters (The Tome of Bill - 5)
Half A Prayer (The Tome of Bill - 6)
Bigfoot Hunters
The Poptart Manifesto
Meeting Misty
Necromantic

To contact Rick (with either undying praise or rude comments) please visit:

Rick's Website:
www.rickgualtieri.com

Facebook Page:
facebook.com/RickGualtieriAuthor

Twitter:
twitter.com/RickGualtieri

Bonus Chapter

Devil Hunters
A Tale of the Crypto Hunter

The golden eagle soared effortlessly above the frozen landscape - its wings barely moving - held aloft by the updraft that preceded the storm front. A clap of thunder sounded in the distance, but the mighty bird paid it no mind. It was preoccupied, as was its norm, with the search for prey.

Something on the ground caught its sharp eyes and it banked its impressive six-foot wingspan to investigate. It moved with the easy grace of a super predator, sure in the mastery of its domain. Soon it spotted what had caught its attention: a fresh kill. Perhaps wolves or even a bear had brought down the great antlered beast below. It did not matter to the eagle. It had few qualms with facing down either opponent over meat. It knew it had little to fear from even the largest of terrestrial predators.

In the fading sunlight, the storm's approach quickened. The great bird began to circle, slowing descending towards the appetizing prize awaiting.

Movement suddenly registered in its sharp vision from down below. A flash of pale yellow appeared and then it saw something step from the brush surrounding the kill. Like many predators, the eagle did not outright fear a lone human; however, its instincts commanded it to be wary of the two-legged things. It continued circling, waiting to see if the intruder would move off. That was when something else caught its eye.

The eagle had no fear of any creature that walked the land. What came from the sky, though, was a different matter. Though it knew instantly that the newcomer was still far above it, the shadow it cast on the ground below dwarfed its own.

Bringing its wings to bear, it made a sharp turn. The prize on the ground wasn't worth it. The creature that had entered the eagle's airspace was an enemy against which it knew it could not win. With one last shriek, the eagle headed west, hoping to try its luck elsewhere.

* * *

"What the hell are you doing?" came the voice from the Bluetooth headset.

"My job," Danni Kent replied, stepping out from the hunting blind and approaching the dead moose that lay before her.

"That's why we set the bait."

"Give me a break, Derek," she said. "This thing's already taken two kids from that village and it's started going after the adults too. It's a man-eater and you know it. The bait isn't going to attract anything more than the normal scavengers." Danni, rolled her eyes. It had been nearly a year since she had joined the team and he *still* acted like she was some kid he needed to be over-protective of.

"We just need to be patient..." Derek replied when another voice drowned his out.

"I see it!"

Danni was tempted to reply, "Told ya so!" but she knew it would be childish. Besides, if the creature really was approaching, she knew it would be wise to free up the radio from unnecessary banter.

"Can you get a shot, Frank?" Derek's voice blared out again.

"No good," came the answer. "Still too far away and the goddamned wind is picking up."

"They don't call them Thunderbirds for nothing," Danni said under her breath. She pushed an errant strand of blonde hair from her face, then lifted her rifle and squinted through the scope, scanning the sky. She didn't see anything.

"Danni..." Derek's voice warned.

"Where is it?" she asked. She lowered the rifle just as the oncoming clouds blotted out the sunlight. The dazzling brightness was immediately replaced by a shape much darker than the clouds above it.

The creature had been using the sun to mask its approach. With its cover gone, Danni could see it in its fullness. It was huge, with a nearly eighteen foot wingspan and a curved beak that looked like it could shatter bone with ease. Worse, though, it was coming at her fast...too fast.

There wasn't time to line up a shot. Her training taking over, Danni threw herself into a hard dive to the left, losing her grip on the gun in the process. Fortunately for her, as big as the creature was, it was incapable of making a quick enough turn to compensate for her movement.

She had just enough time to think, *Where the hell are...*, when she heard the whine of the bullets as they passed just feet above her. Moments later, the reports from the rifle shots reached her ears.

Danni hit the ground and rolled on her back, hoping for the best. She saw a splay of feathers fall from one of the creature's massive wings, but the monstrous bird remained airborne.

Fuck! It had been Derek's idea to split the team up at multiple bait sites so as to cover more ground. Normally it would have been a good idea. The team was spread out, but still near enough to provide cover fire for each other - a useful strategy considering their airborne target. Unfortunately the storm was moving in faster than expected and the erratic wind gusts were playing havoc with their ability to hit a moving target. *Even one as big as a Cessna,* mused Danni, getting back to her feet in time to see the creature banking for another pass at her.

Not afraid of people, she thought. *That's gonna cost you, you ugly son of a bitch.* Despite the danger, she let a small smile play out across her lips. She had been hanging out with Francis a little too much. His attitude was obviously starting to rub off on her. It probably wasn't the healthiest mindset for living a good long life, but still, it was better than running scared.

Speaking of running, though... "Danni, lead it towards me, so I can get a head on shot."

She didn't need to be told twice. Despite its size, the bird was more maneuverable than she would have given it credit for. It was already positioned and building up speed for another approach. She spotted her discarded rifle, immediately determined there wasn't time to retrieve it, then turned and ran toward Derek's position.

* * *

Thunder crashed overhead and at once the storm was upon them. The wind picked up and Danni could feel pinpricks of frozen rain begin to pelt her.

"Just a little more..." Derek's voice came over the headset.

A shriek behind her, though, told her that she didn't have a little more.

Screw this, she thought with a grimace. Still running, she reached into her jacket and drew twin semi-automatic pistols. Throwing herself into a dive, she spun and landed hard on her back, the guns facing upward. There was no chance of missing, the bird took up her entire field of vision.

She squeezed both triggers and unleashed a small volley of hellfire upon the beast. The bullets hit home, but Danni immediately saw she had a new problem: regardless of whether they killed it, the small caliber bullets weren't going to stop the monster bird's momentum. Alive or dead, it was going to slam into her. Between its massive beak and outstretched talons, she knew she was about to be impaled.

* * *

Devil Hunters

Coming Soon